THE RAINBOW TRAIL

Rainbow Trail

Zane Grey

WHITE LION PUBLISHERS LIMITED
London, New York, Sydney and Toronto

First published in Great Britain by
Hodder and Stoughton Limited

Copyright 1915 by Zane Grey
Copyright 1943 by Lina Elise Grey

White Lion edition 1976

ISBN 7274 0091 6

Made and printed in Great Britain
for White Lion Publishers Limited
138 Park Lane, London W1Y 3DD
by Hendington Limited
Deadbrook Lane, Aldershot, Hampshire

995889

FOREWORD

The spell of the desert comes back to me, as it always will come. I see the veils, like purple smoke, in the cañons, and I feel the silence. And it seems that again I must try to pierce both and to get at the strange wild life of the last American wilderness—wild still, almost, as it ever was.

While this romance is an independent story, yet readers of "Riders of the Purple Sage" will find in it an answer to a question often asked.

I wish to say also that this story has appeared serially in a different form in one of the monthly magazines under the title of "The Desert Crucible."

ZANE GREY.

June, 1915.

CONTENTS

CHAP.   PAGE

        FOREWORD IX

I.   RED LAKE 1

II.   THE SAGI 18

III.   KAYENTA 36

IV.   NEW FRIENDS 52

V.   ON THE TRAIL 72

VI.   IN THE HIDDEN VALLEY 90

VII. SAGO-LILIES 109

VIII. THE HOGAN OF NAS TA BEGA 134

IX.   IN THE DESERT CRUCIBLE 155

X.   STONEBRIDGE 159

XI.   AFTER THE TRIAL 182

XII. THE REVELATION 202

XIII. THE STORY OF SURPRISE VALLEY 225

XIV. THE NAVAJO 250

XV. WILD JUSTICE 259

XVI. SURPRISE VALLEY 288

XVII. THE TRAIL TO NONNEZOSHE 306

XVIII. AT THE FOOT OF THE RAINBOW 335

XIX. THE GRAND CAÑON OF THE COLORADO 345

XX. WILLOW SPRINGS 366

        EPILOGUE 371

RED LAKE

SHEFFORD halted his tired horse and gazed with slowly realizing eyes.

A league-long slope of sage rolled and billowed down to Red Lake, a dry red basin, denuded and glistening, a hollow in the desert, a lonely and desolate door to the vast, wild, and broken upland beyond.

All day Shefford had plodded onward with the clear horizon-line a thing unattainable; and for days before that he had ridden the wild bare flats and climbed the rocky desert benches. The great colored reaches and steps had led endlessly onward and upward through dim and deceiving distance.

A hundred miles of desert travel, with its mistakes and lessons and intimations, had not prepared him for what he now saw. He beheld what seemed a world that knew only magnitude. Wonder and awe fixed his gaze, and thought remained aloof. Then that dark and unknown northland flung a menace at him. An irresistible call had drawn him to this seamed and peaked border of Arizona, this broken battlemented wilderness of Utah upland; and at first sight they frowned upon him, as if to warn him not to search for what lay hidden beyond the ranges. But Shefford thrilled with both fear and exultation. That was the country which had been described to him. Far across the red valley, far beyond the ragged line of black mesa and yellow range, lay the wild cañon with its haunting secret.

Red Lake must be his Rubicon. Either he must enter the unknown to seek, to strive, to find, or turn back and fail and never know and be always haunted. A friend's strange story had prompted his singular journey; a beautiful rainbow with its mystery and promise had decided him. Once in his life he had answered a wild call to the kingdom of adventure within him, and once in his life he had been happy. But here in the horizon-wide face of that up-flung and cloven desert he grew cold; he faltered even while he felt more fatally drawn.

As if impelled Shefford started his horse down the sandy trail, but he checked his former far-reaching gaze. It was the month of April, and the waning sun lost heat and brightness. Long shadows crept down the slope ahead of him and the scant sage deepened its gray. He watched the lizards shoot like brown streaks across the sand, leaving their slender tracks; he heard the rustle of pack-rats as they darted into their brushy homes; the whir of a low-sailing hawk startled his horse.

Like ocean waves the slope rose and fell, its hollows choked with sand, its ridge - tops showing scantier growth of sage and grass and weed. The last ridge was a sand-dune, beautifully ribbed and scalloped and lined by the wind, and from its knife-sharp crest a thin wavering sheet of sand blew, almost like smoke. Shefford wondered why the sand looked red at a distance, for here it seemed almost white. It rippled everywhere, clean and glistening, always leading down.

Suddenly Shefford became aware of a house looming out of the bareness of the slope. It dominated that long white incline. Grim, lonely, forbidding, how strangely it harmonized with the surroundings! The structure was octagon - shaped, built of uncut stone, and resembled a fort. There was no door on the sides exposed to Shefford's gaze, but small apertures two-thirds the way up probably served as windows and port-holes. The roof appeared to be made of poles covered with red earth.

Like a huge cold rock on a wide plain this house stood there on the windy slope. It was an outpost of the trader Presbrey, of whom Shefford had heard at Flagstaff and Tuba. No living thing appeared in the limit of Shefford's vision. He gazed shudderingly at the unwelcoming habitation, at the dark eyelike windows, at the sweep of barren slope merging into the vast red valley, at the bold, bleak bluffs. Could any one live here? The nature of that sinister valley forbade a home there, and the spirit of the place hovered in the silence and space. Shefford thought irresistibly of how his enemies would have consigned him to just such a hell. He thought bitterly and mockingly of the narrow congregation that had proved him a failure in the ministry, that

3

had repudiated his ideas of religion and immortality and God, that had driven him, at the age of twenty-four, from the calling forced upon him by his people. As a boy he had yearned to make himself an artist; his family had made him a clergyman; fate had made him a failure. A failure only so far in his life, something urged him to add—for in the lonely days and silent nights of the desert he had experienced a strange birth of hope. Adventure had called him, but it was a vague and spiritual hope, a dream of promise, a nameless attainment that fortified his wilder impulse.

As he rode around a corner of the stone house his horse snorted and stopped. A lean, shaggy pony jumped at sight of him, almost displacing a red long-haired blanket that covered an Indian saddle. Quick thuds of hoofs in sand drew Shefford's attention to a corral made of peeled poles, and here he saw another pony.

Shefford heard subdued voices. He dismounted and walked to an open door. In the dark interior he dimly descried a high counter, a stairway, a pile of bags of flour, blankets, and silver-ornamented objects, but the persons he had heard were not in that part of the house. Around another corner of the octagon-shaped wall he found another open door, and through it saw goat-skins and a mound of dirty sheep-wool, black and brown and white. It was light in this part of the building. When he crossed the threshold he was astounded to see a man struggling with a girl — an Indian girl. She was straining back from him, panting, and uttering low guttural sounds. The man's face was corded and

4

RED LAKE

dark with passion. This scene affected Shefford
strangely. Primitive emotions were new to him.

Before Shefford could speak the girl broke loose
and turned to flee. She was an Indian and this
place was the uncivilized desert, but Shefford knew
terror when he saw it. Like a dog the man rushed
after her. It was instinct that made Shefford strike,
and his blow laid the man flat. He lay stunned a
moment, then raised himself to a sitting posture, his
hand to his face, and the gaze he fixed upon Shefford
seemed to combine astonishment and rage.

"I hope you're not Presbrey," said Shefford,
slowly. He felt awkward, not sure of himself.

The man appeared about to burst into speech, but
repressed it. There was blood on his mouth and
his hand. Hastily he scrambled to his feet. Shefford saw this man's amaze and rage change to
shame. He was tall and rather stout; he had a
smooth tanned face, soft of outline, with a weak
chin; his eyes were dark. The look of him and his
corduroys and his soft shoes gave Shefford an impression that he was not a man who worked hard.
By contrast with the few other worn and rugged
desert men Shefford had met this stranger stood
out strikingly. He stooped to pick up a soft felt
hat and, jamming it on his head, he hurried out.
Shefford followed him and watched him from the
door. He went directly to the corral, mounted the
pony, and rode out, to turn down the slope toward
the south. When he reached the level of the basin,
where evidently the sand was hard, he put the pony
to a lope and gradually drew away.

"Well!" ejaculated Shefford. He did not know

what to make of this adventure. Presently he became aware that the Indian girl was sitting on a roll of blankets near the wall. With curious interest Shefford studied her appearance. She had long, raven-black hair, tangled and disheveled, and she wore a soiled white band of cord above her brow. The color of her face struck him; it was dark, but not red nor bronzed; it almost had a tinge of gold. Her profile was clear-cut, bold, almost stern. Long black eyelashes hid her eyes. She wore a tight-fitting waist garment of material resembling velveteen. It was ripped along her side, exposing a skin still more richly gold than that of her face. A string of silver ornaments and turquoise-and-white beads encircled her neck, and it moved gently up and down with the heaving of her full bosom. Her skirt was some gaudy print goods, torn and stained and dusty. She had little feet, incased in brown moccasins, fitting like gloves and buttoning over the ankles with silver coins.

"Who was that man? Did he hurt you?" inquired Shefford, turning to gaze down the valley where a moving black object showed on the bare sand.

"No savvy," replied the Indian girl.

"Where's the trader Presbrey?" asked Shefford. She pointed straight down into the red valley.

"Toh," she said.

In the center of the basin lay a small pool of water shining brightly in the sunset glow. Small objects moved around it, so small that Shefford thought he saw several dogs led by a child. But it was the distance that deceived him. There was a man down there watering his horses. That reminded Shefford of the duty owing to his own tired and thirsty beast. Whereupon he untied his pack, took off the saddle, and was about ready to start down when the Indian girl grasped the bridle from his hand.

"Me go," she said.

He saw her eyes then, and they made her look different. They were as black as her hair. He was puzzled to decide whether or not he thought her handsome.

"Thanks, but I'll go," he replied, and, taking the bridle again, he started down the slope. At every step he sank into the deep, soft sand. Down a little way he came upon a pile of tin cans; they were everywhere, buried, half buried, and lying loose; and these gave evidence of how the trader lived. Presently Shefford discovered that the Indian girl was following him with her own pony. Looking upward at her against the light, he thought her slender, lithe, picturesque. At a distance he liked her.

He plodded on, at length glad to get out of the drifts of sand to the hard level floor of the valley. This, too, was sand, but dried and baked hard, and red in color. At some season of the year this immense flat must be covered with water. How wide it was, and empty! Shefford experienced again a feeling that had been novel to him—and it was that he was loose, free, unanchored, ready to veer with the wind. From the foot of the slope the water hole had appeared to be a few hundred rods out in the valley. But the small size of the figures made Shefford doubt; and he had to travel many

times a few hundred rods before those figures began
to grow. Then Shefford made out that they were
approaching him.

Thereafter they rapidly increased to normal
proportions of man and beast. When Shefford met
them he saw a powerful, heavily built young man
leading two ponies.

"You're Mr. Presbrey, the trader?" inquired
Shefford.

"Yes, I'm Presbrey, without the Mister," he
replied.

"My name's Shefford. I'm knocking about on
the desert. Rode from beyond Tuba to-day."

"Glad to see you," said Presbrey. He offered his
hand. He was a stalwart man, clad in gray shirt,
overalls, and boots. A shock of tumbled light hair
covered his massive head; he was tanned, but not
darkly, and there was red in his cheeks; under his
shaggy eyebrows were deep, keen eyes; his lips were
hard and set, as if occasion for smiles or words was
rare; and his big, strong jaw seemed locked.

"Wish more travelers came knocking around
Red Lake," he added. "Reckon here's the jumping-
off place."

"It's pretty—lonesome," said Shefford, hesitating
as if at a loss for words.

Then the Indian girl came up. Presbrey addressed her in her own language, which Shefford
did not understand. She seemed shy and would
not answer; she stood with downcast face and eyes.
Presbrey spoke again, at which she pointed down
the valley, and then moved on with her pony toward
the water-hole.

Presbrey's keen eyes fixed on the receding black dot far down that oval expanse.

"That fellow left—rather abruptly," said Shefford, constrainedly. "Who was he?"

"His name's Willetts. He's a missionary. He rode in to-day with this Navajo girl. He was taking her to Blue Cañon, where he lives and teaches the Indians. I've met him only a few times. You see, not many white men ride in here. He's the first white man I've seen in six months, and you're the second. Both the same day!... Red Lake's getting popular! It's queer, though, his leaving. He expected to stay all night. There's no other place to stay. Blue Cañon is fifty miles away."

"I'm sorry to say—no, I'm not sorry, either—but I must tell you I was the cause of Mr. Willetts leaving," replied Shefford.

"How so?" inquired the other.

Then Shefford related the incident following his arrival.

"Perhaps my action was hasty," he concluded, apologetically. "I didn't think. Indeed, I'm surprised at myself."

Presbrey made no comment and his face was as hard to read as one of the distant bluffs.

"But what did the man mean?" asked Shefford, conscious of a little heat. "I'm a stranger out here. I'm ignorant of Indians—how they're controlled. Still I'm no fool. . . . If Willetts didn't mean evil, at least he was brutal."

"He was teaching her religion," replied Presbrey. His tone held faint scorn and implied a joke, but his face did not change in the slightest.

9

Without understanding just why, Shefford felt his conviction justified and his action approved Then he was sensible of a slight shock of wonder and disgust.

"I am—I was a minister of the Gospel," he said to Presbrey. "What you hint seems impossible. I can't believe it."

"I didn't hint," replied Presbrey, bluntly, and it was evident that he was a sincere, but close-mouthed, man. "Shefford, so you're a preacher? . . . Did you come out here to try to convert the Indians?"

"No. I said I *was* a minister. I am no longer. I'm just a — a wanderer."

"I see. Well, the desert's no place for missionaries, but it's good for wanderers. . . . Go water your horse and take him up to the corral. You'll find some hay for him. I'll get grub ready."

Shefford went on with his horse to the pool. The water appeared thick, green, murky, and there was a line of salty crust extending around the margin of the pool. The thirsty horse splashed in and eagerly bent his head. But he did not like the taste. Many times he refused to drink, yet always lowered his nose again. Finally he drank, though not his fill. Shefford saw the Indian girl drink from her hand. He scooped up a handful and found it too sour to swallow. When he turned to retrace his steps she mounted her pony and followed him.

A golden flare lit up the western sky, and silhouetted dark and lonely against it stood the trading-post. Upon his return Shefford found the wind rising, and it chilled him. When he reached the slope thin gray sheets of sand were blowing low, rising, whipping, falling, sweeping along with soft silken rustle. Sometimes the gray veils hid his boots. It was a long, toilsome climb up that yielding, dragging ascent, and he had already been lame and tired. By the time he had put his horse away twilight was everywhere except in the west. The Indian girl left her pony in the corral and came like a shadow toward the house.

Shefford had difficulty in finding the foot of the stairway. He climbed to enter a large loft, lighted by two lamps. Presbrey was there, kneading biscuit dough in a pan.

"Make yourself comfortable," he said.

The huge loft was the shape of a half-octagon. A door opened upon the valley side, and here, too, there were windows. How attractive the place was in comparison with the impressions gained from the outside! The furnishings consisted of Indian blankets on the floor, two beds, a desk and table, several chairs and a couch, a gun-rack full of rifles, innumerable silver-ornamented belts, bridles, and other Indian articles upon the walls, and in one corner a wood-burning stove with teakettle steaming, and a great cupboard with shelves packed full of canned foods.

Shefford leaned in the doorway and looked out. Beneath him on a roll of blankets sat the Indian girl, silent and motionless. He wondered what was in her mind, what she would do, how the trader would treat her. The slope now was a long slant of sheeted moving shadows of sand. Dusk had gathered in the valley. The bluffs loomed black

beyond. A pale star twinkled above. Shefford
suddenly became aware of the intense nature of the
stillness about him. Yet, as he listened to this
silence, he heard an intermittent and immeasurably
low moan, a fitful, mournful murmur. Assuredly
it was only the wind. Nevertheless, it made his
blood run cold. It was a different wind from that
which had made music under the eaves of his
Illinois home. This was a lonely, haunting wind,
with desert hunger in it, and more which he could
not name. Shefford listened to this spirit-brooding
sound while he watched night envelop the valley.
How black, how thick the mantle! Yet it brought
no comforting sense of close-folded protection, of
walls of soft sleep, of a home. Instead there was the
feeling of space, of emptiness, of an infinite hall
down which a mournful wind swept streams of
murmuring sand.

"Well, grub's about ready," said Presbrey.

"Got any water?" asked Shefford.

"Sure. There in the bucket. It's rain-water.
I have a tank here."

Shefford's sore and blistered face felt better after
he had washed off the sand and alkali dust.

"Better not wash your face often while you're
in the desert. Bad plan," went on Presbrey, noting
how gingerly his visitor had gone about his ablutions.
"Well, come and eat."

Shefford marked that if the trader did live a
lonely life he fared well. There was more on the
table than twice two men could have eaten. It
was the first time in four days that Shefford had
sat at a table, and he made up for lost opportunity.

His host's actions indicated pleasure, yet the strange, hard face never relaxed, never changed. When the meal was finished Presbrey declined assistance, had a generous thought of the Indian girl, who, he said, could have a place to eat and sleep down-stairs, and then with the skill and despatch of an accomplished housewife cleared the table, after which work he filled a pipe and evidently prepared to listen.

It took only one question for Shefford to find that the trader was starved for news of the outside world; and for an hour Shefford fed that appetite, even as he had been done by. But when he had talked himself out there seemed indication of Presbrey being more than a good listener.

"How'd you come in?" he asked, presently.

"By Flagstaff—across the Little Colorado—and through Moencopie."

"Did you stop at Moen Ave?"

"No. What place is that?"

"A missionary lives there. Did you stop at Tuba?"

"Only long enough to drink and water my horse. That was a wonderful spring for the desert."

"You said you were a wanderer. . . . Do you want a job? I'll give you one."

"No, thank you, Presbrey."

"I saw your pack. That's no pack to travel with in this country. Your horse won't last, either. Have you any money?"

"Yes, plenty of money."

"Well, that's good. Not that a white man out here would ever take a dollar from you. But you can buy from the Indians as you go. Where are you making for, anyhow?"

Shefford hesitated, debating in mind whether to tell his purpose or not. His host did not press the question.

"I see. Just foot-loose and wandering around," went on Presbrey. "I can understand how the desert appeals to you. Preachers lead easy, safe, crowded, bound lives. They're shut up in a church with a Bible and good people. When once in a lifetime they get loose—they break out."

"Yes, I've broken out—beyond all bounds," replied Shefford, sadly. He seemed retrospective for a moment, unaware of the trader's keen and sympathetic glance, and then he caught himself. "I want to see some wild life. Do you know the country north of here?"

"Only what the Navajos tell me. And they're not much to talk. There's a trail goes north, but I've never traveled it. It's a new trail every time an Indian goes that way, for here the sand blows and covers old tracks. But few Navajos ride in from the north. My trade is mostly with Indians up and down the valley."

"How about water and grass?"

"We've had rain and snow. There's sure to be water. Can't say about grass, though the sheep and ponies from the north are always fat. . . . But, say, Shefford, if you'll excuse me for advising you—don't go north."

"Why?" asked Shefford, and it was certain that he thrilled.

"It's unknown country, terribly broken, as you can see from here, and there are bad Indians hiding in the cañons. I've never met a man who had been over the pass between here and Kayenta. The trip's been made, so there must be a trail. But it's a dangerous trip for any man, let alone a tenderfoot. You're not even packing a gun."

"What's this place Kayenta?" asked Shefford.

"It's a spring. Kayenta means Bottomless Spring. There's a little trading-post, the last and the wildest in northern Arizona. Withers, the trader who keeps it, hauls his supplies in from Colorado and New Mexico. He's never come down this way. I never saw him. Know nothing of him except hearsay. Reckon he's a nervy and strong man to hold that post. If you want to go there, better go by way of Keams Cañon, and then around the foot of Black Mesa. It 'll be a long ride—maybe two hundred miles."

"How far straight north over the pass?"

"Can't say. Upward of seventy-five miles over rough trails, if there are trails at all. . . . I've heard rumors of a fine tribe of Navajos living in there, rich in sheep and horses. It may be true and it may not. But I do know there are bad Indians, halfbreeds and outcasts, hiding in there. Some of them have visited me here. Bad customers! More than that, you'll be going close to the Utah line, and the Mormons over there are unfriendly these days."

"Why?" queried Shefford, again with that curious thrill.

"They are being persecuted by the government."

Shefford asked no more questions and his host vouchsafed no more information on that score. The conversation lagged. Then Shefford inquired about the Indian girl and learned that she lived up the valley somewhere. Presbrey had never seen her before Willetts came with her to Red Lake. And this query brought out the fact that Presbrey was comparatively new to Red Lake and vicinity. Shefford wondered why a lonely six months there had not made the trader old in experience. Probably the desert did not readily give up its secrets. Moreover, this Red Lake house was only an occasionally used branch of Presbrey's main trading-post, which was situated at Willow Springs, fifty miles westward over the mesa.

"I'm closing up here soon for a spell," said Presbrey, and now his face lost its set hardness and seemed singularly changed. It was a difference of light and softness. "Won't be so lonesome over at Willow Springs. . . . I'm being married soon."

"That's fine," replied Shefford, warmly. He was glad for the sake of this lonely desert man. What good a wife would bring into a trader's life!

Presbrey's naïve admission, however, appeared to detach him from his present surroundings, and with his massive head enveloped by a cloud of smoke he lived in dreams.

Shefford respected his host's serene abstraction. Indeed, he was grateful for silence. Not for many nights had the past impinged so closely upon the present. The wound in his soul had not healed, and to speak of himself made it bleed anew. Memory was too poignant; the past was too close; he wanted to forget until he had toiled into the heart of this forbidding wilderness—until time had gone by and he dared to face his unquiet soul. Then he listened to the steadily rising roar of the wind. How strange and hollow! That wind was freighted with heavy sand, and he heard it sweep, sweep, sweep by in gusts, and then blow with dull, steady blast against the walls. The sound was provocative of thought. This moan and rush of wind was no dream—this presence of his in a night-enshrouded and sand-besieged house of the lonely desert was a reality—this adventure was not one of fancy. True indeed, then, must be the wild, strange story that had led him hither. He was going on to seek, to strive, to find. Somewhere northward in the broken fastnesses lay hidden a valley walled in from the world. Would they be there, those lost fugitives whose story had thrilled him? After twelve years would she be alive, a child grown to womanhood in the solitude of a beautiful cañon? Incredible! Yet he believed his friend's story and he indeed knew how strange and tragic life was. He fancied he heard her voice on the sweeping wind. She called to him, haunted him. He admitted the improbability of her existence, but lost nothing of the persistent intangible hope that drove him. He believed himself a man stricken in soul, unworthy, through doubt of God, to minister to the people who had banished him. Perhaps a labor of Hercules, a mighty and perilous work of rescue, the saving of this lost and imprisoned girl, would help him in his trouble. She might be his salvation. Who could tell? Always as a boy and as a man he had fared forth to find the treasure at the foot of the rainbow.

II

THE SAGI

NEXT morning the Indian girl was gone and the tracks of her pony led north. Shefford's first thought was to wonder if he would overtake her on the trail; and this surprised him with the proof of how unconsciously his resolve to go on had formed.

Presbrey made no further attempt to turn Shefford back. But he insisted on replenishing the pack, and that Shefford take weapons. Finally Shefford was persuaded to accept a revolver. The trader bade him good·by and stood in the door while Shefford led his horse down the slope toward the water-hole. Perhaps the trader believed he was watching the departure of a man who would never return. He was still standing at the door of the post when Shefford halted at the pool.

Upon the level floor of the valley lay thin patches of snow which had fallen during the night. The air was biting cold, yet stimulated Shefford while it stung him. His horse drank rather slowly and disgustedly. Then Shefford mounted and reluctantly turned his back upon the trading-post.

As he rode away from the pool he saw a large flock of sheep approaching. They were very closely.

18

even densely, packed, in a solid slow-moving mass,
and coming with a precision almost like a march.
This fact surprised Shefford, for there was not an
Indian in sight. Presently he saw that a dog was
leading the flock, and a little later he discovered
another dog in the rear of the sheep. They were
splendid, long-haired dogs, of a wild-looking shepherd
breed. He halted his horse to watch the procession
pass by. The flock covered fully an acre of ground
and the sheep were black, white, and brown. They
passed him, making a little pattering roar on the
hard-caked sand. The dogs were taking the sheep
in to water.

Shefford went on and was drawing close to the
other side of the basin, where the flat red level was
broken by rising dunes and ridges, when he espied
a bunch of ponies. A shrill whistle told him that
they had seen him. They were wild, shaggy, with
long manes and tails. They stopped, threw up
their heads, and watched him. Shefford certainly
returned the attention. There was no Indian with
them. Presently, with a snort, the leader, which
appeared to be a stallion, trotted behind the others,
seemed to be driving them, and went clear round the
band to get in the lead again. He was taking
them in to water, the same as the dogs had taken
the sheep.

These incidents were new and pleasing to Shefford. How ignorant he had been of life in the
wilderness! Once more he received subtle intimations of what he might learn out in the open; and
it was with a less weighted heart that he faced the
gateway between the huge yellow bluffs on his left

and the slow rise of ground to the black mesa on his right. He looked back in time to see the trading-post, bleak and lonely on the bare slope, pass out of sight behind the bluffs. Shefford felt no fear—he really had little experience of physical fear—but it was certain that he gritted his teeth and welcomeu whatever was to come to him. He had lived a narrow, insulated life with his mind on spiritual things; his family and his congregation and his friends—except that one new friend whose story had enthralled him—were people of quiet religious habit; the man deep down in him had never had a chance. He breathed hard as he tried to imagine the world opening to him, and almost dared to be glad for the doubt that had sent him adrift.

The tracks of the Indian girl's pony were plain in the sand. Also there were other tracks, not so plain, and these Shefford decided had been made by Willetts and the girl the day before. He climbed a ridge, half soft sand and half hard, and saw right before him, rising in striking form, two great yellow buttes, like elephant legs. He rode between them, amazed at their height. Then before him stretched a slowly ascending valley, walled on one side by the black mesa and on the other by low bluffs. For miles a dark-green growth of greasewood covered the valley, and Shefford could see where the green thinned and failed, to give place to sand. He trotted his horse and made good time on this stretch.

The day contrasted greatly with any he had yet experienced. Gray clouds obscured the walls of rock a few miles to the west, and Shefford saw squalls of snow like huge veils dropping down and spreading out. The wind cut with the keenness of a knife. Soon he was chilled to the bone. A squall swooped and roared down upon him, and the wind that bore the driving white pellets of snow, almost like hail, was so freezing bitter cold that the former wind seemed warm in comparison. The squall passed as swiftly as it had come, and it left Shefford so benumbed he could not hold the bridle. He tumbled off his horse and walked. By and by the sun came out and soon warmed him and melted the thin layer of snow on the sand. He was still on the trail of the Indian girl, but hers were now the only tracks he could see.

All morning he gradually climbed, with limited view, until at last he mounted to a point where the country lay open to his sight on all sides except where the endless black mesa ranged on into the north. A rugged yellow peak dominated the landscape to the fore, but it was far away. Red and ragged country extended westward to a huge flat-topped wall of gray rock. Lowering swift clouds swept across the sky, like drooping mantles, and they darkened the sun. Shefford built a little fire out of dead greasewood sticks, and with his blanket round his shoulders he hung over the blaze, scorching his clothes and hands. He had been cold before in his life, but he had never before appreciated fire. This desert blast pierced him. The squall enveloped him, thicker and colder and windier than the other, but, being better fortified, he did not suffer so much. It howled away, hiding the mesa and leaving a white desert behind. Shefford walked on, leading

his horse, until the exercise and the sun had once
more warmed him.

This last squall had rendered the Indian girl's
trail difficult to follow. The snow did not quickly
melt, and, besides, sheep tracks and the tracks of
horses gave him trouble, until at last he was compelled to admit that he could not follow her any
longer. A faint path or trail led north, however, and,
following that, he soon forgot the girl. Every surmounted ridge held a surprise for him. The desert
seemed never to change in the vast whole that en-
compassed him, yet near him it was always changing.
From Red Lake he had seen a peaked, walled, and
cañoned country, as rough as a stormy sea; but
when he rode into that country the sharp and
broken features held to the distance.

He was glad to get out of the sand. Long narrow
flats, gray with grass and dotted with patches of
greasewood, and lined by low bare ridges of yellow
rock, stretched away from him, leading toward the
yellow peak that seemed never to be gained upon.

Shefford had pictures in his mind, pictures of
stone walls and wild valleys and domed buttes, all
of which had been painted in colorful and vivid
words by his friend Venters. He believed he would
recognize the distinctive and remarkable landmarks Venters had portrayed, and he was certain
that he had not yet come upon one of them. This
was his second lonely day of travel and he had
grown more and more susceptible to the influence
of horizon and the different prominent points. He
attributed a gradual change in his feelings to the
loneliness and the increasing wildness. Between

Tuba and Flagstaff he had met Indians and an oc-
casional prospector and teamster. Here he was
alone, and though he felt some strange gladness,
he could not help but see the difference.

He rode on during the gray, lowering, chilly day,
and toward evening the clouds broke in the west,
and a setting sun shone through the rift, burnishing
the desert to red and gold. Shefford's instinctive but
deadened love of the beautiful in nature stirred into
life, and the moment of its rebirth was a melancholy
and sweet one. Too late for the artist's work, but
not too late for his soul!

For a place to make camp he halted near a low
area of rock that lay like an island in a sea of grass.
There was an abundance of dead greasewood for a
camp-fire, and, after searching over the rock, he
found little pools of melted snow in the depressions.
He took off the saddle and pack, watered his horse,
and, hobbling him as well as his inexperience permitted, he turned him loose on the grass.

Then while he built a fire and prepared a meal
the night came down upon him. In the lee of the
rock he was well sheltered from the wind, but the
air was bitter cold. He gathered all the dead
greasewood in the vicinity, replenished the fire, and
rolled in his blanket, back to the blaze. The loneliness and the coyotes did not bother him this night.
He was too tired and cold. He went to sleep at
once and did not awaken until the fire died out.
Then he rebuilt it and went to sleep again. Every
half-hour all night long he repeated this, and was
glad indeed when the dawn broke.

The day began with misfortune. His horse was

gone; it had been stolen, or had worked out of sight, or had broken the hobbles and made off. From a high stone ridge Shefford searched the grassy flats and slopes, all to no purpose. Then he tried to track the horse, but this was equally futile. He had expected disasters, and the first one did not daunt him. He tied most of his pack in the blanket, threw the canteen across his shoulder, and set forth, sure at least of one thing—that he was a very much better traveler on foot than on horseback.

Walking did not afford him the leisure to study the surrounding country; however, from time to time, when he surmounted a bench he scanned the different landmarks that had grown familiar. It took hours of steady walking to reach and pass the yellow peak that had been a kind of goal. He saw many sheep trails and horse tracks in the vicinity of this mountain, and once he was sure he espied an Indian watching him from a bold ridge-top.

The day was bright and warm, with air so clear it magnified objects he knew to be far away. The ascent was gradual; there were many narrow flats connected by steps; and the grass grew thicker and longer. At noon Shefford halted under the first cedar-tree, a lonely, dwarfed shrub that seemed to have had a hard life. From this point the rise of ground was more perceptible, and straggling cedars led the eye on to a purple slope that merged into green of piñon and pine. Could that purple be the sage Venters had so feelingly described, or was it merely the purple of deceiving distance? Whatever it might be, it gave Shefford a thrill and made him think of the strange, shy, and lovely woman

Venters had won out here in this purple - sage country.

He calculated that he had ridden thirty miles the day before and had already traveled ten miles to-day, and therefore could hope to be in the pass before night. Shefford resumed his journey with too much energy and enthusiasm to think of being tired. And he discovered presently that the strag-gling cedars and the slope beyond were much closer than he had judged them to be. He reached the sage to find it gray instead of purple. Yet it was always purple a little way ahead, and if he half shut his eyes it was purple near at hand. He was surprised to find that he could not breathe freely, or it seemed so, and soon made the discovery that the sweet, pungent, penetrating fragrance of sage and cedar had this strange effect upon him. This was an exceedingly dry and odorous forest, where every open space between the clumps of cedars was choked with luxuriant sage. The piñons were higher up on the mesa, and the pines still higher. Shefford appeared to lose himself. There were no trails; the black mesa on the right and the wall of stone on the left could not be seen; but he pushed on with what was either singular confidence or rash impulse. And he did not know whether that slope was long or short.

Once at the summit he saw with surprise that it broke abruptly and the descent was very steep and short on that side. Through the trees he once more saw the black mesa, rising to the dignity of a moun-tain; and he had glimpses of another flat, narrow valley, this time with a red wall running parallel with the mesa. He could not help but hurry down

to get an unobstructed view. His eagerness **was** rewarded by a splendid scene, yet to his regret **he** could not force himself to believe it had any relation to the pictured scenes in his mind. The valley was half a mile wide, perhaps several miles long, and it extended in a curve between the cedar-sloped mesa and a looming wall of red stone. There was not a bird or a beast in sight. He found a well-defined trail, but it had not been recently used. He passed a low structure made of peeled logs and mud, with a dark opening like a door. It did not take him many minutes to learn that the valley was longer than he had calculated. He walked swiftly and steadily, in spite of the fact that the pack had become burdensome. What lay beyond the jutting corner of the mesa had increasing fascination for him and acted as a spur. At last he turned the corner, only to be disappointed at sight of another cedar slope. He had a glimpse of a single black shaft of rock rising far in the distance, and it disappeared as his striding forward made the crest of the slope 'rise toward the sky.

Again his view became restricted, and he lost the sense of a slow and gradual uplift of rock and an increase in the scale of proportion. Half-way up this ascent he was compelled to rest; and again the sun was slanting low when he entered the cedar forest. Soon he was descending, and he suddenly came into the open to face a scene that made his heart beat thick and fast.

He saw lofty crags and cathedral spires, and a wonderful cañon winding between huge beetling red walls. He heard the murmur of flowing water.

26

The trail led down to the cañon floor, which appeared to be level and green and cut by deep washes in red earth. Could this cañon be the mouth of Deception Pass? It bore no resemblance to any place Shefford had heard described, yet somehow he felt rather than saw that it was the portal to the wild fastness he had traveled so far to enter.

Not till he had descended the trail and had dropped his pack did he realize how weary and foot-sore he was. Then he rested. But his eyes roved to and fro, and his mind was active. What a wild and lonesome spot! The low murmur of shallow water came up to him from a deep, narrow cleft. Shadows were already making the cañon seem full of blue haze. He saw a bare slope of stone out of which cedar-trees were growing. And as he looked about him he became aware of a singular and very perceptible change in the lights and shades. The sun was setting; the crags were gold-tipped; the shadows crept upward; the sky seemed to darken swiftly; then the gold changed to red, slowly dulled, and the grays and purples stood out. Shefford was entranced with the beautiful changing effects, and watched till the walls turned black and the sky grew steely and a faint star peeped out. Then he set about the necessary camp tasks.

Dead cedars right at hand assured him a com-fortable night with steady fire; and when he had satisfied his hunger he arranged an easy seat before the blazing logs, and gave his mind over to thought of his weird, lonely environment.

The murmur of running water mingled in har-monious accompaniment with the moan of the wind

27

in the cedars—wild, sweet sounds that were balm
to his wounded spirit! They seemed a part of the
silence, rather than a break in it or a hindrance
to the feeling of it. But suddenly that silence did
break to the rattle of a rock. Shefford listened,
thinking some wild animal was prowling around.
He felt no alarm. Presently he heard the sound
again, and again. Then he recognized the crack
of unshod hoofs upon rock. A horse was coming
down the trail. Shefford rather resented the in-
terruption, though he still had no alarm. He believed he was perfectly safe. As a matter of fact,
he had never in his life been anything but safe and
padded around with wool, hence, never having
experienced peril, he did not know what fear was.

Presently he saw a horse and rider come into
dark prominence on the ridge just above his camp.
They were silhouetted against the starry sky. The
horseman stopped and he and his steed made a
magnificent black statue, somehow wild and strange,
in Shefford's sight. Then he came on, vanished in
the darkness under the ridge, presently to emerge
into the circle of camp-fire light.

He rode to within twenty feet of Shefford and the
fire. The horse was dark, wild-looking, and seemed
ready to run. The rider appeared to be an Indian,
and yet had something about him suggesting the
cowboy. At once Shefford remembered what Presbrey had said about half-breeds. A little shock,
inexplicable to Shefford, rippled over him.

He greeted his visitor, but received no answer.
Shefford saw a dark, squat figure bending forward in
the saddle. The man was tense. All about him

was dark except the glint of a rifle across the saddle. The face under the sombrero was only a shadow. Shefford kicked the fire-logs and a brighter blaze lightened the scene. Then he saw this stranger a little more clearly, and made out an unusually large head, broad dark face, a sinister tight-shut mouth, and gleaming black eyes.

Those eyes were unmistakably hostile. They roved searchingly over Shefford's pack and then over his person. Shefford felt for the gun that Presbrey had given him. But it was gone. He had left it back where he had lost his horse, and had not thought of it since. Then a strange, slow-coming cold agitation possessed Shefford. Something gripped his throat.

Suddenly Shefford was stricken at a menacing movement on the part of the horseman. He had drawn a gun. Shefford saw it shine darkly in the firelight. The Indian meant to murder him. Shefford saw the grim, dark face in a kind of horrible amaze. He felt the meaning of that drawn weapon as he had never felt anything before in his life. And he collapsed back into his seat with an icy, sickening terror. In a second he was dripping wet with cold sweat. Lightning-swift thoughts flashed through his mind. It had been one of his platitudes that he was not afraid of death. Yet here he was a shaking, helpless coward. What had he learned about either life or death? Would this dark savage plunge him into the unknown? It was then that Shefford realized his hollow philosophy and the bitter-sweetness of life. He had a brain and a soul, and between them he might have worked out his salvation. But what were they to this ruthless night-wanderer, this raw and horrible wildness of the desert?

Incapable of voluntary movement, with tongue cleaving to the roof of his mouth, Shefford watched the horseman and the half-poised gun. It was not yet leveled. Then it dawned upon Shefford that the stranger's head was turned a little, his ear to the wind. He was listening. His horse was listening. Suddenly he straightened up, wheeled his horse, and trotted away into the darkness. But he did not climb the ridge down which he had come.

Shefford heard the click of hoofs upon the stony trail. Other horses and riders were descending into the cañon. They had been the cause of his deliverance, and in the relaxation of feeling he almost fainted. Then he sat there, slowly recovering, slowly ceasing to tremble, divining that this situation was somehow to change his attitude toward life.

Three horses, two with riders, moved in dark shapes across the sky - line above the ridge, disappeared as had Shefford's first visitor, and then rode into the light. Shefford saw two Indians—a man and a woman; then with surprise recognized the latter to be the Indian girl he had met at Red Lake. He was still more surprised to recognize in the third horse the one he had lost at the last camp. Shefford rose, a little shaky on his legs, to thank these Indians for a double service. The man slipped from his saddle and his moccasined feet thudded lightly. He was tall, lithe, erect, a singularly graceful figure, and as he advanced Shefford saw a dark face and sharp, dark eyes. The Indian was bareheaded, with his hair bound in a band. He resembled the girl, but appeared to have a finer face.

"How do?" he said, in a voice low and distinct. He extended his hand, and Shefford felt a grip of steel. He returned the greeting. Then the Indian gave Shefford the bridle of the horse, and made signs that appeared to indicate the horse had broken his hobbles and strayed. Shefford thanked him. Thereupon the Indian unsaddled and led the horses away, evidently to water them. The girl remained behind. Shefford addressed her, but she was shy and did not respond. He then set about cooking a meal for his visitors, and was busily engaged at this when the Indian returned without the horses. Presently Shefford resumed his seat by the fire and watched the two eat what he had prepared. They certainly were hungry and soon had the pans and cups empty. Then the girl drew back a little into the shadow, while the man sat with his legs crossed and his feet tucked under him.

His dark face was smooth, yet it seemed to have lines under the surface. Shefford was impressed. He had never seen an Indian who interested him as this one. Looked at superficially, he appeared young, wild, silent, locked in his primeval apathy, just a healthy savage; but looked at more attentively, he appeared matured, even old, a strange, sad, brooding figure, with a burden on his shoulders. Shefford found himself growing curious.

"What place?" asked Shefford, waving his hand toward the dark opening between the black cliffs.

"Sagi," replied the Indian.

That did not mean anything to Shefford, and he

asked if the Sagi was the pass, but the Indian shook
his head.

"Wife?" asked Shefford, pointing to the girl.

The Indian shook his head again. "*Bi-la*," he said.

"What you mean?" asked Shefford. "What
bi-la?"

"Sister," replied the Indian. He spoke the word
reluctantly, as if the white man's language did not
please him, but the clearness and correct pronun-
ciation surprised Shefford.

"What name—what call her?" he went on.

"Glen Naspa."

"What your name?" inquired Shefford, indicat-
ing the Indian.

"Nas Ta Bega," answered the Indian.

"Navajo?"

The Indian bowed with what seemed pride and
stately dignity.

"My name John Shefford. Come far 'way back
toward rising sun. Come stay here long."

Nas Ta Bega's dark eyes were fixed steadily upon
Shefford. He reflected that he could not remember
having felt so penetrating a gaze. But neither the
Indian's eyes nor face gave any clue to his thoughts.

"Navajo no savvy Jesus Christ," said the Indian,
and his voice rolled out low and deep.

Shefford felt both amaze and pain. The Indian
had taken him for a missionary.

"No! . . . Me no missionary," cried Shefford, and
he flung up a passionately repudiating hand.

A singular flash shot from the Indian's dark eyes.
It struck Shefford even at this stinging moment when
the past came back.

"Trade—buy wool—blanket?" queried Nas Ta Bega.

"No," replied Shefford. "Me want ride—walk far." He waved his hand to indicate a wide sweep of territory. "Me sick."

Nas Ta Bega laid a significant finger upon his lungs.

"No," replied Shefford. "Me strong. Sick here." And with motions of his hands he tried to show that his was a trouble of the heart.

Shefford received instant impression of this Indian's intelligent comprehension, but he could not tell just what had given him the feeling. Nas Ta Bega rose then and walked away into the shadow. Shefford heard him working around the dead cedar-tree, where he had probably gone to get fire-wood. Then Shefford heard a splintering crash, which was followed by a crunching, bumping sound. Presently he was astounded to see the Indian enter the lighted circle dragging the whole cedar-tree, trunk first. Shefford would have doubted the ability of two men to drag that tree, and here came Nas Ta Bega, managing it easily. He laid the trunk on the fire, and then proceeded to break off small branches, to place them advantageously where the red coals kindled them into a blaze.

The Indian's next move was to place his saddle, which he evidently meant to use for a pillow. Then he spread a goat-skin on the ground, lay down upon it, with his back to the fire, and, pulling a long-haired saddle-blanket over his shoulders, he relaxed and became motionless. His sister, Glen Naspa, did likewise, except that she stayed farther away from the fire, and she had a larger blanket, which covered her well. It appeared to Shefford that they went to sleep at once.

Shefford felt as tired as he had ever been, but he did not think he could soon drop into slumber, and in fact he did not want to.

There was something in the companionship of these Indians that he had not experienced before. He still had a strange and weak feeling—the aftermath of that fear which had sickened him with its horrible icy grip. Nas Ta Bega's arrival had frightened away that dark and silent prowler of the night; and Shefford was convinced the Indian had saved his life. The measure of his gratitude was a source of wonder to him. Had he cared so much for life? Yes—he had, when face to face with death. That was something to know. It helped him. And he gathered from his strange feelings that the romantic quest which had brought him into the wilderness might turn out to be an antidote for the morbid bitterness of heart.

With new sensations had come new thoughts. Right then it was very pleasant to sit in the warmth and light of the roaring cedar fire. There was a deep-seated ache of fatigue in his bones. What joy it was to rest! He had felt the dry scorch of desert thirst and the pang of hunger. How wonderful to learn the real meaning of water and food! He had just finished the longest, hardest day's work of his life! Had that anything to do with a something almost like peace which seemed to hover near in the shadows, trying to come to him? He had befriended an Indian girl, and now her brother had

34

paid back the service. Both the giving and receiving were somehow sweet to Shefford. They opened up hitherto vague channels of thought. For years he had imagined he was serving people, when he had never lifted a hand. A blow given in the defense of an Indian girl had somehow operated to make a change in John Shefford's existence. It had liberated a spirit in him. Moreover, it had worked its influence outside his mind. The Indian girl and her brother had followed his trail to return his horse, perhaps to guide him safely, but, unknowingly perhaps, they had done infinitely more than that for him. As Shefford's eye wandered over the dark, still figures of the sleepers he had a strange, dreamy premonition, or perhaps only a fancy, that there was to be more come of this fortunate meeting.

For the rest, it was good to be there in the speaking silence, to feel the heat on his outstretched palms and the cold wind on his cheek, to see the black wall lifting its bold outline and the crags reaching for the white stars.

III

KAYENTA

THE stamping of horses awoke Shefford. He saw a towering crag, rosy in the morning light, like a huge red spear splitting the clear blue of sky. He got up, feeling cramped and sore, yet with unfamiliar exhilaration. The whipping air made him stretch his hands to the fire. An odor of coffee and broiled meat mingled with the fragrance of wood smoke. Glen Naspa was on her knees broiling a rabbit on a stick over the red coals. Nas Ta Bega was saddling the ponies. The cañon appeared to be full of purple shadows under one side of dark cliffs and golden streaks of mist on the other where the sun struck high up on the walls.

"Good morning," said Shefford.

Glen Naspa shyly replied in Navajo.

"How," was Nas Ta Bega's greeting.

In daylight the Indian lost some of the dark somberness of face that had impressed Shefford. He had a noble head, in poise like that of an eagle, a bold, clean-cut profile, and stern, close-shut lips. His eyes were the most striking and attractive feature about him; they were coal-black and piercing; the intent look out of them seemed to come from a keen and inquisitive mind.

Shefford ate breakfast with the Indians, and then
helped with the few preparations for departure.
Before they mounted, Nas Ta Bega pointed to horse
tracks in the dust. They were those that had been
made by Shefford's threatening visitor of the night
before. Shefford explained by word and sign, and
succeeded at least in showing that he had been in
danger. Nas Ta Bega followed the tracks a little
way and presently returned.

"Shadd," he said, with an ominous shake of his
head. Shefford did not understand whether he
meant the name of his visitor or something else, but
the menace connected with the word was clear
enough.

Glen Naspa mounted her pony, and it was a
graceful action that pleased Shefford. He climbed
a little stiffly into his own saddle. Then Nas Ta
Bega got up and pointed northward.

"Kayenta?" he inquired.

Shefford nodded and then they were off, with Glen
Naspa in the lead. They did not climb the trail
which they had descended, but took one leading to
the right along the base of the slope. Shefford saw
down into the red wash that bisected the cañon floor.
It was a sheer wall of red clay or loam, a hundred
feet high, and at the bottom ran a swift, shallow
stream of reddish water. Then for a time a high
growth of greasewood hid the surroundings from
Shefford's sight. Presently the trail led out into the
open, and Shefford saw that he was at the neck of a
wonderful valley that gradually widened with great
jagged red peaks on the left and the black mesa, now
a mountain, running away to the right. He turned

to find that the opening of the Sagi could no longer be seen, and he was conscious of a strong desire to return and explore that cañon.

Soon Glen Naspa put her pony to a long, easy, swinging canter and her followers did likewise. As they got outward into the valley Shefford lost the sense of being overshadowed and crowded by the nearness of the huge walls and crags. The trail appeared level underfoot, but at a distance it was seen to climb. Shefford found where it disappeared over the foot of a slope that formed a graceful rising line up to the cedared flank of the mesa. The valley floor, widening away to the north, remained level and green. Beyond rose the jagged range of red peaks, all strangely cut and slanting. These distant deceiving features of the country held Shefford's gaze until the Indian drew his attention to things near at hand. Then Shefford saw flocks of sheep dotting the gray-green valley, and bands of beautiful long-maned, long-tailed ponies.

For several miles the scene did not change except that Shefford imagined he came to see where the upland plain ended or at least broke its level. He was right, for presently the Indian pointed, and Shefford went on to halt upon the edge of a steep slope leading down into a valley vast in its barren gray reaches.

"Kayenta," said Nas Ta Bega.

Shefford at first saw nothing except the monotonous gray valley reaching far to the strange, grotesque monuments of yellow cliff. Then close under the foot of the slope he espied two squat stone houses with red roofs, and a corral with a pool of water shining in the sun.

KAYENTA

The trail leading down was steep and sandy, but it was not long. Shefford's sweeping eyes appeared to take in everything at once—the crude stone structures with their earthen roofs, the piles of dirty wool, the Indians lolling around, the tents, and wagons, and horses, little lazy burros and dogs, and scattered everywhere saddles, blankets, guns, and packs.

Then a white man came out of the door. He waved a hand and shouted. Dust and wool and flour were thick upon him. He was muscular and weather-beaten, and appeared young in activity rather than face. A gun swung at his hip and a row of brass-tipped cartridges showed in his belt. Shefford looked into a face that he thought he had seen before, until he realized the similarity was only the bronze and hard line and rugged cast common to desert men. The gray searching eyes went right through him.

"Glad to see you. Get down and come in. Just heard from an Indian that you were coming. I'm the trader Withers," he said to Shefford. His voice was welcoming and the grip of his hand made Shefford's ache.

Shefford told his name and said he was as glad as he was lucky to arrive at Kayenta.

"Hello! Nas Ta Bega!" exclaimed Withers. His tone expressed a surprise his face did not show. "Did this Indian bring you in?"

Withers shook hands with the Navajo while Shefford briefly related what he owed to him. Then Withers looked at Nas Ta Bega and spoke to him in the Indian tongue.

"Shadd," said Nas Ta Bega.

Withers let out a dry little laugh and his strong hand tugged at his mustache.

"Who's Shadd?" asked Shefford.

"He's a half-breed Ute—bad Indian, outlaw, murderer. He's in with a gang of outlaws who hide in the San Juan country. . . . Reckon you're lucky. How'd you come to be there in the Sagi alone?"

"I traveled from Red Lake. Presbrey, the trader there, advised against it, but I came anyway."

"Well." Withers's gray glance was kind, if it did express the foolhardiness of Shefford's act. "Come into the house. . . . Never mind the horse. My wife will sure be glad to see you."

Withers led Shefford by the first stone house, which evidently was the trading-store, into the second. The room Shefford entered was large, with logs smoldering in a huge open fireplace, blankets covering every foot of floor space, and Indian baskets and silver ornaments everywhere, and strange Indian designs painted upon the whitewashed walls. Withers called his wife and made her acquainted with Shefford. She was a slight, comely little woman, with keen, earnest, dark eyes. She seemed to be serious and quiet, but she made Shefford feel at home immediately. He refused, however, to accept the room offered him, saying that he meant to sleep out under the open sky. Withers laughed at this and said he understood. Shefford, remembering Presbrey's hunger for news of the outside world, told this trader and his wife all he could think of; and he was listened to with that close attention a traveler always gained in the remote places.

"Sure am glad you rode in," said Withers, for the fourth time. "Now you make yourself at home. Stay here—come over to the store—do what you like. I've got to work. To-night we'll talk."

Shefford went out with his host. The store was as interesting as Presbrey's, though much smaller and more primitive. It was full of everything, and smelled strongly of sheep and goats. There was a narrow aisle between sacks of flour and blankets on one side and a high counter on the other. Behind this counter Withers stood to wait upon the buying Indians. They sold blankets and skins and bags of wool, and in exchange took silver money. Then they lingered and with slow, staid reluctance bought one thing and then another—flour, sugar, canned goods, coffee, tobacco, ammunition. The counter was never without two or three Indians leaning on their dark, silver-braceleted arms. But as they were slow to sell and buy and go, so were others slow to come in. Their voices were soft and low and it seemed to Shefford they were whispering. He liked to hear them and to look at the banded heads, the long, twisted rolls of black hair tied with white cords, the still dark faces and watchful eyes, the silver ear-rings, the slender, shapely brown hands, the lean and sinewy shapes, the corduroys with a belt and gun, and the small, close-fitting buckskin moccasins buttoned with coins. These Indians all appeared young, and under the quiet, slow demeanor there was fierce blood and fire.

By and by two women came in, evidently squaw and daughter. The former was a huge, stout Indian with a face that was certainly pleasant if not jolly.

She had the corners of a blanket tied under her chin and in the folds behind on her broad back was a naked Indian baby, round and black of head, brown-skinned, with eyes as bright as beads. When the youngster caught sight of Shefford he made a startled dive into the sack of the blanket. Mani-festly, however, curiosity got the better of fear, for presently Shefford caught a pair of wondering dark eyes peeping at him.

"They're good spenders, but slow," said Withers. "The Navajos are careful and cautious. That's why they're rich. This squaw, Yan As Pa, has flocks of sheep and more mustangs than she knows about."

"Mustangs. So that's what you call the ponies?" replied Shefford.

"Yep. They're mustangs, and mostly wild as jack-rabbits."

Shefford strolled outside and made the acquaint-ance of Withers's helper, a Mormon named Whisner. He was a stockily built man past maturity, and his sun-blistered face and watery eyes told of the open desert. He was engaged in weighing sacks of wool brought in by the Indians. Near by stood a frame-work of poles from which an immense bag was suspended. From the top of this bag protruded the head and shoulders of an Indian who appeared to be stamping and packing wool with his feet. He grinned at the curious Shefford. But Shefford was more interested in the Mormon. So far as he knew, Whisner was the first man of that creed he had ever met, and he could scarcely hide his eagerness. Ven-ters's stories had been of a long-past generation of

Mormons, fanatical, ruthless, and unchangeable. Shefford did not expect to meet Mormons of this kind. But any man of that religion would have interested him. Besides this, Whisner seemed to bring him closer to that wild secret cañon he had come West to find. Shefford was somewhat amazed and discomfited to have his polite and friendly overtures repulsed. Whisner might have been an Indian. He was cold, incommunicative, aloof; and there was something about him that made the sensitive Shefford feel his presence was resented.

Presently Shefford strolled on to the corral, which was full of shaggy mustangs. They snorted and kicked at him. He had a half-formed wish that he would never be called upon to ride one of those wild brutes, and then he found himself thinking that he would ride one of them, and after a while any of them. Shefford did not understand himself, but he fought his natural instinctive reluctance to meet obstacles, peril, suffering.

He traced the white-bordered little stream that made the pool in the corral, and when he came to where it oozed out of the sand under the bluff he decided that was not the spring which had made Kayenta famous. Presently down below the trading-post he saw a trough from which burros were drinking. Here he found the spring, a deep well of eddying water walled in by stones, and the overflow made a shallow stream meandering away between its borders of alkali, like a crust of salt. Shefford tasted the water. It bit, but it was good.

Shefford had no trouble in making friends with the lazy sleepy-eyed burros. They let him pull their long ears and rub their noses, but the mustangs standing around were unapproachable. They had wild eyes; they raised long ears and looked vicious. He let them alone.

Evidently this trading-post was a great deal busier than Red Lake. Shefford counted a dozen Indians lounging outside, and there were others riding away. Big wagons told how the bags of wool were transported out of the wilds and how supplies were brought in. A wide, hard-packed road led off to the east, and another, not so clearly defined, wound away to the north. And Indian trails streaked off in all directions.

Shefford discovered, however, when he had walked off a mile or so across the valley to lose sight of the post, that the feeling of wildness and loneliness returned to him. It was a wonderful country. It held something for him besides the possible rescue of an imprisoned girl from a wild cañon.

That night after supper, when Withers and Shefford sat alone before the blazing logs in the huge fireplace, the trader laid his hand on Shefford's and said, with directness and force:

"I've lived my life in the desert. I've met many men and have been a friend to most. . . . You're no prospector or trader or missionary?"

"No," replied Shefford.

"You've had trouble?"

"Yes."

"Have you come in here to hide? Don't be afraid to tell me. I won't give you away."

"I didn't come to hide."

KAYENTA

"Then no one is after you? You've done no wrong?"

"Perhaps I wronged myself, but no one else," replied Shefford, steadily.

"I reckoned so. Well, tell me, or keep your secret—it's all one to me."

Shefford felt a desire to unburden himself. This man was strong, persuasive, kindly. He drew Shefford.

"You're welcome in Kayenta," went on Withers. "Stay as long as you like. I take no pay from a white man. If you want work I have it aplenty."

"Thank you. That is good. I need to work. We'll talk of it later. . . . But just yet I can't tell you why I came to Kayenta, what I want to do, how long I shall stay. My thoughts put in words would seem so like dreams. Maybe they are dreams. Perhaps I'm only chasing a phantom —perhaps I'm only hunting the treasure at the foot of the rainbow."

"Well, this is the country for rainbows," laughed Withers. "In summer from June to August when it storms we have rainbows that 'll make you think you're in another world. The Navaios have rainbow mountains, rainbow cañons, rainbow bridges of stone, rainbow trails. It sure is rainbow country."

That deep and mystic chord in Shefford thrilled. Here it was again—something tangible at the bottom of his dream.

Withers did not wait for Shefford to say any more, and almost as if he read his visitor's mind he began to talk about the wild country he called home.

He had lived at Kayenta for several years—hard

and profitless years by reason of marauding outlaws. He could not have lived there at all but for the protection of the Indians. His father-in-law had been friendly with the Navajos and Piutes for many years, and his wife had been brought up among them. She was held in peculiar reverence and affection by both tribes in that part of the country. Probably she knew more of the Indians' habits, religion, and life than any white person in the West. Both tribes were friendly and peaceable, but there were bad Indians, half-breeds, and outlaws that made the trading-post a venture Withers had long considered precarious, and he wanted to move and intended to some day. His nearest neighbors in New Mexico and Colorado were a hundred miles distant and at some seasons the roads were impassable. To the north, however, twenty miles or so, was situated a Mormon village named Stonebridge. It lay across the Utah line. Withers did some business with this village, but scarcely enough to warrant the risks he had to run. During the last year he had lost several pack-trains, one of which he had never heard of after it left Stonebridge.

"Stonebridge!" exclaimed Shefford, and he trembled. He had heard that name. In his memory it had a place beside the name of another village Shefford longed to speak of to this trader.

"Yes — Stonebridge," replied Withers. "Ever heard the name?"

"I think so. Are there other villages in—in that part of the country?"

"A few, but not close. Glaze is now only a waterhole. Bluff and Monticello are far north across the

San Juan. . . . There used to be another village—but
that wouldn't interest you."

"Maybe it would," replied Shefford, quietly.

But his hint was not taken by the trader. Withers
suddenly showed a semblance to the aloofness Shefford had observed in Whisner.

"Withers, pardon an impertinence—I am deeply
serious. . . . Are you a Mormon?"

"Indeed I'm not," replied the trader, instantly.

"Are you for the Mormons or against them?"

"Neither. I get along with them. I know them.
I believe they are a misunderstood people."

"That's for them."

"No. I'm only fair-minded."

Shefford paused, trying to curb his thrilling impulse, but it was too strong.

"You said there used to be another village. . . .
Was the name of it—Cottonwoods?"

Withers gave a start and faced round to stare at
Shefford in blank astonishment.

"Say, did you give me a straight story about yourself?" he queried, sharply.

"So far as I went," replied Shefford.

"You're no spy on the lookout for sealed wives?"

"Absolutely not. I don't even know what you
mean by sealed wives."

"Well, it's damn strange that you'd know the
name Cottonwoods. . . . Yes, that's the name of the
village I meant—the one that used to be. It's gone
now, all except a few stone walls."

"What became of it?"

"Torn down by Mormons years ago. They
destroyed it and moved away. I've heard Indians

talk about a grand spring that was there once. It's gone, too. Its name was—let me see—"

"Amber Spring," interrupted Shefford.

"By George, you're right!" rejoined the trader, again amazed. "Shefford, this beats me. I haven't heard that name for ten years. I can't help seeing what a tenderfoot—stranger—you are to the desert. Yet, here you are—speaking of what you should know nothing of. . . . And there's more behind this."

Shefford rose, unable to conceal his agitation.

"Did you ever hear of a rider named Venters?"

"Rider? You mean a cowboy? Venters. No, I never heard that name."

"Did you ever hear of a gunman named Lassiter?" queried Shefford, with increasing emotion.

"No."

"Did you ever hear of a Mormon woman named —Jane Withersteen?"

"No."

Shefford drew his breath sharply. He had followed a gleam—he had caught a fleeting glimpse of it.

"Did you ever hear of a child—a girl—a woman— called Fay Larkin?"

Withers rose slowly with a paling face.

"If you're a spy it 'll go hard with you—though I'm no Mormon," he said, grimly.

Shefford lifted a shaking hand.

"I *was* a clergyman. Now I'm nothing—a wanderer—least of all a spy."

Withers leaned closer to see into the other man's eyes; he looked long and then appeared satisfied.

"I've heard the name Fay Larkin," he said,

slowly. "I reckon that's all I'll say till you tell your story."

Shefford stood with his back to the fire and he turned the palms of his hands to catch the warmth. He felt cold. Withers had affected him strangely. What was the meaning of the trader's somber gravity? Why was the very mention of Mormons attended by something austere and secret?

"My name is John Shefford. I am twenty-four," began Shefford. "My family—"

Here a knock on the door interrupted Shefford.

"Come in," called Withers.

The door opened and like a shadow Nas Ta Bega slipped in. He said something in Navajo to the trader.

"How," he said to Shefford, and extended his hand. He was stately, but there was no mistaking his friendliness. Then he sat down before the fire, doubled his legs under him after the Indian fashion, and with dark eyes on the blazing logs seemed to lose himself in meditation.

"He likes the fire," explained Withers. "Whenever he comes to Kayenta he always visits me like this. . . . Don't mind him. Go on with your story."

"My family were plain people, well-to-do, and very religious," went on Shefford. "When I was a boy we moved from the country to a town called Beaumont, Illinois. There was a college in Beaumont and eventually I was sent to it to study for the ministry. I wanted to be— But never mind that. . . . By the time I was twenty-two I was ready for my career as a clergyman. I preached for a year around

at different places and then got a church in my home
town of Beaumont. I became exceedingly good
friends with a man named Venters, who had recently
come to Beaumont. He was a singular man. His
wife was a strange, beautiful woman, very reserved,
and she had wonderful dark eyes. They had money
and were devoted to each other, and perfectly
happy. They owned the finest horses ever seen in
Illinois, and their particular enjoyment seemed to be
riding. They were always taking long rides. It
was something worth going far for to see Mrs.
Venters on a horse.

"It was through my own love of horses that I
became friendly with Venters. He and his wife
attended my church, and as I got to see more of
them, gradually we grew intimate. And it was not
until I did get intimate with them that I realized
that both seemed to be haunted by the past. They
were sometimes sad even in their happiness. They
drifted off into dreams. They lived back in another
world. They seemed to be listening. Indeed, they
were a singularly interesting couple, and I grew
genuinely fond of them. By and by they had a
little girl whom they named Jane. The coming of
the baby made a change in my friends. They were
happier, and I observed that the haunting shadow
did not so often return.

"Venters had spoken of a journey west that he
and his wife meant to take some time. But after the
baby came he never mentioned his wife in connec-
tion with the trip. I gathered that he felt compelled to go to clear up a mystery or to find something
—I did not make out just what. But eventually,

and it was about a year ago, he told me his story—
the strangest, wildest, and most tragic I ever heard.

"I can't tell it all now. It is enough to say that
fifteen years before he had been a rider for a rich
Mormon woman named Jane Withersteen, of this
village Cottonwoods. She had adopted a beautiful
Gentile child named Fay Larkin. Her interest in
Gentiles earned the displeasure of her churchmen,
and as she was proud there came a breach. Venters
and a gunman named Lassiter became involved in
her quarrel. Finally Venters took to the cañons.
Here in the wilds he found the strange girl he eventually married. For a long time they lived in a wonderful hidden valley, the entrance to which was guarded
by a huge balancing rock. Venters got away with
the girl. But Lassiter and Jane Withersteen and
the child Fay Larkin were driven into the cañon.
They escaped to the valley where Venters had lived.
Lassiter rolled the balancing rock, and, crashing down
the narrow trail, it loosened the weathered walls and
closed the narrow outlet for ever."

IV

NEW FRIENDS

SHEFFORD ended his narrative out of breath, pale, and dripping with sweat. Withers sat leaning forward with an expression of intense interest. Nas Ta Bega's easy, graceful pose had succeeded to one of strained rigidity. He seemed a statue of bronze. Could a few intelligible words, Shefford wondered, have created that strange, listening posture?

"Venters got out of Utah, of course, as you know," went on Shefford. "He got out, knowing —as I feel I would have known—that Jane, Lassiter, and little Fay Larkin were shut up, walled up in Surprise Valley. For years Venters considered it would not have been safe for him to venture to rescue them. He had no fears for their lives. They could live in Surprise Valley. But Venters always intended to come back with Bess and find the valley and his friends. No wonder he and Bess were haunted. However, when his wife had the baby that made a difference. It meant he had to go alone. And he was thinking seriously of starting when I— when there were developments that made it desirable for me to leave Beaumont. Venters's story

haunted me as he had been haunted. I dreamed of
that wild valley—of little Fay Larkin grown to
womanhood—such a woman as Bess Venters was.
And the longing to come was great. . . . And, Withers
—here I am."

The trader reached out and gave Shefford the
grip of a man in whom emotion was powerful, but
deep and difficult to express.

"Listen to this. . . . I wish I could help you. Life
is a queer deal. . . . Shefford, I've got to trust you.
Over here in the wild cañon country there's a village of Mormons' sealed wives. It's in Arizona,
perhaps twenty miles from here, and near the Utah
line. When the United States government began
to persecute, or prosecute, the Mormons for polygamy, the Mormons over here in Stonebridge took
their sealed wives and moved them out of Utah, just
across the line. They built houses, established a
village there. I'm the only Gentile who knows about
it. And I pack supplies every few weeks in to these
women. There are perhaps fifty women, mostly
young—second or third or fourth wives of Mormons
—sealed wives. And I want you to understand that
sealed means *sealed* in all that religion or loyalty
can get out of the word. There are also some old
women and old men in the village, but they hardly
count. And there's a flock of the finest children you
ever saw in your life.

"The idea of the Mormons must have been to
escape prosecution. The law of the government is
one wife for each man—no more. All over Utah
polygamists have been arrested. The Mormons are
deeply concerned. I believe they are a good, law-

abiding people. But this law is a direct blow at their religion. In my opinion they can't obey both. And therefore they have not altogether given up plural wives. Perhaps they will some day. I have no proof, but I believe the Mormons of Stonebridge pay secret night visits to their sealed wives across the line in the lonely, hidden village.

"Now once over in Stonebridge I overheard some Mormons talking about a girl who was named Fay Larkin. I never forgot the name. Later I heard the name in this sealed-wife village. But, as I told you, I never heard of Lassiter or Jane Withersteen. Still if Mormons had found them I would never have heard of it. And Deception Pass—that might be the Sagi. . . . I'm not surprised at your rainbow-chasing adventure. It's a great story. . . . This Fay Larkin I've heard of *might* be your Fay Larkin—I almost believe so. Shefford, I'll help you find out."

"Yes, yes—I must know," replied Shefford. "Oh, I hope, I pray we can find her! But—I'd rather she was dead—if she's not still hidden in the valley."

"Naturally. You've dreamed yourself into rescuing this lost Fay Larkin. . . . But, Shefford, you're old enough to know life doesn't work out as you want it to. One way or another I fear you're in for a bitter disappointment."

"Withers, take me to the village."

"Shefford, you're liable to get in bad out here," said the trader, gravely.

"I couldn't be any more ruined than I am now," replied Shefford, passionately.

"But there's risk in this—risk such as you never had," persisted Withers.

"I'll risk anything."

"Reckon this 's a funny deal for a sheep-trader to have on his hands," continued Withers. "Shefford, I like you. I've a mind to see you through this. It's a damn strange story. . . . I'll tell you what—I will help you. I'll give you a job packing supplies in to the village. I meant to turn that over to a Mormon cowboy—Joe Lake. The job shall be yours, and I'll go with you first trip. Here's my hand on it. . . . Now, Shefford, I'm more curious about you than I was before you told your story. What ruined you? As we're to be partners, you can tell me now. I'll keep your secret. Maybe I can do you good."

Shefford wanted to confess, yet it was hard. Perhaps, had he not been so agitated, he would not have answered to impulse. But this trader was a man—a man of the desert—he would understand.

"I told you I was a clergyman," said Shefford in low voice. "I didn't want to be one, but they made me one. I did my best. I failed. . . . I had doubts of religion—of the Bible—of God, as my Church believed in them. As I grew older thought and study convinced me of the narrowness of religion as my congregation lived it. I preached what I believed. I alienated them. They put me out, took my calling from me, disgraced me, ruined me."

"So that's all!" exclaimed Withers, slowly. "You didn't believe in the God of the Bible. . . . Well, I've been in the desert long enough to know there *is* a God, but probably not the one your Church worships. . . . Shefford, go to the Navajo for a faith!"

Shefford had forgotten the presence of Nas Ta

Bega, and perhaps Withers had likewise. At this juncture the Indian rose to his full height, and he folded his arms to stand with the somber pride of a chieftain while his dark, inscrutable eyes were riveted upon Shefford. At that moment he seemed magnificent. How infinitely more he seemed than just a common Indian who had chanced to befriend a white man! The difference was obscure to Shefford. But he felt that it was there in the Navajo's mind. Nas Ta Bega's strange look was not to be interpreted. Presently he turned and passed from the room.

"By George!" cried Withers, suddenly, and he pounded his knee with his fist. "I'd forgotten."

"What?" ejaculated Shefford.

"Why, that Indian understood every word we said. He knows English. He's educated. Well, if this doesn't beat me. . . . Let me tell you about Nas Ta Bega."

Withers appeared to be recalling something half forgotten.

"Years ago, in fifty-seven, I think, Kit Carson with his soldiers chased the Navajo tribes and rounded them up to be put on reservations. But he failed to catch all the members of one tribe. They escaped up into wild cañons like the Sagi. The descendants of these fugitives live there now and are the finest Indians on earth—the finest because unspoiled by the white man. Well, as I got the story, years after Carson's round-up one of his soldiers guided some interested travelers in here. When they left they took an Indian boy with them to educate. From what I know of Navajos I'm

inclined to think the boy was taken against his
parents' wish. Anyway, he was taken. That boy
was Nas Ta Bega. The story goes that he was
educated somewhere. Years afterward, and perhaps
not long before I came in here, he returned to his
people. There have been missionaries and other
interested fools who have given Indians a white
man's education. In all the instances I know of,
these educated Indians returned to their tribes,
repudiating the white man's knowledge, habits, life,
and religion. I have heard that Nas Ta Bega came
back, laid down the white man's clothes along with
the education, and never again showed that he had
known either.

"You have just seen how strangely he acted.
It's almost certain he heard our conversation.
Well, it doesn't matter. He won't tell. He can
hardly be made to use an English word. Besides,
he's a noble red man, if there ever was one. He
has been a friend in need to me. If you stay long
out here you'll learn something from the Indians.
Nas Ta Bega has befriended you, too, it seems. I
thought he showed unusual interest in you."

"Perhaps that was because I saved his sister—
well, to be charitable, from the rather rude advances
of a white man," said Shefford, and he proceeded
to tell of the incident that occurred at Red Lake.

"Willetts!" exclaimed Withers, with much the
same expression that Presbrey had used. "I never
met him. But I know about him. He's—well, the
Indians don't like him much. Most of the missionaries are good men—good for the Indians, in a
way, but sometimes one drifts out here who is bad.

A bad missionary teaching religion to savages! Queer, isn't it? The queerest part is the white people's blindness—the blindness of those who send the missionaries. Well, I dare say Willetts isn't very good. When Presbrey said that was Willetts's way of teaching religion he meant just what he said If Willetts drifts over here he'll be risking much. . . . This you told me explains Nas Ta Bega's friendliness toward you, and also his bringing his sister Glen Naspa to live with relatives up in the pass. She had been living near Red Lake."

"Do you mean Nas Ta Bega wants to keep his sister far removed from Willetts?" inquired Shefford.

"I mean that," replied Withers, "and I hope he's not too late."

Later Shefford went outdoors to walk and think. There was no moon, but the stars made light enough to cast his shadow on the ground. The dark, illimitable expanse of blue sky seemed to be glittering with numberless points of fire. The air was cold and still. A dreaming silence lay over the land. Shefford saw and felt all these things, and their effect was continuous and remained with him and helped calm him. He was conscious of a burden removed from his mind. Confession of his secret had been like tearing a thorn from his flesh, but, once done, it afforded him relief and a singular realization that out here it did not matter much. In a crowd of men all looking at him and judging him by their standards he had been made to suffer. Here, if he were judged at all, it would be by what he could do, how he sustained himself and helped others.

NEW FRIENDS

He walked far across the valley toward the low
bluffs, but they did not seem to get any closer.
And, finally, he stopped beside a stone and looked
around at the strange horizon and up at the heavens.
He did not feel utterly aloof from them, nor alone in
a waste, nor a useless atom amid incomprehensible
forces. Something like a loosened mantle fell from
about him, dropping down at his feet; and all at
once he was conscious of freedom. He did not understand in the least why abasement left him, but it
was so. He had come a long way, in bitterness, in
despair, believing himself to be what men had
called him. The desert and the stars and the wind,
the silence of the night, the loneliness of this vast
country where there was room for a thousand
cities—these somehow vaguely, yet surely, bade
him lift his head. They withheld their secret, but
they made a promise. The thing which he had been
feeling every day and every night was a strange
enveloping comfort. And it was at this moment
that Shefford, divining whence his help was to come,
embraced all that wild and speaking nature around
and above him and surrendered himself utterly.

"I am young. I am free. I have my life to live."
he said. "I'll be a man. I'll take what comes.
Let me learn here!"

When he had spoken out, settled once and for ever
his attitude toward his future, he seemed to be born
again, wonderfully alive to the influences around him,
ready to trust what yet remained a mystery.

Then his thoughts reverted to Fay Larkin.
Could this girl be known to the Mormons? It was
possible. Fay Larkin was an unusual name. Deep

into Shefford's heart had sunk the story Venters had told. Shefford found that he had unconsciously created a like romance—he had been loving a wild and strange and lonely girl, like beautiful Bess Venters. It was a shock to learn the truth, but, as it had been only a dream, it could hardly be vital.

Shefford retraced his steps toward the post. Halfway back he espied a tall, dark figure moving toward him, and presently the shape and the step seemed familiar. Then he recognized Nas Ta Bega. Soon they were face to face. Shefford felt that the Indian had been trailing him over the sand, and that this was to be a significant meeting. Remembering Withers's revelation about the Navajo, Shefford scarcely knew how to approach him now. There was no difference to be made out in Nas Ta Bega's dark face and inscrutable eyes, yet there was a difference to be felt in his presence. But the Indian did not speak, and turned to walk by Shefford's side. Shefford could not long be silent.

"Nas Ta Bega, were you looking for me?" he asked.

"You had no gun," replied the Indian.

But for his very low voice, his slow speaking of the words, Shefford would have thought him a white man. For Shefford there was indeed an instinct in this meeting, and he turned to face the Navajo.

"Withers told me you had been educated, that you came back to the desert, that you never showed your training. . . . Nas Ta Bega, did you understand all I told Withers?"

"Yes," replied the Indian.

"You won't betray me?"

"I am a Navajo."

60

"Nas Ta Bega, you trail me—you say I had no gun." Shefford wanted to ask this Indian if he cared to be the white man's friend, but the question was not easy to put, and, besides, seemed unnecessary. "I am alone and strange in this wild country. I must learn."

"Nas Ta Bega will show you the trails and the water-holes and how to hide from Shadd."

"For money—for silver you will do this?" inquired Shefford.

Shefford felt that the Indian's silence was a rebuke. He remembered Withers's singular praise of this red man. He realized he must change his idea of Indians.

"Nas Ta Bega, I know nothing. I feel like a child in the wilderness. When I speak it is out of the mouths of those who have taught me. I must find a new voice and a new life. . . . You heard my story to Withers. I am an outcast from my own people. If you will be my friend—be so."

The Indian clasped Shefford's hand and held it in a response that was more beautiful for its silence. So they stood for a moment in the starlight.

"Nas Ta Bega, what did Withers mean when he said go to the Navajo for a faith?" asked Shefford.

"He meant the desert is my mother. . . . Will you go with Nas Ta Bega into the cañons and the mountains?"

"Indeed I will."

They unclasped hands and turned toward the trading-post.

"Nas Ta Bega, have you spoken my tongue to

any other white man since you returned to your
home?" asked Shefford.

"No."

"Why do you—why are you different for me?"

The Indian maintained silence.

"Is it because of—of Glen Naspa?" inquired
Shefford.

Nas Ta Bega stalked on, still silent, but Shefford
divined that, although his service to Glen Naspa
would never be forgotten, still it was not wholly
responsible for the Indian's subtle sympathy.

"Bi Nai! The Navajo will call his white friend
Bi Nai—brother," said Nas Ta Bega, and he spoke
haltingly, not as if words were hard to find, but
strange to speak. "I was stolen from my mother's
hogan and taken to California. They kept me ten
years in a mission at San Bernardino and four years
in a school. They said my color and my hair were
all that was left of the Indian in me. But they
could not see my heart. They took fourteen years
of my life. They wanted to make me a missionary
among my own people. But the white man's ways
and his life and his God are not the Indian's. They
never can be."

How strangely productive of thought for Shefford
to hear the Indian talk! What fatality in this meeting and friendship! Upon Nas Ta Bega had been
forced education, training, religion, that had made
him something more and something less than an
Indian. It was something assimilated from the
white man which made the Indian unhappy and
alien in his own home—something meant to be good
for him and his kind that had ruined him. For

NEW FRIENDS

Shefford felt the passion and the tragedy of this Navajo.

"Bi Nai, the Indian is dying!" Nas Ta Bega's low voice was deep and wonderful with its intensity of feeling. "The white man robbed the Indian of lands and homes, drove him into the deserts, made him a gaunt and sleepless spiller of blood. . . . The blood is all spilled now, for the Indian is broken. But the white man sells him rum and seduces his daughters. . . . He will not leave the Indian in peace with his own God! . . . Bi Nai, the Indian is dying!"

That night Shefford lay in his blankets out under the open sky and the stars. The earth had never meant much to him, and now it was a bed. He had preached of the heavens, but until now had never studied them. An Indian slept beside him. And not until the gray of morning had blotted out the starlight did Shefford close his eyes.

With break of the next day came full, varied, and stirring incidents to Shefford. He was strong, though unskilled at most kinds of outdoor tasks. Withers had work for ten men, if they could have been found. Shefford dug and packed and lifted till he was so sore and tired that rest was a blessing.

He never succeeded in getting on a friendly footing with the Mormon Whisner, though he kept up his agreeable and kindly advances. He listened to the trader's wife as she told him about the Indians, and what he learned he did not forget. And his wonder and respect increased in proportion to his knowledge.

One day there rode into Kayenta the Mormon for

63

whom Withers had been waiting. His name was Joe Lake. He appeared young, and slipped off his superb bay with a grace and activity that were astounding in one of his huge bulk. He had a still, smooth face, with the color of red bronze and the expression of a cherub; big, soft, dark eyes; and a winning smile. He was surprisingly different from Whisner or any Mormon character that Shefford had naturally conceived. His costume was that of the cowboy on active service; and he packed a gun at his hip. The hand-shake he gave Shefford was an ordeal for that young man and left him with his whole right side momentarily benumbed.

"I sure am glad to meet you," he said in a lazy, mild voice. And he was taking friendly stock of Shefford when the bay mustang reached with vicious muzzle to bite at him. Lake gave a jerk on the bridle that almost brought the mustang to his knees. He reared then, snorted, and came down to plant his forefeet wide apart, and watched his master with defiant eyes. This mustang was the finest horse Shefford had ever seen. He appeared quite large for his species, was almost red in color, had a racy and powerful build, and a fine thoroughbred head with dark, fiery eyes. He did not look mean, but he had spirit.

"Navvy, you've sure got bad manners," said Lake, shaking the mustang's bridle. He spoke as if he were chiding a refractory little boy. "Didn't I break you better 'n that? What's this gentleman goin' to think of you? Tryin' to bite my ear off!"

Lake had arrived about the middle of the forenoon, and Withers announced his intention of pack-

ing at once for the trip. Indians were sent out on
the ranges to drive in burros and mustangs. Shefford
had his thrilling expectancy somewhat chilled by
what he considered must have been Lake's reception
of the trader's plan. Lake seemed to oppose him,
and evidently it took vehemence and argument on
Withers's part to make the Mormon tractable. But
Withers won him over, and then he called Shefford
to his side.

"You fellows got to be good friends." he said.
"You'll have charge of my pack-trains. Nas Ta
Bega wants to go with you. I'll feel safer about my
supplies and stock than I've ever been. . . . Joe, I'll
back this stranger for all I'm worth. He's square.
. . . And, Shefford, Joe Lake is a Mormon of the
younger generation. I want to start you right.
You can trust him as you trust me. He's white
clean through. And he's the best horse-wrangler in
Utah."

It was Lake who first offered his hand, and Shefford made haste to meet it with his own. Neither
of them spoke. Shefford intuitively felt an altera-
tion in Lake's regard, or at least a singular increase
of interest. Lake had been told that Shefford had
been a clergyman, was now a wanderer, without
any religion. Again it seemed to Shefford that he
owed a forming of friendship to this singular fact.
And it hurt him. But strangely it came to him that
he had taken a liking to a Mormon.

About one o'clock the pack-train left Kayenta.
Nas Ta Bega led the way up the slope. Following
him climbed half a dozen patient, plodding, heavily
laden burros. Withers came next, and he turned in

nis saddle to wave good-by to his wife. Joe Lake appeared to be busy keeping a red mule and a wild gray mustang and a couple of restive blacks in the trail. Shefford brought up in the rear.

His mount was a beautiful black mustang with three white feet, a white spot on his nose, and a mane that swept to his knees. "His name's Nack-yal," Withers had said. "It means two bits, or twenty-five cents. He ain't worth more." To look at Nack-yal had pleased Shefford very much indeed, but, once upon his back, he grew dubious. The mustang acted queer. He actually looked back at Shefford, and it was a look of speculation and disdain. Shefford took exception to Nack-yal's manner and to his reluctance to go, and especially to a habit the mustang had of turning off the trail to the left. Shefford had managed some rather spirited horses back in Illinois; and though he was willing and eager to learn all over again, he did not enjoy the prospect of Lake and Withers seeing this black mustang make a novice of him. And he guessed that was just what Nack-yal intended to do. However, once up over the hill, with Kayenta out of sight, Nack-yal trotted alcng fairly well, needing only now and then to be pulled back from his strange swinging to the left off the trail.

The pack-train traveled steadily and soon crossed the upland plain to descend into the valley again. Shefford saw the jagged red peaks with an emotion he could not name. The cañons between them were purple in the shadows, the great walls and slopes brightened to red, and the tips were gold in the sun. Shefford forgot all about his mustang and the trail.

NEW FRIENDS

Suddenly with a pound of hoofs Nack-yal seemed to rise. He leaped sidewise out of the trail, came down stiff-legged. Then Shefford shot out of the saddle. He landed so hard that he was stunned for an instant. Sitting up, he saw the mustang bent down, eyes and ears showing fight, and his fore-feet spread. He appeared to be looking at something in the trail. Shefford got up and soon saw what had been the trouble. A long, crooked stick, rather thick and black and yellow, lay in the trail, and any mustang looking for an excuse to jump might have mistaken it for a rattlesnake. Nack-yal appeared disposed to be satisfied, and gave Shefford no trouble in mounting. The incident increased Shefford's dubiousness. These Arizona mustangs were unknown quantities.

Thereafter Shefford had an eye for the trail rather than the scenery, and this continued till the pack-train entered the mouth of the Sagi. Then those wonderful lofty cliffs, with their peaks and towers and spires, loomed so close and so beautiful that he did not care if Nack-yal did throw him. Along here, however, the mustang behaved well, and presently Shefford decided that if it had been otherwise he would have walked. The trail suddenly stood on end and led down into the deep wash, where some days before he had seen the stream of reddish water. This day there appeared to be less water and it was not so red. Nack-yal sank deep as he took short and careful steps down. The burros and other mustangs were drinking, and Nack-yal followed suit. The Indian, with a hand clutching his mustang's mane, rode up a steep, sandy slope on the other side that Shefford would not have believed any horse could climb. The burros plodded up and over the rim, with Withers calling to them. Joe Lake swung his rope and cracked the flanks of the gray mare and the red mule; and the way the two kicked was a revelation and a warning to Shefford. When his turn came to climb the trail he got off and walked, an action that Nack-yal appeared fully to appreciate.

From the head of this wash the trail wound away up the widening cañon, through greasewood flats and over greasy levels and across sandy stretches. The looming walls made the valley look narrow, yet it must have been half a mile wide. The slopes under the cliffs were dotted with huge stones and cedar-trees. There were deep indentations in the walls, running back to form box cañons, choked with green of cedar and spruce and piñon. These notches haunted Shefford, and he was ever on the lookout for more of them.

Withers came back to ride just in advance and began to talk.

"Reckon this Sagi Cañon is your Deception Pass," he said. "It's sure a queer hole. I've been lost more than once, hunting mustangs in here. I've an idea Nas Ta Bega knows all this country. He just pointed out a cliff-dwelling to me. See it? . . . There 'way up in that cave of the wall."

Shefford saw a steep, rough slope leading up to a bulge of the cliff, and finally he made out strange little houses with dark, eyelike windows. He wanted to climb up there. Withers called his attention to more caves with what he believed were the ruins of cliff-dwellings. And as they rode along the trader

NEW FRIENDS

showed him remarkable formations of rock where
the elements were slowly hollowing out a bridge.
They came presently to a region of intersecting
cañons, and here the breaking of the trail up and
down the deep washes took Withers back to his
task with the burros and gave Shefford more concern than he liked with Nack-yal. The mustang
grew unruly and was continually turning to the left.
Sometimes he tried to climb the steep slope. He had
to be pulled hard away from the opening cañons on
the left. It seemed strange to Shefford that the
mustang never swerved to the right. This habit of
Nack-yal's and the increasing caution needed on the
trail took all of Shefford's attention. When he dismounted, however, he had a chance to look around,
and more and more he was amazed at the increasing
proportions and wildness of the Sagi.

He came at length to a place where a fallen tree
blocked the trail. All of the rest of the pack-train
had jumped the log. But Nack-yal balked. Shefford dismounted, pulled the bridle over the mustang's head, and tried to lead him. Nack-yal, however, refused to budge. Whereupon Shefford got a
stick and, remounting, he gave the balky mustang
a cut across the flank. Then something violent happened. Shefford received a sudden propelling jolt,
and then he was rising into the air, and then falling.
Before he alighted he had a clear image of Nack-yal
in the air above him, bent double, and seemingly
possessed of devils. Then Shefford hit the ground
with no light thud. He was thoroughly angry when
he got dizzily upon his feet, but he was not quick
enough to catch the mustang. Nack-yal leaped

easily over the log and went on ahead, dragging his
bridle. Shefford hurried after him, and the faster he
went just by so much the cunning Nack-yal accelerated his gait. As the pack-train was out of sight
somewhere ahead, Shefford could not call to his companions to halt his mount, so he gave up trying, and
walked on now with free and growing appreciation of
his surroundings.

The afternoon had waned. The sun blazed low
in the west in a notch of the cañon ramparts, and
one wall was darkening into purple shadow while
the other shone through a golden haze. It was a
weird, wild world to Shefford, and every few strides
he caught his breath and tried to realize actuality
was not a dream.

Nack-yal kept about a hundred paces to the fore
and ever and anon he looked back to see how his
new master was progressing. He varied these occa-
sions by reaching down and nipping a tuft of grass.
Evidently he was too intelligent to go on fast enough
to be caught by Withers. Also he kept continually
looking up the slope to the left as if seeking a way to
climb out of the valley in that direction. Shefford
thought it was well the trail lay at the foot of a
steep slope that ran up to unbroken bluffs.

The sun set and the cañon lost its red and its gold
and deepened its purple. Shefford calculated he had
walked five miles, and though he did not mind the
effort, he would rather have ridden Nack-yal into
camp. He mounted a cedar ridge, crossed some
sandy washes, turned a corner of bold wall to enter
a wide, green level. The mustangs were rolling and
snorting. He heard the bray of a burro. A bright

blaze of camp-fire greeted him, and the dark figure
of the Indian approached to intercept and catch
Nack-yal. When he stalked into camp Withers
wore a beaming smile, and Joe Lake, who was on his
knees making biscuit dough in a pan, stopped proceedings and drawled:

"Reckon Nack-yal bucked you off."

"Bucked! Was that it? Well, he separated himself from me in a new and somewhat painful manner
—to me."

"Sure, I saw that in his eye," replied Lake; and
Withers laughed with him.

"Nack-yal never was well broke," he said. "But
he's a good mustang, nothing like Joe's Navvy or
that gray mare Dynamite. All this Indian stock
will buck on a man once in a while."

"I'll take the bucking along with the rest," said
Shefford.

Both men liked his reply, and the Indian smiled
for the first time.

Soon they all sat round a spread tarpaulin and ate
like wolves. After supper came the rest and talk
before the camp-fire. Joe Lake was droll; he said
the most serious things in a way to make Shefford
wonder if he was not joking. Withers talked about
the cañon, the Indians, the mustangs, the scorpions
running out of the heated sand; and to Shefford
it was all like a fascinating book. Nas Ta Bega
smoked in silence, his brooding eyes upon the fire.

V

ON THE TRAIL

SHEFFORD was awakened next morning by a
sound he had never heard before—the plunging
of hobbled horses on soft turf. It was clear daylight, with a ruddy color in the sky and a tinge of
red along the cañon rim. He saw Withers, Lake,
and the Indian driving the mustangs toward camp.

The burros appeared lazy, yet willing. But the
mustangs and the mule Withers called Red and the
gray mare Dynamite were determined not to be
driven into camp. It was astonishing how much
action they had, how much ground they could cover
with their forefeet hobbled together. They were
exceedingly skilful; they lifted both forefeet at once,
and then plunged. And they all went in different
directions. Nas Ta Bega darted in here and there
to head off escape.

Shefford pulled on his boots and went out to help.
He got too close to the gray mare and, warned by a
yell from Withers, he jumped back just in time to
avoid her vicious heels. Then Shefford turned his
attention to Nack-yal and chased him all over the
flat in a futile effort to catch him. Nas Ta Bega
came to Shefford's assistance and put a rope over
Nack-yal's head.

"Don't ever get behind one of these mustangs, said Withers, warningly, as Shefford came up. "You might be killed. . . . Eat your bite now. We'll soon be out of here."

Shefford had been late in awakening. The others had breakfasted. He found eating somewhat difficult in the excitement that ensued. Nas Ta Bega held ropes which were round the necks of Red and Dynamite. The mule showed his cunning and always appeared to present his heels to Withers, who tried to approach him with a pack-saddle. The patience of the trader was a revelation to Shefford. And at length Red was cornered by the three men, the pack-saddle was strapped on, and then the packs. Red promptly bucked the packs off, and the work had to be done over again. Then Red dropped his long ears and seemed ready to be tractable.

When Shefford turned his attention to Dynamite he decided that this was his first sight of a wild horse. The gray mare had fiery eyes that rolled and showed the white. She jumped straight up, screamed, pawed, bit, and then plunged down to shoot her hind hoofs into the air as high as her head had been. She was amazingly agile and she seemed mad to kill something. She dragged the Indian about, and when Joe Lake got a rope on her hind foot she dragged them both. They lashed her with the ends of the lassoes, which action only made her kick harder. She plunged into camp, drove Shefford flying for his life, knocked down two of the burros, and played havoc with the unstrapped packs. Withers ran to the assistance of Lake, and the two of them hauled back with all their strength and weight. They were both powerful and heavy men. Dynamite circled round and finally, after kicking the camp-fire to bits, fell down on her haunches in the hot embers. "Let—her—set—there!" panted Withers. And Joe Lake shouted, "Burn up, you durn coyote!" Both men appeared delighted that she had brought upon herself just punishment. Dynamite sat in the remains of the fire long enough to get burnt, and then she got up and meekly allowed Withers to throw a tarpaulin and a roll of blankets over her and tie them fast.

Lake and Withers were sweating freely when this job was finished.

"Say, is that a usual morning's task with the pack-animals?" asked Shefford.

"They're all pretty decent to-day, except Dynamite," replied Withers. "She's got to be worked out."

Shefford felt both amusement and consternation. The sun was just rising over the ramparts of the cañon, and he had already seen more difficult and dangerous work accomplished than half a dozen men of his type could do in a whole day. He liked the outlook of his new duty as Withers's assistant, but he felt helplessly inefficient. Still, all he needed was experience. He passed over what he anticipated would be pain and peril—the cost was of no moment.

Soon the pack-train was on the move, with the Indian leading. This morning Nack-yal began his strange swinging off to the left, precisely as he had done the day before. It got to be annoying to Shefford, and he lost patience with the mustang and jerked him sharply round. This, however, had no great effect upon Nack-yal.

As the train headed straight up the cañon Joe Lake dropped back to ride beside Shefford. The Mormon had been amiable and friendly.

"Flock of deer up that draw," he said, pointing up a narrow side cañon.

Shefford gazed to see a half-dozen small, brown, long-eared objects, very like burros, watching the pack-train pass.

"Are they deer?" he asked, delightedly.

"Sure are," replied Joe, sincerely. "Get down and shoot one. There's a rifle in your saddle-sheath."

Shefford had already discovered that he had been armed this morning, a matter which had caused him reflection. These animals certainly looked like deer; he had seen a few deer, though not in their native wild haunts; and he experienced the thrill of the hunter. Dismounting, he drew the rifle out of the sheath and started toward the little cañon.

"Hyar! Where you going with that gun?" yelled Withers. "That's a bunch of burros. . . . Joe's up to his old tricks. Shefford, look out for Joe!"

Rather sheepishly Shefford returned to his mustang and sheathed the rifle, and then took a long look at the animals up the draw. They resembled deer, but upon second glance they surely were burros.

"Durn me! Now if I didn't think they sure were deer!" exclaimed Joe. He appeared absolutely sincere and innocent. Shefford hardly knew how to take this likable Mormon, but vowed he would be on his guard in the future.

Nas Ta Bega soon led the pack-train toward the left wall of the cañon, and evidently intended to scale it. Shefford could not see any trail, and the wall appeared steep and insurmountable. But upon nearing the cliff he saw a narrow broken trail leading zigzag up over smooth rock, weathered slope, and through cracks.

"Spread out, and careful now!" yelled Withers.

The need of both advices soon became manifest to Shefford. The burros started stones rolling, making danger for those below. Shefford dismounted and led Nack-yal ard turned aside many a rolling rock. The Indian and the burros, with the red mule leading, climbed steadily. But the mustangs had trouble. Joe's spirited bay had to be coaxed to face the ascent; Nack-yal balked at every difficult step; and Dynamite slipped on a flat slant of rock and slid down forty feet. Withers and Lake with ropes hauled the mare out of the dangerous position. Shefford, who brought up the rear, saw all the action, and it was exciting, but his pleasure in the climb was spoiled by sight of blood and hair on the stones. The ascent was crooked, steep, and long, and when Shefford reached the top of the wall he was glad to rest. It made him gasp to look down and see what he had surmounted. The cañon floor, green and level, lay a thousand feet below; and the wild burros which had followed on the trail looked like rabbits.

Shefford mounted presently, and rode out upon a wide, smooth trail leading into a cedar forest. There were bunches of gray sage in the open places. The air was cool and crisp, laden with a sweet fragrance. He saw Lake and Withers bobbing along, now on one side of the trail, now on the other, and they kept to a steady trot. Occasionally the Indian and his bright-red saddle-blanket showed in an opening of the cedars.

It was level country, and there was nothing for Shefford to see except cedar and sage, an outcropping of red rock in places, and the winding trail. Mocking-birds made melody everywhere. Shefford seemed full of a strange pleasure, and the hours flew by. Nack-yal still wanted to be everlastingly turning off the trail, and, moreover, now he wanted to go faster. He was eager, restless, dissatisfied.

At noon the pack-train descended into a deep draw, well covered with cedar and sage. There was plenty of grass and shade, but no water. Shefford was surprised to see that every pack was removed; however, the roll of blankets was left on Dynamite.

The men made a fire and began to cook a noonday meal. Shefford, tired and warm, sat in a shady spot and watched. He had become all eyes. He had almost forgotten Fay Larkin; he had forgotten his trouble; and the present seemed sweet and full. Presently his ears were filled by a pattering roar and, looking up the draw, he saw two streams of sheep and goats coming down. Soon an Indian shepherd appeared, riding a fine mustang. A cream-colored colt bounded along behind, and presently a shaggy dog came in sight. The Indian dismounted at the camp, and his flock spread by in two white and black streams. The dog went with them. Withers and Joe shook hands with the Indian, whom Joe called "Navvy," and Shefford lost no time in doing likewise. Then Nas Ta Bega came in, and he and the Navajo talked. When the meal was ready all of them sat down round the canvas. The shepherd did not tie his horse.

Presently Shefford noticed that Nack-yal had returned to camp and was acting strangely. Evidently he was attracted by the Indian's mustang or the cream-colored colt. At any rate, Nack-yal hung around, tossed his head, whinnied in a low, nervous manner, and looked strangely eager and wild. Shefford was at first amused, then curious. Nack-yal approached too close to the mother of the colt, and she gave him a sounding kick in the ribs. Nack-yal uttered a plaintive snort and backed away, to stand, crestfallen, with all his eagerness and fire vanished.

Nas Ta Bega pointed to the mustang and said something in his own tongue. Then Withers addressed the visiting Indian, and they exchanged some words, whereupon the trader turned to Shefford.

"I bought Nack-yal from this Indian three years ago. This mare is Nack-yal's mother. He was born over here to the south. That's why he always swung left off the trail. He wanted to go home. Just now he recognized his mother and she whaled away and gave him a whack for his pains. She's got a colt now and probably didn't recognize Nack-yal. But he's broken-hearted."

The trader laughed, and Joe said, "You can't tell what these durn mustangs will do." Shefford felt sorry for Nack-yal, and when it came time to saddle him again found him easier to handle than ever before. Nack-yal stood with head down, broken-spirited.

Shefford was the first to ride up out of the draw,

and once upon the top of the ridge he halted to gaze, wide-eyed and entranced. A rolling, endless plain sloped down beneath him, and led him on to a distant round-topped mountain. To the right a red cañon opened its jagged jaws, and away to the north rose a whorled and strange sea of curved ridges, crags, and domes.

Nas Ta Bega rode up then, leading the pack-train. "Bi Nai, that is Na-tsis-an," he said, pointing to the mountain. "Navajo Mountain. And there in the north are the cañons."

Shefford followed the Indian down the trail and ,oon lost sight of that wide green-and-red wilderness. Nas Ta Bega turned at an intersecting trail, rode down into the cañon, and climbed out on the other side. Shefford got a glimpse now and then of the black dome of the mountain, but for the most part the distant points of the country were hidden. They crossed many trails, and went up and down the sides of many shallow cañons. Troops of wild mustangs whistled at them, srood on ridge-tops to watch, and then dashed away with manes and tails flying.

Withers rode forward presently and halted the pack-train. He had some conversation with Nas Ta Bega, whereupon the Indian turned his horse and trotted back, to disappear in the cedars.

"I'm some worried," explained Withers. "Joe thinks he saw a bunch of horsemen trailing us. My eyes are bad and I can't see far. The Indian will find out. I took a roundabout way to reach the village because I'm always dodging Shadd."

This communication lent an added zest to the

journey. Shefford could hardly believe the truth that his eyes and his ears brought to his consciousness. He turned in behind Withers and rode down the rough trail, helping the mustang all in his power. It occurred to him that Nack-yal had been entirely different since that meeting with his mother in the draw. He turned no more off the trail; he answered readily to the rein; he did not look afar from every ridge. Shefford conceived a liking for the mustang.

Withers turned sidewise in his saddle and let his mustang pick the way.

"Another time we'll go up round the base of the mountain, where you can look down on the grandest scene in the world," said he. "Two hundred miles of wind-worn rock, all smooth and bare, without a single straight line—cañons, caves, bridges—the most wonderful country in the world! Even the Indians haven't explored it. It's haunted, for them, and they have strange gods. The Navajos will hunt on this side of the mountain, but not on the other. That north side is consecrated ground. My wife has long been trying to get the Navajos to tell her the secret of Nonnezoshe. Nonnezoshe means Rainbow Bridge. The Indians worship it, but as far as she can find out only a few have ever seen it. I imagine it 'd be worth some trouble."

"Maybe that's the bridge Venters talked about— the one overarching the entrance to Surprise Valley," said Shefford.

"It might be," replied the trader. "You've got a good chance of finding out. Nas Ta Bega is the man. You stick to that Indian. . . . Well, we start

'down here into this cañon, and we go down *some*, 1
reckon. In half an hour you'll see sago-lilies and
Indian paint-brush and vermilion cactus."

About the middle of the afternoon the pack-train
and its drivers arrived at the hidden Mormon village.
Nas Ta Bega had not returned from his scout back
along the trail.

Shefford's sensibilities had all been overstrained,
but he had left in him enthusiasm and appreciation
that made the situation of this village a fairyland.
It was a valley, a cañon floor, so long that he could
not see the end, and perhaps a quarter of a mile wide.
The air was hot, still, and sweetly odorous of unfamiliar flowers. Piñon and cedar trees surrounded
the little log and stone houses, and along the walls of
the cañon stood sharp-pointed, dark-green spruce-
trees. These walls were singular of shape and color.
They were not imposing in height, but they waved
like the long, undulating swell of a sea. Every foot
of surface was perfectly smooth, and the long curved
lines of darker tinge that streaked the red followed
the rounded line of the slope at the top. Far above,
yet overhanging, were great yellow crags and peaks,
and between these, still higher, showed the pine-
fringed slope of Navajo Mountain with snow in the
sheltered places, and glistening streams, like silver
threads, running down.

All this Shefford noticed as he entered the valley
from round a corner of wall. Upon nearer view he
saw and heard a host of children, who, looking up to
see the intruders, scattered like frightened quail.
Long gray grass covered the ground, and here and

there wide, smooth paths had been worn. A swift and murmuring brook ran through the middle of the valley, and its banks were bordered with flowers.

Withers led the way to one side near the wall, where a clump of cedar-trees and a dark, swift spring boiling out of the rocks and banks of amber moss with purple blossoms made a beautiful camp site. Here the mustangs were unsaddled and turned loose without hobbles. It was certainly unlikely that they would leave such a spot. Some of the burros were unpacked, and the others Withers drove off into the village.

"Sure's pretty nice," said Joe, wiping his sweaty face. "I'll never want to leave. It suits me to lie on this moss. . . . Take a drink of that spring."

Shefford complied with alacrity and found the water cool and sweet, and he seemed to feel it all through him. Then he returned to the mossy bank. He did not reply to Joe. In fact, all his faculties were absorbed in watching and feeling, and he lay there long after Joe went off to the village. The murmur of water, the hum of bees, the songs of strange birds, the sweet, warm air, the dreamy summer somnolence of the valley—all these added drowsiness to Shefford's weary lassitude, and he fell asleep. When he awoke Nas Ta Bega was sitting near him and Joe was busy near a camp-fire.

"Hello, Nas Ta Bega!" said Shefford. "Was there any one trailing us?"

The Navajo nodded.

Joe raised his head and with forceful brevity said, "Shadd."

"Shadd!" echoed Shefford, remembering the dark,

sinister face of his visitor that night in the Sagi. "Joe, is it serious—his trailing us?"

"Well, I don't know how durn serious it is, but I'm scared to death," replied Lake. "He and his gang will hold us up somewhere on the way home."

Shefford regarded Joe with both concern and doubt. Joe's words were at variance with his looks.

"Say, pard, can you shoot a rifle?" queried Joe.

"Yes. I'm a fair shot at targets."

The Mormon nodded his head as if pleased. "That's good. These outlaws are all poor shots with a rifle. So'm I. But I can handle a six-shooter. I reckon we'll make Shadd sweat if he pushes us."

Withers returned, driving the burros, all of which had been unpacked down to the saddles. Two gray-bearded men accompanied him. One of them appeared to be very old and venerable, and walked with a stick. The other had a sad-lined face and kind, mild blue eyes. Shefford observed that Lake seemed unusually respectful. Withers introduced these Mormons merely as Smith and Henninger. They were very cordial and pleasant in their greetings to Shefford. Presently another, somewhat younger, man joined the group, a stalwart, jovial fellow with ruddy face. There was certainly no mistaking his kindly welcome as he shook Shefford's hand. His name was Beal. The three stood round the camp-fire for a while, evidently glad of the presence of fellow-men and to hear news from the outside. Finally they went away, taking Joe with them. Withers took up the task of getting supper where Joe had been made to leave it.

"Shefford, listen," he said, presently, as he knelt before the fire. "I told them right out that you'd been a Gentile clergyman—that you'd gone back on your religion. It impressed them and you've been well received. I'll tell the same thing over at Stonebridge. You'll get in right. Of course I don't expect they'll make a Mormon of you. But they'll try to. Meanwhile you can be square and friendly all the time you're trying to find your Fay Larkin. To-morrow you'll meet some of the women. They're good souls, but, like any women, crazy for news. Think what it is to be shut up in here between these walls!"

"Withers, I'm intensely interested," replied Shefford, "and excited, too. Shall we stay here long?"

"I'll stay a couple of days, then go to Stonebridge with Joe. He'll come back here, and when you both feel like leaving, and if Nas Ta Bega thinks it safe, you'll take a trail over to some Indian hogans and pack me out a load of skins and blankets. . . . My boy, you've all the time there is, and I wish you luck. This isn't a bad place to loaf. I always get sentimental over here. Maybe it's the women. Some of them are pretty, and one of them— Shefford, they call her the Sago Lily. Her first name is Mary, I'm told. Don't know her last name. She's lovely. And I'll bet you forget Fay Larkin in a flash. Only —be careful. You drop in here with rather peculiar credentials, so to speak—as my helper and as a man with no religion! You'll not only be fully trusted, but you'll be welcome to these lonely women. So be careful. Remember it's my secret belief they are sealed wives and are visited occasionally at night

by their husbands. I don't *know* this, but **I believe it.** And you're not supposed to dream of that."

"How many men in the village?" asked Shefford.

"Three. You met them."

"Have they wives?" asked Shefford, curiously.

"Wives! Well, I guess. But only one each that I know of. Joe Lake is the only unmarried Mormon I've met."

"And no men—strangers, cowboys, outlaws—ever come to this village?"

"Except to Indians, it seems to be a secret so far," replied the trader, earnestly. "But it can't be kept secret. I've said that time after time over in Stonebridge. With Mormons it's 'sufficient unto the day is the evil thereof.'"

"What 'll happen when outsiders do learn and ride in here?"

"There'll be trouble—maybe bloodshed. Mormon women are absolutely good, but they're human, and want and need a little life. And, strange to say, Mormon men are pig-headedly jealous. . . . Why, if some of the cowboys I knew in Durango would ride over here there'd simply be hell. But that's a long way, and probably this village will be deserted before news of it ever reaches Colorado. There's more danger of Shadd and his gang coming in. Shadd's half Piute. He must know of this place. And he's got some white outlaws in his gang. . . . Come on. Grub's ready, and I'm too hungry to talk."

Later, when shadows began to gather in the valley and the lofty peaks above were gold in the sunset glow, Withers left camp to look after the straying mustangs, and Shefford strolled to and fro under the cedars. The lights and shades in the Sagi that first night had moved him to enthusiastic watchfulness, but here they were so weird and beautiful that he was enraptured. He actually saw great shafts of gold and shadows of purple streaming from the peaks down into the valley. It was day on the heights and twilight in the valley. The swiftly changing colors were like rainbows.

While he strolled up and down several women came to the spring and filled their buckets. They wore shawls or hoods and their garments were somber, but, nevertheless, they appeared to have youth and comeliness. They saw him, looked at him curiously, and then, without speaking, went back on the well-trodden path. Presently down the path appeared a woman—a girl in lighter garb. It was almost white. She was shapely and walked with free, graceful step, reminding him of the Indian girl, Glen Naspa. This one wore a hood shaped like a huge sunbonnet and it concealed her face. She carried a bucket. When she reached the spring and went down the few stone steps Shefford saw that she did not have on shoes. As she braced herself to lift the bucket her bare foot clung to the mossy stone. It was a strong, sinewy, beautiful foot, instinct with youth. He was curious enough, he thought, but the awakening artist in him made him more so. She dragged at the full bucket and had difficulty in lifting it out of the hole. Shefford strode forward and took the bucket-handle from her.

"Won't you let me help you?" he said, lifting the bucket. "Indeed—it's very heavy."

"Oh—thank you," she said, without raising her head. Her voice seemed singularly young and sweet. He had not heard a voice like it. She moved down the path and he walked beside her. He felt embarrassed, yet more curious than ever; he wanted to say something, to turn and look at her, but he kept on for a dozen paces without making up his mind.

Finally he said: "Do you really carry this heavy bucket? Why, it makes my arm ache."

"Twice every day—morning and evening," she replied. "I'm very strong."

Then he stole a look out of the corner of his eye, and, seeing that her face was hidden from him by the hood, he turned to observe her at better advantage. A long braid of hair hung down her back. In the twilight it gleamed dull gold. She came up to his shoulder. The sleeve nearest him was rolled up to her elbow, revealing a fine round arm. Her hand, like her foot, was brown, strong, and well shaped. It was a hand that had been developed by labor. She was full-bosomed, yet slender, and she walked with a free stride that made Shefford admire and wonder.

They passed several of the little stone and log houses, and women greeted them as they went by, and children peered shyly from the doors. He kept trying to think of something to say, and, failing in that, determined to have one good look under the hood before he left her.

"You walk lame," she said, solicitously. "Let me carry the bucket now—please. My house is near."

"Am I lame? . . . Guess so, a little," he replied. "It was a hard ride for me. But I'll carry the bucket just the same."

They went on under some piñon-trees, down a path to a little house identical with the others, except that it had a stone porch. Shefford smelled fragrant wood-smoke and saw a column curling from the low, flat, stone chimney. Then he set the bucket down on the porch.

"Thank you, Mr. Shefford," she said.

"You know my name?" he asked.

"Yes. Mr. Withers spoke to my nearest neighbor and she told me."

"Oh, I see. And you—"

He did not go on and she did not reply. When she stepped upon the porch and turned he was able to see under the hood. The face there was in shadow, and for that very reason he answered to ungovernable impulse and took a step closer to her. Dark, grave, sad eyes looked down at him, and he felt as if he could never draw his own glance away. He seemed not to see the rest of her face, and yet felt that it was lovely. Then a downward movement of the hood hid from him the strange eyes and the shadowy loveliness.

"I—I beg your pardon," he said, quickly, drawing back. "I'm rude. . . . Withers told me about a girl he called—he said looked like a sago-lily. That's no excuse to stare under your hood. But I—I was curious. I wondered if—"

He hesitated, realizing how foolish his talk was. She stood a moment, probably watching him, but he could not be sure, for her face was hidden.

"They call me that," she said. "But my name is Mary."

"Mary—what?" he asked.

"Just Mary," she said, simply. "Good night."

He did not say good night and could not have told why. She took up the bucket and went into the dark house. Shefford hurried away into the gathering darkness.

VI

SHEFFORD had hardly seen her face, yet he was more interested in a woman than he had ever been before. Still, he reflected, as he returned to camp, he had been under a long strain, he was unduly excited by this new and adventurous life, and these, with the mystery of this village, were perhaps accountable for a state of mind that could not last.

He rolled in his blankets on the soft bed of moss and he saw the stars through the needle-like fringe of the piñons. It seemed impossible to fall asleep. The two domed peaks split the sky, and back of them, looming dark and shadowy, rose the mountain. There was something cold, austere, and majestic in their lofty presence, and they made him feel alone, yet not alone. He raised himself to see the quiet forms of Withers and Nas Ta Bega prone in the starlight, and their slow, deep breathing was that of tired men. A bell on a mustang rang somewhere off in the valley and gave out a low, strange, reverberating echo from wall to wall. When it ceased a silence set in that was deader than any silence he had ever felt, but gradually he became aware of the low murmur of the brook. For the rest there was no sound of wind, no bark of dog or yelp of coyote, no sound of voice in the village.

He tried to sleep, but instead thought of this girl who was called the Sago Lily. He recalled everything incident to their meeting and the walk to her home. Her swift, free step, her graceful poise, her shapely form—the long braid of hair, dull gold in the twilight, the beautiful bare foot and the strong round arm—these he thought of and recalled vividly. But of her face he had no idea except the shadowy, haunting loveliness, and that grew more and more difficult to remember. The tone of her voice and what she had said—how the one had thrilled him and the other mystified! It was her voice that had most attracted him. There was something in it besides music—what, he could not tell—sadness, depth, something like that in Nas Ta Bega's—a beauty springing from disuse. But this seemed absurd. Why should he imagine her voice one that had not been used as freely as any other woman's? She was a Mormon; very likely, almost surely, she was a sealed wife. His interest, too, was absurd, and he tried to throw it off, or imagine it one he might have felt in any other of these strange women of the hidden village.

But Shefford's intelligence and his good sense, which became operative when he was fully roused and set the situation clearly before his eyes, had no effect upon his deeper, mystic, and primitive feelings. He saw the truth and he felt something that he could not name. He would not be a fool, but there was no harm in dreaming. And unquestionably, beyond all doubt, the dream and the romance that had lured him to the wilderness were here, hanging over him like the shadows of the great peaks. His heart swelled with emotion when he thought of how the black and incessant despair of the past was gone. So he embraced any attraction that made him forget and think and feel; some instinct stronger than intelligence bade him drift.

Joe's rolling voice awoke him next morning and he rose with a singular zest. When or where in his life had he awakened in such a beautiful place? Almost he understood why Venters and Bess had been haunted by memories of Surprise Valley. The morning was clear, cool, sweet; the peaks were dim and soft in rosy cloud; shafts of golden sunlight shot down into the purple shadows. Mocking-birds were singing. His body was sore and tired from the unaccustomed travel, but his heart was full, happy. His spirit wanted to run, and he knew there was something out there waiting to meet it. The Indian and the trader and the Mormon all meant more to him this morning. He had grown a little overnight. Nas Ta Bega's deep "Bi Nai" rang in his ears, and the smiles of Withers and Joe were greetings. He had friends; he had work; and there was rich, strange, and helpful life to live. There was even a difference in the mustang Nack-yal. He came readily; he did not look wild; he had a friendly eye; and Shefford liked him more.

"What is there to do?" asked Shefford, feeling equal to a hundred tasks.

"No work," replied the trader, with a laugh, and he drew Shefford aside. "I'm in no hurry. I like it

here. And Joe never wants to leave. To-day you
can meet the women. Make yourself popular. I've
already made you that. These women are most all
young and lonesome. Talk to them. Make them
like you. Then some day you may be safe to ask
questions. Last night I wanted to ask old Mother
Smith if she ever heard the name Fay Larkin. But
I thought better of it. If there's a girl here or at
Stonebridge of that name we'll learn it. If there's
mystery we'd better go slow. Mormons are hell on
secret and mystery, and to pry into their affairs
is to queer yourself. My advice is—just be as nice
as you can be, and let things happen."

Fay Larkin! All in a night Shefford had forgotten
her. Why? He pondered over the matter, and
then the old thrill, the old desire, came back.

"Shefford, what do you think Nas Ta Bega said
to me last night?" asked Withers in lower voice.

"Haven't any idea," replied Shefford, curiously.

"We were sitting beside the fire. I saw you
walking under the cedars. You seemed thoughtful.
That keen Indian watched you, and he said to me in
Navajo, 'Bi Nai has lost his God. He has come far
to find a wife. Nas Ta Bega is his brother.' . . .
He meant he'll find both God and wife for you. I
don't know about that, but I say take the Indian as
he thinks he is—your brother. Long before I knew
Nas Ta Bega well my wife used to tell me about
him. He's a sage and a poet—the very spirit of
this desert. He's worth cultivating for his own
sake. But more—remember, if Fay Larkin is still
shut in that valley the Navajo will find her for
you."

"I shall take Nas Ta Bega as my brother—and be proud," replied Shefford.

"There's another thing. Do you intend to confide in Joe?"

"I hadn't thought of that."

"Well, it might be a good plan. But wait until you know him better and he knows you. He's ready to fight for you now. He's taken your trouble to heart. You wouldn't think Joe is deeply religious. Yet he is. He may never breathe a word about religion to you. . . . Now, Shefford, go ahead. You've struck a trail. It's rough, but it 'll make a man of you. It 'll lead somewhere."

"I'm singularly fortunate—I—who had lost all friends. Withers, I am grateful. I'll prove it. I'll show—"

Withers's upheld hand checked further speech, and Shefford realized that beneath the rough exterior of this desert trader there was fine feeling. These men of crude toil and wild surroundings were beginning to loom up large in Shefford's mind.

The day began leisurely. The men were yet at breakfast when the women of the village began to come one by one to the spring. Joe Lake made friendly and joking remarks to each. And as each one passed on down the path he poised a biscuit in one hand and a cup of coffee in the other, and with his head cocked sidewise like an owl he said, "Reckon I've got to get me a woman like her."

Shefford saw and heard, yet he was all the time half unconsciously watching with strange eagerness for a white figure to appear. At last he saw her— the same girl with the hood, the same swift step: **A**

little shock or quiver passed over him, and at the
moment all that was explicable about it was something associated with regret.

Joe Lake whistled and stared.

"I haven't met her," he muttered.

"That's the Sago Lily," said Withers.

"Reckon I'm going to carry that bucket," went
on Joe.

"And queer yourself with all the other women
who've been to the spring? Don't do it, Joe,"
advised the trader.

"But her bucket's bigger," protested Joe, weakly.

"That's true. But you ought to know Mormons.
If she'd come first, all right. As she didn't—why,
don't single her out."

Joe kept his seat. The girl came to the spring.
A low "good morning" came from under the hood.
Then she filled her bucket and started home. Shefford observed that this time she wore moccasins
and she carried the heavy bucket with ease. When
she disappeared he had again the vague, inexplicable
sensation of regret.

Joe Lake breathed heavily. "Reckon I've got
to get me a woman like her," he said. But the
former jocose tone was lacking and he appeared
thoughtful.

Withers first took Shefford to the building used
for a school. It was somewhat larger than the other
houses, had only one room with two doors and
several windows. It was full of children of all
sizes and ages, sitting on rude board benches.

There were half a hundred of them, sturdy,

healthy, rosy boys and girls, clad in home-made garments. The young woman teacher was as embarrassed as her pupils were shy, and the visitors withdrew without having heard a word of lessons.

Withers then called upon Smith, Henninger, and Beal, and their wives. Shefford found himself cordially received, and what little he did say showed him how he would be listened to when he cared to talk. These folk were plain and kindly, and he found that there was nothing about them to dislike. The men appeared mild and quiet, and when not conversing seemed austere. The repose of the women was only on the surface; underneath he felt their intensity. Especially in many of the younger women, whom he met in the succeeding hour, did he feel this power of restrained emotion. This surprised him, as did also the fact that almost every one of them was attractive and some of them were exceedingly pretty. He became so interested in them all as a whole that he could not individualize one. They were as widely different in appearance and temperament as women of any other class, but it seemed to Shefford that one common trait united them—and it was a strange, checked yearning for something that he could not discover. Was it happiness? They certainly seemed to be happy, far more so than those millions of women who were chasing phantoms. Were they really sealed wives, as Withers believed, and was this unnatural wifehood responsible for the strange intensity? At any rate he returned to camp with the conviction that he had stumbled upon a remarkable situation.

He had been told the last names of only three

women, and their husbands were in the village. The names of the others were Ruth, Rebecca, Joan—he could not recall them all. They were the mothers of these beautiful children. The fathers, as far as he was concerned, were as intangible as myths. Shefford was an educated clergyman, a man of the world, and, as such, knew women in his way. Mormons might be strange and different, yet the fundamental truth was that all over the world mothers of children were wives; there was a relation between wife and mother that did not need to be named to be felt; and he divined from this that, whatever the situation of these lonely and hidden women, they knew themselves to be wives. Shefford absolutely satisfied himself on that score. If they were miserable they certainly did not show it, and the question came to him how just was the criticism of uninformed men? His judgment of Mormons had been established by what he had heard and read, rather than what he knew. He wanted now to have an open mind. He had studied the totemism and exogamy of the primitive races, and here was his opportunity to understand polygamy. One wife for one man—that was the law. Mormons broke it openly; Gentiles broke it secretly. Mormons acknowledged all their wives and protected their children; Gentiles acknowledged one wife only. Unquestionably the Mormons were wrong, but were not the Gentiles still more wrong?

The following day Joe Lake appeared reluctant to start for Stonebridge with Withers.

"Joe, you'd better come along," said the trader.

dryly. "I reckon you've seen a little too much of the Sago Lily."

Lake offered no reply, but it was evident from his sober face that Withers had not hit short of the mark. Withers rode off, with a parting word to Shefford, and finally Joe somberly mounted his bay and trotted down the valley. As Nas Ta Bega had gone off somewhere to visit Indians, Shefford was left alone.

He went into the village and made himself useful and agreeable. He made friends with the children and he talked to the women until he was hoarse. Their ignorance of the world was a spur to him, and never in his life had he had such an attentive audience. And as he showed no curiosity, asked no difficult questions, gradually what reserve he had noted wore away, and the end of the day saw him on a footing with them that Withers had predicted.

By the time several like days had passed it seemed from the interest and friendliness of these women that he might have lived long among them. He was possessed of wit and eloquence and information, which he freely gave, and not with selfish motive. He liked these women; he liked to see the somber shade pass from their faces, to see them brighten. He had met the girl Mary at the spring and along the path, but he had not yet seen her face. He was always looking for her, hoping to meet her, and confessed to himself that the best of the day for him were the morning and evening visits she made to the spring. Nevertheless, for some reason hard to divine, he was reluctant to seek her deliberately.

Always while he had listened to her neighbors' talk, he had hoped they might let fall something about her. But they did not. He received an impression that she was not so intimate with the others as he had supposed. They all made one big family. Still, she seemed a little outside. He could bring no proofs to strengthen this idea. He merely felt it, and many of his feelings were independent of intelligent reason. Something had been added to curiosity, that was sure.

It was his habit to call upon Mother Smith in the afternoons. From the first her talk to him hinted of a leaning toward thought of making him a Mormon. Her husband and the other men took up her cue and spoke of their religion, casually at first, but gradually opening their minds to free and simple discussion of their faith. Shefford lent respectful attention. He would rather have been a Mormon than an atheist, and apparently they considered him the latter, and were earnest to save his soul. Shefford knew that he could never be one any more than the other. He was just at sea. But he listened, and he found them simple in faith, blind, perhaps, but loyal and good. It was noteworthy that Mother Smith happened to be the only woman in the village who had ever mentioned religion to him. She was old, of a past generation; the young women belonged to the present. Shefford pondered the significant difference.

Every day made more steadfast his impression of the great mystery that was like a twining shadow round these women, yet in the same time many little ideas shifted and many new characteristics became manifest. This last was of course the result of acquaintance; he was learning more about the villagers. He gathered from keen interpretation of subtle words and looks that here in this lonely village, the same as in all the rest of the world where women were together, there were cliques, quarrels, dislikes, loves, and jealousies. The truth, once known to him, made him feel natural and fortified his confidence to meet the demands of an increasingly interesting position. He discovered, with a somewhat grim amusement, that a clergyman's experience in a church full of women had not been entirely useless.

One afternoon he let fall a careless remark that was a subtle question in regard to the girl Mary, whom Withers called the Sago Lily. In response he received an answer couched in the sweet poisoned honey of woman's jealousy. He said no more. Certain ideas of his were strengthened, and straightway he became thoughtful.

That afternoon late, as he did his camp chores, he watched for her. But she did not come. Then he decided to go to see her. But even the decision and the strange thrill it imparted did not change his reluctance.

Twilight was darkening the valley when he reached her house, and the shadows were thick under the piñons. There was no light in the door or window. He saw a white shape on the porch, and as he came down the path it rose. It was the girl Mary, and she appeared startled.

"Good evening," he said. "It's Shefford. May I stay and talk a little while?"

She was silent for so long that he began to feel awkward.

"I'd be glad to have you," she replied, finally.

There was a bench on the porch, but he preferred to sit upon a blanket on the step.

"I've been getting acquainted with everybody— except you," he went on.

"I have been here," she replied.

That might have been a woman's speech, but it certainly had been made in a girl's voice. She was neither shy nor embarrassed nor self-conscious. As she stood back from him he could not see her face in the dense twilight.

"I've been wanting to call on you."

She made some slight movement. Shefford felt a strange calm, yet he knew the moment was big and potent.

"Won't you sit here?" he asked.

She complied with his wish, and then he saw her face, though dimly, in the twilight. And it struck him mute. But he had no glimpse such as had flashed upon him from under her hood that other night. He thought of a white flower in shadow, and received his first impression of the rare and perfect lily Withers had said graced the wild cañons. She was only a girl. She sat very still, looking straight before her, and seemed to be waiting, listening. Shefford saw the quick rise and fall of her bosom.

"I want to talk," he began, swiftly, hoping to put her at her ease. "Every one here has been good to me and I've talked—oh, for hours and hours. But the thing in my mind I haven't spoken of. I've never asked any questions. That makes my part so

strange. I want to tell why I came out here. I
need some one who will keep my secret, and perhaps
help me. . . . Would you?"

"Yes, if I could," she replied.

"You see I've got to trust you, or one of these
other women. You're all Mormons. I don't mean
that's anything against you. I believe you're all
good and noble. But the fact makes—well, makes
a liberty of speech impossible. What can I do?"

Her silence probably meant that she did not know.
Shefford sensed less strain in her and more excitement. He believed he was on the right track and
did not regret his impulse. Even had he regretted
it he would have gone on, for opposed to caution and
intelligence was his driving mystic force.

Then he told her the truth about his boyhood,
his ambition to be an artist, his renunciation to his
father's hope, his career as a clergyman, his failure
in religion, and the disgrace that had made him a
wanderer.

"Oh—I'm sorry!" she said. The faint starlight
shone on her face, in her eyes, and if he ever saw
beauty and soul he saw them then. She seemed
deeply moved. She had forgotten herself. She betrayed girlhood then—all the quick sympathy, the
wonder, the sweetness of a heart innocent and un-
tutored. She looked at him with great, starry,
questioning eyes, as if they had just become aware
of his presence, as if a man had been strange to her.

"Thank you. It's good of you to be sorry," he
said. "My instinct guided me right. Perhaps
you'll be my friend."

"I will be—if I can," she said.

IN THE HIDDEN VALLEY

"But *can* you be?"

"I don't know. I never had a friend. I . . . But, sir, I mustn't talk of myself. . . . Oh, I'm afraid I can't help you."

How strange the pathos of her voice! Almost he believed she was in need of help or sympathy or love. But he could not wholly trust a judgment formed from observation of a class different from hers.

"Maybe you *can* help me. Let's see," he said. "I don't seek to make you talk of yourself. But —you're a human being—a girl—almost a woman. You're not dumb. But even a nun can talk."

"A nun? What is that?"

"Well—a nun is a sister of mercy—a woman consecrated to God—who has renounced the world. In some ways you Mormon women here resemble nuns. It is sacrifice that nails you in this lonely valley. . . . You see—how I talk! One word, one thought brings another, and I speak what perhaps should be unsaid. And it's hard, because I feel I could unburden myself to you."

"Tell me what you want," she said.

Shefford hesitated, and became aware of the rapid pound of his heart. More than anything he wanted to be fair to this girl. He saw that she was warming to his influence. Her shadowy eyes were fixed upon him. The starlight, growing brighter, shone on her golden hair and white face.

"I'll tell you presently," he said. "I've trusted you. I'll trust you with all. . . . But let me have my own time. This is so strange a thing, my wanting to confide in you. It's selfish, perhaps. I have my own ax to grind. I hope I won't wrong you.

That's why I'm going to be perfectly frank. I might wait for days to get better acquainted. But the impulse is on me. I've been so interested in all you Mormon women. The fact—the meaning of this hidden village is so—so terrible to me. But that's none of my business. I have spent my afternoons and evenings with these women at the different cottages. You do not mingle with them. They are lonely, but have not such loneliness as yours. I have passed here every night. No light—no sound. I can't help thinking. Don't censure me or be afraid or draw within yourself just because I must think. I may be all wrong. But I'm curious. I wonder about you. Who are you? Mary—Mary what? Maybe I really don't want to know. I came with selfish motive and now I'd like to—to—what shall I say? Make your life a little less lonely for the while I'm here. That's all. It needn't offend. And if you accept it, how much easier I can tell you my secret. You are a Mormon and I—well, I am only a wanderer in these wilds. But—we might help each other. . . . Have I made a mistake?"

"No—no," she cried, almost wildly.

"We can be friends then. You will trust me, help me?"

"Yes, if I dare."

"Surely you may dare what the other women would?"

She was silent.

And the wistfulness of her silence touched him. He felt contrition. He did not stop to analyze his own emotions, but he had an inkling that once this strange situation was ended he would have food for reflection. What struck him most now was the girl's blanched face, the strong, nervous clasp of her hands, the visible tumult of her bosom. Excitement alone could not be accountable for this. He had not divined the cause for such agitation. He was puzzled, troubled, and drawn irresistibly. He had not said what he had planned to say. The moment had given birth to his speech, and it had flowed. What was guiding him?

"Mary," he said, earnestly, "tell me—have you mother, father, sister, brother? Something prompts me to ask that."

"All dead—gone—years ago," she answered.

"How old are you?"

"Eighteen, I think. I'm not sure."

"You *are* lonely."

His words were gentle and divining.

"O God!" she cried. "Lonely!"

Then as a man in a dream he beheld her weeping. There was in her the unconsciousness of a child and the passion of a woman. He gazed out into the dark shadows and up at the white stars, and then at the bowed head with its mass of glinting hair. But her agitation was no longer strange to him. A few gentle and kind words had proved her undoing. He knew then that whatever her life was, no kindness or sympathy entered it. Presently she recovered, and sat as before, only whiter of face it seemed, and with something tragic in her dark eyes. She was growing cold and still again, aloof, more like those other Mormon women.

"I understand," he said. "I'm not sorry I spoke. I felt your trouble, whatever it is. . . . Do not retreat into your cold shell, I beg of you. . . . Let me trust you with my secret."

He saw her shake out of the cold apathy. She wavered. He felt an inexplicable sweetness in the power his voice seemed to have upon her. She bowed her head in acquiescence. And Shefford began his story. Did she grow still, like stone, or was that only his vivid imagination? He told her of Venters and Bess—of Lassiter and Jane—of little Fay Larkin—of the romance, and then the tragedy of Surprise Valley.

"So, when my Church disowned me," he concluded, "I conceived the idea of wandering into the wilds of Utah to save Fay Larkin from that cañon prison. It grew to be the best and strongest desire of my life. I think if I could save her that it would save me. I never loved any girl. I can't say that I love Fay Larkin. How could I when I've never seen her—when she's only a dream girl? But I believe if she were to become a reality—a flesh-and-blood girl—that I would love her."

That was more than Shefford had ever confessed to any one, and it stirred him to his depths. Mary bent her head on her hands in strange, stonelike rigidity.

"So here I am in the cañon country," he continued. "Withers tells me it is a country of rainbows, both in the evanescent air and in the changeless stone. Always as a boy there had been for me some haunting promise, some treasure at the foot of the rainbow. I shall expect the curve of a rainbow to lead me down into Surprise Valley. A dreamer, you will call me. But I have had strange dreams come true. . . . Mary, do you think *this* dream will come true?"

She was silent so long that he repeated his question.

"Only—in heaven," she whispered.

He took her reply strangely and a chill crept over him.

"You think my plan to seek to strive, to find—you, think that idle, vain?"

"I think it noble. . . . Thank God I've met a man like you!"

"Don't praise me!" he exclaimed, hastily. "Only help me. . . . Mary, will you answer a few little questions, if I swear by my honor I'll never reveal what you tell me?"

"I'll try."

He moistened his lips. Why did she seem so strange, so far away? The hovering shadows made him nervous. Always he had been afraid of the dark. His mood now admitted of unreal fancies.

"Have you ever heard of Fay Larkin?" he asked, very low.

"Yes."

"Was there only one Fay Larkin?"

"Only one."

"Did you—ever see her?"

"Yes," came the faint reply.

He was grateful. How she might be breaking faith with creed or duty! He had not dared to hope so much. All his inner being trembled at the portent of his next query. He had not dreamed it would be so hard to put, or would affect him so powerfully. A warmth, a glow, a happiness pervaded his spirit; and the chill, the gloom were as if they had never been.

"Where is Fay Larkin now?" he asked, huskily.

He bent over her, touched her, leaned close to catch her whisper.

"She is—dead!"

Slowly Shefford rose, with a sickening shock, and then in bitter pain he strode away into the starlight.

VII

SAGO-LILIES

THE Indian returned to camp that night, and early the next day, which was Sunday, Withers rode in, accompanied by a stout, gray-bearded personage wearing a long black coat.

"Bishop Kane, this is my new man, John Shefford," said the trader.

Shefford acknowledged the introduction with the respectful courtesy evidently in order, and found himself being studied intently by clear blue eyes. The bishop appeared old, dry, and absorbed in thought; he spoke quaintly, using in every speech some Biblical word or phrase; and he had an air of authority. He asked Shefford to hear him preach at the morning service, and then he went off into the village.

"Guess he liked your looks," remarked Withers.

"He certainly sized me up," replied Shefford.

"Well, what could you expect? Sure I never heard of a deal like this—a handsome young fellow left alone with a lot of pretty Mormon women! You'll understand when you learn to know Mormons. Bishop Kane's a square old chap. Crazy on religion, maybe, but otherwise he's a good fellow. I made the best stand I could for you. The Mormons over at Stonebridge were huffy because I hadn't consulted them before fetching you over here. If I had, of course you'd never have gotten here. It was Joe Lake who made it all right with them. Joe's well thought of, and he certainly stood up for you."

"I owe him something, then," replied Shefford. "Hope my obligations don't grow beyond me. Did you leave Joe at Stonebridge?"

"Yes. He wanted to stay, and I had work there that 'll keep him awhile. Shefford, we got news of Shadd—bad news. The half-breed's cutting up rough. His gang shot up some Piutes over here across the line. Then he got run out of Durango a few weeks ago for murder. A posse of cowboys trailed him. But he slipped them. He's a fox. You know he was trailing us here. He left the trail, Nas Ta Bega said. I learned at Stonebridge that Shadd is well disposed toward Mormons. It takes the Mormons to handle Indians. Shadd knows of this village and that's why he shunted off our trail. But he might hang down in the pass and wait for us. I think I'd better go back to Kayenta alone, across country. You stay here till Joe and the Indian think it safe to leave. You'll be going up on the slope of Navajo to load a pack-train, and from there it may be well to go down West Cañon to Red Lake, and home over the divide, the way you came. Joe 'll decide what's best. And you might as well buckle on a gun and get used to it. Sooner or later you'll have to shoot your way through."

Shefford did not respond with his usual enthusiasm, and the omission caused the trader to scrutinize him closely.

"What's the matter?" he queried. "There's no light in your eye to-day. You look a little shady."

"I didn't rest well last night," replied Shefford. "I'm depressed this morning. But I'll cheer up directly."

"Did you get along with the women?"

"Very well indeed. And I've enjoyed myself. It's a strange, beautiful place."

"Do you like the women?"

"Yes."

"Have you seen much of the Sago Lily?"

"No. I carried her bucket one night—and saw her only once again. I've been with the other women most of the time."

"It's just as well you didn't run often into Mary. Joe's sick over her. I never saw a girl with a face and form to equal hers. There's danger here for any man, Shefford. Even for you who think you've turned your back on the world! Any of these Mormon women may fall in love with you. They *can't* love their husbands. That's how I figure it. Religion holds them, not love. And the peculiar thing is this: they're second, third, or fourth wives, all sealed. That means their husbands are old, have picked them out for youth and physical charms, have chosen the very opposite to their first wives, and then have hidden them here in this lonely hole. . . . Did you ever imagine so terrible a thing?"

"No, Withers, I did not."

"Maybe that's what depressed you. Anyway, my hunch is worth taking. Be as nice as you can, Shefford. Lord knows it would be good for these poor women if every last one of them fell in love with

111

you. That won't hurt them so long as you keep your head. Savvy? Perhaps I seem rough and coarse to a man of your class. Well, that may be. But human nature is human nature. And in this strange and beautiful place you might love an Indian girl, let alone the Sago Lily. That's all. I sure feel better with that load off my conscience. Hope I don't offend."

"No indeed. I thank you, Withers," replied Shefford, with his hand on the trader's shoulder. "You are right to caution me. I seem to be wild—thirsting for adventure—chasing a gleam. In these unstable days I can't answer for my heart. But I can for my honor. These unfortunate women are as safe with me as — as they are with you and Joe."

Withers uttered a blunt laugh.

"See here, son, look things square in the eye. Men of violent, lonely, toilsome lives store up hunger for the love of woman. Love of a *strange* woman, if you want to put it that way. It's nature. It seems all the beautiful young women in Utah are corralled in this valley. When I come over here I feel natural, but I'm not happy. I'd like to make love to—to that flower-faced girl. And I'm not ashamed to own it. I've told Molly, my wife, and she understands. As for Joe, it's much harder for him. Joe never has had a wife or sweetheart. I tell you he's sick, and if I'd stay here a month I'd be sick."

Withers had spoken with fire in his eyes, with grim humor on his lips, with uncompromising brutal truth. What he admitted was astounding to Shefford, but, once spoken, not at all strange. The

trader was a man who spoke his inmost thought.
And what he said suddenly focused Shefford's mental
vision clear and whole upon the appalling significance
of the tragedy of those women, especially of the girl
whose life was lonelier, sadder, darker than that of
the others.

"Withers, trust me," replied Shefford.

"All right. Make the best of a bad job," said
the trader, and went off about his tasks.

Shefford and Withers attended the morning service, which was held in the school-house. Exclusive
of the children every inhabitant of the village was
there. The women, except the few eldest, were
dressed in white and looked exceedingly well.
Manifestly they had bestowed care upon this
Sabbath morning's toilet. One thing surely this
dress occasion brought out, and it was evidence that
the Mormon women were not poor, whatever their
misfortunes might be. Jewelry was not wanting, nor
fine lace. And they all wore beautiful wild flowers
of a kind unknown to Shefford. He received many a
bright smile. He looked for Mary, hoping to see her
face for the first time in the daylight, but she sat
far forward and did not turn. He saw her graceful
white neck, the fine lines of her throat, and her
colorless cheek. He recognized her, yet in the light
she seemed a stranger.

The service began with a short prayer and was followed by the singing of a hymn. Nowhere had
Shefford heard better music or sweeter voices. How
deeply they affected him! Had any man ever fallen
into a stranger adventure than this? He had only to

shut his eyes to believe it all a creation of his fancy—
the square log cabin with its red mud between the
chinks and a roof like an Indian hogan—the old
bishop in his black coat, standing solemnly, his hand
beating time to the tune—the few old women, digni-
fied and stately—the many young women, fresh and
handsome, lifting their voices.

Shefford listened intently to the bishop's sermon.
In some respects it was the best he had ever heard.
In others it was impossible for an intelligent man to
regard seriously. It was very long, lasting an hour
and a half, and the parts that were helpful to Shefford came from the experience and wisdom of a man
who had grown old in the desert. The physical
things that had molded characters of iron, the obstacles that only strong, patient men could have
overcome, the making of homes in a wilderness,
showed the greatness of this alien band of Mormons.
Shefford conceded greatness to them. But the
strange religion—the narrowing down of the world
to the soil of Utah, the intimations of prophets on
earth who had direct converse with God, the austere self-conscious omnipotence of this old bishop—
these were matters that Shefford felt he must understand better, and see more favorably, if he were not
to consider them impossible.

Immediately after the service, forgetting that his
intention had been to get the long-waited-for look
at Mary in the light of the sun, Shefford hurried
back to camp and to a secluded spot among the
cedars. Strikingly it had come to him that the
fault he had found in Gentile religion he now found
in the Mormon religion. An old question returned

to haunt him—were all religions the same in blindness? As far as he could see, religion existed to uphold the founders of a Church, a creed. The Church
of his own kind was a place where narrow men and
women went to think of their own salvation. They
did not go there to think of others. And now
Shefford's keen mind saw something of Mormonism
and found it wanting. Bishop Kane was a sincere,
good, mistaken man. He believed what he preached,
but that would not stand logic. He taught blindness and mostly it appeared to be directed at the
women. Was there no religion divorced from power,
no religion as good for one man as another, no religion in the spirit of brotherly love? Nas Ta Bega's
"Bi Nai" (brother)—that was love, if not religion,
and perhaps the one and the other were the same.
Shefford kept in mind an intention to ask Nas Ta
Bega what he thought of the Mormons.

Later, when opportunity afforded, he did speak
to the Indian. Nas Ta Bega threw away his
cigarette and made an impressive gesture that con-
veyed as much sorrow as scorn.

"The first Mormon said God spoke to him and
told him to go to a certain place and dig. He went
there and found the Book of Mormon. It said
follow me, marry many wives, go into the desert
and multiply, send your sons out into the world and
bring us young women, many young women. And
when the first Mormon became strong with many
followers he said again: Give to me part of your
labor—of your cattle and sheep—of your silver—that
I may build me great cathedrals for you to worship
in. And I will commune with God and make it

right and good that you have more wives. That is what the bishop preached. That is Mormonism."

"Nas Ta Bega, you mean the Mormons are a great and good people blindly following a leader?"

"Yes. And the leader builds for himself—not for them."

"That is not religion. He has no God but himself."

"They have no God. They are blind like the Mokis who have the creeping growths on their eyes. They have no God they can see and hear and feel, who is with them day and night."

It was late in the afternoon when Bishop Kane rode through the camp and halted on his way to speak to Shefford. He was kind and fatherly.

"Young man, are you open to faith?" he questioned, gravely.

"I think I am," replied Shefford, thankful he could answer readily.

"Then come into the fold. You are a lost sheep. 'Away on the desert I heard its cry.' . . . God bless you. Visit me when you ride to Stonebridge."

He flicked his horse with a cedar branch and trotted away beside the trader, and presently the green-choked neck of the valley hid them from view. Shefford could not have said that he was glad to be left behind, and yet neither was he sorry.

That Sabbath evening as he sat quietly with Nas Ta Bega, watching the sunset gilding the peaks, he was visited by three of the young Mormon women —Ruth, Joan, and Hester. They deliberately sought him and merrily led him off to the village and to the evening service of singing and prayer. Afterward

he was surrounded and made much of. He had
been popular before, but this was different. When
he thoughtfully wended his way campward under
the quiet stars he realized that the coming of Bishop
Kane had made a subtle change in the women. That
change was at first hard to define, but from every
point by which he approached it he came to the same
conclusion—the bishop had not objected to his
presence in the village. The women became natural,
free, and unrestrained. A dozen or twenty young
and attractive women thrown much into companionship with one man. He might become a Mormon.
The idea made him laugh. But upon reflection it
was not funny; it sobered him. What a situation!
He felt instinctively that he ought to fly from this
hidden valley. But he could not have done it, even
had he ... been in the trader's employ. The thing
was provokingly seductive. It was like an Arabian
Nights' tale. What would these strange, fatally
bound women do? Would any one of them become
involved in sweet toils such as were possible to him?
He was no fool. Already eyes had flashed and lips
had smiled.

A thousand like thoughts whirled through his
mind. And when he had calmed down somewhat
two things were not lost upon him—an intricate and
fascinating situation, with no end to its possibilities,
threatened and attracted him—and the certainty
that, whatever change the bishop had inaugurated,
it had made these poor women happier. The latter
fact weighed more with Shefford than fears for himself. His word was given to Withers. He would
have felt just the same without having bound him

self. Still, in the light of the trader's blunt philosophy, and of his own assurance that he was no fool, Shefford felt it incumbent upon him to accept a belief that there were situations no man could resist without an anchor. The ingenuity of man could not have devised a stranger, a more enticing, a more overpoweringly fatal situation. Fatal in that it could not be left untried! Shefford gave in and clicked his teeth as he let himself go. And suddenly he thought of her whom these bitter women called the Sago Lily.

The regret that had been his returned with thought of her. The saddest disillusion of his life, the keenest disappointment, the strangest pain, would always be associated with her. He had meant to see her face once, clear in the sunlight, so that he could always remember it, and then never go near her again. And now it came to him that if he did see much of her these other women would find him like the stone wall in the valley. Folly! Perhaps it was, but she would be safe, maybe happier. When he decided, it was certain that he trembled.

Then he buried the memory of Fay Larkin.

Next day Shefford threw himself with all the boy left in him into the work and play of the village. He helped the women and made games for the children. And he talked or listened. In the early evening he called on Ruth, chatted awhile, and went on to see Joan, and from her to another. When the valley became shrouded in darkness he went unseen down the path to Mary's lonely home.

She was there, a white shadow against the black.

When she replied to his greeting her voice seemed full, broken, eager to express something that would not come. She was happier to see him than she should have been, Shefford thought. He talked, swiftly, eloquently, about whatever he believed would interest her. He stayed long, and finally left, not having seen her face except in pale starlight and shadow; and the strong clasp of her hand remained with him as he went away under the piñons.

Days passed swiftly. Joe Lake did not return. The Indian rode in and out of camp, watered and guarded the pack-burros and the mustangs. Shefford grew strong and active. He made garden for the women; he cut cords of fire-wood; he dammed the brook and made an irrigation ditch; he learned to love these fatherless children, and they loved him.

In the afternoons there was leisure for him and for the women. He had no favorites, and let the occasion decide what he should do and with whom he should be. They had little parties at the cottages and picnics under the cedars. He rode up and down the valley with Ruth, who could ride a horse as no other girl he had ever seen. He climbed with Hester. He walked with Joan. Mostly he contrived to include several at once in the little excursions, though it was not rare for him to be out alone with one.

It was not a game he was playing. More and more, as he learned to know these young women, he liked them better, he pitied them, he was good for them. It shamed him, hurt him, somehow, to see how they tried to forget something when they were with him.

Not improbably a little of it was coquetry, as natural as a laugh to any pretty woman. But that was not what hurt him. It was to see Ruth or Rebecca, as the case might be, full of life and fun, thoroughly enjoying some jest or play, all of a sudden be strangely recalled from the wholesome pleasure of a girl to become a deep and somber woman. The crimes in the name of religion! How he thought of the blood and the ruin laid at the door of religion. He wondered if that were so with Nas Ta Bega's religion, and he meant to find out some day. The women he liked best he imagined the least religious, and they made less effort to attract him.

Every night in the dark he went to Mary's home and sat with her on the porch. He never went inside. For all he knew, his visits were unknown to her neighbors. Still, it did not matter to him if they found out. To her he could talk as he had never talked to any one. She liberated all his thought and fancy. He filled her mind.

As there had been a change in the other women, so was there in Mary; however, it had no relation to the bishop's visit. The time came when Shefford could not but see that she lived and dragged through the long day for the sake of those few hours in the shadow of the stars with him. She seldom spoke. She listened. Wonderful to him—sometimes she laughed—and it seemed the sound was a ghost of childhood pleasure. When he stopped to consider that she might fall in love with him he drove the thought from him. When he realized that his folly had become sweet and that the sweetness imperiously drew him, he likewise cast off that

120

SAGO-LILIES

thought. The present was enough. And if he had
any treasures of mind and heart he gave them to
her.

She never asked him to stay, but she showed that
she wanted him to. That made it hard to go.
Still, he never stayed late. The moment of parting
was like a break. Her good-by was sweet, low
music; it lingered on his ear; it bade him come
to-morrow night; and it sent him away into the
valley to walk under the stars, a man fighting
against himself.

One night at parting, as he tried to see her face
in the wan glow of a clouded moon, he said:

"I've been trying to find a sago-lily."

"Have you never seen one?" she asked.

"No." He meant to say something with a double meaning, in reference to her face and the name
of the flower, but her unconsciousness made him
hold his tongue. She was wholly unlike the other
women.

"I'll show you where the lilies grow," she said.

"When?"

"To-morrow. Early in the afternoon I'll come
to the spring. Then I'll take you."

Next morning Joe Lake returned and imparted
news that was perturbing to Shefford. Reports of
Shadd had come in to Stonebridge from different
Indian villages; Joe was not inclined to linger long
at the camp, and favored taking the trail with the
pack-train.

Shefford discovered that he did not want to
leave the valley, and the knowledge made him re-

121

flective. That morning he did not go into the village, and stayed in camp alone. A depression weighed upon him. It was dispelled, however, early in the afternoon by the sight of a slender figure in white swiftly coming down the path to the spring. He had an appointment with Mary to go to see the sago-lilies; everything else slipped his mind.

Mary wore the long black hood that effectually concealed her face. It made of her a woman, a Mormon woman, and strangely belied the lithe form and the braid of gold hair.

"Good day," she said, putting down her bucket. "Do you still want to go—to see the lilies?"

"Yes," replied Shefford, with a short laugh.

"Can you climb?"

"I'll go where you go."

Then she set off under the cedars and Shefford stalked at her side. He was aware that Nas Ta Bega watched them walk away. This day, so far, at least, Shefford did not feel talkative; and Mary had always been one who mostly listened. They came at length to a place where the wall rose in low, smooth swells, not steep, but certainly at an angle Shefford would not of his own accord have attempted to scale.

Light, quick, and sure as a mountain-sheep Mary went up the first swell to an offset above. Shefford, in amaze and admiration, watched the little moccasins as they flashed and held on to the smooth rock.

When he essayed to follow her he slipped and came to grief. A second attempt resulted in like failure. Then he backed away from the wall, to run forward fast and up the slope, only to slip, half-way up, and fall again.

He made light of the incident, but she was solici-
tous. When he assured her he was unhurt she
said he had agreed to go where she went.

"But I'm not a—a bird," he protested.

"Take off your boots. Then you can climb.
When we get over the wall it 'll be easy," she said.

In his stocking-feet he had no great difficulty
walking up the first bulge of the walls. And from
there she led him up the strange waves of wind-worn
rock. He could not attend to anything save the
red, polished rock under him, and so saw little.
The ascent was longer than he would have imagined,
and steep enough to make him pant, but at last a
huge round summit was reached

From here he saw down into the valley where the
village lay. But for the lazy columns of blue
smoke curling up from the piñons the place would
have seemed uninhabited. The wall on the other
side was about level with the one upon which he
stood. Beyond rose other walls and cliffs, up and
up to the great towering peaks between which the
green-and-black mountain loomed. Facing the
other way, Shefford had only a restricted view.
There were low crags and smooth stone ridges, between which were aisles green with cedar and piñon.
Shefford's companion headed toward one of these,
and when he had followed her a few steps he could
no longer see down into the valley. The Mormon
village where she lived was as if it were lost, and
when it vanished Shefford felt a difference. Scarcely
had the thought passed when Mary removed the
dark hood. Her small head glistened like gold in
the sunlight.

Shefford caught up with her and walked at her side, but could not bring himself at once deliberately to look at her. They entered a narrow, low-walled lane where cedars and piñons grew thickly, their fragrance heavy in the warm air, and flowers began to show in the grassy patches.

"This is Indian paint-brush," she said, pointing to little, low, scarlet flowers. A gray sage-bush with beautiful purple blossoms she called purple sage, another bush with yellow flowers she named buck-brush, and there were vermilion cacti and low, flat mounds of lavender daisies which she said had no name. A whole mossy bank was covered with lace like green leaves and tiny blossoms the color of violets, which she called loco.

"Loco? Is this what makes the horses go crazy when they eat it?" he asked.

"It is, indeed," she said, laughing.

When she laughed it was impossible not to look at her. She walked a little in advance. Her white cheek and temple seemed framed in the gold of her hair. How white her skin! But it was like pearl, faintly veined and flushed. The profile, clear-cut and pure, appeared cold, almost stern. He knew now that she was singularly beautiful, though he had yet to see her full face.

They walked on. Quite suddenly the lane opened out between two rounded bluffs, and Shefford looked down upon a grander and more awe-inspiring scene than ever he had viewed in his dreams.

What appeared to be a green mountainside sloped endlessly down to a plain, and that rolled and billowed away to a boundless region of strangely carved rock. The greatness of the scene could not be grasped in a glance. The slope was long; the plain not as level as it seemed to be on first sight; here and there round, red rocks, isolated and strange, like lonely castles, rose out of the green. Beyond the green all the earth seemed naked, showing smooth, glistening bones. It was a formidable wall of rock that flung itself up in the distance, carved into a thousand cañons and walls and domes and peaks, and there was not a straight nor a broken nor a jagged line in all that wildness. The color low down was red, dark blue, and purple in the clefts, yellow upon the heights, and in the distance rainbow-hued. A land of curves and color!

Shefford uttered an exclamation.

"That's Utah," said Mary. "I come often to sit here. You see that winding blue line. There. . . . That's San Juan Cañon. And the other dark line, that's Escalante Cañon. They wind down into this great purple chasm—'way over here to the left—and that's the Grand Cañon. They say not even the Indians have been in there."

Shefford had nothing to say. The moment was one of subtle and vital assimilation. Such places as this to be unknown to men! What strength, what wonder, what help, what glory, just to sit there an hour, slowly and appallingly to realize! Something came to Shefford from the distance, out of the purple cañons and from those dim, wind-worn peaks. He resolved to come here to this promontory again and again, alone and in humble spirit, and learn to know why he had been silenced, why peace pervaded his soul.

It was with this emotion upon him that he turned to find his companion watching him. Then for the first time he saw her face fully, and was thrilled that chance had reserved the privilege for this moment. It was a girl's face he saw, flower-like, lovely and pure as a Madonna's, and strangely, tragically sad. The eyes were large, dark gray, the color of the sage. They were as clear as the air which made distant things close, and yet they seemed full of shadows, like a ruffled pool under midnight stars. They disturbed him. Her mouth had the sweet curves and redness of youth, but it showed bitterness, pain, and repression.

"Where are the sago-lilies?" he asked, suddenly.

"Farther down. It's too cold up here for them. Come," she said.

He followed her down a winding trail—down and down till the green plain rose to blot out the scrawled wall of rock, down into a verdant cañon where a brook made swift music over stones, where the air was sultry and hot, laden with the fragrant breath of flower and leaf. This was a cañon of summer, and it bloomed.

The girl bent and plucked something from the grass.

"Here's a white lily," she said. "There are three colors. The yellow and pink ones are deeper down in the cañons."

Shefford took the flower and regarded it with great interest. He had never seen such an exquisite thing. It had three large petals, curving cuplike, of a whiteness purer than new-fallen snow, and a heart of rich, warm gold. Its fragrance was so faint as to be almost indistinguishable, yet of a haunting, unforgetable sweetness. And even while he looked at it the petals drooped and their whiteness shaded and the gold paled. In a moment the flower was wilted.

"I don't like to pluck the lilies," said Mary. "They die so swiftly."

Shefford saw the white flowers everywhere in the open, sunny places along the brook. They swayed with stately grace in the slow, warm wind. They seemed like three-pointed stars shining out of the green. He bent over one with a particularly lofty stem, and after a close survey of it he rose to look at her face. His action was plainly one of comparison. She laughed and said it was foolish for the women to call her the Sago Lily. She had no coquetry; she spoke as she would have spoken of the stones at her feet; she did not know that she was beautiful. Shefford imagined there was some resemblance in her to the lily—the same whiteness, the same rich gold, and, more striking than either, a strange, rare quality of beauty, of life, intangible as something fleeting, the spirit that had swiftly faded from the plucked flower. Where had the girl been born— what had her life been? Shefford was intensely curious about her. She seemed as different from any other women he had known as this rare cañon lily was different from the tame flowers at home.

On the return up the slope she outstripped him. She climbed lightly and tirelessly. When he reached her upon the promontory there was a stain of red in her cheeks and her expression had changed.

"Let's go back up over the rocks," she said. "I've not climbed for—for so long."

"I'll go where you go," he replied.

Then she was off, and he followed. She took to the curves of the bare rocks and climbed. He sensed a spirit released in her. It was so strange, so keen, so wonderful to be with her, and when he did catch her he feared to speak lest he break this mood. Her eyes grew dark and daring, and often she stopped to look away across the wavy sea of stones to something beyond the great walls. When they got high the wind blew her hair loose and it flew out, a golden stream, with the sun bright upon it. He saw that she changed her direction, which had been in line with the two peaks, and now she climbed toward the heights. They came to more difficult ascent, where the stone still held to the smooth curves, yet was marked by steep bulges and slants and crevices. Here she became a wild thing. She ran, she leaped, she would have left him far behind had he not called. Then she appeared to remember him and waited.

Her face had now lost its whiteness; it was flushed, rosy, warm.

"Where—did you—ever learn—to run over rocks —this way?" he panted.

"All my life I've climbed," she said. "Ah! it's so good to be up on the walls again—to feel the wind —to see!"

Thereafter he kept close to her, no matter what the effort. He would not miss a moment of her, if he could help it. She was wonderful. He imagined she must be like an Indian girl, or a savage who loved the lofty places and the silence. When she leaped she uttered a strange, low, sweet cry of wild-

ness and exultation. Shefford guessed she was a
girl freed from her prison, forgetting herself, living
again youthful hours. Still she did not forget him.
She waited for him at the bad places, lent him a
strong hand, and sometimes let it stay long in his
clasp. Tireless and agile, 'sure-footed as a goat,
fleet and wild she leaped and climbed and ran until
Shefford marveled at her. This adventure was
indeed fulfilment of a dream. Perhaps she might
lead him to the treasure at the foot of the rainbow.
But that thought, sad with memory daring forth
from its grave, was irrevocably linked with a girl
who was dead. He could not remember her, in the
presence of this wonderful creature who was as
strange as she was beautiful. When Shefford reached
for the brown hand stretched forth to help him in a
leap, when he felt its strong clasp, the youth and
vitality and life of it, he had the fear of a man who
was running toward a precipice and who could not
draw back. This was a climb, a lark, a wild race
to the Mormon girl, bound now in the village, and
by the very freedom of it she betrayed her bonds.
To Shefford it was also a wild race, but toward one
sure goal he dared not name.

They went on, and at length, hand in hand, even
where no steep step or wide fissure gave reason for
the clasp. But she seemed unconscious. They
were nearing the last height, a bare eminence, when
she broke from him and ran up the smooth stone.
When he surmounted it she was standing on the very
summit, her arms wide, her full breast heaving, her
slender body straight as an Indian's, her hair flying
in the wind and blazing in the sun. She seemed to

embrace the west, to reach for something afar, to offer herself to the wind and distance. Her face was scarlet from the exertion of the climb, and her broad brow was moist. Her eyes had the piercing light of an eagle's, though now they were dark. Shefford instinctively grasped the essence of this strange spirit, primitive and wild. She was not the woman who had met him at the spring. She had dropped some side of her with that Mormon hood, and now she stood totally strange.

She belonged up here, he divined. She was a part of that wildness. She must have been born and brought up in loneliness, where the wind blew and the peaks loomed and silence held dominion. The sinking sun touched the rim of the distant wall, and as if in parting regret shone with renewed golden fire. And the girl was crowned as with a glory.

Shefford loved her then. Realizing it, he thought he might have loved her before, but that did not matter when he was certain of it now. He trembled a little, fearfully, though without regret. Everything pertaining to his desert experience had been strange—this the strangest of all.

The sun sank swiftly, and instantly there was a change in the golden light. Quickly it died out. The girl changed as swiftly. She seemed to remember herself, and sat down as if suddenly weary. Shefford went closer and seated himself beside her.

"The sun has set. We must go," she said. But she made no movement.

"Whenever you are ready," replied he.

Just as the blaze had died out of her eyes, so the

SAGO-LILIES

flush faded out of her face. The whiteness stole back, and with it the sadness. He had to bite his tongue to keep from telling her what he felt, to keep from pouring out a thousand questions. But the privilege of having seen her, of having been with her when she had forgotten herself—that he believed was enough. It had been wonderful; it had made him love her. But it need not add to the tragedy of her life, whatever that was. He tried to eliminate himself. And he watched her.

Her eyes were fixed upon the gold-rimmed ramparts of the distant wall in the west. Plain it was how she loved that wild upland. And there seemed to be some haunting memory of the past in her gaze—some happy part of life, agonizing to think of now.

"We must go," she said, and rose.

Shefford rose to accompany her. She looked at him, and her haunting eyes seemed to want him to know that he had helped her to forget the present, to remember girlhood, and that somehow she would always associate a wonderful happy afternoon with him. He divined that her silence then was a Mormon seal on lips.

"Mary, this has been the happiest, the best, the most revealing day of my life," he said, simply.

Swiftly, as if startled, she turned and faced down the slope. At the top of the wall above the village she put on the dark hood, and with it that somber something which was Mormon.

Twilight had descended into the valley, and shadows were so thick Shefford had difficulty in finding Mary's bucket. He filled it at the spring, and made offer to carry it home for her, which she declined.

"You'll come to-night—later?" she asked.

"Yes," he replied, hurriedly promising. Then he watched her white form slowly glide down the path to disappear in the shadows.

Nas Ta Bega and Joe were busy at the camp-fire. Shefford joined them. This night he was uncommunicative. Joe peered curiously at him in the flare of the blaze. Later, after the meal, when Shefford appeared restless and strode to and fro, Joe spoke up gruffly:

"Better hang round camp to-night."

Shefford heard, but did not heed. Nevertheless, the purport of the remark, which was either jealousy or admonition, haunted him with the possibility of its meaning.

He walked away from the camp-fire, under the dark piñons, out into the starry open; and every step was hard to take, unless it pointed toward the home of the girl whose beauty and sadness and mystery had bewitched him. After what seemed hours he took the well-known path toward her cabin, and then every step seemed lighter. He divined he was rushing to some fate—he knew not what.

The porch was in shadow. He peered in vain for the white form against the dark background. In the silence he seemed to hear his heart-beats thick and muffled.

Some distance down the path he heard the sound of hoofs. Withdrawing into the gloom of a cedar, he watched. Soon he made out moving horses with riders. They filed past him to the number of half a score. Like a flash of fire the truth burned him. Mormons come for one of those mysterious night visits to sealed wives!

Shefford stalked far down the valley, into the lonely silence and the night shadows under the walls.

VIII

THE home of Nas Ta Bega lay far up the cedared slope, with the craggy yellow cliffs and the black cañons and the pine-fringed top of Navajo Mountain behind, and to the fore the vast, rolling descent of cedar groves and sage flats and sandy washes. No dim, dark range made bold outline along the horizon; the stretch of gray and purple and green extended to the blue line of sky.

Down the length of one sage level Shefford saw a long lane where the brush and the grass had been beaten flat. This, the Navajo said, was a track where the young braves had raced their mustangs and had striven for supremacy before the eyes of maidens and the old people of the tribe.

"Nas Ta Bega, did you ever race here?" asked Shefford.

"I am a chief by birth. But I was stolen from my home, and now I cannot ride well enough to race the braves of my tribe," the Indian replied, bitterly.

In another place Joe Lake halted his horse and called Shefford's attention to a big yellow rock lying along the trail. And then he spoke in Navajo to the Indian.

134

"I've heard of this stone—Isende Aha," said Joe, after Nas Ta Bega had spoken. "Get down, and let's see."

Shefford dismounted, but the Indian kept his seat in the saddle.

Joe placed a big hand on the stone and tried to move it. According to Shefford's eye measurement the stone was nearly oval, perhaps three feet high, by a little over two in width. Joe threw off his sombrero, took a deep breath, and, bending over, clasped the stone in his arms. He was an exceedingly heavy and powerful man, and it was plain to Shefford that he meant to lift the stone if that were possible. Joe's broad shoulders strained, flattened; his arms bulged, his joints cracked, his neck corded, and his face turned black. By gigantic effort he lifted the stone and moved it about six inches. Then as he released his hold he fell, and when he sat up his face was wet with sweat.

"Try it," he said to Shefford, with his lazy smile "See if you can heave it."

Shefford was strong, and there had been a time when he took pride in his strength. Something in Joe's supreme effort and in the gloom of the Indian's eyes made Shefford curious about this stone. He bent over and grasped it as Joe had done. He braced himself and lifted with all his power, until a red blur obscured his sight and shooting stars seemed to explode in his head. But he could not even stir the stone.

"Shefford, maybe you'll be able to heft it some day," observed Joe. Then he pointed to the stone and addressed Nas Ta Bega.

The Indian shook his head and spoke for a moment.

"This is the Isende Aha of the Navajos," explained Joe. "The young braves are always trying to carry this stone. As soon as one of them can carry it he is a man. He who carries it farthest is the biggest man. And just so soon as any Indian can no longer lift it he is old. Nas Ta Bega says the stone has been carried two miles in his lifetime. His own father carried it the length of six steps."

"Well! It's plain to me that I am not a man," said Shefford, "or else I am old."

Joe Lake drawled his lazy laugh and, mounting, rode up the trail. But Shefford lingered beside the Indian.

"Bi Nai," said Nas Ta Bega, "I am a chief of my tribe, but I have never been a man. I never lifted that stone. See what the pale-face education has done for the Indian!"

The Navajo's bitterness made Shefford thoughtful. Could greater injury be done to man than this—to rob him of his heritage of strength?

Joe drove the bobbing pack-train of burros into the cedars where the smoke of the hogans curled upward, and soon the whistling of mustangs, the barking of dogs, the bleating of sheep, told of his reception. And presently Shefford was in the midst of an animated scene. Great, woolly, fierce dogs, like wolves, ran out to meet the visitors. Sheep and goats were everywhere, and little lambs scarcely able to walk, with others frisky and frolicsome. There were pure-white lambs, and some that appeared to be painted, and some so beautiful with their fleecy white all except black faces or ears or tails or feet. They ran right under Nack-yal's legs and bumped against Shefford, and kept bleating their thin-piped welcome. Under the cedars surrounding the several hogans were mustangs that took Shefford's eye. He saw an iron-gray with white mane and tail sweeping to the ground; and a fiery black, wilder than any other beast he had ever seen; and a pinto as wonderfully painted as the little lambs; and, most striking of all, a pure, cream-colored mustang with grace and fine lines and beautiful mane and tail, and, strange to see, eyes as blue as azure. This albino mustang came right up to Shefford, an action in singular contrast with that of the others, and showed a tame and friendly spirit toward him and Nack-yal. Indeed, Shefford had reason to feel ashamed of Nack-yal's temper or jealousy.

The first Indians to put in an appearance were a flock of children, half naked, with tangled manes of raven-black hair and skin like gold bronze. They appeared bold and shy by turns. Then a little, sinewy man, old and beaten and gray, came out of the principal hogan. He wore a blanket round his bent shoulders. His name was Hosteen Doetin, and it meant gentle man. His fine, old, wrinkled face lighted with a smile of kindly interest. His squaw followed him, and she was as venerable as he. Shefford caught a glimpse of the shy, dark Glen Naspa, Nas Ta Bega's sister, but she did not come out. Other Indians appeared, coming from adjacent hogans.

Nas Ta Bega turned the mustangs loose among those Shefford had noticed, and presently there rose a snorting, whistling, kicking, plunging mêlée. A cloud of dust hid them, and then a thudding of swift hoofs told of a run through the cedars. Joe Lake began picking over stacks of goat-skins and bags of wool that were piled against the hogan.

"Reckon we'll have one grand job packing out this load," he growled. "It's not so heavy, but awkward to pack."

It developed, presently, from talk with the old Navajo, that this pile was only a half of the load to be packed to Kayenta, and the other half was round the corner of the mountain in the camp of Piutes. Hosteen Doetin said he would send to the camp and have the Piutes bring their share over. The suggestion suited Joe, who wanted to save his burros as much as possible. Accordingly, a messenger was despatched to the Piute camp. And Shefford, with time on his hands and poignant memory to combat, decided to recall his keen interest in the Navajo, and learn, if possible, what the Indian's life was like. What would a day of his natural life be?

In the gray of dawn, when the hush of the desert night still lay deep over the land, the Navajo stirred in his blanket and began to chant to the morning light. It began very soft and low, a strange, broken murmur, like the music of a brook, and as it swelled that weird and mournful tone was slowly lost in one of hope and joy. The Indian's soul was coming out of night, blackness, the sleep that resembled death, into the day, the light that was life.

Then he stood in the door of his hogan, his blanket around him, and faced the east.

138

THE HOGAN OF NAS TA BEGA

Night was lifting out of the clefts and ravines, the rolling cedar ridges and the sage flats were softly gray, with thin veils like smoke mysteriously rising and vanishing; the colorless rocks were changing. A long, horizon-wide gleam of light, rosiest in the center, lay low down in the east and momentarily brightened. One by one the stars in the deep-blue sky paled and went out and the blue dome changed and lightened. Night had vanished on invisible wings and silence broke to the music of a mockingbird. The rose in the east deepened; a wisp of cloud turned gold; dim distant mountains showed dark against the red; and low down in a notch a rim of fire appeared. Over the soft ridges and valleys crept a wondrous transfiguration. It was as if every blade of grass, every leaf of sage, every twig of cedar, the flowers, the trees, the rocks came to life at sight of the sun. The red disk rose, and a golden fire burned over the glowing face of that lonely waste.

The Navajo, dark, stately, inscrutable, faced the sun—his god. This was his Great Spirit. The desert was his mother, but the sun was his life. To the keeper of the winds and rains, to the master of light, to the maker of fire, to the giver of life the Navajo sent up his prayer:

Of all the good things of the Earth let me always have plenty.
Of all the beautiful things of the Earth let me always have plenty.
Peacefully let my horses go and peacefully let my sheep go.
God of the Heavens, give me many sheep and horses.
God of the Heavens, help me to talk straight.
Goddess of the Earth, my Mother, let me walk straight.
Now all is well, now all is well, now all is well, now all is well,

Hope and faith were his.

A chief would be born to save the vanishing tribe of Navajos. A bride would rise from a wind—kiss of the lilies in the moonlight.

He drank from the clear, cold spring bubbling from under mossy rocks. He went into the cedars, and the tracks in the trails told him of the visitors of night. His mustangs whistled to him from the ridge-tops, standing clear with heads up and manes flying, and then trooped down through the sage. The shepherd-dogs, guardians of the flocks, barked him a welcome, and the sheep bleated and the lambs pattered round him.

In the hogan by the warm, red fire his women baked his bread and cooked his meat. And he satisfied his hunger. Then he took choice meat to the hogan of a sick relative, and joined in the song and the dance and the prayer that drove away the evil spirit of illness. Down in the valley, in a sandy, sunny place, was his corn-field, and here he turned in the water from the ditch, and worked awhile, and went his contented way.

He loved his people, his women, and his children. To his son he said: "Be bold and brave. Grow like the pine. Work and ride and play that you may be strong. Talk straight. Love your brother. Give half to your friend. Honor your mother that you may honor your wife. Pray and listen to your gods."

Then with his gun and his mustang he climbed the slope of the mountain. He loved the solitude, but he was never alone. There were voices on the wind and steps on his trail. The lofty pine, the lichened rock, the tiny bluebell, the seared crag—all whispered their secrets. For him their spirits spoke. In the morning light Old Stone Face, the mountain, was a red god calling him to the chase. He was a brother of the eagle, at home on the heights where the winds swept and the earth lay revealed below.

In the golden afternoon, with the warm sun on his back and the blue cañons at his feet, he knew the joy of doing nothing. He did not need rest, for he was never tired. The sage-sweet breath of the open was thick in his nostrils, the silence that had so many whisperings was all about him, the loneliness of the wild was his. His falcon eye saw mustang and sheep, the puff of dust down on the cedar level, the Indian riding on a distant ridge, the gray walls, and the blue clefts. Here was home, still free, still wild, still untainted. He saw with the eyes of his ancestors. He felt them around him. They had gone into the elements from which their voices came on the wind. They were the watchers on his trails.

At sunset he faced the west, and this was his prayer:

> Great Spirit, God of my Fathers,
> Keep my horses in the night.
> Keep my sheep in the night.
> Keep my family in the night.
> Let me wake to the day.
> Let me be worthy of the light.
> Now all is well, now all is well,
> Now all is well, now all is well.

And he watched the sun go down and the gold sink from the peaks and the red die out of the west and the gray shadows creep out of the cañons to meet the twilight and the slow, silent, mysterious approach of night with its gift of stars.

Night fell. The white stars blinked. The wind sighed in the cedars. The sheep bleated. The shepherd-dogs bayed the mourning coyotes. And the Indian lay down in his blankets with his dark face tranquil in the starlight. All was well in his lonely world. Phantoms hovered, illness lingered, injury and pain and death were there, the shadow of a strange white hand flitted across the face of the moon—but now all was well—the Navajo had prayed to the god of his Fathers. Now all was well!

And this, thought Shefford in revolt, was what the white man had killed in the Indian tribes, was reaching out now to kill in this wild remnant of the Navajos. The padre, the trapper, the trader, the prospector, and the missionary—so the white man had come, some of him good, no doubt, but more of him evil; and the young brave learned a thirst that could never be quenched at the cold, sweet spring of his forefathers, and the young maiden burned with a fever in her blood, and lost the sweet, strange, wild fancies of her tribe.

Joe Lake came to Shefford and said, "Withers told me you had a mix-up with a missionary at Red Lake."

"Yes, I regret to say," replied Shefford.

"About Glen Naspa?"

"Yes, Nas Ta Bega's sister."

"Withers just mentioned it. Who was the missionary?"

"Willetts, so Presbrey, the trader, said."

"What 'd he look like?"

Shefford recalled the smooth, brown face, the dark eyes, the weak chin, the mild expression, and the soft, lax figure of the missionary.

"Can't tell by what you said," went on Joe. "But I'll bet a peso to a horse-hair that's the fellow who's been here. Old Hosteen Doetin just told me. First visits he ever had from the priest with the long gown. That's what he called the missionary. These old fellows will never forget what's come down from father to son about the Spanish padres. Well, anyway, Willetts has been here twice after Glen Naspa. The old chap is impressed, but he doesn't want to let the girl go. I'm inclined to think Glen Naspa would as lief go as stay. She may be a Navajo, but she's a girl. She won't talk much."

"Where's Nas Ta Bega?" asked Shefford.

"He rode off somewhere yesterday. Perhaps to the Piute camp. These Indians are slow. They may take a week to pack that load over here. But if Nas Ta Bega or some one doesn't come with a message to-day I'll ride over there myself."

"Joe, what do you think about this missionary?" queried Shefford, bluntly.

"Reckon there's not much to think, unless you see him or find out something. I heard of Willetts before Withers spoke of him. He's friendly with Mormons. I understand he's worked for Mormon interests, someway or other. That's on the quiet. Savvy? This matter of him coming after Glen

Naspa, reckon that's all right. The missionaries all go after the young people. What 'd be the use to try to convert the old Indians? No, the missionary's work is to educate the Indian, and, of course, the younger he is the better."

"You approve of the missionary?"

"Shefford, if you understood a Mormon you wouldn't ask that. Did you ever read or hear of Jacob Hamblin? . . . Well, he was a Mormon missionary among the Navajos. The Navajos were as fierce as Apaches till Hamblin worked among them. He made them friendly to the white man."

"That doesn't prove he made converts of them," replied Shefford, still bluntly.

"No. For the matter of that, Hamblin let religion alone. He made presents, then traded with them, then taught them useful knowledge. Mormon or not, Shefford, I'll admit this: a good man, strong with his body, and learned in ways with his hands, with some knowledge of medicine, can better the condition of these Indians. But just as soon as he begins to preach his religion, then his influence wanes. That's natural. These heathen have their ideals, their gods."

"Which the white man should leave them!" replied Shefford, feelingly.

"That's a matter of opinion. But don't let's argue. . . . Willetts is after Glen Naspa. And if I know Indian girls he'll persuade her to go to his school."

"Persuade her!" Then Shefford broke off and related the incident that had occurred at Red Lake.

"Reckon any means justifies the end," replied Joe,

imperturbably. "Let him talk love to her or rope
her or beat her, so long as he makes a Christian of
her."

Shefford felt a hot flush and had difficulty in controlling himself. From this single point of view the
Mormon was impossible to reason with.

"That, too, is a matter of opinion. We won't
discuss it," continued Shefford. "But—if old Hosteen Doetin objects to the girl leaving, and if Nas
Ta Bega does the same, won't that end the matter?"

"Reckon not. The end of the matter is Glen
Naspa. If she wants to go she'll go."

Shefford thought best to drop the discussion.
For the first time he had occasion to be repelled by
something in this kind and genial Mormon, and he
wanted to forget it. Just as he had never talked
about men to the sealed wives in the hidden valley,
so he could not talk of women to Joe Lake.

Nas Ta Bega did not return that day, but next
morning a messenger came calling Lake to the
Piute camp. Shefford spent the morning high on
the slope, learning more with every hour in the
silence and loneliness, that he was stronger of soul
than he had dared to hope, and that the added
pain which had come to him could be borne.

Upon his return toward camp, in the cedar grove,
he caught sight of Glen Naspa with a white man.
They did not see him. When Shefford recognized
Willetts an embarrassment as well as an instinct
made him halt and step into a bushy, low-branched
cedar. It was not his intention to spy on them.
He merely wanted to avoid a meeting. But the
missionary's hand on the girl's arm and her up-

lifted head, her pretty face, strange, intent, troubled, struck Shefford with an unusual and irresistible curiosity. Willetts was talking earnestly; Glen Naspa was listening intently. Shefford watched long enough to see that the girl loved the missionary, and that he reciprocated or was pretending. His manner scarcely savored of pretense, Shefford concluded, as he slipped away under the trees.

He did not go at once into camp. He felt troubled, and wished that he had not encountered the two. His duty in the matter, of course, was to tell Nas Ta Bega what he had seen. Upon reflection Shefford decided to give the missionary the benefit of a doubt; and if he really cared for the Indian girl, and admitted or betrayed it, to think all the better of him for the fact. Glen Naspa was certainly pretty enough, and probably lovable enough, to please any lonely man in this desert. The pain and the yearning in Shefford's heart made him lenient. He had to fight himself—not to forget, for that was impossible—but to keep rational and sane when a white flower-like face haunted him and a voice called.

The cracking of hard hoofs on stones caused him to turn toward camp, and as he emerged from the cedar grove he saw three Indian horsemen ride into the cleared space before the hogans. They were superbly mounted and well armed, and impressed him as being different from Navajos. Perhaps they were Piutes. They dismounted and led the mustangs down to the pool below the spring. Shefford saw another mustang, standing bridle down and carrying a pack behind the saddle. Some squaws with children hanging behind their skirts were standing at the door of Hosteen Doetin's hogan. Shefford glanced in to see Glen Naspa, pale, quiet, almost sullen. Willetts stood with his hands spread. The old Navajo's seamed face worked convulsively as he tried to lift his bent form to some semblance of dignity, and his voice rolled out, sonorously: "Me no savvy Jesus Christ! Me hungry! . . . Me no eat Jesus Christ!"

Shefford drew back as if he had received a blow. That had been Hosteen Doetin's reply to the importunities of the missionary. The old Navajo could work no longer. His sons were gone. His squaw was worn out. He had no one save Glen Naspa to help him. She was young, strong. He was hungry. What was the white man's religion to him?

With long, swift stride Shefford entered the hogan. Willetts, seeing him, did not look so mild as Shefford had him pictured in memory, nor did he appear surprised. Shefford touched Hosteen Doetin's shoulder and said, "Tell me."

The aged Navajo lifted a shaking hand.

"Me no savvy Jesus Christ! Me hungry! . . . Me no eat Jesus Christ!"

Shefford then made signs that indicated the missionary's intention to take the girl away.

"Him come—big talk—Jesus—all Jesus. . . . Me no want Glen Naspa go," replied the Indian.

Shefford turned to the missionary.

"Willetts, is he a relative of the girl?"

"There's some blood tie, I don't know what. But it's not close," replied Willetts.

"Then don't you think you'd better wait till Nas Ta Bega returns? He's her brother."

"What for?" demanded Willetts. "That Indian may be gone a week. She's willing to go."

Shefford looked at the girl.

"Glen Naspa, do you want to go?"

She was shy, ashamed, and silent, but manifestly willing to accompany the missionary. Shefford pondered a moment. How he hoped Nas Ta Bega would come back! It was thought of the Indian that made Shefford stubborn. What his stand ought to be was hard to define, unless he answered to impulse; and here in the wilds he had become imbued with the idea that his impulses and instincts were no longer false.

"Willetts, what do you want with the girl?" queried Shefford, coolly, and at the question he seemed to find himself. He peered deliberately and searchingly into the other's face. The missionary's gaze shifted and a tinge of red crept up from under his collar.

"Absurd thing to ask a missionary!" he burst out, impatiently.

"Do you care for Glen Naspa?"

"I care as God's disciple—who cares to save the soul of heathen," he replied, with the lofty tone of prayer.

"Has Glen Naspa no—no other interest in you—except to be taught religion?"

The missionary's face flamed, and his violent tremor showed that under his exterior there was a different man.

"What right have you to question me?" he demanded. "You're an adventurer—an outcast. I've my duty here. I'm a missionary with Church and state and government behind me."

"Yes, I'm an outcast," replied Shefford, bitterly. "And you may be all you say. But we're alone now out here on the desert. And this girl's brother is absent. You haven't answered me yet. . . . Is there anything between you and Glen Naspa except religion?"

"No, you insulting beggar!"

Shefford had forced the reply that he had expected and which damned the missionary beyond any consideration.

"Willetts, you are a liar!" said Shefford, steadily.

"And what are you?" cried Willetts, in shrill fury. "I've heard all about you. Heretic! Atheist! Driven from your Church! Hated and scrorned for your blasphemy!"

Then he gave way to ungovernable rage, and cursed Shefford as a religious fanatic might have cursed the most debased of sinners. Shefford heard with the blood beating, strangling the pulse in his ears. Somehow this missionary had learned his secret—most likely from the Mormons in Stonebridge. And the terms of disgrace were coals of fire upon Shefford's head. Strangely, however, he did not bow to them, as had been his humble act in the past, when his calumniators had arraigned and flayed him. Passion burned in him now, and hate, for the first time in his life, made a tiger of him. And these raw emotions, new to him, were difficult to control.

"You can't take the girl," he replied, when the other had ceased. "Not without her brother's consent."

"I will take her!"

Shefford threw him out of the hogan and strode after him. Willetts had stumbled. When he straightened up he was white and shaken. He groped for the bridle of his horse while keeping his eyes upon Shefford, and when he found it he whirled quickly, mounted, and rode off. Shefford saw him halt a moment under the cedars to speak with the three strange Indians, and then he galloped away. It came to Shefford then that he had been unconscious of the last strained moment of that encounter. He seemed all cold, tight, locked, and was amazed to find his hand on his gun. Verily the wild environment had liberated strange instincts and impulses, which he had answered. That he had no regrets proved how he had changed.

Shefford heard the old woman scolding. Peering into the hogan, he saw Glen Naspa flounce sullenly down, for all the world like any other thwarted girl. Hosteen Doetin came out and pointed down the slope at the departing missionary.

"Heap talk Jesus—all talk—all Jesus!" he exclaimed, contemptuously. Then he gave Shefford a hard rap on the chest. "Small talk—heap man!"

The matter appeared to be adjusted for the present. But Shefford felt that he had made a bitter enemy, and perhaps a powerful one.

He prepared and ate his supper alone that evening, for Joe Lake and Nas Ta Bega did not put in an appearance. He observed that the three strange Indians, whom he took for Piutes, kept to themselves, and, so far as he knew, had no intercourse with any one at the camp. This would not have seemed unusual, considering the taciturn habit of Indians, had he not remembered seeing Willetts speak to the trio. What had he to do with them? Shefford was considering the situation with vague doubts when, to his relief, the three strangers rode off into the twilight. Then he went to bed.

He was awakened by violence. It was the gray hour before dawn. Dark forms knelt over him. A cloth pressed down hard over his mouth. Strong hands bound it while other strong hands held him. He could not cry out. He could not struggle. A heavy weight, evidently a man, held down his feet. Then he was rolled over, securely bound, and carried, to be thrown like a sack over the back of a horse.

All this happened so swiftly as to be bewildering. He was too astounded to be frightened. As he hung head downward he saw the legs of a horse and a dim trail. A stirrup swung to and fro, hitting him in the face. He began to feel exceedingly uncomfortable, with a rush of blood to his head, and cramps in his arms and legs. This kept on and grew worse for what seemed a long time. Then the horse was stopped and a rude hand tumbled him to the ground. Again he was rolled over on his face. Strong fingers plucked at his clothes, and he believed he was being searched. His captors were as silent as if they had been dumb. He felt when they took his pocketbook and his knife and all that he had. Then they cut, tore, and stripped off all his clothing. He was lifted, carried a few steps, and dropped upon what seemed a soft, low mound, and left lying there, still tied and naked. Shefford heard the rustle of sage and the dull thud of hoofs as his assailants went away.

His first sensation was one of immeasurable relief. He had not been murdered. Robbery was nothing. And though roughly handled, he had not been hurt. He associated the assault with the three strange visitors of the preceding day. Still, he had no proof of that. Not the slightest clue remained to help him ascertain who had attacked him.

It might have been a short while or a long one, his mind was so filled with growing conjectures, but a time came when he felt cold. As he lay face down, only his back felt cold at first. He was grateful that he had not been thrown upon the rocks. The ground under him appeared soft, spongy, and gave somewhat as he breathed. He had really sunk down a little in this pile of soft earth. The day was not far off, as he could tell by the brightening of the gray. He began to suffer with the cold, and then slowly he seemed to freeze and grow numb. In an effort to roll over upon his back he discovered that his position, or his being bound, or the numbness of his muscles was responsible for the fact that he could not move. Here was a predicament. It began to look serious. What would a few hours of the powerful sun do to his uncovered skin? Somebody would trail and find him· still, he might not be found soon.

He saw the sky lighten, turn rosy and then gold. The sun shone upon him, but some time elapsed before he felt its warmth. All of a sudden a pain, like a sting, shot through his shoulder. He could not see what caused it; probably a bee. Then he felt another upon his leg, and about simultaneously with it a tiny, fiery stab in his side. A sickening sensation pervaded his body, slowly moving, as if poison had entered the blood of his veins. Then a puncture, as from a hot wire, entered the skin of his breast. Unmistakably it was a bite. By dint of great effort he twisted his head to see a big red ant on his breast. Then he heard a faint sound, so exceedingly faint that he could not tell what it was like. But presently his strained ears detected a low, swift, rustling, creeping sound, like the slipping rattle of an infinite number of tiny bits of moving gravel. Then it was a sound like the seeping of wind-blown sand. Several hot bites occurred at once. And then with his head twisted he saw a red stream of ants pour out of the mound and spill over his quivering flesh.

In an instant he realized his position. He had been dropped intentionally upon an ant-heap, which had sunk with his weight, wedging him between the crusts. At the mercy of those terrible desert ants! A frantic effort to roll out proved futile, as did another and another. His violent muscular contractions infuriated the ants, and in an instant he was writhing in pain so horrible and so unendurable that he nearly fainted. But he was too strong to faint suddenly. A bath of vitriol, a stripping of his skin and red embers of fire thrown upon raw flesh, could not have equaled this. There was fury in the bites and poison in the fangs of these ants. Was this an Indian's brutal trick or was it the missionary's revenge? Shefford realized that it would kill him soon. He sweat what seemed blood, although perhaps the blood came from the bites. A strange, hollow, buzzing roar filled his ears, and it must have been the pouring of the angry ants from their mound.

Then followed a time that was hell—worse than fire, for fire would have given merciful death—agony under which his physical being began spasmodically to jerk and retch—and his eyeballs turned and his breast caved in.

A cry rang through the roar in his ears. "Bi Nai! Bi Nai!"

His fading sight seemed to shade round the dark face of Nas Ta Bega.

Then powerful hands dragged him from the mound, through the grass and sage, rolled him over and over, and brushed his burning skin with strong, swift sweep.

IX

THAT hard experience was but the beginning of many cruel trials for John Shefford.

He never knew who his assailants were, nor their motive other than robbery; and they had gotten little, for they had not found the large sum of money sewed in the lining of his coat. Joe Lake declared it was Shadd's work, and the Mormon showed the stern nature that lay hidden under his habitual mild manner. Nas Ta Bega shook his head and would not tell what he thought. But a somber fire burned in his eyes.

The three started with a heavily laden pack-train and went down the mountain slope into West Cañon. The second day they were shot at from the rim walls. Lake was wounded, hindering the swift flight necessary to escape deeper into the cañon. Here they hid for days, while the Mormon recovered and the Indian took stealthy trips to try to locate the enemy. Lack of water and grass for the burros drove them on. They climbed out of a side cañon, losing several burros on a rough trail, and had proceeded to within half a day's journey of Red Lake when they were attacked while making camp in a

155

cedar grove. Shefford sustained an exceedingly
painful injury to his leg, but, fortunately, the bullet
went through without breaking a bone. With that
burning pain there came to Shefford the meaning of
fight, and his rifle grew hot in his hands. Night
alone saved the trio from certain fatality. Under
the cover of darkness the Indian helped Shefford to
escape. Joe Lake looked out for himself. The
pack-train was lost, and the mustangs, except Nack-
yal.

Shefford learned what it meant to lie out at night,
listening for pursuit, cold to his marrow, sick with
dread, and enduring frightful pain from a ragged
bullet-hole. Next day the Indian led him down
into the red basin, where the sun shone hot and the
sand reflected the heat. They had no water. A
wind arose and the valley became a place of flying
sand. Through a heavy, stifling pall Nas Ta Bega
somehow got Shefford to the trading-post at Red
Lake. Presbrey attended to Shefford's injury and
made him comfortable. Next day Joe Lake limped
in, surly and somber, with the news that Shadd and
eight or ten of his outlaw gang had gotten away with
the pack-train.

In short time Shefford was able to ride, and with
his companions went over the pass to Kayenta.
Withers already knew of his loss, and all he said
was that he hoped to meet Shadd some day.

Shefford showed a reluctance to go again to the
hidden village in the silent cañon with the rounded
walls. The trader appeared surprised, but did not
press the point. And Shefford meant sooner or
later to tell him, yet never quite reached the point.

The early summer brought more work for the little post, and Shefford toiled with the others. He liked the outdoor tasks, and at night was grateful that he was too tired to think. Then followed trips to Durango and Bluff and Monticello. He rode fifty miles a day for many days. He knew how a man fares who packs light and rides far and fast. When the Indian was with him he got along well, but Nas Ta Bega would not go near the towns. Thus many mishaps were Shefford's fortune.

Many and many a mile he trailed his mustang, for Nack-yal never forgot the Sagi, and always headed for it when he broke his hobbles. Shefford accompanied an Indian teamster in to Durango with a wagon and four wild mustangs. Upon the return, with a heavy load of supplies, accident put Shefford in charge of the outfit. In despair he had to face the hardest task that could have been given him—to take care of a crippled Indian, catch, water, feed, harness, and drive four wild mustangs that did not know him and tried to kill him at every turn, and to get that precious load of supplies home to Kayenta. That he accomplished it proved to him the possibilities of a man, for both endurance and patience. From that time he never gave up in the front of any duty.

In the absence of an available Indian he rode to Durango and back in record time. Upon one occasion he was lost in a cañon for days, with no food and little water. Upon another he went through a sand-storm in the open desert, facing it for forty miles and keeping to the trail. When he rode in to Kayenta that night the trader, in grim praise, said there was no worse to endure. At Monticello Shefford stood off a band of desperadoes, and this time Shefford experienced a strange, sickening shock in the wounding of a man. Later he had other fights, but in none of them did he know whether or not he had shed blood.

The heat of midsummer came, when the blistering sun shone, and a hot blast blew across the sand, and the furious storms made floods in the washes. Day and night Shefford was always in the open, and any one who had ever known him in the past would have failed to recognize him now.

In the early fall, with Nas Ta Bega as companion, he set out to the south of Kayenta upon long-neglected business of the trader. They visited Red Lake, Blue Cañon, Keams Cañon, Oribi, the Moki villages, Tuba, Moencopie, and Moen Ave. This trip took many weeks and gave Shefford all the opportunity he wanted to study the Indians, and the conditions nearer to the border of civilization. He learned the truth about the Indians and the missionaries.

Upon the return trip he rode over the trail he had followed alone to Red Lake and thence on to the Sagi, and it seemed that years had passed since he first entered this wild region which had come to be home, years that had molded him in the stern and fiery crucible of the desert.

X

IN October Shefford arranged for a hunt in the Cresaw Mountains with Joe Lake and Nas Ta Bega. The Indian had gone home for a short visit, and upon his return the party expected to start. But Nas Ta Bega did not come back. Then the arrival of a Piute with news that excited Withers and greatly perturbed Lake convinced Shefford that something was wrong.

The little trading-post seldom saw such disorder; certainly Shefford had never known the trader to neglect work. Joe Lake threw a saddle on a mustang he would have scorned to notice in an ordinary moment, and without a word of explanation or farewell rode hard to the north on the Stonebridge trail.

Shefford had long since acquired patience. He was curious, but he did not care particularly what was in the wind. However, when Withers came out and sent an Indian to drive up the horses Shefford could not refrain from a query.

"I hate to tell you," replied the trader.

"Go on," added Shefford, quickly.

"Did I tell you about the government sending a

159

Supreme Court judge out to Utah to prosecute the polygamists?"

"No," replied Shefford.

"I forgot to, I reckon. You've been away a lot. Well, there's been hell up in Utah for six months. Lately this judge and his men have worked down into southern Utah. He visited Bluff and Monticello a few weeks ago. . . . Now what do you think?"

"Withers! Is he coming to Stonebridge?"

"He's there now. Some one betrayed the whereabouts of the hidden village over in the cañon. All the women have been arrested and taken to Stonebridge. The trial begins to-day."

"Arrested!" echoed Shefford, blankly. "Those poor, lonely, good women? What on earth for?"

"Sealed wives!" exclaimed Withers, tersely. "This judge is after the polygamists. They say he's absolutely relentless."

"But—women can't be polygamists. Their husbands are the ones wanted."

"Sure. But the prosecutors have got to find the sealed wives—the second wives—to find the lawbreaking husbands. That 'll be a job, or I don't know Mormons. . . . Are you going to ride over to Stonebridge with me?"

Shefford shrank at the idea. Months of toil and pain and travail had not been enough to make him forget the strange girl he had loved. But he had remembered only at poignant intervals, and the lapse of time had made thought of her a dream like that sad dream which had lured him into the desert. With the query of the trader came a bitter-sweet regret.

"Better come with me," said Withers. "Have you forgotten the Sago Lily? She'll be put on trial. . . . That girl—that child! . . . Shefford, you know she hasn't any friends. And now no Mormon man dare protect her, for fear of prosecution."

"I'll go," replied Shefford, shortly.

The Indian brought up the horses. Nack-yal was thin from his long travel during the hot summer, but he was as hard as iron, and the way he pointed his keen nose toward the Sagi showed how he wanted to make for the upland country, with its clear springs and valleys of grass. Withers mounted his bay and with a hurried farewell to his wife spurred the mustang into the trail. Shefford took time to get his weapons and the light pack he always carried, and then rode out after the trader.

The pace Withers set was the long, steady lope to which these Indian mustangs had been trained all their lives. In an hour they reached the mouth of the Sagi, and at sight of it it seemed to Shefford that the hard half-year of suffering since he had been there had disappeared. Withers, to Shefford's regret, did not enter the Sagi. He turned off to the north and took a wild trail into a split of the red wall, and wound in and out, and climbed a crack so narrow that the light was obscured and the cliffs could be reached from both sides of a horse.

Once up on the wild plateau, Shefford felt again in a different world from the barren desert he had lately known. The desert had crucified him and had left him to die or survive, according to his spirit and his strength. If he had loved the glare, the endless level, the deceiving distance, the shifting sand, it had certainly not been as he loved this softer, wilder, more intimate upland. With the red peaks shining up into the blue, and the fragrance of cedar and piñon, and the purple sage and flowers and grass and splash of clear water over stones— with these there came back to him something that he had lost and which had haunted him.

It seemed he had returned to this wild upland of color and cañons and lofty crags and green valleys and silent places with a spirit gained from victory over himself in the harsher and sterner desert below. And, strange to him, he found his old self, the dreamer, the artist, the lover of beauty, the searcher for he knew not what, come to meet him on the fragrant wind.

He felt this, saw the old wildness with glad eyes, yet the greater part of his mind was given over to the thought of the unfortunate women he expected to see in Stonebridge.

Withers was harder to follow, to keep up with, than an Indian. For one thing he was a steady and tireless rider, and for another there were times when he had no mercy on a horse. Then an Indian always found easier steps in a trail and shorter cuts. Withers put his mount to some bad slopes, and Shefford had no choice but to follow. But they crossed the great broken bench of upland without mishap, and came out upon a promontory of a plateau from which Shefford saw a wide valley and the dark-green alfalfa fields of Stonebridge.

Stonebridge lay in the center of a fertile valley surrounded by pink cliffs. It must have been a very old town, certainly far older than Bluff or

STONEBRIDGE

Monticello, though smaller, and evidently it had
been built to last. There was one main street, very
wide, that divided the town and was crossed at
right angles by a stream spanned by a small natural
stone bridge. A line of poplar-trees shaded each
foot-path. The little log cabins and stone houses
and cottages were half hidden in foliage now tinted
with autumn colors. Toward the center of the town
the houses and stores and shops fronted upon the
street and along one side of a green square, or plaza.
Here were situated several edifices, the most prominent of which was a church built of wood, whitewashed, and remarkable, according to Withers, for
the fact that not a nail had been used in its con-
struction. Beyond the church was a large, low
structure of stone, with a split-shingle roof, and
evidently this was the town hall.

Shefford saw, before he reached the square, that
this day in Stonebridge was one of singular action
and excitement for a Mormon village. The town
was full of people and, judging from the horses
hitched everywhere and the big canvas-covered
wagons, many of the people were visitors. A crowd
surrounded the hall—a dusty, booted, spurred, shirt-
sleeved and sombreroed assemblage that did not
wear the hall-mark Shefford had come to associate
with Mormons. They were riders, cowboys, horse-
wranglers, and some of them Shefford had seen in
Durango. Navajos and Piutes were present, also,
but they loitered in the background.

Withers drew Shefford off to the side where, under
a tree, they hitched their horses.

"Never saw Stonebridge full of a riffraff gang

like this to-day," said Withers. "I'll bet the Mormons are wild. There's a tough outfit from Durango. If they can get anything to drink—or if they've got it —Stonebridge will see smoke to-day! . . . Come on. I'll get in that hall."

But before Withers reached the hall he started violently and pulled up short, then, with apparent unconcern, turned to lay a hand upon Shefford. The trader's face had blanched and his eyes grew hard and shiny, like flint. He gripped Shefford's arm.

"Look! Over to your left!" he whispered. "See that gang of Indians there—by the big wagon. See the short Indian with the chaps. He's got a face big as a ham, dark, fierce. That's Shadd! . . . You ought to know him. Shadd and his outfit here! How's that for nerve? But he pulls a rein with the Mormons."

Shefford's keen eye took in a lounging group of ten or twelve Indians and several white men. They did not present any great contrast to the other groups except that they were isolated, appeared quiet and watchful, and were all armed. A bunch of lean, racy mustangs, restive and spirited, stood near by in charge of an Indian. Shefford had to take a second and closer glance to distinguish the half-breed. At once he recognized in Shadd the broad-faced squat Indian who had paid him a threatening visit that night long ago in the mouth of the Sagi. A fire ran along Shefford's veins and seemed to concentrate in his breast. Shadd's dark, piercing eyes alighted upon Shefford and rested there. Then the half-breed spoke to one of his white outlaws and pointed at Shefford. His action attracted the attention of others in the gang, and for a moment Shefford and Withers were treated to a keen-eyed stare.

The trader cursed low. "Maybe I wouldn't like to mix it with that damned breed," he said. "But what chance have we with that gang? Besides, we're here on other and more important business. All the same, before I forget, let me remind you that Shadd has had you spotted ever since you came out here. A friendly Piute told me only lately. Shefford, did any Indian between here and Flagstaff ever see that bunch of money you persist in carrying?"

"Why, yes, I suppose so—'way back in Tuba, when I first came out," replied Shefford.

"Huh! Well, Shadd's after that. . . . Come on now, let's get inside the hall."

The crowd opened for the trader, who appeared to be known to everybody. A huge man with a bushy beard blocked the way to a shut door.

"Hello, Meade!" said Withers. "Let us in."

The man opened the door, permitted Withers and Shefford to enter, and then closed it.

Shefford, coming out of the bright glare of sun into the hall, could not see distinctly at first. His eyes blurred. He heard a subdued murmur of many voices. Withers appeared to be affected with the same kind of blindness, for he stood bewildered a moment. But he recovered sooner than Shefford. Gradually the darkness shrouding many obscure forms lifted. Withers drew him through a crowd of men and women to one side of the hall, and squeezed along a wall to a railing where progress was stopped.

Then Shefford raised his head to look with bated breath and strange curiosity.

The hall was large and had many windows. Men were in consultation upon a platform. Women to the number of twenty sat close together upon benches. Back of them stood another crowd. But the women on the benches held Shefford's gaze. They were the prisoners. They made a somber group. Some were hooded, some veiled, all clad in dark garments except one on the front bench, and she was dressed in white. She wore a long hood that concealed her face. Shefford recognized the hood and then the slender shape. She was Mary—she whom her jealous neighbors had named the Sago Lily. At sight of her a sharp pain pierced Shefford's breast. His eyes were blurred when he forced them away from her, and it took a moment for him to see clearly.

Withers was whispering to him or to some one near at hand, but Shefford did not catch the meaning of what was said. He paid more attention; however, Withers ceased speaking. Shefford gazed upon the crowd back of him. The women were hooded and it was not possible to see what they looked like. There were many stalwart, clean-cut, young Mormons of Joe Lake's type, and these men appeared troubled, even distressed and at a loss. There was little about them resembling the stern, quiet, somber austerity of the more matured men, and nothing at all of the strange, aloof, serene impassiveness of the gray-bearded old patriarchs. These venerable men were the Mormons of the old school, the sons of the pioneers, the ruthless fanatics. Instinctively

Shefford felt that it was in them that polygamy was embodied; they were the husbands of the sealed wives. He conceived an absorbing curiosity to learn if his instinct was correct; and hard upon that followed a hot, hateful eagerness to see which one was the husband of Mary.

"There's Bishop Kane," whispered Withers, nudging Shefford. "And there's Waggoner with him."

Shefford saw the bishop, and then beside him a man of striking presence.

"Who's Waggoner?" asked Shefford, as he looked.

"He owns more than any Mormon in southern Utah," replied the trader. "He's the biggest man in Stonebridge, that's sure. But I don't know his relation to the Church. They don't call him elder or bishop. But I'll bet he's some pumpkins. He never had any use for me or any Gentile. A close-fisted, tight-lipped Mormon—a skinflint if I ever saw one! Just look him over."

Shefford had been looking, and considered it unlikely that he would ever forget this individual called Waggoner. He seemed old, sixty at least, yet at that only in the prime of a wonderful physical life. Unlike most of the others, he wore his grizzled beard close-cropped, so close that it showed the lean, wolfish line of his jaw. All his features were of striking sharpness. His eyes, of a singularly brilliant blue, were yet cold and pale. The brow had a serious, thoughtful cast; long furrows sloped down the cheeks. It was a strange, secretive face, full of a power that Shefford had not seen in another man's, full of intelligence and thought that had not been used as Shefford had known them used among men.

167

The face mystified him. It had so much more than the strange aloofness so characteristic of his fellows.

"Waggoner had five wives and fifty-five children before the law went into effect," whispered Withers. "Nobody knows and nobody will ever know how many he's got now. That's my private opinion."

Somehow, after Withers told that, Shefford seemed to understand the strange power in Waggoner's face. Absolutely it was not the force, the strength given to a man from his years of control of men. Shefford, long schooled now in his fair-mindedness, fought down the feelings of other years, and waited with patience. Who was he to judge Waggoner or any other Mormon? But whenever his glance strayed back to the quiet, slender form in white, when he realized again and again the appalling nature of this court, his heart beat heavy and labored within his breast.

Then a bustle among the men upon the platform appeared to indicate that proceedings were about to begin. Some men left the platform; several sat down at a table upon which were books and papers, and others remained standing. These last were all roughly garbed, in riding-boots and spurs, and Shefford's keen eye detected the bulge of hidden weapons. They looked like deputy-marshals upon duty.

Somebody whispered that the judge's name was Stone. The name fitted him. He was not young, and looked a man suited to the prosecution of these secret Mormons. He had a ponderous brow, a deep, cavernous eye that emitted gleams but betrayed no color or expression. His mouth was the saving human feature of his stony face.

Shefford took the man upon the judge's right hand to be a lawyer, and the one on his left an officer of court, perhaps a prosecuting attorney. Presently this fellow pounded upon the table and stood up as if to address a court-room. Certainly he silenced that hallful of people. Then he perfunctorily and briefly stated that certain women had been arrested upon suspicion of being sealed wives of Mormon polygamists, and were to be herewith tried by a judge of the United States Court. Shefford felt how the impressive words affected that silent hall of listeners, but he gathered from the brief preliminaries that the trial could not be otherwise than a crude, rapid investigation, and perhaps for that the more sinister.

The first woman on the foremost bench was led forward by a deputy to a vacant chair on the platform just in front of the judge's table. She was told to sit down, and showed no sign that she had heard. Then the judge courteously asked her to take the chair. She refused. And Stone nodded his head as if he had experienced that sort of thing before. He stroked his chin wearily, and Shefford conceived an idea that he was a kind man, if he was a relentless judge.

"Please remove your veil," requested the prosecutor.

The woman did so, and proved to be young and handsome. Shefford had a thrill as he recognized her. She was Ruth, who had been one of his best-known acquaintances in the hidden village. She

was pale, angry, almost sullen, and her breast heaved.
She had no shame, but she seemed to be outraged.
Her dark eyes, scornful and blazing, passed over the
judge and his assistants, and on to the crowd behind
the railing. Shefford, keen as a blade, with all his
faculties absorbed, fancied he saw Ruth stiffen and
change slightly as her glance encountered some one
in that crowd. Then the prosecutor in deliberate
and chosen words enjoined her to kiss the Bible
handed to her and swear to tell the truth. How
strange for Shefford to see her kiss the book which
he had studied for so many years! Stranger still
to hear the low murmur from the listening audience
as she took the oath!

"What is your name?" asked Judge Stone, leaning back and fixing the cavernous eyes upon her.

"Ruth Jones," was the cool reply.

"How old are you?"

"Twenty."

"Where were you born?" went on the judge. He
allowed time for the clerk to record her answers.

"Panguitch, Utah."

"Were your parents Mormons?"

"Yes."

"Are you a Mormon?"

"Yes."

"Are you a married woman?"

"No."

The answer was instant, cold, final. It seemed
to be truth. Almost Shefford believed she spoke
truth. The judge stroked his chin and waited a
moment, and then hesitatingly he went on.

"Have you—any children?"

"No." And the blazing eyes met tne cavernous ones.

That about the children was true enough, Shefford thought, and he could have testified to it.

"You live in the hidden village near this town?"

"Yes."

"What is the name of this village?"

"It has none."

"Did you ever hear of Fre-donia, another village far west of here?"

"Yes."

"It is in Arizona, near the Utah line. There are few men there. Is it the same kind of village as this one in which you live?"

"Yes."

"What does Fre-donia mean? The name—has it any meaning?"

"It means free women."

The judge maintained silence for a moment, turned to whisper to his assistants, and presently, without glancing up, said to the woman:

"That will do."

Ruth was led back to the bench, and the woman next to her brought forward. This was a heavier person, with the figure and step of a matured woman. Upon removing her bonnet she showed the plain face of a woman of forty, and it was striking only in that strange, stony aloofness noted in the older men. Here, Shefford thought, was the real Mormon, different in a way he could not define from Ruth. This woman seated herself in the chair and calmly faced her prosecutors. She manifested no emotion whatever. Shefford remembered her and could not see any change in her deportment. This trial appeared to be of little moment to her and she took the oath as if doing so had been a habit all her life.

"What is your name?" asked Judge Stone, glancing up from a paper he held.

"Mary Danton."

"Family or married name?"

"My husband's name was Danton."

"Was. Is he living?"

"No."

"Where did you live when you were married to him?"

"In St. George, and later here in Stonebridge."

"You were both Mormons?"

"Yes."

"Did you have any children by him?"

"Yes."

"How many?"

"Two."

"Are they living?"

"One of them is living."

Judge Stone bent over his paper and then slowly raised his eyes to her face.

"Are you married now?"

"No."

Again the judge consulted his notes, and held a whispered colloquy with the two men at his table.

"Mrs. Danton, when you were arrested there were five children found in your home. To whom do they belong?"

"Me."

"Are you their mother?"

"Yes."

"Your husband Danton is the father of only one, the eldest, according to your former statement. Is that correct?"

"Yes."

"Who, then, is the father—or who are the fathers, of your other children?"

"I do not know."

She said it with the most stony-faced calmness, with utter disregard of what significance her words had. A strong, mystic wall of cold flint insulated her. Strangely it came to Shefford how impossible either to doubt or believe her. Yet he did both! Judge Stone showed a little heat.

"You don't know the father of one or all of these children?" he queried, with sharp rising inflection of voice.

"I do not."

"Madam, I beg to remind you that you are under oath."

The woman did not reply.

"These children are nameless, then—illegitimate?"

"They are."

"You swear you are not the sealed wife of some Mormon?"

"I swear."

"How do you live—maintain yourself?"

"I work."

"What at?"

"I weave, sew, bake, and work in my garden."

"My men made note of your large and comfortable cabin, even luxurious, considering this country. How is that?"

"My husband left me comfortable."

Judge Stone shook a warning finger at the defendant.

"Suppose I were to sentence you to jail for perjury? For a year? Far from your home and children! Would you speak—tell the truth?"

"I am telling the truth. I can't speak what I don't know. . . . Send me to jail."

Baffled, with despairing, angry impatience, Judge Stone waved the woman away.

"That will do for her. Fetch the next one," he said.

One after another he examined three more women, and arrived, by various questions and answers different in tone and temper, at precisely the same point as had been made in the case of Mrs. Danton. Thereupon the proceedings rested a few moments while the judge consulted with his assistants.

Shefford was grateful for this respite. He had been worked up to an unusual degree of interest, and now, as the next Mormon woman to be examined was she whom he had loved and loved still, he felt rise in him emotion that threatened to make him conspicuous unless it could be hidden. The answers of these Mormon women had been not altogether unexpected by him, but once spoken in cold blood under oath, how tragic, how appallingly significant of the shadow, the mystery, the yoke that bound them! He was amazed, saddened. He felt bewildered. He needed to think out the meaning of the falsehoods of women he knew to be good and noble. Surely religion, instead of fear and loyalty, was the foundation and the strength of this disgrace, this sacrifice. Absolutely, shame was not in these women,

174

though they swore to shameful facts. They had been coached to give these baffling answers, every one of which seemed to brand them, not the brazen mothers of illegitimate offspring, but faithful, unfortunate sealed wives. To Shefford the truth was not in their words, but it sat upon their somber brows.

Was it only his heightened imagination, or did the silence and the suspense grow more intense when a deputy led that dark-hooded, white-clad, slender woman to the defendant's chair? She did not walk with the poise that had been manifest in the other women, and she sank into the chair as if she could no longer stand.

"Please remove your hood," requested the prosecutor.

How well Shefford remembered the strong, shapely hands! He saw them tremble at the knot of ribbon, and that tremor was communicated to him in a sympathy which made his pulses beat. He held his breath while she removed the hood. And then there was revealed, he thought, the loveliest and the most tragic face that ever was seen in a court-room.

A low, whispering murmur that swelled like a wave ran through the hall. And by it Shefford divined, as clearly as if the fact had been blazoned on the walls, that Mary's face had been unknown to these villagers. But the name Sago Lily had not been unknown; Shefford heard it whispered on all sides.

The murmuring subsided. The judge and his assistants stared at Mary. As for Shefford, there was no need of his personal feeling to make the

situation dramatic. Not improbably Judge Stone
had tried many Mormon women. But manifestly
this one was different. Unhooded, Mary appeared
to be only a young girl, and a court, confronted suddenly with her youth and the suspicion attached to
her, could not but have been shocked. Then her
beauty made her seem, in that somber company,
indeed the white flower for which she had been
named. But, more likely, it was her agony that
bound the court into silence which grew painful.
Perhaps the thought that flashed into Shefford's
mind was telepathic; it seemed to him that every
watcher there realized that in this defendant the
judge had a girl of softer mold, of different spirit,
and from her the bitter truth could be wrung.

Mary faced the court and the crowd on that side
of the platform. Unlike the other women, she did
not look at or seem to see any one behind the railing.
Shefford was absolutely sure there was not a man or
a woman who caught her glance. She gazed afar,
with eyes strained, humid, fearful.

When the prosecutor swore her to the oath her
lips were seen to move, but no one heard her speak.

"What is your name?" asked the judge.

"Mary." Her voice was low, with a slight tremor.

"What's your other name?"

"I won't tell."

Her singular reply, the tones of her voice, her
manner before the judge, marked her with strange
simplicity. It was evident that she was not ac-
customed to questions.

"What were your parents' names?"

"I won't tell," she replied, very low.

176

Judge Stone did not press the point. Perhaps he wanted to make the examination as easy as possible for her or to wait till she showed more composure.

"Were your parents Mormons?" he went on.

"No, sir." She added the sir with a quaint respect, contrasting markedly with the short replies of the women before her.

"Then you were not born a Mormon?"

"No, sir."

"How old are you?"

"Seventeen or eighteen. I'm not sure."

"You don't know your exact age?"

"No."

"Where were you born?"

"I won't tell."

"Was it in Utah?"

"Yes, sir."

"How long have you lived in this state?"

"Always—except last year."

"And that's been over in the hidden village where you were arrested?"

"Yes."

"But you often visited here—this town Stonebridge?"

"I never was here—till yesterday."

Judge Stone regarded her as if his interest as a man was running counter to his duty as an officer. Suddenly he leaned forward.

"Are you a Mormon *now?*" he queried, forcibly.

"No, sir," she replied, and here her voice rose a little clearer.

It was an unexpected reply. Judge Stone stared at her. The low buzz ran through the listening crowd. And as for Shefford, he was astounded. When his wits flashed back and he weighed her words and saw in her face truth as clear as light, he had the strangest sensation of joy. Almost it flooded away the gloom and pain that attended this ordeal.

The judge bent his head to his assistants as if for counsel. All of them were eager where formerly they had been weary. Shefford glanced around at the dark and somber faces, and a slow wrath grew within him. Then he caught a glimpse of Waggoner. The steel-blue, piercing intensity of the Mormon's gaze impressed him at a moment when all that older generation of Mormons looked as hard and immutable as iron. Either Shefford was over-excited and mistaken or the hour had become fraught with greater suspense. The secret, the mystery, the power, the hate, the religion of a strange people were thick and tangible in that hall. For Shefford the feeling of the presence of Withers on his left was entirely different from that of the Mormon on his other side. If there was not a shadow there, then the sun did not shine so brightly as it had shone when he entered. The air seemed clogged with nameless passion.

"I gather that you've lived mostly in the country —away from people?" the judge began.

"Yes, sir," replied the girl.

"Do you know anything about the government of the United States?"

"No, sir."

He pondered again, evidently weighing his queries, leading up to the fatal and inevitable question.

Still, his interest in this particular defendant had become visible.

"Have you any idea of the consequences of perjury?"

"No, sir."

"Do you understand what perjury is?"

"It's to lie."

"Do you tell lies?"

"No, sir."

"Have you ever told a single lie?"

"Not—yet," she replied, almost whispering.

It was the answer of a child and affected the judge. He fussed with his papers. Perhaps his task was not easy; certainly it was not pleasant. Then he leaned forward again and fixed those deep, cavernous eyes upon the sad face.

"Do you understand what a sealed wife is?"

"I've never been told."

"But you know there *are* sealed wives in Utah?"

"Yes, sir; I've been told that."

Judge Stone halted there, watching her. The hall was silent except for faint rustlings and here and there deep breaths drawn guardedly. The vital question hung like a sword over the white-faced girl. Perhaps she divined its impending stroke, for she sat like a stone with dilating, appealing eyes upon her executioner.

"Are you a sealed wife?" he flung at her.

She could not answer at once. She made effort, but the words would not come. He flung the question again, sternly.

"No!" she cried.

And then there was silence. That poignant word

179

quivered in Shefford's heart. He believed it was a lie. It seemed he would have known it if this hour was the first in which he had ever seen the girl. He heard, he felt, he sensed the fatal thing. The beautiful voice had lacked some quality before present. And the thing wanting was something subtle, an essence, a beautiful ring—the truth. What a hellish thing to make that pure girl a liar—a perjurer! The heat deep within Shefford kindled to fire.

"You are not married?" went on Judge Stone.

"No, sir," she answered, faintly.

"Have you ever been married?"

"No, sir."

"Do you expect ever to be married?"

"Oh! No, sir."

She was ashen pale now, quivering all over, with her strong hands clasping the black hood, and she could no longer meet the judge's glance.

"Have you — any — any children?" the judge asked, haltingly. It was a hard question to get out.

"No."

Judge Stone leaned far over the table, and that his face was purple showed Shefford he was a man. His big fist clenched.

"Girl, you're not going to swear you, too, were visited—over there by men . . . You're not going to swear that?"

"Oh—no, sir!"

Judge Stone settled back in his chair, and while he wiped his moist face that same foreboding murmur, almost a menace, moaned through the hall.

Shefford was sick in his soul and afraid of himself.

He did not know this spirit that flamed up in him. His helplessness was a most hateful fact.

"Come—confess you are a sealed wife," called her interrogator.

She maintained silence, but shook her head.

Suddenly he seemed to leap forward.

"Unfortunate child! Confess."

That forced her to lift her head and face him, yet still she did not speak. It was the strength of despair. She could not endure much more.

"Who is your husband?" he thundered at her.

She rose wildly, terror-stricken. It was terror that dominated her, not of the stern judge, for she took a faltering step toward him, lifting a shaking hand, but of some one or of some thing far more terrible than any punishment she could have received in the sentence of a court. Still she was not proof against the judge's will. She had weakened, and the terror must have been because of that weakening.

"Who is the Mormon who visits you?" he thundered, relentlessly.

"I—never—knew—his—name."

"But you'd know his face. I'll arrest every Mormon in this country and bring him before you. You'd know his face?"

"Oh, I wouldn't. I *couldn't* tell! . . . I—never—saw his face—in the light!"

The tragic beauty of her, the certainty of some monstrous crime to youth and innocence, the presence of an agony and terror that unfathomably seemed not to be for herself—these transfixed the court and the audience, and held them silenced, till she reached out blindly and then sank in a heap to the floor.

XI

AFTER THE TRIAL

SHEFFORD might have leaped over the railing but for Withers's restraining hand, and when there appeared to be some sign of kindness in those other women for the unconscious girl Shefford squeezed through the crowd and got out of the hall.

The gang outside that had been denied admittance pressed upon Shefford, with jest and curious query, and a good nature that jarred upon him. He was far from gentle as he jostled off the first importuning fellows; the others, gaping at him, opened a lane for him to pass through.

Then there was a hand laid on his shoulder that he did not shake off. Nas Ta Bega loomed dark and tall beside him. Neither the trader nor Joe Lake nor any white man Shefford had met influenced him as this Navajo.

"Nas Ta Bega! you here, too. I guess the whole country is here. We waited at Kayenta. What kept you so long?"

The Indian, always slow to answer, did not open his lips till he drew Shefford apart from the noisy crowd.

"Bi Nai, there is sorrow in the hogan of Hosteen Doetin," he said.

AFTER THE TRIAL

"Glen Naspa!" exclaimed Shefford.

"My sister is gone from the home of her brother. She went away alone in the summer."

"Blue Cañon! She went to the missionary. Nas Ta Bega, I thought I saw her there. But I wasn't sure. I didn't want to make sure. I was afraid it might be true."

"A brave who loved my sister trailed her there."

"Nas Ta Bega, will you—will we go find her, take her home?"

"No. She will come home some day."

What bitter sadness and wisdom in his words!

"But, my friend, that damned missionary—" began Shefford, passionately. The Indian had met him at a bad hour.

"Willetts is here. I saw him go in there," interrupted Nas Ta Bega, and he pointed to the hall.

"Here! He gets around a good deal," declared Shefford. "Nas Ta Bega, what are you going to do to him?"

The Indian held his peace and there was no telling from his inscrutable face what might be in his mind. He was dark, impassive. He seemed a wise and bitter Indian, beyond any savagery of his tribe, and the suffering Shefford divined was deep.

"He'd better keep out of my sight," muttered Shefford, more to himself than to his companion.

"The half-breed is here," said Nas Ta Bega.

"Shadd? Yes, we saw him. There! He's still with his gang. Nas Ta Bega, what are they up to?"

"They will steal what they can."

"Withers says Shadd is friendly with the Mormons."

183

THE RAINBOW TRAIL

"Yes, and with the missionary, too."

"With Willetts?"

"I saw them talk together—strong talk."

"Strange. But maybe it's not so strange. Shadd is known well in Monticello and Bluff. He spends money there. They are afraid of him, but he's welcome just the same. Perhaps everybody knows him. It 'd be like him to ride into Kayenta. But, Nas Ta Bega, I've got to look out for him, because Withers says he's after me."

"Bi Nai wears a scar that is proof," said the Indian.

"Then it must be he found out long ago I had a little money."

"It might be. But, Bi Nai, the half-breed has a strange step on your trail."

"What do you mean?" demanded Shefford.

"Nas Ta Bega cannot tell what he does not know," replied the Navajo. "Let that be. We shall know some day. Bi Nai, there is sorrow to tell that is not the Indian's. . . . Sorrow for my brother!"

Shefford lifted his eyes to the Indian's, and if he did not see sadness there he was much deceived.

"Bi Nai, long ago you told a story to the trader. Nas Ta Bega sat before the fire that night. You did not know he could understand your language. He listened. And he learned what brought you to the country of the Indian. That night he made you his brother. . . . All his lonely rides into the cañons have been to find the little golden-haired child, the lost girl—Fay Larkin. . . . Bi Nai, I have found the girl you wanted for your sweetheart."

Shefford was bereft of speech. He could not see

184

steadily, and the last solemn words of the Indian seemed far away.

"Bi Nai, I have found Fay Larkin," repeated Nas Ta Bega.

"Fay Larkin!" gasped Shefford, shaking his head. "But—she's dead."

"It would be less sorrow for Bi Nai if she were dead."

Shefford clutched at the Indian. There was something terrible to be revealed. Like an aspen-leaf in the wind he shook all over. He divined the revelation—divined the coming blow—but that was as far as his mind got.

"She's in there," said the Indian, pointing toward the hall.

"Fay Larkin?" whispered Shefford.

"Yes, Bi Nai."

"My God! *How* do you know? Oh, I could have seen. I've been blind. . . . Tell me, Indian. Which one?"

"Fay Larkin is the Sago Lily."

Shefford strode away into a secluded corner of the square, where in the shade and quiet of the trees he suffered a storm of heart and mind. During that short or long time—he had no idea how long—the Indian remained with him. He never lost the feeling of Nas Ta Bega close beside him. When the period of acute pain left him and some order began to replace the tumult in his mind he felt in Nas Ta Bega the same quality—silence or strength or help— that he had learned to feel in the deep cañons and the lofty crags. He realized then that the Indian

185

was indeed a brother. And Shefford needed him.
What he had to fight was more fatal than suffering
and love—it was hate rising out of the unsuspected
dark gulf of his heart—the instinct to kill—the murder in his soul. Only now did he come to understand Jane Withersteen's tragic story and the passion
of Venters and what had made Lassiter a gun-man.

The desert had transformed Shefford. The elements had entered into his muscle and bone, into
the very fiber of his heart. Sun, wind, sand, cold,
storm, space, stone, the poison cactus, the racking
toil, the terrible loneliness—the iron of the desert
man, the cruelty of the desert savage, the wildness
of the mustang, the ferocity of hawk and wolf, the
bitter struggle of every surviving thing—these were
as if they had been melted and merged together and
now made a dark and passionate stream that was
his throbbing blood. He realized what he had
become and gloried in it, yet there, looking on with
grave and earnest eyes, was his old self, the man of
reason, of intellect, of culture, who had been a good
man despite the failure and shame of his life. And
he gave heed to the voice of warning, of conscience.
Not by revengefully seeking the Mormon who had
ruined Fay Larkin and blindly dealing a wild justice
could he help this unfortunate girl. This fierce, new-
born strength and passion must be tempered by
reason, lest he become merely elemental, a man
answering wholly to primitive impulses. In the
darkness of that hour he mined deep into his heart,
understood himself, trembled at the thing he faced,
and won his victory. He would go forth from that
hour a man. He might fight, and perhaps there was

death in the balance, but hate would never overthrow him.

Then when he looked at future action he felt a strange, unalterable purpose to save Fay Larkin. She was very young—seventeen or eighteen, she had said—and there could be, there must be some happiness before her. It had been his dream to chase a rainbow—it had been his determination to find her in the lost Surprise Valley. Well, he had found her. It never occurred to him to ask Nas Ta Bega how he had discovered that the Sago Lily was Fay Larkin. The wonder was, Shefford thought, that he had so long been blind himself. How simply everything worked out now! Every thought, every recollection of her was proof. Her strange beauty like that of the sweet and rare lily, her low voice that showed the habit of silence, her shapely hands with the clasp strong as a man's, her lithe form, her swift step, her wonderful agility upon the smooth, steep walls, and the wildness of her upon the heights, and the haunting, brooding shadow of her eyes when she gazed across the cañons—all these fitted so harmoniously the conception of a child lost in a beautiful Surprise Valley and growing up in its wildness and silence, tutored by the sad love of broken Jane and Lassiter. Yes, to save her had been Shefford's dream, and he had loved that dream. He had loved the dream and he had loved the child. The secret of her hiding-place as revealed by the story told him and his slow growth from dream to action—these had strangely given Fay Larkin to him. Then had come the bitter knowledge that she was dead. In the light of this subsequent revelation how easy

to account for his loving Mary, too. Never would
she be Mary again to him! Fay Larkin and the
Sago Lily were one and the same. She was here,
near him, and he was powerless for the present to
help her or to reveal himself. She was held back
there in that gloomy hall among those somber
Mormons, alien to the women, bound in some fatal
way to one of the men, and now, by reason of her
weakness in the trial, surely to be hated. Thinking
of her past and her present, of the future, and that
secret Mormon whose face she had never seen, Shefford felt a sinking of his heart, a terrible cold pang
in his breast, a fainting of his spirit. She had sworn
she was no sealed wife. But had she not lied? So,
then, how utterly powerless he was!

But here to save him, to uplift him, came that
strange mystic insight which had been the gift of
the desert to him. She was not dead. He had
found her. What mattered obstacles, even that implacable creed to which she had been sacrificed, in
the face of this blessed and overwhelming truth?
It was as mighty as the love suddenly dawning upon
him. A strong and terrible and deathly sweet wind
seemed to fill his soul with the love of her. It was
her fate that had drawn him; and now it was her
agony, her innocence, her beauty, that bound him
for all time. Patience and cunning and toil, passion
and blood, the unquenchable spirit of a man to save—
these were nothing to give—life itself were little,
could he but free her.

Patience and cunning! His sharpening mind cut
these out as his greatest assets for the present. And
his thoughts flashed like light through his brain. . . .

Judge Stone and his court would fail to convict any Mormon in Stonebridge, just the same as they had failed in the northern towns. They would go away, and Stonebridge would fall to the slow, sleepy tenor of its former way. The hidden village must become known to all men, honest and outlawed, in that country, but this fact would hardly make any quick change in the plans of the Mormons. They did not soon change. They would send the sealed wives back to the cañon and, after the excitement had died down, visit them as usual. Nothing, perhaps, would ever change these old Mormons but death.

Shefford resolved to remain in Stonebridge and ingratiate himself deeper into the regard of the Mormons. He would find work there, if the sealed wives were not returned to the hidden village. In case the women went back to the valley Shefford meant to resume his old duty of driving Withers's pack-trains. Wanting that opportunity, he would find some other work, some excuse to take him there.

In due time he would reveal to Fay Larkin that he knew her. How the thought thrilled him! She might deny, might persist in her fear, might fight to keep her secret. But he would learn it—hear her story—hear what had become of Jane Withersteen and Lassiter—and if they were alive, which now he believed he would find them—and he would take them and Fay out of the country.

The duty, the great task, held a grim fascination for him. He had a foreboding of the cost; he had a dark realization of the force he meant to oppose. There were duty here and pity and unselfish love, but these alone did not actuate Shefford. Mystic-ally fate seemed again to come like a gleam and bid him follow.

When Shefford and Nas Ta Bega returned to the town hall the trial had been ended, the hall was closed, and only a few Indians and cowboys remained in the square, and they were about to depart. On the street, however, and the paths and in the doorways of stores were knots of people, talking earnestly. Shefford walked up and down, hoping to meet Withers or Joe Lake. Nas Ta Bega said he would take the horses to water and feed and then return.

There were indications that Stonebridge might experience some of the excitement and perhaps violence common to towns like Monticello and Durango. There was only one saloon in Stonebridge, and it was full of roystering cowboys and horse-wranglers. Shefford saw the bunch of mustangs, in charge of the same Indian, that belonged to Shadd and his gang. The men were inside, drinking. Next door was a tavern called Hopewell House, a stone structure of some pretensions. There were Indians lounging outside. Shefford entered through a wide door and found himself in a large bare room, boarded like a loft, with no ceiling except the roof. The place was full of men and noise. Here he encountered Joe Lake talking to Bishop Kane and other Mormons. Shefford got a friendly greeting from the bishop, and then was well received by the strangers, to whom Joe introduced him.

"Have you seen Withers?" asked Shefford.

"Reckon he's around somewhere," replied Joe. "Better hang up here, for he'll drop in sooner or later."

"When are you going back to Kayenta?" went on Shefford.

"Hard to say. We'll have to call off our hunt. Nas Ta Bega is here, too."

"Yes, I've been with him."

The older Mormons drew aside, and then Joe mentioned the fact that he was half starved. Shefford went with him into another clapboard room, which was evidently a dining-room. There were half a dozen men at the long table. The seat at the end was a box, and scarcely large enough or safe enough for Joe and Shefford, but they risked it.

"Saw you in the hall," said Joe. "Hell—wasn't it?"

"Joe, I never knew how much I dared say to you, so I don't talk much. But, it *was* hell," replied Shefford.

"You needn't be so scared of me," spoke up Joe, testily.

That was the first time Shefford had heard the Mormon speak that way.

"I'm not scared, Joe. But I like you—respect you. I can't say so much of—of your people."

"Did you stick out the whole mix?" asked Joe.

"No. I had enough when—when they got through with Mary." Shefford spoke low and dropped his head. He heard the Mormon grind his teeth. There was silence for a little space while neither man looked at the other.

"Reckon the judge was pretty decent," presently said Joe.

"Yes, I thought so. He might have—" But Shefford did not finish that sentence. "How'd the thing end?"

191

"It ended all right."

"Was there no conviction—no sentence?" Shefford felt a curious eagerness.

"Naw," he snorted. "That court might have saved its breath."

"I suppose. Well, Joe, between you and me, as old friends now, that trial established one fact, even if it couldn't be proved. . . . Those women *are* sealed wives."

Joe had no reply for that. He looked gloomy, and there was a stern line in his lips. To-day he seemed more like a Mormon.

"Judge Stone knew that as well as I knew," went on Shefford. "Any man of penetration could have seen it. What an ordeal that was for good women to go through! I know they're good. And there they were swearing to—"

"Didn't it make me sick?" interrupted Joe in a kind of growl. "Reckon it made Judge Stone sick, too. After Mary went under he conducted that trial like a man cuttin' out steers at a round-up. He wanted to get it over. He never forced any question. . . . Bad job to ride down Stonebridge way! It's out of creation. There's only six men in the party, with a poor lot of horses. Really, government officers or not, they're not safe. And they've taken a hunch."

"Have they left already?" inquired Shefford.

"Were packed an hour ago. I didn't see them go, but somebody said they went. Took the trail for Bluff, which sure is the only trail they could take, unless they wanted to go to Colorado by way of Kayenta. That might have been the safest trail."

192

"Joe, what might happen to them?" asked Shefford, quietly, with eyes on the Mormon.

"Aw, you know that rough trail. Bad on horses. Weathered slopes—slipping ledges—a rock might fall on you any time. Then Shadd's here with his gang. And bad Piutes."

"What became of the women?" Shefford asked, presently.

"They're around among friends."

"Where are their children?"

"Left over there with the old women. Couldn't be fetched over. But there are some pretty young babies in that bunch—need their mothers."

"I should—think so," replied Shefford, constrainedly. "When will their mothers get back to them?"

"To-night, maybe, if this mob of cow-punchers and wranglers get out of town. . . . It's a bad mix, Shefford, here's a hunch on that. These fellows will get full of whisky. And trouble might come if they —approach the women."

"You mean they might get drunk enough to take the oaths of those poor women—take the meaning literally—pretend to believe the women what they swore they were?"

"Reckon you've got the hunch," replied Joe, gloomily.

"My God! man, that would be horrible!" exclaimed Shefford.

"Horrible or not, it's liable to happen. The women can be kept here yet awhile. Reckon there won't be any trouble here. It'll be over there in the valley. Shefford, getting the women over there safe is a job that's been put to me. I've got a bunch

193

of fellows already. Can I count on you? I'm glad to say you're well thought of. Bishop Kane liked you, and what he says goes."

"Yes, Joe, you can count on me," replied Shefford.

They finished their meal then and repaired to the big office-room of the house. Several groups of men were there and loud talk was going on outside. Shefford saw Withers talking to Bishop Kane and two other Mormons, both strangers to Shefford. The trader appeared to be speaking with unwonted force, emphasizing his words with energetic movements of his hands.

"Reckon something's up," whispered Joe, hoarsely. "It's been in the air all day."

Withers must have been watching for Shefford.

"Here's Shefford now," he said to the trio of Mormons, as Joe and Shefford reached the group. "I want you to hear him speak for himself."

"What's the matter?" asked Shefford.

"Give me a hunch and I'll put in my say-so," said Joe Lake.

"Shefford, it's the matter of a good name more than a job," replied the trader. "A little while back I told the bishop I meant to put you on the pack job over to the valley—same as when you first came to me. Well, the bishop was pleased and said he might put something in your way. Just now I ran in here to find you—not wanted. When I kicked I got the straight hunch. Willetts has said things about you. One of them—the one that sticks in my craw—was that you'd do anything, even pretend to be inclined toward Mormonism, just to be among those Mormon women over there. Willetts is your enemy. And he's worse than I thought. Now I want you to tell Bishop Kane *why* this missionary is bitter toward you."

"Gentlemen, I knocked him down," replied Shefford, simply.

"What for?" inquired the bishop, in surprise and curiosity.

Shefford related the incident which had occurred at Red Lake and that now seemed again to come forward fatefully.

"You insinuate he had evil intent toward the Indian girl?" queried Kane.

"I insinuate nothing. I merely state what led to my acting as I did."

"Principles of religion, sir?"

"No. A man's principles."

Withers interposed in his blunt way, "Bishop, did you ever see Glen Naspa?"

"No."

"She's the prettiest Navajo in the country. Willetts was after her, that's all."

"My dear man, I can't believe that of a Christian missionary. We've known Willetts for years. He's a man of influence. He has money back of him. He's doing a good work. You hint of a love relation."

"No, I don't hint," replied Withers, impatiently. "I know. It's not the first time I've known a missionary to do this sort of thing. Nor is it the first time for Willetts. Bishop Kane, I live among the Indians. I see a lot I never speak of. My work is to trade with the Indians, that's all. But I'll not have Willetts or any other damned hypocrite run

down my friend here. John Shefford is the finest
young man that ever came to me in the desert. And
he's got to be put right before you all or I'll not set
foot in Stonebridge again. . . . Willetts was after
Glen Naspa. Shefford punched him. And later
threw him out of the old Indian's hogan up on the
mountain. That explains Willetts's enmity. He
was after the girl."

"What's more, gentlemen, he *got* her," added
Shefford. "Glen Naspa has not been home for six
months. I saw her at Blue Cañon. . . . I would like
to face this Willetts before you all."

"Easy enough," replied Withers, with a grim
chuckle. "He's just outside."

The trader went out; Joe Lake followed at his
heels and the three Mormons were next; Shefford
brought up the rear and lingered in the door while
his eye swept the crowd of men and Indians. His
feeling was in direct contrast to his movements.
He felt the throbbing of fierce anger. But it seemed
a face came between him and his passion—a sweet
and tragic face that would have had power to check
him in a vastly more critical moment than this. And
in an instant he had himself in hand, and, strangely,
suddenly felt the strength that had come to him.

Willetts stood in earnest colloquy with a short,
squat Indian—the half-breed Shadd. They leaned
against a hitching-rail. Other Indians were there,
and outlaws. It was a mixed group, rough and hard-
looking.

"Hey, Willetts!" called the trader, and his loud,
ringing voice, not pleasant, stilled the movement
and sound.

AFTER THE TRIAL

When Willetts turned, Shefford was half-way across the wide walk. The missionary not only saw him, but also Nas Ta Bega, who was striding forward. Joe Lake was ahead of the trader, the Mormons followed with decision, and they all confronted Willetts. He turned pale. Shadd had cautiously moved along the rail, nearer to his gang, and then they, with the others of the curious crowd, drew closer.

"Willetts, here's Shefford. Now say it to his face!" declared the trader. He was angry and evidently wanted the fact known, as well as the situation.

Willetts had paled, but he showed boldness. For an instant Shefford studied the smooth face, with its sloping lines, the dark, wine-colored eyes.

"Willetts, I understand you've maligned me to Bishop Kane and others," began Shefford, curtly.

"I called you an atheist," returned the missionary, harshly.

"Yes, and more than that. And I told these men *why* you vented your spite on me."

Willetts uttered a half-laugh, an uneasy, contemptuous expression of scorn and repudiation.

"The charges of such a man as you are can't hurt me," he said.

The man did not show fear so much as disgust at the meeting. He seemed to be absorbed in thought, yet no serious consideration of the situation made itself manifest. Shefford felt puzzled. Perhaps there was no fire to strike from this man. The desert had certainly not made him flint. He had not toiled or suffered or fought.

But *I* can hurt you," thundered Shefford, with startling suddenness. "Here! Look at this Indian! Do you know him? Glen Naspa's brother. Look at him. Let us see you face him while I accuse you. . . . You made love to Glen Naspa—took her from her home!"

"Harping infidel!" replied Willetts, hoarsely. "So that's your game. Well, Glen Naspa came to my school of her own accord and she will say so."

"Why will she? Because you blinded the simple Indian girl. . . . Willetts, I'll waste little more time on you."

And swift and light as a panther Shefford leaped upon the man and, fastening powerful hands round the thick neck, bore him to his knees and bent back his head over the rail. There was a convulsive struggle, a hard flinging of arms, a straining wrestle, and then Willetts was in a dreadful position. Shefford held him in iron grasp.

"You damned, white-livered hypocrite—I'm liable to kill you!" cried Shefford. "I watched you and Glen Naspa that day up on the mountain. I saw you embrace her. I saw that she loved you. Tell *that*, you liar! That 'll be enough."

The face of the missionary turned purple as Shefford forced his head back over the rail.

"I'll *kill* you, man," repeated Shefford, piercingly. "Do you want to go to your God unprepared? Say you made love to Glen Naspa—tell that you persuaded her to leave her home. Quick!"

Willetts raised a shaking hand and then Shefford relaxed the paralyzing grip and let his head come forward. The half-strangled man gasped out a few

198

incoherent words that his livid, guilty face made unnecessary.

Shefford gave him a shove and he fell into the dust at the feet of the Navajo.

"Gentlemen, I leave him to Nas Ta Bega," said Shefford, with a strange change from passion to calmness.

Late that night, when the roystering visitors had gone or were deep in drunken slumber, a melancholy and strange procession filed out of Stonebridge. Joe Lake and his armed comrades were escorting the Mormon women back to the hidden valley. They were mounted on burros and mustangs, and in all that dark and somber line there was only one figure which shone white under the pale moon.

At the starting, until that white-clad figure had appeared, Shefford's heart had seemed to be in his throat; and thereafter its beat was muffled and painful in his breast. Yet there was some sad sweetness in the knowledge that he could see her now, be near her, watch over her.

By and by the overcast clouds drifted and the moon shone bright. The night was still; the great dark mountain loomed to the stars; the numberless waves of rounded rock that must be crossed and circled lay deep in shadow. There was only a steady pattering of light hoofs.

Shefford's place was near the end of the line, and he kept well back, riding close to one woman and then another. No word was spoken. These sealed wives rode where their mounts were led or driven, as blind in their hoods as veiled Arab women in palanquins. And their heads drooped wearily and their shoulders bent, as if under a burden. It took an hour of steady riding to reach the ascent to the plateau, and here, with the beginning of rough and smooth and shadowed trail, the work of the escort began. The line lengthened out and each man kept to the several women assigned to him. Shefford had three, and one of them was the girl he loved. She rode as if the world and time and life were naught to her. As soon as he dared trust his voice and his control he meant to let her know the man whom perhaps she had not forgotten was there with her, a friend. Six months! It had been a lifetime to him. Surely eternity to her! Had she forgotten? He felt like a coward who had basely deserted her. Oh—had he only known!

She rode a burro that was slow, continually blocking the passage for those behind, and eventually it became lame. Thus the other women forged ahead. Shefford dismounted and stopped her burro. It was a moment before she noted the halt, and twice in that time Shefford tried to speak and failed. What poignant pain, regret, love made his utterance fail!

"Ride my horse," he finally said, and his voice was not like his own.

Obediently and wearily she dismounted from the burro and got up on Nack-yal. The stirrups were long for her and he had to change them. His fingers were all thumbs as he fumbled with the buckles.

Suddenly he became aware that there had been a subtle change in her. He knew it without looking up and he seemed to be unable to go on with his task. If his life had depended upon keeping his head lowered he could not have done it. The listlessness of her drooping form was no longer manifest. The peak of the dark hood pointed toward him: He knew then that she was gazing at him.

Never so long as he lived would that moment be forgotten! They were alone. The others had gotten so far ahead that no sound came back. The stillness was so deep it could be felt. The moon shone with white, cold radiance and the shining slopes of smooth stone waved away, crossed by shadows of piñons.

Then she leaned a little toward him. One swift hand flew up to tear the black hood back so that she could see. In its place flashed her white face. And her eyes were like the night.

"*You!*" she whispered.

His blood came leaping to sting neck and cheek and temple. What dared he interpret from that single word? Could any other word have meant so much?

"No—one—else," he replied, unsteadily.

Her white hand flashed again to him, and he met it with his own. He felt himself standing cold and motionless in the moonlight. He saw her, wonderful, with the deep, shadowy eyes, and a silver sheen on her hair. And as he looked she released her hand and lifted it, with the other, to her hood. He saw the shiny hair darken and disappear—and then the lovely face with its sad eyes and tragic lips.

He drew Nack-yal's bridle forward, and led him up the moonlit trail.

XII

THE REVELATION

THE following afternoon cowboys and horse-wranglers, keen-eyed as Indians for tracks and trails, began to arrive in the quiet valley to which the Mormon women had been returned.

Under every cedar clump there were hobbled horses, packs, and rolled bedding in tarpaulins. Shefford and Joe Lake had pitched camp in the old site near the spring. The other men of Joe's escort went to the homes of the women; and that afternoon, as the curious visitors began to arrive, these homes became barred and dark and quiet, as if they had been closed and deserted for the winter. Not a woman showed herself.

Shefford and Joe, by reason of the location of their camp and their alertness, met all the new-comers. The ride from Stonebridge was a long and hard one, calculated to wear off the effects of the whisky imbibed by the adventure-seekers. This fact alone saved the situation. Nevertheless, Joe expected trouble. Most of the visitors were decent, good-natured fellows, merely curious, and simple enough to believe that this really was what the Mormons had claimed—a village of free women. But there were those among them who were coarse, evil minded, and dangerous.

By supper-time there were two dozen or more of these men in the valley, camped along the west wall. Fires were lighted, smoke curled up over the cedars, gay songs disturbed the usual serenity of the place. Later in the early twilight the curious visitors, by twos and threes, walked about the village, peering at the dark cabins and jesting among themselves. Joe had informed Shefford that all the women had been put in a limited number of cabins, so that they could be protected. So far as Shefford saw or heard there was no unpleasant incident in the village; however, as the sauntering visitors returned toward their camps they loitered at the spring, and here developments threatened.

In spite of the fact that the majority of these cowboys and their comrades were decent-minded and beginning to see the real relation of things, they were not disposed to be civil to Shefford. They were certainly not Mormons. And his position, apparently as a Gentile, among these Mormons was one open to criticism. They might have been jealous, too; at any rate, remarks were passed in his hearing, meant for his ears, that made it exceedingly trying for him not to resent. Moreover, Joe Lake's increasing impatience rendered the situation more difficult. Shefford welcomed the arrival of Nas Ta Bega. The Indian listened to the loud talk of several loungers round the camp-fire; and thereafter he was like Shefford's shadow, silent, somber, watchful.

Nevertheless, it did not happen to be one of the

riendly and sarcastic cowboys that precipitated the
crisis. A horse-wrangler named Hurley, a man of
bad repute, as much outlaw as anything, took up
the bantering.

"Say, Shefford, what in the hell's your job here,
anyway?" he queried as he kicked a cedar branch
into the camp-fire. The brightening blaze showed
him swarthy, unshaven, a large-featured, ugly man.

"I've been doing odd jobs for Withers," replied
Shefford. "Expect to drive pack-trains in here for
a while."

"You must stand strong with these Mormons.
Must be a Mormon yerself?"

"No," replied Shefford, briefly.

"Wal, I'm stuck on your job. Do you need a
packer? I can throw a diamond-hitch better 'n any
feller in this country."

"I don't need help."

"Mebbe you'll take me over to see the ladies " he
went on, with a coarse laugh.

Shefford did not show that he had heard. Hurley
waited, leering as he looked from the keen listeners to
Shefford.

"Want to have them all yerself, eh?" he jeered.

Shefford struck him—sent him tumbling heavily,
like a log. Hurley, cursing as he half rose, jerked
his gun out. Nas Ta Bega, swift as light, kicked the
gun out of his hand. And Joe Lake picked it up.

Deliberately the Mormon cocked the weapon and
stood over Hurley.

"Get up!" he ordered, and Shefford heard the
ruthless Mormon in him then.

Hurley rose slowly. Then Joe prodded him in

the middle with the cocked gun. Shefford, startled, expected the gun to go off. So did the others, especially Hurley, who shrank in panic from the dark Mormon.

"Rustle!" said Joe, and gave the man a harder prod. Assuredly the gun did not have a hair-trigger.

"Joe, mebbe it's loaded!" protested one of the cowboys.

Hurley shrank back, and turned to hurry away, with Joe close after him. They disappeared in the darkness. A constrained silence was maintained around the camp-fire for a while. Presently some of the men walked off and others began to converse. Everybody heard the sound of hoofs passing down the trail. The patter ceased, and in a few moments Lake returned. He still carried Hurley's gun.

The crowd dispersed then. There was no indication of further trouble. However, Shefford and Joe and Nas Ta Bega divided the night in watches, so that some one would be wide awake.

Early next morning there was an exodus from the village of the better element among the visitors. "No fun hangin' round hyar," one of them expressed it, and as good-naturedly as they had come they rode away. Six or seven of the desperado class remained behind, bent on mischief; and they were reinforced by more arrivals from Stonebridge. They avoided the camp by the spring, and when Shefford and Lake attempted to go to them they gave them a wide berth. This caused Joe to assert that they were up to some dirty work. All morning they lounged around under the cedars, keeping out of sight, and evidently the reinforcement from Stone-bridge had brought liquor. When they gathered together at their camp, half drunk, all noisy, some wanting to swagger off into the village and others trying to hold them back, Joe Lake said, grimly, that somebody was going to get shot. Indeed, Shefford saw that there was every likelihood of bloodshed.

"Reckon we'd better take to one of the cabins," said Joe.

Thereupon the three repaired to the nearest cabin, and, entering, kept watch from the windows. During a couple of hours, however, they did not see or hear anything of the ruffians. Then came a shot from over in the village, a single yell, and, after that, a scattering volley. The silence and suspense which followed were finally broken by hoof-beats. Nas Ta Bega called Joe and Shefford to the window he had been stationed at. From here they saw the unwelcome visitors ride down the trail, to disappear in the cedars toward the outlet of the valley. Joe, who had numbered them, said that all but one of them had gone.

"Reckon he got it," added Joe.

So indeed it turned out; one of the men, a well-known rustler named Harker, had been killed, by whom no one seemed to know. He had brazenly tried to force his way into one of the houses, and the act had cost him his life. Naturally Shefford, never free from his civilized habit of thought, remarked apprehensively that he hoped this affair would not cause the poor women to be arrested again and haled before some rude court.

"Law!" grunted Joe. "There ain't any. The

nearest sheriff is in Durango. That's Colorado. And he'd give us a medal for killing Harker. It was a good job, for it 'll teach these rowdies a lesson."

The Mormons, notwithstanding their indifference to the killing of the desperado, gave him decent burial and prayed for his soul.

Next day the old order of life was resumed in the village. And the arrival of a heavily laden pack-train, under the guidance of Withers, attested to the fact that the Mormons meant not only to continue to live in the valley, but also to build and plant and enlarge. This was good news to Shefford. At least the village could be made less lonely. And there was plenty of work to give him excuse for staying there. Furthermore, Withers brought a message from Bishop Kane to the effect that the young man was offered a place as teacher in the school, in co-operation with the Mormon teachers. Shefford experienced no twinge of conscience when he accepted.

It was the fourth evening after the never-to-be-forgotten moonlight ride to the valley that Shefford passed under the dark piñon-trees on his way to Fay Larkin's cottage. He paused in the gloom and memory beset him. The six months were annihilated, and it was the night he had fled. But now all was silent. He seemed to be trying to drag himself back. A beginning must be made. Only how to meet her—what to say—what to conceal!

He tapped on the door and she came out. After all, it was a meeting vastly different from what his feeling made him imagine it might have been. She was nervous, frightened, as were all the other women, for that matter. She was alone in the cottage. He made haste to reassure her about the improbability of any further trouble such as had befallen the last week. As he had always done on those former visits to her, he talked rapidly, using all his wit, and here his emotion made him eloquent; he avoided personalities, except to tell about his prospects of work in the village, and he sought above all to lead her mind from thought of herself and her condition. Before he left her he had the gladness of knowing he had succeeded.

When he said good night he felt the strange falsity of his position. He did not expect to be able to keep up the deception for long. That roused him, and half the night he lay awake, thinking. Next day he was the life of the work and study and play in that village. Kindness and good-will did not need inspiration, but it was keen, deep passion that made him a plotter for influence and friendship. Was there a woman in the village whom he might trust, in case he needed one? And his instinct guided him to her whom he had liked well—Ruth. Ruth Jones she had called herself at the trial, and when Shefford used the name she laughed mockingly. Ruth was not very religious, and sometimes she was bitter and hard. She wanted life, and here she was a prisoner in a lonely valley. She welcomed Shefford's visits. He imagined that she had slightly changed, and whether it was the added six months with its trouble and pain or a growing revolt he could not tell. After a time he divined that the inevitable retrogression had set in: she had not enough faith to uphold the burden she had accepted, nor the courage to cast it off. She was ready to love him. That did not frighten Shefford, and if she did love him he was not so sure it would not be an anchor for her. He saw her danger, and then he became what he had never really been in all the days of his ministry—the real helper. Unselfishly, for her sake, he found power to influence her; and selfishly, for the sake of Fay Larkin, he began slowly to win her to a possible need.

The days passed swiftly. Mormons came and went, though in the open day, as laborers; new cabins went up, and a store, and other improvements. Some part of every evening Shefford spent with Fay, and these visits were no longer unknown to the village. Women gossiped, in a friendly way about Shefford, but with jealous tongues about the girl. Joe Lake told Shefford the run of the village talk. Anything concerning the Sago Lily the droll Mormon took to heart. He had been hard hit, and admitted it. Sometimes he went with Shefford to call upon her, but he talked little and never remained long. Shefford had anticipated antagonism on the part of Joe; however, he did not find it.

Shefford really lived through the busy day for that hour with Fay in the twilight. And every evening seemed the same. He would find her in the dark, alone, silent, brooding, hopeless. Her mood did not puzzle him, but how to keep from plunging her deeper into despair baffled him. He exhausted all his powers trying to do for her what he had been able to do for Ruth. Yet he failed. Something had blunted her. The shadow of that baneful trial hovered over her, and he came to sense a strange terror in her. It was mostly always present. Was she thinking of Jane Withersteen and Lassiter, left dead or imprisoned in the valley from which she had been brought so mysteriously? Shefford wearied his brain revolving these questions. The fate of her friends, and the cross she bore—of these was tragedy born, but the terror—that Shefford divined came of waiting for the visit of the Mormon whose face she had never seen. Shefford prayed that he might never meet this man. Finally he grew desperate. When he first arrived at the girl's home she would speak, she showed gladness, relief, and then straightway she dropped back into the shadow of her gloom. When he got up to go then there was a wistfulness, an unspoken need, an unconscious reliance, in her reluctant good night.

Then the hour came when he reached his limit. He must begin his revelation.

"You never ask me anything—let alone about myself," he said.

"I'd like to hear," she replied, timidly.

"Do I strike you as an unhappy man?"

"No, indeed."

"Well, how *do* I strike you?"

This was an entirely new tack he had veered to.

"Very good and kind to us women," she said.

"I don't know about that. If I am so, it doesn't bring me happiness. . . . Do you remember what I told you once, about my being a preacher—disgrace, ruin, and all that—and my rainbow-chasing dream out here after a—a lost girl?"

"I—remember all—you said," she replied, very low.

"Listen." His voice was a little husky, but behind it there seemed a tide of resistless utterance. "Loss of faith and name did not send me to this

wilderness. But I had love—love for that lost girl,
Fay Larkin. I dreamed about her till I loved her. I
dreamed that I would find her—my treasure—at the
foot of a rainbow. Dreams! . . . When you told
me she was dead I accepted that. There was truth
in your voice. I respected your reticence. But
something died in me then. I lost myself, the best
of me, the good that might have uplifted me. I
went away, down upon the barren desert, and there
I rode and slept and grew into another and a harder
man. Yet, strange to say, I never forgot her,
though my dreams were done. As I toiled and suffered and changed I loved her—if not her, the thought
of her—more and more. Now I have come back to
these walled valleys—to the smell of piñon, to the
flowers in the nooks, to the wind on the heights, to
the silence and loneliness and beauty. And here
the dreams come back and *she* is *with* me always.
Her spirit is all that keeps me kind and good, as
you say I am. But I suffer, I long for her alive.
If I love her dead, how could I love her living! Always I torture myself with the vain dream that—that
she *might* not be dead. I have never been anything
but a dreamer. And here I go about my work by
day and lie awake at night with that lost girl in my
mind. . . . I love her. Does that seem strange to you?
But it would not if you understood. Think. I had
lost faith, hope. I set myself a great work—to find
Fay Larkin. And by the fire and the iron and the
blood that I felt it would cost to save her some faith
must come to me again. . . . My work is undone—
I've never saved her. But listen, how strange it is
to feel—now—as I let myself go—that just the lov-

ing her and the living here in the wildness that holds
her somewhere have brought me hope again. Some
faith must come, too. It was through her that I
met this Indian, Nas Ta Bega. He has saved my
life—taught me much. What would I ever have
learned of the naked and vast earth, of the sublimity
of the wild uplands, of the storm and night and sun,
if I had not followed a gleam she inspired? In my
hunt for a lost girl perhaps I wandered into a place
where I shall find a God and my salvation. Do you
marvel that I love Fay Larkin—that she is not dead
to me? Do you marvel that I love her, when I *know*,
were she alive, chained in a cañon, or bound, or lost
in any way, my destiny would lead me to her, and
she should be saved?"

Shefford ended, overcome with emotion. In the
dusk he could not see the girl's face, but the white
form that had drooped so listlessly seemed now
charged by some vitalizing current. He knew he
had spoken irrationally; still he held it no dishonor
to have told her he loved her as one dead. If she
took that love to the secret heart of living Fay Larkin,
then perhaps a spirit might light in her darkened
soul. He had no thought yet that Fay Larkin might
ever belong to him. He divined a crime—he had
seen her agony. And this avowal of his was only
one step toward her deliverance.

Softly she rose, retreating into the shadow.

"Forgive me if I—I disturb you, distress you," he
said. "I wanted to tell you. She was—somehow
known to you. I am not happy. And are *you*
happy? . . . Let her memory be a bond between us.
. . . Good night."

THE REVELATION

"Good night."

Faintly as the faintest whisper breathed her reply, and, though it came from a child forced into womanhood, it whispered of girlhood not dead, of sweet incredulity, of amazed tumult, of a wondering, frantic desire to run and hide, of the bewilderment incident to a first hint of love.

Shefford walked away into the darkness. The whisper filled his soul. Had a word of love ever been spoken to that girl? Never—not the love which had been on his lips. Fay Larkin's lonely life spoke clearly in her whisper.

Next morning as the sun gilded the looming peaks and shafts of gold slanted into the valley she came swiftly down the path to the spring.

Shefford paused in his task of chopping wood. Joe Lake, on his knees, with his big hands in a pan of dough, lifted his head to stare. She had left off the somber black hood, and, although that made a vast difference in her, still it was not enough to account for what struck both men.

"Good morning," she called, brightly.

They both answered, but not spontaneously. She stopped at the spring and with one sweep of her strong arm filled the bucket and lifted it. Then she started back down the path and, pausing opposite the camp, set the bucket down.

"Joe, do you still pride yourself on your sour dough?" she asked.

"Reckon I do," replied Joe, with a grin.

"I've heard your boasts, but never tasted your bread," she went on.

"I'll ask you to eat with us some day."

"Don't forget," she replied.

And then shyly she looked at Shefford. She was like the fresh dawn, and the gold of the sun shone on her head.

"Have you chopped all that wood—so early?" she asked.

"Sure," replied Shefford, laughing. "I have to get up early to keep Joe from doing all the camp chores."

She smiled, and then to Shefford she seemed to gleam, to be radiant.

"It 'd be a lovely morning to climb—'way high."

"Why—yes—it would," replied Shefford, awkwardly. "I wish I didn't have my work."

"Joe, will *you* climb with me some day?"

"I should smile I will," declared Joe.

"But I can run right up the walls."

"I reckon. Mary, it wouldn't surprise me to see you fly."

"Do you mean I'm like a cañon swallow or an angel?"

Then, as Joe stared speechlessly, she said good-by and, taking up the bucket, went on with her swift, graceful step.

"She's perked up," said the Mormon, staring after her. "Never heard her say more'n yes or no till now."

"She did seem—bright," replied Shefford.

He was stunned. What had happened to her? To-day this girl had not been Mary, the sealed wife, or the Sago Lily, alien among Mormon women. Then it flashed upon him—she was Fay Larkin.

She who had regarded herself as dead had come back to life. In one short night what had transformed her—what had taken place in her heart? Shefford dared not accept, nor allow lodgment in his mind, a thrilling idea that he had made her forget her misery.

"Shefford, did you ever see her like that?" asked Joe.

"Never."

"Haven't you—something to do with it?"

"Maybe I have. I—I hope so."

"Reckon you've seen how she's faded—since the trial?"

"No," replied Shefford, swiftly. "But I've not seen her face in daylight since then."

"Well, take my hunch," said Joe, soberly. "She's begun to fade like the cañon lily when it's broken. And she's going to die unless—"

"Why. man!" ejaculated Shefford. "Didn't you see—"

"Sure I see," interrupted the Mormon. "I see a lot you don't. She's so white you can look through her. She's grown thin, all in a week. She doesn't eat. Oh, I know, because I've made it my business to find out. It's no news to the women. But they'd like to see her die. And she will die unless—"

"My God!" exclaimed Shefford, huskily. "I never noticed—I never thought. . . . Joe, hasn't she any friends?"

"Sure. You and Ruth—and me. Maybe Nas Ta Bega, too. He watches her a good deal."

"We can do so little, when she needs so much."

"Nobody can help her, unless it's you," went on the Mormon. "That's plain talk. She seemed different this morning. Why, she was alive—she talked—she smiled. . . . Shefford, if you cheer her up I'll go to hell for you!"

The big Mormon, on his knees, with his hands in a pan of dough, and his shirt all covered with flour, presented an incongruous figure of a man actuated by pathos and passion. Yet the contrast made his emotion all the simpler and stronger. Shefford grew closer to Joe in that moment.

"Why do you think *I* can cheer her, help her?" queried Shefford.

"I don't know. But she's different with you. It's not that you're a Gentile, though, for all the women are crazy about you. You talk to her. You have power over her, Shefford. I feel that. She's only a kid."

"Who is she, Joe? Where did she come from?" asked Shefford, very low, with his eyes cast down.

"I don't know. I can't find out. Nobody knows. It's a mystery—to all the younger Mormons, anyway."

Shefford burned to ask questions about the Mormon whose sealed wife the girl was, but he respected Joe too much to take advantage of him in a poignant moment like this. Besides, it was only jealousy that made him burn to know the Mormon's identity, and jealousy had become a creeping, insidious, growing fire. He would be wise not to add fuel to it. He rejected many things before he thought of one that he could voice to his friend.

"Joe, it's only her body that belongs to—to . . . Her soul is lost to—"

"John Shefford, let that go. My mind's tired.

THE REVELATION

I've been taught so and so, and I'm not bright.
But, after all, men are much alike. The thing with
you and me is this—we don't want to see *her* grave!"

Love spoke there. The Mormon had seized upon
the single elemental point that concerned him and
his friend in their relation to this unfortunate girl.
His simple, powerful statement united them; it gave
the lie to his hint of denseness; it stripped the truth
naked. It was such a wonderful thought-provok-
ing statement that Shefford needed time to ponder
how deep the Mormon was. To what limit would he
go? Did he mean that here, between two men who
loved the same girl, class, duty, honor, creed were
nothing if they stood in the way of her deliverance
and her life?

"Joe Lake, you Mormons are impossible," said
Shefford, deliberately. "You don't want to see
her grave. So long as she lives—remains on the
earth—white and gold like the flower you call her,
that's enough for you. It's her body you think of.
And that's the great and horrible error in your
religion. . . . But death of the soul is infinitely worse
than death of the body. I have been thinking of
her soul. . . . So here we stand, you and I. You to
save her life—I to save her soul! What will you
do?"

"Why, John, I'd turn Gentile," he said, with terrible softness. It was a softness that scorned Shefford for asking, and likewise it flung defiance at his
creed and into the face of hell.

Shefford felt the sting and the exaltation.

"And I'd be a Mormon," he said.

"All right. We understand each other. Reckon

217

there won't be any call for such extremes. I haven't
an idea what you mean—what can be done. But
I say, go slow, so we won't all find graves. First
cheer her up somehow. Make her want to live. But
go slow, John. *And don't be with her late!*"

That night Shefford found her waiting for him in
the moonlight—a girl who was as transparent as
crystal-clear water, who had left off the somber
gloom with the black hood, who tremulously embraced happiness without knowing it, who was one
moment timid and wild like a half-frightened fawn,
and the next, exquisitely half-conscious of what it
meant to be thought dead, but to be alive, to be
awakening, wondering, palpitating, and to be loved.
Shefford lived the hour as a dream and went back
to the quiet darkness under the cedars to lie wide-
eyed, trying to recall all that she had said. For she
had talked as if utterance had long been dammed
behind a barrier of silence.

There followed other hours like that one, indescribable hours, so sweet they stung, and in which,
keeping pace with his love, was the nobler stride
of a spirit that more every day lightened her burden.

The thing he had to do, sooner or later, was to tell
her he knew she was Fay Larkin, not dead, but alive,
and that, not love nor religion, but sacrifice, nailed
her down to her martyrdom. Many and many a
time he had tried to force himself to tell her, only
to fail. He hated to risk ending this sweet, strange,
thoughtless, girlish mood of hers. It might not be
soon won back—perhaps never. How could he tell
what chains bound her? And so as he vacillated

between Joe's cautious advice to go slow and his own pity the days and weeks slipped by.

One haunting fear kept him sleepless half the nights and sick even in his dreams, and it was that the Mormon whose sealed wife she was might come, surely would come, some night. Shefford could bear it. But what would that visit do to Fay Larkin? Shefford instinctively feared the awakening in the girl of womanhood, of deeper insight, of a spiritual realization of what she was, of a physical dawn.

He might have spared himself needless torture. One day Joe Lake eyed him with penetrating glance.

"Reckon you don't have to sleep right on that Stonebridge trail," said the Mormon, significantly.

Shefford felt the blood burn his neck and face. He had pulled his tarpaulin closer to the trail, and his motive was as an open page to the keen Mormon.

"Why?" asked Shefford.

"There won't be any Mormons riding in here soon —by night—to visit the women," replied Joe, bluntly. "Haven't you figured there might be government spies watching the trails?"

"No, I haven't."

"Well, take a hunch, then," added the Mormon, gruffly, and Shefford divined, as well as if he had been told, that warning word had gone to Stonebridge. Gone despite the fact that Nas Ta Bega had reported every trail free of watchers! There was no sign of any spies, cowboys, outlaws, or Indians in the vicinity of the valley. A passionate gratitude to the Mormon overcame Shefford; and the unreasonableness of it, the nature of it, perturbed him greatly. But, something hammered into his brain.

if he loved one of these sealed wives, how could he help being jealous?

The result of Joe's hint was that Shefford put off the hour of revelation, lived in his dream, helped the girl grow farther and farther away from her trouble, until that inevitable hour arrived when he was driven by accumulated emotion as much as the exigency of the case.

He had not often walked with her beyond the dark shade of the piñons round the cottage, but this night, when he knew he must tell her, he led her away down the path, through the cedar grove to the west end of the valley where it was wild and lonely and sad and silent.

The moon was full and the great peaks were crowned as with snow. A coyote uttered his cutting cry. There were a few melancholy notes from a night bird of the stone walls. The air was clear and cold, with a tang of frost in it. Shefford gazed about him at the vast, uplifted, insulating walls, and that feeling of his which was more than a sense told him how walls like these and the silence and shadow and mystery had been nearly all of Fay Larkin's life. He felt them all in her.

He stopped out in the open, near the line where dark shadow of the wall met the silver moonlight on the grass, and here, by a huge flat stone where he had come often alone and sometimes with Ruth, he faced Fay Larkin in the spirit to tell her gently that he knew her, and sternly to force her secret from her.

"Am I your friend?" he began.

"Ah!—my only friend," she said.

"Do you trust me, believe I mean well by you, want to help you?"

"Yes, indeed."

"Well, then, let me speak of you. You know one topic we've never touched upon. You!"

She was silent, and looked wonderingly, a little fearfully, at him, as if vague, disturbing thoughts were entering the fringe of her mind.

"Our friendship is a strange one, is it not?" he went on.

"How do I know? I never had any other friendship. What do you mean by strange?"

"Well, I'm a young man. You're a—a married woman. We are together a good deal—and like to be."

"Why is that strange?" she asked.

Suddenly Shefford realized that there was nothing strange in what was natural. A remnant of sophistication clung to him and that had spoken. He needed to speak to her in a way which in her simplicity she would understand.

"Never mind strange. Say that I am interested in you, and, as you're not happy, I want to help you. And say that your neighbors are curious and oppose my idea. Why do they?"

"They're jealous and want you themselves," she replied, with sweet directness. "They've said things I don't understand. But I felt they—they hated in me what would be all right in themselves."

Here to simplicity she added truth and wisdom, as an Indian might have expressed them. But shame was unknown to her, and she had as yet only vague perceptions of love and passion. Shefford began to realize the quickness of her mind, that she was indeed awakening.

"They are jealous—were jealous before I ever came here. That's only human nature. I was trying to get to a point. Your neighbors are curious. They oppose me. They hate you. It's all bound up in the—the fact of your difference from them, your youth, beauty, that you're not a Mormon, that you nearly betrayed their secret at the trial in Stonebridge."

"Please—please don't—speak of that!" she faltered.

"But I must," he replied, swiftly. "That trial was a torture to you. It revealed so much to me. . . . I know you are a sealed wife. I know there has been a crime. I know you've sacrificed yourself. I know that love and religion have nothing to do with—what you are. . . . Now, is not all that true?"

"I must not tell," she whispered.

"But I shall *make* you tell," he replied, and his voice rang.

"Oh no, you cannot," she said.

"I can—with just one word!"

Her eyes were great, starry, shadowy gulfs, dark in the white beauty of her face. She was calm now. She had strength. She invited him to speak the word, and the wistful, tremulous quiver of her lips was for his earnest thought of her.

"Wait—a—little," said Shefford, unsteadily. "I'll come to that presently. Tell me this—have you ever thought of being free?"

"Free!" she echoed, and there was singular depth and richness in her voice. That was the first spark of fire he had struck from her. "Long ago, the minute I was unwatched, I'd have leaped from a wall had I dared. Oh, I wasn't afraid. I'd love to die that way. But I never dared."

"Why?" queried Shefford, piercingly.

She was silent then.

"Suppose I offered to give you freedom that meant life?"

"I—couldn't—take it."

"Why?"

"Oh, my friend, don't ask me any more."

"I know, I can see—you want to tell me—you need to tell."

"But I daren't."

"Won't you trust me?"

"I do—I do."

"Then tell me."

"No—no—oh no!"

The moment had come. How sad, tragic, yet glorious for him! It would be like a magic touch upon this lovely, cold, white ghost of Fay Larkin, transforming her into a living, breathing girl. He held his love as a thing aloof, and, as such, intangible because of the living death she believed she lived, it had no warmth and intimacy for them. What might it not become with a lightning flash of revelation? He dreaded, yet he was driven to speak. He waited, swallowing hard, fighting the tumultuous storm of emotion, and his eyes dimmed.

"What did I come to this country for?" he asked, suddenly, in ringing, powerful voice.

"To find a girl," she whispered.

"I've found her!"

THE RAINBOW TRAIL

She began to shake. He saw a white hand go to her breast.

"Where is Surprise Valley? . . . How were you taken from Jane Withersteen and Lassiter? . . . I know they're alive. But where?"

She seemed to turn to stone.

"Fay!—*Fay Larkin!* . . . I KNOW YOU!" he cried, brokenly.

She slipped off the stone to her knees, swayed forward blindly with her hands reaching out, her head falling back to let the moon fall full upon the beautiful, snow-white, tragically convulsed face.

XIII

THE STORY OF SURPRISE VALLEY

". . . OH, I remember so well! Even now I dream of it sometimes. I hear the roll and crash of falling rock—like thunder. . . . We rode and rode. Then the horses fell. Uncle Jim took me in his arms and started up the cliff. Mother Jane climbed close after us. They kept looking back. Down there in the gray valley came the Mormons. I see the first one now. He rode a white horse. That was Tull. Oh, I remember so well! And I was five or six years old.

"We climbed up and up and into dark cañons and wound in and out. Then there was the narrow white trail, straight up, with the little cut steps and the great, red, ruined walls. I looked down over Uncle Jim's shoulder. I saw Mother Jane dragging herself up. Uncle Jim's blood spotted the trail. He reached a flat place at the top and fell with me. Mother Jane crawled up to us.

"Then she cried out and pointed. Tull was 'way below, climbing the trail. His men came behind him. Uncle Jim went to a great, tall rock and leaned against it. There was a bloody hole in his hand. He pushed the rock. It rolled down, banging the loose walls. They crashed and crashed—then all was terrible thunder and red smoke. I couldn't hear—I couldn't see.

"Uncle Jim carried me down and down out of the dark and dust into a beautiful valley all red and gold, with a wonderful arch of stone over the entrance.

"I don't remember well what happened then for what seemed a long, long time. I can feel how the place looked, but not so clear as it is now in my dreams. I seem to see myself with the dogs, and with Mother Jane, learning my letters, marking with red stone on the walls.

"But I remember now how I felt when I first understood we were shut in for ever. Shut in Surprise Valley where Venters had lived so long. I was glad. The Mormons would never get me. I was seven or eight years old then. From that time all is clear in my mind.

"Venters had left supplies and tools and grain and cattle and burros, so we had a good start to begin life there. He had killed off the wildcats and kept the coyotes out, so the rabbits and quail multiplied till there were thousands of them. We raised corn and fruit, and stored what we didn't use. Mother Jane taught me to read and write with the soft red stone that marked well on the walls.

"The years passed. We kept track of time pretty well. Uncle Jim's hair turned white and Mother Jane grew gray. Every day was like the one before. Mother Jane cried sometimes and Uncle Jim was sad because they could never be able to get me out of the valley. It was long before they stopped looking and listening for some one. Venters would come back, Uncle Jim always said. But Mother Jane did not think so.

"I loved Surprise Valley. I wanted to stay there always. I remembered Cottonwoods, how the children there hated me, and I didn't want to go back. The only unhappy times I ever had in the valley were when Ring and Whitie, my dogs, grew old and died. I roamed the valley. I climbed to every nook upon the mossy ledges. I learned to run up the steep cliffs. I could almost stick on the straight walls. Mother Jane called me a wild girl. We had put away the clothes we wore when we got there, to save them, and we made clothes of skins. I always laughed when I thought of my little dress—how I grew out of it. I think Uncle Jim and Mother Jane talked less as the years went by. And after I'd learned all she could teach me we didn't talk much. I used to scream into the caves just to hear my voice, and the echoes would frighten me.

"The older I grew the more I was alone. I was always running round the valley. I would climb to a high place and sit there for hours, doing nothing. I just watched and listened. I used to stay in the cliff-dwellers' caves and wonder about them. I loved to be out in the wind. And my happiest time was in the summer storms with the thunder echoes under the walls. At evening it was such a quiet place—after the night bird's cry, no sound. The quiet made me sad, but I loved it. I loved to watch the stars as I lay awake.

"So it was beautiful and happy for me there till— till . . .

"Two years or more ago there was a bad storm, and one of the great walls caved. The walls were always weathering, slipping. Many and many a time have I heard the rumble of an avalanche, but most of them were in other cañons. This slide in the valley made it possible, Uncle Jim said, for men to get down into the valley. But we could not climb out unless helped from above. Uncle Jim never rested well after that. But it never worried me.

"One day, over a year ago, while I was across the valley, I heard strange shouts, and then screams. I ran to our camp. I came upon men with ropes and guns. Uncle Jim was tied, and a rope was round his neck. Mother Jane was lying on the ground. I thought she was dead until I heard her moan. I was not afraid. I screamed and flew at Uncle Jim to tear the ropes off him. The men held me back. They called me a pretty cat. Then they talked together, and some were for hanging Lassiter—that was the first time I ever knew any name for him but Uncle Jim—and some were for leaving him in the valley. Finally they decided to hang him. But Mother Jane pleaded so and I screamed and fought so that they left off. Then they went away and we saw them climb out of the valley.

"Uncle Jim said they were Mormons, and some among them had been born in Cottonwoods. I was not told why they had such a terrible hate for him. He said they would come back and kill him. Uncle Jim had no guns to fight with.

"We watched and watched. In five days they did come back, with more men, and some of them wor—

black masks. They came to our cave with ropes and guns. One was tall. He had a cruel voice. The others ran to obey him. I could see white hair and sharp eyes behind the mask. The men caught me and brought me before him.

"He said Lassiter had killed many Mormons. He said Lassiter had killed his father and should be hanged. But Lassiter would be let live and Mother Jane could stay with him, both prisoners there in the valley, if I would marry the Mormon. I must marry him, accept the Mormon faith, and bring up my children as Mormons. If I refused they would hang Lassiter, leave the heretic Jane Withersteen alone in the valley, and take me and break me to their rule.

"I agreed. But Mother Jane absolutely forbade me to marry him. Then the Mormons took me away. It nearly killed me to leave Uncle Jim and Mother Jane. I was carried and lifted out of the valley, and rode a long way on a horse. They brought me here, to the cabin where I live, and I have never been away except that—that time—to—Stonebridge. Only little by little did I learn my position. Bishop Kane was kind, but stern, because I could not be quick to learn the faith.

"I am not a sealed wife. But they're trying to make me one. The master Mormon—he visited me often—at night—till lately. He threatened me. He never told me a name—except Saint George. I don't—know him—except his voice. I never—saw his face—in the light!"

Fay Larkin ended her story. Toward its close

Shefford had grown involuntarily restless, and when her last tragic whisper ceased all his body seemed shaken with a terrible violence of his joy. He strode to and fro in the dark shadow of the stone. The receding blood left him cold, with a pricking, sickening sensation over his body, but there seemed to be an overwhelming tide accumulating deep in his breast—a tide of passion and pain. He dominated the passion, but the ache remained. And he returned to the quiet figure on the stone.

"Fay Larkin!" he exclaimed, with a deep breath of relief that the secret was disclosed. "So you're not a wife! . . . You're free! Thank Heaven! But I felt it was sacrifice. I knew there had been a crime. For crime it is. You child! You can't understand what crime. Oh, almost I wish you and Jane and Lassiter had never been found. But that's wrong of me. One year of agony—that shall not ruin your life. Fay, I will take you away."

"Where?" she whispered.

"Away from this Mormon country—to the East," he replied, and he spoke of what he had known, of travel, of cities, of people, of happiness possible for a young girl who had spent all her life hidden between the narrow walls of a silent, lonely valley—he spoke swiftly and eloquently till he lost his breath.

There was an instant of flashing wonder and joy on her white face, and then the radiance paled, the glow died. Her soul was the darker for that one strange, leaping glimpse of a glory not for such as she.

"I must stay here," she said, shudderingly.

"Fay!—How strange to *say* Fay aloud to *you!*— Fay, do you know the way to Surprise Valley?"

"I don't know where it is, but I could go straight to it," she replied.

"Take me there. Show me your beautiful valley. Let me see where you ran and climbed and spent so many lonely years."

"Ah, how I'd love to! But I dare not. And why should you want me to take you? We can run and climb here."

"I want to—I mean to save Jane Withersteen and Lassiter," he declared.

She uttered a little cry of pain. "Save them?"

"Yes, save them. Get them out of the valley, take them out of the country, far away where they and *you*—"

"But I can't go," she wailed. "I'm afraid. I'm bound. It *can't* be broken. If I dared—if I tried to go they would catch me. They would hang Uncle Jim and leave Mother Jane alone there to starve."

"Fay, Lassiter and Jane both will starve—at least they will die there if we do not save them. You have been terribly wronged. You're a slave. You're not a wife."

"They—said I'll be burned in hell if I don't marry him. . . . Mother Jane never taught me about God. I don't know. But *he*—he said God was there. I dare not break it."

"Fay, you have been deceived by old men. Let them have their creed. But *you* mustn't accept it."

"John, what is God to you?"

"Dear child, I—I am not sure of that myself," he replied, huskily. "When all this trouble is behind us, surely I can help you to understand and you can help me. The fact that you are alive—that Lassiter

231

and Jane are alive—that I shall save you all—that
lifts me up. I tell you—Fay Larkin will be my
salvation."

"Your words trouble me. Oh, I shall be torn one
way and another. . . . But, John, I daren't run away.
I will not tell you where to find Lassiter and Mother
Jane."

"I shall find them. I have the Indian. He found
you for me. Nas Ta Bega will find Surprise Valley."

"Nas Ta Bega! . . . Oh, I remember. There was
an Indian with the Mormons who found us. But he
was a Piute."

"Nas Ta Bega never told me how he learned about
you. That he learned was enough. And, Fay, he
will find Surprise Valley. He will save Uncle Jim
and Mother Jane."

Fay's hands clasped Shefford's in strong, trembling pressure; the tears streamed down her white
cheeks; a tragic and eloquent joy convulsed her face.

"Oh, my friend, save them! But I can't go. . . .
Let them keep me! Let him kill me!"

"Him! Fay—he shall not harm you," replied
Shefford in passionate earnestness.

She caught the hand he had struck out with.

"You talk—you look like Uncle Jim when he spoke
of the Mormons," she said. "Then I used to be
afraid of him. He was so different. John, you
must not do anything about me. Let me be. It's
too late. He—and his men—they would hang you.
And I couldn't bear that. I've enough to bear
without losing my friend. Say you won't watch and
wait—for—for him."

Shefford had to promise her. Like an Indian she

gave expression to primitive feeling, for it certainly never occurred to her that, whatever Shefford might do, he was not the kind of man to wait in hiding for an enemy. Fay had faltered through her last speech and was now weak and nervous and frightened. Shefford took her back to the cabin.

"Fay, don't be distressed," he said. "I won't do anything right away. You can trust me. I won't be rash. I'll consult you before I make a move. I haven't any idea what I could do, anyway. . . . You must bear up. Why, it looks as if you're sorry I found you."

"Oh! I'm glad!" she whispered.

"Then if you're glad you mustn't break down this way again. Suppose some of the women happened to run into us."

"I won't again. It's only you—you surprised me so. I used to think how I'd like you to know—I wasn't really dead. But now—it's different. It hurts me here. Yet I'm glad—if my being alive makes you—a little happier."

Shefford felt that he had to go then. He could not trust himself any further.

"Good night, Fay," he said.

"Good night, John," she whispered. "I promise —to be good to-morrow."

She was crying softly when he left her. Twice he turned to see the dim, white, slender form against the gloom of the cabin. Then he went on under the piñons, blindly down the path, with his heart as heavy as lead. That night as he rolled in his blanket and stretched wearily he felt that he would never be able to sleep. The wind in the cedars made him shiver. The great stars seemed relentless, passionless, white eyes, mocking his little destiny and his pain. The huge shadow of the mountain resembled the shadow of the insurmountable barrier between Fay and him.

Her pitiful, childish promise to be good was in his mind when he went to her home on the next night. He wondered how she would be, and he realized a desperate need of self-control.

But that night Fay Larkin was a different girl. In the dark, before she spoke, he felt a difference that afforded him surprise and relief. He greeted her as usual. And then it seemed, though not at all clearly, that he was listening to a girl, strangely and unconsciously glad to see him, who spoke with deeper note in her voice, who talked where always she had listened, whose sadness was there under an eagerness, a subdued gaiety as new to her, as sweet as it was bewildering. And he responded with emotion, so that the hour passed swiftly, and he found himself back in camp, in a kind of dream, unable to remember much of what she had said, sure only of this strange sweetness suddenly come to her.

Upon the following night, however, he discovered what had wrought this singular change in Fay Larkin. She loved him and she did not know it. How passionately sweet and sad and painful was that realization for Shefford! The hour spent with her then was only a moment.

He walked under the stars that night and they shed a glorious light upon him. He tried to think, to plan, but the sweetness of remembered word or look made mental effort almost impossible. He got as far as the thought that he would do well to drift, to wait till she learned she loved him, and then, perhaps, she could be persuaded to let him take her and Lassiter and Jane away together.

And from that night he went at his work and the part he played in the village with a zeal and a cunning that left him free to seek Fay when he chose.

Sometimes in the afternoon, always for a while in the evening, he was with her. They climbed the walls, and sat upon a lonely height to look afar; they walked under the stars, and the cedars, and the shadows of the great cliffs. She had a beautiful mind. Listening to her, he imagined he saw down into beautiful Surprise Valley with all its weird shadows, its colored walls and painted caves, its golden shafts of morning light and the red haze at sunset; and he felt the silence that must have been there, and the singing of the wind in the cliffs, and the sweetness and fragrance of the flowers, and the wildness of it all. Love had worked a marvelous transformation in this girl who had lived her life in a cañon. The burden upon her did not weigh heavily. She could not have an unhappy thought. She spoke of the village, of her Mormon companions, of daily happenings, of Stonebridge, of many things in a matter-of-fact way that showed how little they occupied her mind. She even spoke of sealed wives in a kind of dreamy abstraction. Something had possession of her, something as strong as the nature which had developed her, and in its power she, in her simplicity, was utterly unconscious, a watching and feeling girl. A strange, witching, radiant beauty lurked in her smile. And Shefford heard her laugh in his dreams.

The weeks slipped by. The black mountain took on a white cap of snow; in the early mornings there was ice in the crevices on the heights and frost in the valley. In the sheltered cañons where sunshine seemed to linger it was warm and pleasant, so that winter did not kill the flowers.

Shefford waited so long for Fay's awakening that he believed it would never come, and, believing, had not the heart to force it upon her. Then there was a growing fear with him. What would Fay Larkin do when she awakened to the truth? Fay was indeed like that white and fragile lily which bloomed in the silent, lonely cañons, but the same nature that had created it had created her. Would she droop as the lily would in a furnace blast? More than that, he feared a sudden flashing into life of strength, power, passion, hate. She did not hate yet because she did not yet realize love. She was utterly innocent of any wrong having been done her. More and more he began to fear, and a foreboding grew upon him. He made up his mind to broach the subject of Surprise Valley and of escaping with Lassiter and Jane; still, every time he was with Fay the girl and her beauty and her love were so wonderful that he put off the ordeal till the next night. As time flew by he excused his vacillation on the score that winter was not a good time to try to cross the desert. There was no grass for the mustangs, except in well-known valleys, and these he must shun. Spring would soon come. So the days passed, and he loved Fay more all the time, desperately living out to its limit the sweetness of every moment with her, and paying for his bliss in the increasing trouble that beset him when once away from her charm.

One starry night, about ten o'clock, he went, as was his custom, to drink at the spring. Upon his return to the cedars Nas Ta Bega, who slept under the same tree with him, had arisen, with his blanket hanging half off his shoulder.

"Listen," said the Indian.

Shefford took one glance at the dark, somber face, with its inscrutable eyes, now so strange and piercing, and then, with a kind of cold excitement, he faced the way the Indian looked, and listened. But he heard only the soft moan of the night wind in the cedars.

Nas Ta Bega kept the rigidity of his position for a moment, and then he relaxed, and stood at ease. Shefford knew the Indian had made a certainty of what must have been a doubtful sound. And Shefford leaned his ear to the wind and strained his hearing.

Then the soft night breeze brought a faint patter —the slow trot of horses on a hard trail Some one was coming into the village at a late hour. Shefford thought of Joe Lake. But Joe lay right behind him, asleep in his blankets. It could not be Withers, for the trader was in Durango at that time. Shefford thought of Willetts and Shadd.

'Who's coming?" he asked low of the Indian.

Nas Ta Bega pointed down the trail without speaking.

Shefford peered through the white dim haze of starlight and presently he made out moving figures. Horses, with riders—a string of them—one—two— three—four—five—and he counted up to eleven. Eleven horsemen riding into the village! He was amazed, and suddenly keenly anxious. This visit might be one of Shadd's raids.

"Shadd's gang!" he whispered.

"No, Bi Nai," replied Nas Ta Bega, and he drew Shefford farther into the shade of the cedars. His voice, his action, the way he kept a hand on Shefford's shoulder, all this told much to the young man.

Mormons come on a night visit! Shefford realized it with a slight shock. Then swift as a lightning flash he was rent by another shock—one that brought cold moisture to his brow and to his heart a flame of hell.

He was shaking when he sank down to find the support of a log. Like a shadow the Indian silently moved away. Shefford watched the eleven horses pass the camp, go down the road, to disappear in the village. They vanished, and the soft clip-clops of hoofs died away. There was nothing left to prove he had not dreamed.

Nothing to prove it except this sudden terrible demoralization of his physical and spiritual being! While he peered out into the valley, toward the black patch of cedars and piñons that hid the cabins, moments and moments passed, and in them he was gripped with cold and fire.

Was the Mormon who had abducted Fay—the

man with the cruel voice—was he among those eleven horsemen? He might not have been. What a torturing hope! But vain—vain, for inevitably he must be among them. He was there in the cabin already. He had dismounted, tied his horse, had knocked on her door. Did he need to knock? No, he would go in, he would call her in that cruel voice, and then . . .

Shefford pulled a blanket from his bed and covered his cold and trembling body. He had sunk down off the log, was leaning back upon it. The stars were pale, far off, and the valley seemed unreal. He found himself listening—listening with sick and terrible earnestness, trying to hear against the thrum and beat of his heart, straining to catch a sound in all that cold, star-blanched, silent valley. But he could hear no sound. It was as if death held the valley in its perfect silence. How he hated that silence! There ought to have been a million horrible, bellowing demons making the night hideous. Did the stars serenely look down upon the lonely cabins of these exiles? Was there no thunderbolt to drop down from that dark and looming mountain upon the silent cabin where tragedy had entered? In all the world, under the sea, in the abysmal caves, in the vast spaces of the air, there was no such terrible silence as this. A scream, a long cry, a moan—these were natural to a woman, and why did not one of these sealed wives, why did not Fay Larkin, damn this everlasting acquiescent silence? Perhaps she would fly out of her cabin, come running along the path. Shefford peered into the bright patches of starlight and into the shadows of the cedars. But he

saw no moving form in the open, no dim white shape
against the gloom. And he heard no sound—not
even a whisper of wind in the branches overhead.

Nas Ta Bega returned to the shade of the cedars
and, lying down on his blankets, covered himself and
went to sleep. The fact seemed to bring bitter reality to Shefford. Nothing was going to happen. The
valley was to be the same this night as any other
night. Shefford accepted the truth. He experienced a kind of self-pity. The night he had thought
so much about, prepared for, and had forgotten had,
now arrived. Then he threw another blanket round
him, and, cold, dark, grim, he faced that lonely vigil,
meaning to sit there, wide-eyed, to endure and to
wait.

Jealousy and pain, following his frenzy, abided
with him long hours, and when they passed he
divined that selfishness passed with them. What he
suffered then was for Fay Larkin and for her sisters
in misfortune. He grew big enough to pity these
fanatics. The fiery, racing tide of blood that had
made of him only an animal had cooled with thought
of others. Still he feared that stultifying thing which
must have been hate. What a tempest had raged
within him! This blood of his, that had received a
stronger strain from his desert life, might in a single
moment flood out reason and intellect and make him
a vengeful man. So in those starlit hours that
dragged interminably he looked deep into his heart
and tried to fortify himself against a dark and evil
moment to come.

Midnight—and the valley seemed a tomb! Did
he alone keep wakeful? The sky was a darker blue,

the stars burned a whiter fire, the peaks stood looming and vast, tranquil sentinels of that valley, and the wind rose to sigh, to breathe, to mourn through the cedars. It was a sad music. The Indian lay prone, dark face to the stars. Joe Lake lay prone, sleeping as quietly, with his dark face exposed to the starlight. The gentle movement of the cedar branches changed the shape of the bright patches on the grass where shadow and light met. The walls of the valley waved upward, dark below and growing paler, to shine faintly at the rounded rims. And there was a tiny, silvery tinkle of running water over stones.

Here was a little nook of the vast world. Here were tranquillity, beauty, music, loneliness, life. Shefford wondered—did he alone keep watchful? Did he feel that he could see dark, wide eyes peering into the gloom? And it came to him after a time that he was not alone in his vigil, nor was Fay Larkin alone in her agony. There was some one else in the valley, a great and breathing and watchful spirit. It entered into Shefford's soul and he trembled. What had come to him? And he answered—only added pain and new love, and a strange strength from the firmament and the peaks and the silence and the shadows.

The bright belt with its three radiant stars sank behind the western wall and there was a paler gloom upon the valley.

Then a few lights twinkled in the darkness that enveloped the cabins; a woman's laugh strangely broke the silence, profaning it, giving the lie to that somber yoke which seemed to consist of the very shadows; the voices of men were heard, and then the slow clip-clop of trotting horses on the hard trail.

Shefford saw the Mormons file out into the paling starlight, ride down the valley, and vanish in the gray gloom. He was aware that the Indian sat up to watch the procession ride by, and that Joe turned over, as if disturbed.

One by one the stars went out. The valley became a place of gray shadows. In the east a light glowed. Shefford sat there, haggard and worn, watching the coming of the dawn, the kindling of the light; and had the power been his the dawn would never have broken and the rose and gold never have tipped the lofty peaks.

Shefford attended to his camp chores as usual. Several times he was aware of Joe's close scrutiny, and finally, without looking at him, Shefford told of the visit of the Mormons. A violent expulsion of breath was Joe's answer and it might have been a curse. Straightway Joe ceased his cheery whistling and became as somber as the Indian. The camp was silent; the men did not look at one another. While they sat at breakfast Shefford's back was turned toward the village· he had not looked in that direction since dawn.

"Ugh!" suddenly exclaimed Nas Ta Bega.

Joe Lake muttered low and deep, and this time there was no mistake about the nature of his speech. Shefford did not have the courage to turn to see what had caused these exclamations. He knew since to-day had dawned that there was calamity in the air.

"Shefford, I reckon if I know women there's a

little hell coming to you," said the Mormon, significantly.

Shefford wheeled as if a powerful force had turned
him on a pivot. He saw Fay Larkin. She seemed
to be almost running. She was unhooded and her
bright hair streamed down. Her swift, lithe action
was without its usual grace. She looked wild, and
she almost fell crossing the stepping-stones of the
brook.

Joe hurried to meet her, took hold of her arm and
spoke, but she did not seem to hear him. She drew
him along with her, up the little bench under the
cedars straight toward Shefford. Her face held a
white, mute agony, as if in the hour of strife it had
hardened into marble. But her eyes were dark-
purple fire—windows of an extraordinarily intense
and vital life. In one night the girl had become a
woman. But the blight Shefford had dreaded to see
—the withering of the exquisite soul and spirit and
purity he had considered inevitable, just as inevitable as the death of something similar in the flower
she resembled, when it was broken and defiled—
nothing of this was manifest in her. Straight and
swiftly she came to him back in the shade of the
cedars and took hold of his hands.

"Last night—*he came!*" she said.

"Yes—Fay—I—I know," replied Shefford, haltingly.

He was tremblingly conscious of amaze at her—of
something wonderful in her. She did not heed Joe,
who stepped aside a little; she did not see Nas Ta
Bega, who sat motionless on a log, apparently ob-
livious to her presence.

243

"You knew he came?"

"Yes, Fay. I was awake when—they rode in. I watched them. I sat up all night. I saw them ride away."

"If you knew when he came why didn't you run to me—to get to me before he did?"

Her question was unanswerable. It had the force of a blow. It stunned him. Its sharp, frank directness sprang from a simplicity and a strength that had not been nurtured in the life he had lived. So far men had wandered from truth and nature!

"I came to you as soon as I was able," she went on. "I must have fainted. I just had to drag myself around. . . . And now I can tell you."

He was powerless to reply, as if she had put another unanswerable question. What did she mean to tell him? What might she not tell him? She loosed her hands from his and lifted them to his shoulders, and that was the first conscious action of feeling, of intimacy, which she had ever shown. It quite robbed Shefford of strength, and in spite of his sorrow there was an indefinable thrill in her touch. He looked at her, saw the white-and-gold beauty that was hers yesterday and seemed changed to-day, and he recognized Fay Larkin in a woman he did not know.

"Listen! He came—"

"Fay, don't—tell me," interrupted Shefford.

"I *will* tell you," she said.

Did the instinct of love teach her how to mitigate his pain? Shefford felt that, as he felt the new-born strength in her.

"Listen," she went on. "He came when I was

undressing for bed. I heard the horse. He knocked
on the door. Something terrible happened to me
then. I felt sick and my head wasn't clear. I
remember next—his being in the room—the lamp
was out—I couldn't see very well. He thought I
was sick and he gave me a drink and let the air blow
in on me through the window. I remember I lay
back in the chair and I thought. And I listened.
When would you come? I didn't feel that you could
leave me there alone with him. For his coming was
different this time. That pain like a blade in my
side!... When it came I was not the same. I loved
you. I understood then. I belonged to you. I
couldn't let him touch me. I had never been his
wife. When I realized this—that he was there, that
you might suffer for it—I cried right out.

"He thought I was sick. He worked over me.
He gave me medicine. And then he prayed. I saw
him, in the dark, on his knees, praying for me.
That seemed strange. Yet he was kind, so kind
that I begged him to let me go. I was not a
Mormon. I couldn't marry him. I begged him
to let me go.

"Then he thought I had been deceiving him. He
fell into a fury. He talked for a long time. He
called upon God to visit my sins upon me. He
tried to make me pray. But I wouldn't. And then
—I fought him. I'd have screamed for you had he
not smothered me. I got weak. . . . And you never
came. I know I thought you would come. But
you didn't. Then I—I gave out. And after—
some time—I must have fainted."

"Fay! For Heaven's sake, how could I come to
245.

you?" burst out Shefford, hoarse and white with remorse, passion, pain.

"If I'm any man's wife I'm yours. It's a thing you *feel*, isn't it? I know that now. . . . But I want to know what to do?"

"Fay!" he cried, huskily.

"I'm sick of it all. If it weren't for you I'd climb the wall and throw myself off. That would be easy for me. I'd love to die that way. All my life I've been high up on the walls. To fall would be nothing!"

"Oh, you mustn't talk like that!"

"Do you love me?" she asked, with a low and deathless sweetness.

"Love you? With all my heart! Nothing can change that!"

"Do you want me—as you used to want the Fay Larkin lost in Surprise Valley? Do you love me that way? I understand things better than before, but still—not all. I *am* Fay Larkin. I think I must have dreamed of you all my life. I was glad when you came here. I've been happy lately. I forgot— till last night. Maybe it needed that to make me see I've loved you all the time. . . . And I fought him like a wildcat! . . . Tell me the truth. I *feel* I'm yours. Is that true? If I'm not—I'll not live another hour. Something holds me up. I am the same. . . . Do you want me?"

"Yes, Fay Larkin, I want you," replied Shefford, steadily, with his grip on her arms.

"Then take me away. I don't want to live here another hour."

"Fay, I'll take you. But it can't be done at once.

We must plan. I need help. There are Lassiter and Jane to get out of Surprise Valley. Give me time, dear—give me time. It 'll be a hard job. And we must plan so we can positively get away. Give me time, Fay."

"Suppose *he* comes back?" she queried. with a singular depth of voice.

"We'll have to risk that," replied Shefford, miserably. "But—he won't come soon."

"He said he would," she flashed.

Shefford seemed to freeze inwardly with her words. Love had made her a woman and now the woman in her was speaking. She saw the truth as he could not see it. And the truth was nature. She had been hidden all her life from the world, from knowledge as he had it, yet when love betrayed her womanhood to her she acquired all its subtlety.

"If I wait and he *does* come will you keep me from him?" she asked.

"How can I? I'm staking all on the chance of his not coming soon. . . . But, Fay, if he does come and I don't give up our secret—how on earth can I keep you from him?" demanded Shefford.

"If you love me you will do it," she said, as simply as if she were fate.

"But how?" cried Shefford, almost beside himself.

"You are a man. Any man would save the woman who loves him from—from— Oh, from a beast! . . . How would Lassiter do it?"

"Lassiter!"

"*You can kill him!*"

It was there, deep and full in her voice, the strength of the elemental forces that had surrounded her, primitive passion and hate and love, as they were in woman in the beginning.

"My God!" Shefford cried aloud with his spirit when all that was red in him sprang again into a flame of hell. That was what had been wrong with him last night. He could kill this stealthy night-rider, and now, face to face with Fay, who had never been so beautiful and wonderful as in this hour when she made love the only and the sacred thing of life, now he had it in him to kill. Yet, murder—even to kill a brute—that was not for John Shefford, not the way for him to save a woman. Reason and wisdom still fought the passion in him. If he could but cling to them—have them with him in the dark and contending hour!

She leaned against him now, exhausted, her soul in her eyes, and they saw only him. Shefford was all but powerless to resist the longing to take her into his arms, to hold her to his heart, to let himself go. Did not her love give her to him? Shefford gazed helplessly at the stricken Joe Lake, at the somber Indian, as if from them he expected help.

"I know him now," said Fay, breaking the silence with startling suddenness.

"What!"

"I've seen him in the light. I flashed a candle in his face. I saw it. I know him now. He was there at Stonebridge with us, and I never knew him. But I know him now. His name is—"

"For God's sake don't tell me who he is!" implored Shefford.

Ignorance was Shefford's safeguard against him-self. To make a name of this heretofore intangible man, to give him an identity apart from the crowd, to be able to recognize him—that for Shefford would be fatal.

"Fay—tell me—no more," he said, brokenly. "I love you and I will give you my life. Trust me. I swear I'll save you."

"Will you take me away soon?"

"Yes."

She appeared satisfied with that and dropped her hands and moved back from him. A light flitted over her white face, and her eyes grew dark and humid, losing their fire in changing, shadowing thought of submission, of trust, of hope.

"I can lead you to Surprise Valley," she said. "I feel the way. It's there!" And she pointed to the west.

"Fay, we'll go—soon. I must plan. I'll see you to-night. Then we'll talk. Run home now, before some of the women see you here."

She said good-by and started away under the cedars, out into the open where her hair shone like gold in the sunlight, and she took the stepping-stones with her old free grace, and strode down the path swift and lithe as an Indian. Once she turned to wave a hand.

Shefford watched her with a torture of pride, love, hope, and fear contending within him.

XIV

THE NAVAJO

THAT morning a Piute rode into the valley. Shefford recognized him as the brave whc had been in love with Glen Naspa. The moment Nas Ta Bega saw this visitor he made a singular motion with his hands—a motion that somehow to Shefford suggested despair—and then he waited, somber and statuesque, for the messenger to come to him. It was the Piute who did all the talking, and that was brief. Then the Navajo stood motionless, with his hands crossed over his breast. Shefford drew near and waited.

"Bi Nai," said the Navajo, "Nas Ta Bega said his sister would come home some day. . . . Glen Naspa is in the hogan of her grandfather."

He spoke in his usual slow, guttural voice, and he might have been bronze for all the emotion he expressed; yet Shefford instinctively felt the despair that had been hinted to him, and he put his hand on the Indian's shoulder.

"If I am the Navajo's brother, then I am brother to Glen Naspa," he said. "I will go with you to the hogan of Hosteen Doetin."

Nas Ta Bega went away into the valley for the

horses. Shefford hurried to the village, made his
excuses at the school, and then called to explain to
Fay that trouble of some kind had come to the
Indian.

Soon afterward he was riding Nack-yal on the
rough and winding trail up through the broken
country of cliffs and cañons to the great league-long
sage and cedar slope of the mountain. It was weeks
since he had ridden the mustang. Nack-yal was fat
and lazy. He loved his master, but he did not like
the climb, and so fell far behind the lean and wiry
pony that carried Nas Ta Bega. The sage levels
were as purple as the haze of the distance, and there
was a bitter-sweet tang on the strong, cool wind.
The sun was gold behind the dark line of fringe on
the mountain-top. A flock of sheep swept down one
of the sage levels, looking like a narrow stream of
white and black and brown. It was always amazing
for Shefford to see how swiftly these Navajo sheep
grazed along. Wild mustangs plunged out of the
cedar clumps and stood upon the ridges, whistling
defiance or curiosity, and their manes and tails
waved in the wind.

Shefford mounted slowly to the cedar bench in
the midst of which were hidden the few hogans.
And he halted at the edge to·dismount and take a
look at that downward-sweeping world of color, of
wide space, at the wild desert upland which from
there unrolled its magnificent panorama.

Then he passed on into the cedars. How strange
to hear the lambs bleating again! Lambing-time
had come early, but still spring was there in the new
green of grass, in the bright upland flower. He led

his mustang out of the cedars into the cleared circle. It was full of colts and lambs, and there were the shepherd-dogs and a few old rams and ewes. But the circle was a quiet place this day. There were no Indians in sight. Shefford loosened the saddle-girths on Nack-yal and, leaving him to graze, went toward the hogan of Hosteen Doetin. A blanket was hung across the door. Shefford heard a low chanting. He waited beside the door till the covering was pulled in, then he entered.

Hosteen Doetin met him, clasped his hand. The old Navajo could not speak; his fine face was working in grief; tears streamed from his dim old eyes and rolled down his wrinkled cheeks. His sorrow was no different from a white man's sorrow. Beyond him Shefford saw Nas Ta Bega standing with folded arms, somehow terrible in his somber impassiveness. At his feet crouched the old woman, Hosteen Doetin's wife, and beside her, prone and quiet, half covered with a blanket, lay Glen Naspa.

She was dead. To Shefford she seemed older than when he had last seen her. And she was beautiful. Calm, cold, dark, with only bitter lips to give the lie to peace! There was a story in those lips.

At her side, half hidden under the fold of blanket, lay a tiny bundle. Its human shape startled Shefford. Then he did not need to be told the tragedy. When he looked again at Glen Naspa's face he seemed to understand all that had made her older, to feel the pain that had lined and set her lips.

She was dead, and she was the last of Nas Ta Bega's family. In the old grandfather's agony, in the wild chant of the stricken grandmother, in the brother's stern and terrible calmness Shefford felt more than the death of a loved one. The shadow of ruin, of doom, of death hovered over the girl and her family and her tribe and her race. There was no consolation to offer these relatives of Glen Naspa. Shefford took one more fascinated gaze at her dark, eloquent, prophetic face, at the tragic tiny shape by her side, and then with bowed head he left the hogan.

Outside he paced to and fro, with an aching heart for Nas Ta Bega; with something of the white man's burden of crime toward the Indian weighing upon his soul.

Old Hosteen Doetin came to him with shaking hands and words memorable of the time Glen Naspa left his hogan.

"Me no savvy Jesus Christ. Me hungry. Me no eat Jesus Christ!"

That seemed to be all of his trouble that he could express to Shefford. He could not understand the religion of the missionary, this Jesus Christ who had called his granddaughter away. And the great fear of an old Indian was not death, but hunger. Shefford remembered a custom of the Navajos, a thing barbarous looked at with a white man's mind. If an old Indian failed on a long march he was inclosed by a wall of stones, given plenty to eat and drink, and left there to die in the desert. Not death did he fear, but hunger! Old Hosteen Doetin expected to starve, now that the young and strong squaw of his family was gone.

Shefford spoke in his halting Navajo and assured the old Indian that Nas Ta Bega would never let him starve.

At sunset Shefford stood with Nas Ta Bega facing the west. The Indian was magnificent in repose. He watched the sun go down upon the day that had seen the burial of the last of his family. He resembled an impassive destiny, upon which no shocks fell. He had the light of that flaring golden sky in his face, the majesty of the mountain in his mien, the silence of the great gulf below on his lips. This educated Navajo, who had reverted to the life of his ancestors, found in the wildness and loneliness of his environment a strength no white teaching could ever have given him. Shefford sensed in him a measureless grief, an impenetrable gloom, a tragic acceptance of the meaning of Glen Naspa's ruin and death—the vanishing of his race from the earth. Death had written the law of such bitter truth round Glen Naspa's lips, and the same truth was here in the grandeur and gloom of the Navajo.

"Bi Nai," he said, with the beautiful sonorous roll in his voice, "Glen Naspa is in her grave and there are no paths to the place of her sleep. Glen Naspa is gone."

"Gone! Where? Nas Ta Bega, remember I lost my own faith, and I have not yet learned yours."

"The Navajo has one mother—the earth. Her body has gone to the earth and it will become dust. But her spirit is in the air. It shall whisper to me from the wind. I shall hear it on running waters. It will hide in the morning music of a mocking-bird and in the lonely night cry of the cañon hawk. Her blood will go to make the red of the Indian flowers and her soul will rest at midnight in the lily that opens only to the moon. She will wait in the shadow for me, and live in the great mountain that is my home, and for ever step behind me on the trail."

"You will kill Willetts?" demanded Shefford.

"The Navajo will not seek the missionary."

"But if you meet him you'll kill him?"

"Bi Nai, would Nas Ta Bega kill after it is too late? What good could come? The Navajo is above revenge."

"If he crosses my trail I think I couldn't help but kill him," muttered Shefford in a passion that wrung the threat from him.

The Indian put his arm round the white man's shoulders.

"Bi Nai, long ago I made you my brother. And now you make me your brother. Is it not so? Glen Naspa's spirit calls for wisdom, not revenge. Willetts must be a bad man. But we'll let him live. Life will punish him. Who knows if he was all to blame? Glen Naspa was only one pretty Indian girl. There are many white men in the desert. She loved a white man when she was a baby. The thing was a curse. . . . Listen, Bi Nai, and the Navajo will talk.

"Many years ago the Spanish padres, the first white men, came into the land of the Indian. Their search was for gold. But they were not wicked men. They did not steal and kill. They taught the Indian many useful things. They brought him horses. But when they went away they left him unsatisfied with his life and his god.

"Then came the pioneers. They crossed the great river and took the pasture-lands and the hunting-grounds of the Indian. They drove him backward, and the Indian grew sullen. He began to fight. The white man's government made treaties with the Indian, and these were broken. Then war came—fierce and bloody war. The Indian was driven to the waste places. The stream of pioneers, like a march of ants, spread on into the desert. Every valley where grass grew, every river, became a place for farms and towns. Cattle choked the water-holes where the buffalo and deer had once gone to drink. The forests in the hills were cut and the springs dried up. And the pioneers followed to the edge of the desert.

"Then came the prospectors, mad, like the padres for the gleam of gold. The day was not long enough for them to dig in the creeks and the cañons; they worked in the night. And they brought weapons and rum to the Indian, to buy from him the secret of the places where the shining gold lay hidden.

"Then came the traders. And they traded with the Indian. They gave him little for much, and that little changed his life. He learned a taste for the sweet foods of the white man. Because he could trade for a sack of flour he worked less in the field. And the very fiber of his bones softened.

"Then came the missionaries. They were prose-lytizers for converts to their religion. The mission-aries are good men. There may be a bad missionary, like Willetts, the same as there are bad men in other callings, or bad Indians. They say Shadd is a half-breed. But the Piutes can tell you he is a full-blood, and he, like me, was sent to a white man's school. In the beginning the missionaries did well for the Indian. They taught him cleaner ways of living, better farming, useful work with tools—many good things. But the wrong to the Indian was the undermining of his faith. It was not humanity that sent the missionary to the Indian. Humanity would have helped the Indian in his ignorance of sickness and work, and left him his god. For to trouble the Indian about his god worked at the roots of his nature.

"The beauty of the Indian's life is in his love of the open, of all that is nature, of silence, freedom, wildness. It is a beauty of mind and soul. The Indian would have been content to watch and feel. To a white man he might be dirty and lazy—content to dream life away without trouble or what the white man calls evolution. The Indian might seem cruel because he leaves his old father out in the desert to die. But the old man wants to die that way, alone with his spirits and the sunset. And the white man's medicine keeps his old father alive days and days after he ought to be dead. Which is more cruel? The Navajos used to fight with other tribes, and then they were stronger men than they are to-day.

"But leaving religion, greed, and war out of the question, contact with the white man would alone have ruined the Indian. The Indian and the white man cannot mix. The Indian brave learns the habits of the white man, acquires his diseases, and has not the mind or body to withstand them. The Indian girl learns to love the white man—and that is death of her Indian soul, if not of life.

"So the red man is passing. Tribes once powerful have died in the life of Nas Ta Bega. The curse of the white man is already heavy upon my race in the south. Here in the north, in the wildest corner of the desert, chased here by the great soldier, Carson, the Navajo has made his last stand.

"Bi Nai, you have seen the shadow in the hogan of Hosteen Doetin. Glen Naspa has gone to her grave, and no sisters, no children, will make paths to the place of her sleep. Nas Ta Bega will never have a wife—a child. He sees the end. It is the sunset of the Navajo. . . . Bi Nai, the Navajo is dying—dying —dying!"

XV

WILD JUSTICE

A CRESCENT moon hung above the lofty peak over the valley and a train of white stars ran along the bold rim of the western wall. A few young frogs peeped plaintively. The night was cool, yet had a touch of balmy spring, and a sweeter fragrance, as if the cedars and piñons had freshened in the warm sun of that day.

Shefford and Fay were walking in the aisles of moonlight and the patches of shade, and Nas Ta Bega, more than ever a shadow of his white brother, followed them silently.

"Fay, it's growing late. Feel the dew?" said Shefford. "Come, I must take you back."

"But the time's so short. I have said nothing that I wanted to say," she replied.

"Say it quickly, then, as we go."

"After all, it's only—will you take me away soon?"

"Yes, very soon. The Indian and I have talked. But we've made no plan yet. There are only three ways to get out of this country. By Stonebridge, by Kayenta and Durango, and by Red Lake. We must choose one. All are dangerous. We must lose time finding Surprise Valley. I hoped the Indian could find it. Then we'd bring Lassiter and Jane here and hide them near till dark, then take you and go. That would give us a night's start. But you must help us to Surprise Valley."

"I can go right to it, blindfolded, or in the dark. . . . Oh, John, hurry! I dread the wait. *He* might come again."

"Joe says—they won't come very soon."

"Is it far—where we're going—out of the country?"

"Ten days' hard riding."

"Oh! That night ride to and from Stonebridge nearly killed me. But I could walk very far, and climb for ever."

"Fay, we'll get out of the country if I have to carry you."

When they arrived at the cabin Fay turned on the porch step and, with her face nearer a level with his, white and sweet in the moonlight, with her eyes shining and unfathomable, she was more than beautiful.

"You've never been inside my house," she said. "Come in. I've something for you."

"But it's late," he remonstrated. "I suppose you've got me a cake or pie—something to eat. You women all think Joe and I have to be fed."

"No. You'd never guess. Come in," she said, and the rare smile on her face was something Shefford would have gone far to see.

"Well, then, for a minute."

He crossed the porch, the threshold, and entered her home. Her dim, white shape moved in the darkness. And he followed into a room where the moon shone through the open window, giving soft, mellow, shadowy light. He discerned objects, but not clearly, for his senses seemed absorbed in the strange warmth and intimacy of being for the first time with her in her home.

"No, it's not good to eat," she said, and her laugh was happy. "Here—"

Suddenly she abruptly ceased speaking. Shefford saw her plainly, and the slender form had stiffened, alert and strained. She was listening.

"What was that?" she whispered.

"I didn't hear anything," he whispered back.

He stepped softly nearer the open window and listened.

Clip-clop! clip-clop! clip-clop! Hard hoofs on the hard path outside!

A strong and rippling thrill went over Shefford. In the soft light her eyes seemed unnaturally large and black and fearful.

Clip-clop! clip-clop!

The horse stopped outside. Then followed a metallic clink of spur against stirrup—thud of boots on hard ground—heavy footsteps upon the porch.

A swift, cold contraction of throat, of breast, convulsed Shefford. His only thought was that he could not think.

"Ho—Mary!"

A voice liberated both Shefford's muscle and mind —a voice of strange, vibrant power. Authority of religion and cruelty of will—these Mormon attributes constituted that power. And Shefford suffered a transformation which must have been ordered by demons. That sudden flame seemed to

261

curl and twine and shoot along his veins with blast-ing force. A rancorous and terrible cry leaped to his lips.

"Ho—Mary!" Then came a heavy tread across the threshold of the outer room.

Shefford dared not look at Fay. Yet, dimly, from the corner of his eye, he saw her, a pale shadow, turned to stone, with her arms out. If he looked, if he made sure of that, he was lost. When had he drawn his gun? It was there, a dark and glinting thing in his hand. He must fly—not through cowardice and fear, but because in one more moment he would kill a man. Swift as the thought he dove through the open window. And, leaping up, he ran under the dark piñons toward camp.

Joe Lake had been out late himself. He sat by the fire, smoking his pipe. He must have seen or heard Shefford coming, for he rose with unwonted alacrity, and he kicked the smoldering logs into a flickering blaze.

Shefford, realizing his deliverance, came panting, staggering into the light. The Mormon uttered an exclamation. Then he spoke, anxiously, but what he said was not clear in Shefford's thick and throb-bing ears. He dropped his pipe, a sign of perturba-tion, and he stared.

But Shefford, without a word, lunged swiftly away into the shadow of the cedars. He found relief in action. He began a steep ascent of the east wall, a dangerous slant he had never dared even in day-light, and he climbed it without a slip. Danger, steep walls, perilous heights, night, and black cañon the same—these he never thought of. But something drove him to desperate effort, that the hours might seem short.

The red sun was tipping the eastern wall when he returned to camp, and he was neither calm nor sure of himself nor ready for sleep or food. Only he had put the night behind him.

The Indian showed no surprise. But Joe Lake's jaw dropped and his eyes rolled. Moreover, Joe bore a singular aspect, the exact nature of which did not at once dawn upon Shefford.

"By God! you've got nerve—or you're crazy!" he ejaculated, hoarsely.

Then it was Shefford's turn to stare. The Mormon was haggard, grieved, frightened, and utterly amazed. He appeared to be trying to make certain of Shefford's being there in the flesh and then to find reason for it.

"I've no nerve and I am crazy," replied Shefford. "But, Joe—what do you mean? Why do you look at me like that?"

"I reckon if I get your horse that 'll square us. Did you come back for him? You'd better hit the trail quick."

"It's you now who 're crazy," burst out Shefford.

"Wish to God I was," replied Joe.

It was then Shefford realized catastrophe, and cold fear gnawed at his vitals, so that he was sick.

"Joe, what has happened?" he asked, with the blood thick in his heart.

"Hadn't you better tell me?" demanded the Mormon, and a red wave blotted out the haggard shade of his face.

263

"You talk like a fool," said Shefford, sharply, and he strode right up to Joe.

"See here, Shefford, we've been pards. You're making it hard for me. Reckon you ain't square."

Shefford shot out a long arm and his hand clutched the Mormon's burly shoulder.

"Why am I not square? What do you mean?"

Joe swallowed hard and gave himself a shake. Then he eyed his comrade steadily.

"I was afraid you'd kill him. I reckon I can't blame you. I'll help you get away. . . . And I'm a Mormon! Do you take the hunch? . . . But don't deny you killed him!"

"Killed whom?" gasped Shefford.

"Her husband!"

Shefford seemed stricken by a slow, paralyzing horror. The Mormon's changing face grew huge and indistinct and awful in his sight. He was clutched and shaken in Joe's rude hands, yet scarcely felt them. Joe seemed to be bellowing at him, but the voice was far off. Then Shefford began to see, to hear through some cold and terrible deadness that had come between him and everything.

"Say *you* killed him!" hoarsely supplicated the Mormon.

Shefford had not yet control of speech. Something in his gaze appeared to drive Joe frantic.

"Damn you! Tell me quick. Say *you* killed him! . . . If you want to know my stand, why, I'm glad! . . . Shefford, don't look so stony! . . . For *her* sake, say you killed him!"

Shefford stood with a face as gray and still as stone. With a groan the Mormon drew away from

264

him and sank upon a log. He bowed his head; his broad shoulders heaved; husky sounds came from him. Then with a violent wrench he plunged to his feet and shook himself like a huge, savage dog.

"Reckon it's no time to weaken," he said, huskily, and with the words a dark, hard, somber bitterness came to his face.

"Where—is—she?" whispered Shefford.

"Shut up in the school-house," he replied.

"Did she—did she—"

"She neither denied nor confessed."

"Have you—seen her?"

"Yes."

"How did—she look?"

"Cool and quiet as the Indian there. . . . Game as hell! She always had stuff in her."

"Oh, Joe! . . . It's unbelievable!" cried Shefford. "That lovely, innocent girl! She couldn't — she couldn't."

"She's fixed him. Don't think of that. It's too late. We ought to have saved her."

"God! . . . She begged me to hurry—to take her away."

"Think what we can do *now* to save her," cut in the Mormon.

Shefford sustained a vivifying shock. "To save her?" he echoed.

"Think, man!"

"Joe, I can hit the trail and let you tell them I killed him," burst out Shefford in panting excitement.

"Reckon I can."

"So help me God I'll do it!"

The Mormon turned a dark and austere glance upon Shefford.

"You mustn't leave her. She killed him for your sake. . . . You must fight for her now—save her—take her away."

"But the law!"

"Law!" scoffed Joe. "In these wilds men get killed and there's no law. But if she's taken back to Stonebridge those iron-jawed old Mormons will make law enough to—to . . . Shefford, the thing is—get her away. Once out of the country, she's safe. Mormons keep their secrets."

"I'll take her. Joe, will you help me?"

Shefford, even in his agitation, felt the Mormon's silence to be a consent that need not have been asked. And Shefford had a passionate gratefulness toward his comrade. That stultifying and blinding prejudice which had always seemed to remove a Mormon outside the pale of certain virtue suffered final eclipse; and Joe Lake stood out a man, strange and crude, but with a heart and a soul.

"Joe, tell me what to do," said Shefford, with a simplicity that meant he needed only to be directed.

"Pull yourself together. Get your nerve back," replied Joe. "Reckon you'd better show yourself over there. No one saw you come in this morning —your absence from camp isn't known. It's better you seem curious and shocked like the rest of us. Come on. We'll go over. And afterward we'll get the Indian, and plan."

They left camp and, crossing the brook, took the shaded path toward the village. Hope of saving Fay, the need of all his strength and nerve and cun-

ning to effect that end, gave Shefford the supreme
courage to overcome his horror and fear. On that
short walk under the piñons to Fay's cabin he had
suffered many changes of emotion, but never anything like this change which made him fierce and
strong to fight, deep and crafty to plan, hard as iron
to endure.

The village appeared very quiet, though groups
of women stood at the doors of cabins. If they
talked, it was very low. Henninger and Smith, two
of the three Mormon men living in the village, were
standing before the closed door of the school-house.
A tigerish feeling thrilled Shefford when he saw them
on guard there. Shefford purposely avoided looking
at Fay's cabin as long as he could keep from it.
When he had to look he saw several hooded, whispering women in the yard, and Beal, the other Mormon
man, standing in the cabin door. Upon the porch
lay the long shape of a man, covered with blankets.

Shefford experienced a horrible curiosity.

"Say, Beal, I've fetched Shefford over," said
Lake. "He's pretty much cut up."

Beal wagged a solemn head, but said nothing.
His mind seemed absent or steeped in gloom, and he
looked up as one silently praying.

Joe Lake strode upon the little porch and, reaching
down, he stripped the blanket from the shrouded
form.

Shefford saw a sharp, cold, ghastly face. "Waggoner!" he whispered.

"Yes," replied Lake.

Waggoner! Shefford remembered the strange
power in his face, and, now that life had gone, that

power was stripped of all disguise. Death, in Shefford's years of ministry, had lain under his gaze many times and in a multiplicity of aspects, but never before had he seen it stamped so strangely. Shefford did not need to be told that here was a man who believed he had conversed with God on earth, who believed he had a divine right to rule women, who had a will that would not yield itself to death utterly. Waggoner, then, was the devil who had come masked to Surprise Valley, had forced a martyrdom upon Fay Larkin. And this was the Mormon who had made Fay Larkin a murderess. Shefford had hated him living, and now he hated him dead. Death here was robbed of all nobility, of pathos, of majesty. It was only retribution. Wild justice! But alas! that it had to be meted out by a white-souled girl whose innocence was as great as the unconscious savagery which she had assimilated from her lonely and wild environment. Shefford laid a despairing curse upon his own head, and a terrible remorse knocked at his heart. He had left her alone, this girl in whom love had made the great change—like a coward he had left her alone. That curse he visited upon himself because he had been the spirit and the motive of this wild justice, and his should have been the deed.

Joe Lake touched Shefford's arm and pointed at the haft of a knife protruding from Waggoner's breast. It was a wooden haft. Shefford had seen it before somewhere.

Then he was struck with what perhaps Joe meant him to see—the singular impression the haft gave of one sweeping, accurate, powerful stroke. A strong arm had driven that blade home. The haft was sunk deep; there was a little depression in the cloth; no blood showed; and the weapon looked as if it could not be pulled out. Shefford's thought went fatally and irresistibly to Fay Larkin's strong arm. He saw her flash that white arm and lift the heavy bucket from the spring with an ease he wondered at. He felt the strong clasp of her hand as she had given it to him in a flying leap across a crevice upon the walls. Yes, her fine hand and the round, strong arm possessed the strength to have given that blade its singular directness and force. The marvel was not in the physical action. It hid inscrutably in the mystery of deadly passion rising out of a gentle and sad heart.

Joe Lake drew up the blanket and shut from Shefford's fascinated gaze that spare form, that accusing knife, that face of strange, cruel power.

"Anybody been sent for?" asked Lake of Beal.

"Yes. An Indian boy went for the Piute. We'll send him to Stonebridge," replied the Mormon.

"How soon do you expect any one here from Stonebridge?"

"To-morrow, mebbe by noon."

"Meantime what's to be done with—this?"

"Elder Smith thinks the body should stay right here where it fell till they come from Stonebridge."

"Waggoner was found here, then?"

"Right here."

"Who found him?"

"Mother Smith. She came over early. An' the sight made her scream. The women all came runnin'. Mother Smith had to be put to bed."

'Who found—Mary?"

"See here, Joe, I told you all I knowed once before," replied the Mormon, testily.

"I've forgotten. Was sort of bewildered. Tell me again. . . . Who found—her?"

"The women folks. She laid right inside the door, in a dead faint. She hadn't undressed. There was blood on her hands an' a cut or scratch. The women fetched her to. But she wouldn't talk. Then Elder Smith come an' took her. They've got her locked up."

Then Joe led Shefford away from the cabin farther on into the village. When they were halted by the somber, grieving women it was Joe who did the talking. They passed the school-house, and here Shefford quickened his step. He could scarcely bear the feeling that rushed over him. And the Mormon gripped his arm as if he understood.

"Shefford, which one of these younger women do you reckon your best friend? Ruth?" asked Lake, earnestly.

"Ruth, by all means. Just lately I haven't seen her often. But we've been close friends. I think she'd do much for me."

"Maybe there'll be a chance to find out. Maybe we'll need Ruth. Let's have a word with her. I haven't seen her out among the women."

They stopped at the door of Ruth's cabin. It was closed. When Joe knocked there came a sound of footsteps inside, a hand drew aside the window-blind, and presently the door opened. Ruth stood there, dressed in somber hue. She was a pretty, slender, blue-eyed, brown-haired young woman.

Shefford imagined from her pallor and the set look of shock upon her face, that the tragedy had affected her more powerfully than it had the other women. When he remembered that she had been more friendly with Fay Larkin than any other neighbor, he made sure he was right in his conjecture.

"Come in," was Ruth's greeting.

"No. We just wanted to say a word. I noticed you've not been out. Do you know—all about it?"

She gave them a strange glance.

"Any of the women folks been in?" added Joe.

"Hester ran over. She told me through the window. Then I barred my door to keep the other women out."

"What for?" asked Joe, curiously.

"Please come in," she said, in reply.

They entered, and she closed the door after them. The change that came over her then was the loosing of restraint.

"Joe—what will they do with Mary?" she queried, tensely.

The Mormon studied her with dark, speculative eyes. "Hang her!" he rejoined in brutal harshness.

"O Mother of Saints!" she cried, and her hands went up.

"You're sorry for Mary, then?" asked Joe, bluntly.

"My heart is breaking for her."

"Well, so's Shefford's," said the Mormon, huskily. "And mine's kind of damn shaky."

Ruth glided to Shefford with a woman's swift softness.

"You've been my good—my best friend. You

271

were hers, too. Oh, I know!... Can't you do something for her?"

"I hope to God I can," replied Shefford.

Then the three stood looking from one to the other, in a strong and subtly realizing moment, drawn together.

"Ruth," whispered Joe, hoarsely, and then he glanced fearfully around, at the window and door, as if listeners were there. It was certain that his dark face had paled. He tried to whisper more, only to fail. Shefford divined the weight of Mormonism that burdened Joe Lake then. Joe was faithful to a love for Fay Larkin, noble in friendship to Shefford, desperate in a bitter strait with his own manliness, but the power of that creed by which he had been raised struck his lips mute. For to speak on meant to be false to that creed. Already in his heart he had decided, yet he could not voice the thing.

"Ruth"—Shefford took up the Mormon's unfinished whisper—"if we plan to save her—if we need you—will you help?"

Ruth turned white, but an instant and splendid fire shone in her eyes.

"Try me," she whispered back. "I'll change places with her—so you can get her away. They can't do much to me."

Shefford wrung her hands. Joe licked his lips and found his voice: "We'll come back later." Then he led the way out and Shefford followed. They were silent all the way back to camp.

Nas Ta Bega sat in repose where they had left him, a thoughtful, somber figure. Shefford went directly to the Indian, and Joe tarried at the camp-fire, where he raked out some red embers and put one upon the bowl of his pipe. He puffed clouds of white smoke, then found a seat beside the others.

"Shefford, go ahead. Talk. It 'll take a deal of talk. I'll listen. Then I'll talk. It 'll be Nas Ta Bega who makes the plan out of it all."

Shefford launched himself so swiftly that he scarcely talked coherently. But he made clear the points that he must save Fay, get her away from the village, let her lead him to Surprise Valley, rescue Lassiter and Jane Withersteen, and take them all out of the country.

Joe Lake dubiously shook his head. Manifestly the Surprise Valley part of the situation presented a new and serious obstacle. It changed the whole thing. To try to take the three out by way of Kayenta and Durango was not to be thought of, for reasons he briefly stated. The Red Lake trail was the only one left, and if that were taken the chances were against Shefford. It was five days over sand to Red Lake—impossible to hide a trail—and even with a day's start Shefford could not escape · the hard-riding men who would come from Stonebridge. Besides, after reaching Red Lake, there were days and days of desert-travel needful to avoid places like Blue Cañon, Tuba, Moencopie, and the Indian villages.

"We'll have to risk all that," declared Shefford, desperately.

"It's a fool risk," retorted Joe. "Listen. By to-morrow noon all of Stonebridge, more or less, will be riding in here. You've got to get away to-night

with the girl—or never! And to-morrow you've
got to find that Lassiter and the woman in Surprise
Valley. This valley must be back, deep in the cañon
country. Well, you've got to come out this way
again. No trail through here would be safe. Why,
you'd put all your heads in a rope! . . . You mustn't
come through this way. It 'll have to be tried across
country, off the trails, and that means hell—day-
and-night travel, no camp, no feed for horses—
maybe no water. Then you'll have the best trackers
in Utah like hounds on your trail."

When the Mormon ceased his forceful speech there
was a silence fraught with hopeless meaning. He
bowed his head in gloom. Shefford, growing sick
again to his marrow, fought a cold, hateful sense of
despair.

"Bi Nai!" In his extremity he called to the
Indian.

"The Navajo has heard," replied Nas Ta Bega,
strangely speaking in his own language.

With a long, slow heave of breast Shefford felt his
despair leave him. In the Indian lay his salvation.
He knew it. Joe Lake caught the subtle spirit of the
moment and looked up eagerly.

Nas Ta Bega stretched an arm toward the east,
and spoke in Navajo. But Shefford, owing to the
hurry and excitement of his mind, could not trans-
late. Joe Lake listened, gave a violent start, leaped
up with all his big frame quivering, and then fired
question after question at the Indian. When the
Navajo had replied to all, Joe drew himself up as if
facing an irrevocable decision which would wring
his very soul. What did he cast off in that moment?

What did he grapple with? Shefford had no means
to tell, except by the instinct which baffled him.
But whether the Mormon's trial was one of spiritual
rending or the natural physical fear of a perilous,
virtually impossible venture, the fact was he was
magnificent in his acceptance of it. He turned to
Shefford, white, cold, yet glowing.

"Nas Ta Bega believes he can take you down a
cañon to the big river—the Colorado. He knows
the head of this cañon. Nonnezoshe Boco it's called
—cañon of the rainbow bridge. He has never been
down it. Only two or three living Indians have ever
seen the great stone bridge. But all have heard
of it. They worship it as a god. There's water
runs down this cañon and water runs to the river.
Nas Ta Bega thinks he can take you down to the
river."

"Go on," cried Shefford. breathlessly, as Joe
paused.

"The Indian plans this way. God, it's great! . . .
If only I can do my end! . . . He plans to take mustangs to-day and wait with them for you to-night
or to-morrow till you come with the girl. You'll
go get Lassiter and the woman out of Surprise Valley. Then you'll strike east for Nonnezoshe Boco.
If possible, you must take a pack of grub. You
may be days going down—and waiting for me at the
mouth of the cañon, at the river."

"Joe! Where will you be?"

"I'll ride like hell for Kayenta, get another horse
there, and ride like hell for the San Juan River.
There's a big flatboat at the Durango crossing. I'll
go down the San Juan in that—into the big river.

I'll drift down by day, tie up by night, and watch for you at the mouth of every cañon till I come to Nonnezoshe Boco."

Shefford could not believe the evidence of his ears. He knew the treacherous San Juan River. He had heard of the great, sweeping, terrible red Colorado and its roaring rapids.

"Oh, it seems impossible!" he gasped. "You'll just lose your life for nothing."

"The Indian will turn the trick, I tell you. Take my hunch. It's nothing for me to drift down a swift river. I worked a ferry-boat once."

Shefford, to whom flying straws would have seemed stable, caught the inflection of defiance and daring and hope of the Mormon's spirit.

"What then—after you meet us at the mouth of Nonnezoshe Boco?" he queried.

"We'll all drift down to Lee's Ferry. That's at the head of Marble Cañon. We'll get out on the south side of the river, thus avoiding any Mormons at the ferry. Nas Ta Bega knows the country. It's open desert—on the other side of these plateaus. He can get horses from Navajos. Then you'll strike south for Willow Springs."

"Willow Springs? That's Presbrey's trading-post," said Shefford.

"Never met him. But he'll see you safe out of the Painted Desert. . . . The thing that worries me most is how not to miss you all at the mouth of Nonnezoshe. You must have sharp eyes. But I forget the Indian. A bird couldn't pass him. . . . And suppose Nonnezoshe Boco has a steep-walled, narrow mouth opening into a rapids! . . . Whew!

Well, the Indian will figure that, too. Now, let's put our heads together and plan how to turn this end of the trick here. Getting the girl!"

After a short colloquy it was arranged that Shefford would go to Ruth and talk to her of the aid she had promised. Joe averred that this aid could be best given by Ruth going in her somber gown and hood to the school-house, and there, while Joe and Shefford engaged the guards outside, she would change apparel and places with Fay and let her come forth.

"What 'll they do to Ruth?" demanded Shefford. "We can't accept her sacrifice if she's to suffer—or be punished."

"Reckon Ruth has a strong hunch that she can get away with it. Did you notice how strange she said that? Well, they can't do much to her. The bishop may damn her soul. But—Ruth—"

Here Lake hesitated and broke off. Not improbably he had meant to say that of all the Mormon women in the valley Ruth was the least likely to suffer from punishment inflicted upon her soul.

"Anyway, it's our only chance," went on Joe, "unless we kill a couple of men. Ruth will gladly take what comes to help you."

"All right; I consent," replied Shefford, with emotion. "And now after she comes out—the supposed Ruth—what then?"

"You can be natural-like. Go with her back to Ruth's cabin. Then stroll off into the cedars. Then climb the west wall. Meanwhile Nas Ta Bega will ride off with a pack of grub and Nack-yal and several other mustangs. He'll wait for you or you'll wait for him, as the case may be, at some appointed place. When you're gone I'll jump my horse and hit the trail for Kayenta and the San Juan."

"Very well; that's settled," said Shefford, soberly. "I'll go at once to see Ruth. You and Nas Ta Bega decide on where I'm to meet him."

"Reckon you'd do just as well to walk round and come up to Ruth's from the other side—instead of going through the village," suggested Joe.

Shefford approached Ruth's cabin in a round-about way; nevertheless, she saw him coming before he got there and, opening the door, stood pale, composed, and quietly bade him enter. Briefly, in low and earnest voice, Shefford acquainted her with the plan.

"You love her so much," she said, wistfully, wonderingly.

"Indeed I do. Is it too much to ask of you to do this thing?" he asked.

"Do it?" she queried, with a flash of spirit. "Of course I'll do it."

"Ruth, I can't thank you. I can't. I've only a faint idea what you're risking. That distresses me. I'm afraid of what may happen to you."

She gave him another of the strange glances. "I don't risk so much as you think," she said, significantly.

"Why?"

She came close to him, and her hands clasped his arms and she looked up at him, her eyes darkening and her face growing paler. "Will you swear to keep my secret?" she asked, very low.

"Yes, I swear."

"I was one of Waggoner's sealed wives!"

"God Almighty!" broke out Shefford, utterly overwhelmed.

"Yes. That's why I say I don't risk so much. I will make up a story to tell the bishop and everybody. I'll tell that Waggoner was jealous, that he was brutal to Mary, that I believed she was goaded to her mad deed, that I thought she ought to be free. They'll be terrible. But what can they do to me? My husband is dead . . . and if I have to go to hell to keep from marrying another married Mormon. I'll go!"

In that low, passionate utterance Shefford read the death-blow to the old Mormon polygamous creed. In the uplift of his spirit, in the joy at this revelation, he almost forgot the stern matter at hand. Ruth and Joe Lake belonged to a younger generation of Mormons. Their nobility in this instance was in part a revolt at the conditions of their lives. Doubt was knocking at Joe Lake's heart, and conviction had come to this young sealed wife, bitter and hopeless while she had been fettered, strong and mounting now that she was free. In a flash of inspiration Shefford saw the old order changing. The Mormon creed might survive, but that part of it which was an affront to nature, a horrible yoke on women's necks, was doomed. It could not live. It could never have survived more than a generation or two of religious fanatics. Shefford had marked a different force and religious fervor in the younger Mormons. and now he understood them.

"Ruth, you talk wildly," he said. "But I understand. I see. You are free and you're going to stay free. . . . It stuns me to think of that man of many wives. What did you feel when you were told he was dead?"

I dare not think of that. It makes me wicked. And he was good to me. . . . Listen. Last night about midnight he came to my window and woke me. I got up and let him in. He was in a terrible state. I thought he was crazy. He walked the floor and called on his saints and prayed. When I wanted to light a lamp he wouldn't let me. He was afraid I'd see his face. But I saw well enough in the moonlight. And I knew something had happened. So I soothed and coaxed him. He had been a man as close-mouthed as a stone. Yet then I got him to talk. . . . He had gone to Mary's, and upon entering, thought he heard some one with her. She didn't answer him at first. When he found her in her bedroom she was like a ghost. He accused her. Her silence made him furious. Then he berated her, brought down the wrath of God upon her, threatened her with damnation. All of which she never seemed to hear. But when he tried to touch her she flew at him like a she-panther. That's what he called her. She said she'd kill him! And she drove him out of her house. . . . He was all weak and unstrung, and I believe scared, too, when he came to me. She must have been a fury. Those quiet, gentle women are furies when they're once roused. Well, I was hours up with him and finally he got over it. He didn't pray any more. He paced the room. It was just daybreak when he said the wrath of God had come to him. I tried to keep him from going back to Mary. But he went. . . . An hour later the women ran to tell me he had been found dead at Mary's door."

"Ruth—she was mad—driven—she didn't know what she—was doing," said Shefford, brokenly.

"She was always a strange girl, more like an Indian than any one I ever knew. We called her the Sago Lily. I gave her the name. She was so sweet, lovely, white and gold, like those flowers. . . . And to think! Oh, it's horrible for her! You must save her. If you get her away there never will be anything come of it. The Mormons will hush it up."

"Ruth, time is flying," rejoined Shefford, hurriedly. "I must go back to Joe. You be ready for us when we come. Wear something loose, easily thrown off, and don't forget the long hood."

"I'll be ready and watching," she said. "The sooner the better, I'd say."

He left her and returned toward camp in the same circling route by which he had come. The Indian had disappeared and so had his mustang. This significant fact augmented Shefford's hurried, thrilling excitement. But one glance at Joe's face changed all that to a sudden numbness, a sinking of his heart.

"What is it?" he queried.

"Look there!" exclaimed the Mormon.

Shefford's quick eye caught sight of horses and men down the valley. He saw several Indians and three or four white men. They were making camp.

"Who are they?" demanded Shefford.

"Shadd and some of his gang. Reckon that Piute told the news. By to-morrow the valley will

be full as a horse-wrangler's corral. . . . Lucky Nas
Ta Bega got away before that gang rode in. Now
things won't look as queer as they might have
looked. The Indian took a pack of grub, six mustangs, and my guns. Then there was your rifle
in your saddle-sheath. So you'll be well heeled in
case you come to close quarters. Reckon you can
look for a running fight. For now, as soon as your
flight is discovered, Shadd will hit your trail. He's
in with the Mormons. You know him—what
you'll have to deal with. But the advantage will
all be yours. You can ambush the trail."

"We're in for it. And the sooner we're off the
better," replied Shefford, grimly.

"Reckon that's gospel. Well—come on!"

The Mormon strode off, and Shefford, catching up
with him, kept at his side. Shefford's mind was
full, but Joe's dark and gloomy face did not invite
communication. They entered the piñon grove and
passed the cabin where the tragedy had been en-
acted. A tarpaulin had been stretched across the
front porch. Beal was not in sight, nor were any
of the women.

"I forgot," said Shefford, suddenly. "Where am
I to meet the Indian?"

"Climb the west wall, back of camp," replied
Joe. "Nas Ta Bega took the Stonebridge trail.
But he'll leave that, climb the rocks, then hide the
outfit and come back to watch for you. Reckon
he'll see you when you top the wall."

They passed on into the heart of the village. Joe
tarried at the window of a cabin, and passed a few
remarks to a woman there, and then he inquired

WILD JUSTICE

for Mother Smith at her house. When they left here the Mormon gave Shefford a nudge. Then they separated, Joe going toward the school-house, while Shefford bent his steps in the direction of Ruth's home.

Her door opened before he had a chance to knock. He entered. Ruth, white and resolute, greeted him with a wistful smile.

"All ready?" she asked.

"Yes. Are you?" he replied, low-voiced.

"I've only to put on my hood. I think luck favors you. Hester was here and she said Elder Smith told some one that Mary hadn't been offered anything to eat yet. So I'm taking her a little. It 'll be a good excuse for me to get in the school-house to see her. I can throw off this dress and she can put it on in a minute. Then the hood. I mustn't forget to hide her golden hair. You know how it flies. But this is a big hood. . . . Well, I'm ready now. And—this 's our last time together."

"Ruth, what can I say—how can I thank you?"

"I don't want any thanks. It 'll be something to think of always—to make me happy. . . . Only I'd like to feel you—you cared a little."

The wistful smile was there, a tremor on the sad lips, and a shadow of soul-hunger in her eyes. Shefford did not misunderstand her. She did not mean love, although it was a yearning for real love that she mutely expressed.

"Care! I shall care all my life," he said, with strong feeling. "I shall never forget you."

"It's not likely I'll forget you. . . . Good-by, John!"

283

Shefford took her in his arms and held her close. "Ruth—good-by!" he said, huskily.

Then he released her. She adjusted the hood and, taking up a little tray which held food covered with a napkin, she turned to the door. He opened it and they went out.

They did not speak another word.

It was not a long walk from Ruth's home to the school-house, yet if it were to be measured by Shefford's emotion the distance would have been unending. The sacrifice offered by Ruth and Joe would have been noble under any circumstances had they been Gentiles or persons with no particular religion, but, considering that they were Mormons, that Ruth had been a sealed wife, that Joe had been brought up under the strange, secret, and binding creed, their action was no less than tremendous in its import. Shefford took it to mean vastly more than loyalty to him and pity for Fay Larkin. As Ruth and Joe had arisen to this height, so perhaps would other young Mormons have arisen. It needed only the situation, the climax, to focus these long-insulated, slow-developing and inquiring minds upon the truth—that one wife, one mother of children, for one man at one time was a law of nature, love, and righteousness. Shefford felt as if he were marching with the whole younger generation of Mormons, as if somehow he had been a humble instrument in the working out of their destiny, in the awakening that was to eliminate from their religion the only thing which kept it from being as good for man, and perhaps as true, as any other religion.

And then suddenly he turned the corner of the

school-house to encounter Joe talking with the Mormon Henninger. Elder Smith was not present.

"Why, hello, Ruth!" greeted Joe. "You've fetched Mary some dinner. Now that's good of you."

"May I go in?" asked Ruth.

"Reckon so," replied Henninger, scratching his head. He appeared to be tractable, and probably was good-natured under pleasant conditions. "She ought to have somethin' to eat. An' nobody 'pears to have remembered thet—we're so set up."

He unbarred the huge, clumsy door and allowed Ruth to pass in.

"Joe, you can go in if you want," he said. "But hurry out before Elder Smith comes back from his dinner."

Joe mumbled something, gave a husky cough, and then went in.

Shefford experienced great difficulty in presenting to this mild Mormon a natural and unagitated front. When all his internal structure seemed to be in a state of turmoil he did not see how it was possible to keep the fact from showing in his face. So he turned away and took aimless steps here and there.

"'Pears like we'd hev rain," observed Henninger. "It's right warm an' them clouds are onseasonable."

"Yes," replied Shefford. "Hope so. A little rain would be good for the grass."

"Joe tells me Shadd rode in, an' some of his fellers."

"So I see. About eight in the party."

Shefford was gritting his teeth and preparing to endure the ordeal of controlling his mind and expression when the door opened and Joe stalked out.

He had his sombrero pulled down so that it hid the upper half of his face. His lips were a shade off healthy color. He stood there with his back to the door.

"Say, what Mary needs is quiet—to be left alone," he said. "Ruth says if she rests, sleeps a little, she won't get fever. . . . Henninger, don't let anybody disturb her till night."

"All right, Joe," replied the Mormon. "An' I take it good of Ruth an' you to concern yourselves."

A slight tap on the inside of the door sent Shefford's pulses to throbbing. Joe opened it with a strong and vigorous sweep that meant more than the mere action.

"Ruth—reckon you didn't stay long," he said, and his voice rang clear. "Sure you feel sick and weak. Why, seeing her flustered even me!"

A slender, dark-garbed woman wearing a long black hood stepped uncertainly out. She appeared to be Ruth. Shefford's heart stood still because she looked so like Ruth. But she did not step steadily, she seemed dazed, she did not raise the hooded head.

"Go home," said Joe, and his voice rang a little louder. "Take her home, Shefford. Or, better, walk her round some. She's faintish. . . . And see here, Henninger—"

Shefford led the girl away with a hand in apparent carelessness on her arm. After a few rods she walked with a freer step and then a swifter. He found it necessary to make that hold on her arm a real one, so as to keep her from walking too fast. No one, however, appeared to observe them. When

they passed Ruth's house then Shefford began to
lose his fear that this was not Fay Larkin. He was
far from being calm or clear-sighted. He thought
he recognized that free step; nevertheless, he could
not make sure. When they passed under the trees,
crossed the brook, and turned down along the west
wall, then doubt ceased in Shefford's mind. He
knew this was not Ruth. Still, so strange was his
agitation, so keen his suspense, that he needed con-
firmation of ear, of eye. He wanted to hear her
voice, to see her face. Yet just as strangely there
was a twist of feeling, a reluctance, a sadness that
kept off the moment.

They reached the low, slow-swelling slant of wall
and started to ascend. How impossible not to
recognize Fay Larkin now in that swift grace and
skill on the steep wall! Still, though he knew her,
he perversely clung to the unreality of the moment.
But when a long braid of dead-gold hair tumbled
from under the hood, then his heart leaped. That
identified Fay Larkin. He had freed her. He was
taking her away. Then a sadness embittered his
joy.

As always before, she distanced him in the ascent
to the top. She went on without looking back.
But Shefford had an irresistible desire to look again
and the last time at this valley where he had suffered and loved so much.

XVI

SURPRISE VALLEY

FROM the summit of the wall the plateau waved away in red and yellow ridges, with here and there little valleys green with cedar and piñon.

Upon one of these ridges, silhouetted against the sky, appeared the stalking figure of the Indian. He had espied the fugitives. He disappeared in a niche, and presently came again into view round a corner of cliff. Here he waited, and soon Shefford and Fay joined him.

"Bi Nai, it is well," he said.

Shefford eagerly asked for the horses, and Nas Ta Bega silently pointed down the niche, which was evidently an opening into one of the shallow cañons. Then he led the way, walking swiftly. It was Shefford, and not Fay, who had difficulty in keeping close to him. This speed caused Shefford to become more alive to the business, instead of the feeling, of the flight. The Indian entered a crack between low cliffs—a very narrow cañon full of rocks and clumps of cedars—and in a half-hour or less he came to where the mustangs were halted among some cedars. Three of the mustangs, including Nack-yal, were saddled; one bore a small pack, and the remaining two had blankets strapped on their backs.

"Fay, can you ride in that long skirt?" asked Shefford. How strange it seemed that his first words to her were practical when all his impassioned thought had been only mute! But the instant he spoke he experienced a relief, a relaxation.

"I'll take it off," replied Fay, just as practically. And in a twinkling she slipped out of both waist and skirt. She had worn them over the short white-flannel dress with which Shefford had grown familiar.

As Nack-yal appeared to be the safest mustang for her to ride, Shefford helped her upon him and then attended to the stirrups. When he had adjusted them to the proper length he drew the bridle over Nack-yal's head and, upon handing it to her, found himself suddenly looking into her face. She had taken off the hood, too. The instant their eyes met he realized that she was strangely afraid to meet his glance, as he was to meet hers. That seemed natural. But her face was flushed and there were unmistakable signs upon it of growing excitement, of mounting happiness. Save for that fugitive glance she would have been the Fay Larkin of yesterday. How he had expected her to look he did not know, but it was not like this. And never had he felt her strange quality of simplicity so powerfully.

"Have you ever been here—through this little cañon?" he asked.

"Oh yes, lots of times."

"You'll be able to lead us to Surprise Valley, you think?"

"I know it. I shall see Uncle Jim and Mother Jane before sunset!"

"I hope—you do," he replied, a little shakily "Perhaps we'd better not tell them of the—the—about what happened last night."

Her beautiful, grave, and troubled glance returned to meet his, and he received a shock that he considered was amaze. And after more swift consideration he believed he was amazed because that look, instead of betraying fear or gloom or any haunting shadow of darkness, betrayed apprehension for him —grave, sweet, troubled love for him. She was not thinking of herself at all—of what he might think of her, of a possible gulf between them, of a vast and terrible change in the relation of soul to soul. He experienced a profound gladness. Though he could not understand her, he was happy that the horror of Waggoner's death had escaped her. He loved her, he meant to give his life to her, and right then and there he accepted the burden of her deed and meant to bear it without ever letting her know of the shadow between them.

"Fay, we'll forget—what's behind us," he said. "Now to find Surprise Valley. Lead on. Nack-yal is gentle. Pull him the way you want to go. We'll follow."

Shefford mounted the other saddled mustang, and they set off, Fay in advance. Presently they rode out of this cañon up to level cedar-patched, solid rock, and here Fay turned straight west. Evidently she had been over the ground before. The heights to which he had climbed with her were up to the left, great slopes and looming promontories. And the course she chose was as level and easy as any he could have picked out in that direction.

SURPRISE VALLEY

When a mile or more of this up-and-down travel had been traversed Fay halted and appeared to be at fault. The plateau was losing its rounded, smooth, wavy characteristics, and to the west grew bolder, more rugged, more cut up into low crags and buttes. After a long, sweeping glance Fay headed straight for this rougher country. Thereafter from time to time she repeated this action.

"Fay, how do you know you're going in the right direction?" asked Shefford, anxiously.

"I never forget any ground I've been over. I keep my eyes close ahead. All that seems strange to me is the wrong way. What I've seen before must be the right way, because I saw it when they brought me from Surprise Valley."

Shefford had to acknowledge that she was following an Indian's instinct for ground he had once covered.

Still Shefford began to worry, and finally dropped back to question Nas Ta Bega.

"Bi Nai, she has the eye of a Navajo," replied the Indian. "Look! Iron-shod horses have passed here. See the marks in the stone?"

Shefford indeed made out faint cut tracks that would have escaped his own sight. They had been made long ago, but they were unmistakable.

"She's following the trail by memory—she must remember the stones, trees, sage, cactus," said Shefford in surprise.

"Pictures in her mind," replied the Indian.

Thereafter the farther she progressed the less at fault she appeared and the faster she traveled. She made several miles an hour, and about the middle

291

THE RAINBOW TRAIL

of the afternoon entered upon the more broken region of the plateau. View became restricted. Low walls, and ruined cliffs of red rock with cedars at their base, and gullies growing into cañons and cañons opening into larger ones—these were passed and crossed and climbed and rimmed in travel that grew more difficult as the going became wilder. Then there was a steady ascent, up and up all the time, though not steep, until another level, green with cedar and piñon, was reached.

It reminded Shefford of the forest near the mouth of the Sagi. It was so dense he could not see far ahead of Fay, and often he lost sight of her entirely. Presently he rode out of the forest into a strip of purple sage. It ended abruptly, and above that abrupt line, seemingly far away, rose a long, red wall. Instantly he recognized that to be the opposite wall of a cañon which as yet he could not see.

Fay was acting strangely and he hurried forward. She slipped off Nack-yal and fell, sprang up and ran wildly, to stand upon a promontory, her arms uplifted, her hair a mass of moving gold in the wind, her attitude one of wild and eloquent significance.

Shefford ran, too, and as he ran the red wall in his eager sight seemed to enlarge downward, deeper and deeper, and then it merged into a strip of green.

Suddenly beneath him yawned a red-walled gulf, a deceiving gulf seen through transparent haze, a softly shining green-and-white valley, strange, wild, beautiful, like a picture in his memory.

"Surprise Valley!" he cried, in wondering recognition.

Fay Larkin waved her arms as if they were wings

292

to carry her swiftly downward, and her plaintive cry
fitted the wildness of her manner and the lonely
height where she leaned.

Shefford drew her back from the rim.

"Fay, we are here," he said. "I recognize the
valley. I miss only one thing—the arch of stone."

His words seemed to recall her to reality.

"The arch? That fell when the wall slipped, in
the great avalanche. See! There is the place.
We can get down there. Oh, let us hurry!"

The Indian reached the rim and his falcon gaze
swept the valley. "Ugh!" he exclaimed. He, too,
recognized the valley that he had vainly sought
for half a year.

"Bring the lassos," said Shefford.

With Fay leading, they followed the rim toward
the head of the valley. Here the wall had caved in,
and there was a slope of jumbled rock a thousand
feet wide and more than that in depth. It was easy
to descend because there were so many rocks waist-
high that afforded a handhold. Shefford marked,
however, that Fay never took advantage of these.
More than once he paused to watch her. Swiftly
she went down; she stepped from rock to rock;
lightly she crossed cracks and pits; she ran along
the sharp and broken edge of a long ledge; she
poised on a pointed stone and, sure-footed as a
mountain-sheep, she sprang to another that had
scarce surface for a foothold; her moccasins flashed,
seemed to hold wondrously on any angle; and when
a rock tipped or slipped with her she leaped to a
surer stand. Shefford watched her performance, so
swift, agile, so perfectly balanced, showing such

293

wonderful accord between eye and foot; and then when he swept his gaze down upon that wild valley where she had roamed alone for twelve years he marveled no more.

The farther down he got the greater became the size of rocks, until he found himself amid huge pieces of cliff as large as houses. He lost sight of Fay entirely, and he anxiously threaded a narrow, winding, descending way between the broken masses. Finally he came out upon flat rock again. Fay stood on another rim, looking down. He saw that the slide had moved far out into the valley, and the lower part of it consisted of great sections of wall. In fact, the base of the great wall had just moved out with the avalanche, and this much of it held its vertical position. Looking upward, Shefford was astounded and thrilled to see how far he had descended, how the walls leaned like a great, wide, curving, continuous rim of mountain.

"Here! Here!" called Fay. "Here's where they got down—where they brought me up. Here are the sticks they used. They stuck them in this crack, down to that ledge."

Shefford ran to her side and looked down. There was a narrow split in this section of wall and it was perhaps sixty feet in depth. The floor of rock below led out in a ledge, with a sheer drop to the valley level.

As Shefford gazed, pondering on a way to descend lower, the Indian reached his side. He had no sooner looked than he proceeded to act. Selecting one of the sticks, which were strong pieces of cedar, well hewn and trimmed, he jammed it between the walls of the crack till it stuck fast. Then sitting astride this one he jammed in another some three feet below. When he got down upon that one it was necessary for Shefford to drop him a third stick. In a comparatively short time the Indian reached the ledge below. Then he called for the lassos. Shefford threw them down. His next move was an attempt to assist Fay, but she slipped out of his grasp and descended the ladder with a swiftness that made him hold his breath. Still, when his turn came, her spirit so governed him that he went down as swiftly, and even leaped sheer the last ten feet.

Nas Ta Bega and Fay were leaning over the ledge. "Here's the place," she said, excitedly. "Let me down on the rope."

It took two thirty-foot lassos tied together to reach the floor of the valley. Shefford folded his vest, put it round Fay, and slipped a loop of the lasso under her arms. Then he and Nas Ta Bega lowered her to the grass below. Fay, throwing off the loop, bounded away like a wild creature, uttering the strangest cries he had ever heard, and she disappeared along the wall.

"I'll go down," said Shefford to the Indian. "You stay here to help pull us up."

Hand over hand Shefford descended, and when his feet touched the grass he experienced a shock of the most singular exultation.

"In Surprise Valley!" he breathed, softly. The dream that had come to him with his friend's story, the years of waiting, wondering, and then the long, fruitless, hopeless search in the desert uplands—these were in his mind as he turned along the wall where

Fay had disappeared. He faced a wide terrace, green with grass and moss and starry with strange white flowers, and dark-foliaged, spear-pointed spruce-trees. Below the terrace sloped a bench covered with thick copse, and this merged into a forest of dwarf oaks, and beyond that was a beautiful strip of white aspens, their leaves quivering in the stillness. The air was close, sweet, warm, fragrant, and remarkably dry. It reminded him of the air he had smelled in dry caves under cliffs. He reached a point from where he saw a meadow dotted with red-and-white-spotted cattle and little black burros. There were many of them. And he remembered with a start the agony of toil and peril Venters had endured bringing the progenitors of this stock into the valley. What a strange, wild, beautiful story it all was! But a story connected with this valley could not have been otherwise.

Beyond the meadow, on the other side of the valley, extended the forest, and that ended in the rising bench of thicket, which gave place to green slope and mossy terrace of sharp-tipped spruces—and all this led the eye irresistibly up to the red wall where a vast, dark, wonderful cavern yawned, with its rust-colored streaks of stain on the wall, and the queer little houses of the cliff-dwellers, with their black, vacant, silent windows speaking so weirdly of the unknown past.

Shefford passed a place where the ground had been cultivated, but not as recently as the last six months. There was a scant shock of corn and many meager standing stalks. He became aware of a low, whining hum and a fragrance overpowering in its sweetness. And there round another corner of wall he came upon an orchard all pink and white in blossom and melodious with the buzz and hum of innumerable bees.

He crossed a little stream that had been dammed, went along a pond, down beside an irrigation-ditch that furnished water to orchard and vineyard, and from there he strode into a beautiful cove between two jutting corners of red wall. It was level and green and the spruces stood gracefully everywhere. Beyond their dark trunks he saw caves in the wall.

Suddenly the fragrance of blossom was overwhelmed by the stronger fragrance of smoke from a wood fire. Swiftly he strode under the spruces. Quail fluttered before him as tame as chickens. Big gray rabbits scarcely moved out of his way. The branches above him were full of mockingbirds. And then—there before him stood three figures.

Fay Larkin was held close to the side of a magnificent woman, barbarously clad in garments made of skins and pieces of blanket. Her face worked in noble emotion. Shefford seemed to see the ghost of that fair beauty Venters had said was Jane Withersteen's. Her hair was gray. Near her sto d a lean, stoop-shouldered man whose long hair was perfectly white. His gaunt face was bare of beard. It had strange, sloping, sad lines. And he was staring with mild, surprised eyes.

The moment held Shefford mute till sight of Fay Larkin's tear-wet face broke the spell. He leaped forward and his strong hands reached for the woman and the man.

"Jane Withersteen! . . . Lassiter! I have found you!"

"Oh, sir, who are you?" she cried, with rich and deep and quivering voice. "This child came running—screaming. She could not speak. We thought she had gone mad—and escaped to come back to us."

"I am John Shefford," he replied, swiftly. "I am a friend of Bern Venters—of his wife Bess. I learned your story. I came west. I've searched a year. I found Fay. And we've come to take you away."

"You found Fay? But that masked Mormon who forced her to sacrifice herself to save us! . . . What of him? It's not been so many long years—I remember what my father was—and Dyeı and Tull —all those cruel churchmen."

"Waggoner is dead," replied Shefford.

"Dead? She is free! Oh, what—how did he die?"

"He was killed."

"Who did it?"

"That's no matter," replied Shefford, stonily, and he met her gaze with steady eyes. "He's out of the way. Fay was never his wife. Fay's free. We've come to take you out of the country. We must hurry. We'll be tracked—pursued. But we've horses and an Indian guide. We'll get away. . . . I think it better to leave here at once. There's no telling how soon we'll be hunted. Get what things you want to take with you."

"Oh—yes—Mother Jane, let us hurry!" cried Fay. "I'm so full—I can't talk—my heart hurts so!"

Jane Withersteen's face shone with an exceedingly radiant light, and a glory blended with a terrible fear in her eyes.

"Fay! my little Fay!"

Lassiter had stood there with his mild, clear blue eyes upon Shefford.

"I shore am glad to see you-all," he drawled, and extended his hand as if the meeting were casual. "What 'd you say your name was?"

Shefford repeated it as he met the proffered hand.

"How's Bern an' Bess?" Lassiter inquired.

"They were well, prosperous, happy when last I saw them. . . . They had a baby."

"Now ain't thet fine? . . . Jane, did you hear? Bess has a baby. An', Jane, didn't I always say Bern would come back to get us out? Shore it's just the same."

How cool, easy, slow, and mild this Lassiter seemed! Had the man grown old, Shefford wondered? The past to him manifestly was only yesterday, and the danger of the present was as nothing. Looking in Lassiter's face, Shefford was baffled. If he had not remembered the greatness of this old gun-man he might have believed that the lonely years in the valley had unbalanced his mind. In an hour like this coolness seemed inexplicable—assuredly would have been impossible in an ordinary man. Yet what hid behind that drawling coolness? What was the meaning of those long, sloping, shadowy lines of the face? What spirit lay in the deep, mild, clear eyes? Shefford experienced a sudden check to what had been his first growing impression of a drifting, broken old man.

THE RAINBOW TRAIL

"Lassiter, pack what little you can carry mustn't be much—and we'll get out of here," said Shefford.

"I shore will. Reckon I ain't a-goin' to need a pack-train. We saved the clothes we wore in here. Jane never thought it no use. But I figgered we might need them some day. They won't be stylish, but I reckon they'll do better 'n these skins. An' there's an old coat thet was Venters's."

The mild, dreamy look became intensified in Lassiter's eyes.

"Did Venters have any hosses when you knowed him?" he asked.

"He had a farm full of horses," replied Shefford, with a smile. "And there were two blacks—the grandest horses I ever saw. Black Star and Night! You remember, Lassiter?"

"Shore. I was wonderin' if he got the blacks out. They must be growin' old by now. . . . Grand hosses, they was. But Jane had another hoss, a big devil of a sorrel. His name was Wrangle. Did Venters ever tell you about him—an' thet race with Jerry Card?"

"A hundred times!" replied Shefford.

"Wrangle run the blacks off their legs. But Jane never would believe thet. An' I couldn't change her all these years. . . . Reckon mebbe we'll get to see them blacks?"

"Indeed, I hope—I believe you will," replied Shefford, feelingly.

"Shore won't thet be fine. Jane, did you hear? Black Star an' Night are livin' an' we'll get to see them."

But Jane Withersteen only clasped Fay in her

300

arms, and looked at Lassiter with wet and glistening eyes.

Shefford told them to hurry and come to the cliff where the ascent from the valley was to be made. He thought best to leave them alone to make their preparations and bid farewell to the cavern home they had known for so long.

Then he strolled back along the wall, loitering here to gaze into a cave, and there to study crude red paintings in the nooks. And sometimes he halted thoughtfully and did not see anything. At length he rounded a corner of cliff to espy Nas Ta Bega sitting upon the ledge, reposeful and watchful as usual. Shefford told the Indian they would be climbing out soon, and then he sat down to wait and let his gaze rove over the valley.

He might have sat there a long while, so sad and reflective and wondering was his thought, but it seemed a very short time till Fay came in sight with her free, swift grace, and Lassiter and Jane some distance behind. Jane carried a small bundle and Lassiter had a sack over his shoulder that appeared no inconsiderable burden.

"Them beans shore is heavy," he drawled, as he deposited the sack upon the ground.

Shefford curiously took hold of the sack and was amazed to find that a second and hard muscular effort was required to lift it.

"Beans?" he queried.

"Shore," replied Lassiter.

"That's the heaviest sack of beans I ever saw. Why —it's not possible it can be. . . . Lassiter, we've a long, rough trail. We've got to pack light."

"Wal, I ain't a-goin' to leave this here sack behind. Reckon I've been all of twelve years in fillin' it," he declared, mildly.

Shefford could only stare at him.

"Fay may need them beans," went on Lassiter.

"Why?"

"Because they're gold."

"Gold!" ejaculated Shefford.

"Shore. An' they represent some work. Twelve years of diggin' an' washin'!"

Shefford laughed constrainedly. "Well, Lassiter, that alters the case considerably. A sack of gold nuggets or grains, or beans, as you call them, certainly must not be left behind. . . . Come, now, we'll tackle this climbing job."

He called up to the Indian and, grasping the rope, began to walk up the first slant, and then by dint of hand-over-hand effort and climbing with knees and feet he succeeded, with Nas Ta Bega's help, in making the ledge. Then he let down the rope to haul up the sack and bundle. That done, he directed Fay to fasten the noose round her as he had fixed it before. When she had complied he called to her to hold herself out from the wall while he and Nas Ta Bega hauled her up.

"Hold the rope tight," replied Fay. "I'll walk up."

And to Shefford's amaze and admiration, she virtually walked up that almost perpendicular wall by slipping her hands along the rope and stepping as she pulled herself up. There, if never before, he saw the fruit of her years of experience on steep slopes. Only such experience could have made the feat possible.

Jane had to be hauled up, and the task was a painful one for her. Lassiter's turn came then, and he showed more strength and agility than Shefford had supposed him capable of. From the ledge they turned their attention to the narrow crack with its ladder of sticks. Fay had already ascended and now hung over the rim, her white face and golden hair framed vividly in the narrow stream of blue sky above.

"Mother Jane! Uncle Jim! You are so slow," she called.

"Wal, Fay, we haven't been second cousins to a cañon squirrel all these years," replied Lassiter.

This upper half of the climb bid fair to be as difficult for Jane, if not so painful, as the lower. It was necessary for the Indian to go up and drop the rope, which was looped around her, and then, with him pulling from above and Shefford assisting Jane as she climbed, she was finally gotten up without mishap. When Lassiter reached the level they rested a little while and then faced the great slide of jumbled rocks. Fay led the way, light, supple, tireless, and Shefford never ceased looking at her. At last they surmounted the long slope and, winding along the rim, reached the point where Fay had led out of the cedars.

Nas Ta Bega, then, was the one to whom Shefford looked for every decision or action of the immediate future. The Indian said he had seen a pool of water in a rocky hole, that the day was spent, that here was a little grass for the mustangs, and it would be well to camp right there. So while Nas Ta Bega attended to the mustangs Shefford set about such prepara-

tions for camp and supper as their light pack afforded. The question of beds was easily answered,
for the mats of soft needles under piñon and cedar
would be comfortable places to sleep.

When Shefford felt free again the sun was setting.
Lassiter and Jane were walking under the trees.
The Indian had returned to camp. But Fay was
missing. Shefford imagined he knew where to find
her, and upon going to the edge of the forest he saw
her sitting on the promontory. He approached her,
drawn in spite of a feeling that perhaps he ought
to stay away.

"Fay, would you rather be alone?" he asked.

His voice startled her.

"I want you," she replied, and held out her hand.
Taking it in his own, he sat beside her.

The red sun was at their backs. Surprise Valley
lay hazy, dusky, shadowy beneath them. The opposite wall seemed fired by crimson flame, save far
down at its base, which the sun no longer touched.
And the dark line of red slowly rose, encroaching
upon the bright crimson. Changing, transparent,
yet dusky veils seemed to float between the walls;
long, red rays, where the sun shone through notch
or crack in the rim, split the darker spaces; deep
down at the floor the forest darkened, the strip of
aspen paled, the meadow turned gray; and all under
the shelves and in the great caverns a purple gloom
deepened. Then the sun set. And swiftly twilight
was there below while day lingered above. On
the opposite wall the fire died and the stone grew
cold.

A cañon night-hawk voiced his lonely, weird, and

melancholy cry, and it seemed to pierce and mark the silence.

A pale star, peering out of a sky that had begun to turn blue, marked the end of twilight. And all the purple shadows moved and hovered and changed till, softly and mysteriously, they embraced black night.

Beautiful, wild, strange, silent Surprise Valley! Shefford saw it before and beneath him, a dark abyss now, the abode of loneliness. He imagined faintly what was in Fay Larkin's heart. For the last time she had seen the sun set there and night come with its dead silence and sweet mystery and phantom shadows, its velvet blue sky and white trains of stars.

He, who had dreamed and longed and searched, found that the hour had been incalculable for him in its import.

XVII

WHEN Shefford awoke next morning and sat up on his bed of piñon boughs the dawn had broken cold with a ruddy gold brightness under the trees. Nas Ta Bega and Lassiter were busy around a camp-fire; the mustangs were haltered near by; Jane Withersteen combed out her long, tangled tresses with a crude wooden comb; and Fay Larkin was not in sight. As she had been missing from the group at sunset, so she was now at sunrise. Shefford went out to take his last look at Surprise Valley.

On the evening before the valley had been a place of dusky red veils and purple shadows, and now it was pink-walled, clear and rosy and green and white, with wonderful shafts of gold slanting down from the notched eastern rim. Fay stood on the promontory, and Shefford did not break the spell of her silent farewell to her wild home. A strange emotion abided with him and he knew he would always, all his life, regret leaving Surprise Valley.

Then the Indian called.

"Come, Fay," said Shefford, gently.

And she turned away with dark, haunted eyes and a white, still face.

306

The somber Indian gave a silent gesture for Shefford to make haste. While they had breakfast the mustangs were saddled and packed. And soon all was in readiness for the flight. Fay was given Nack-yal, Jane the saddled horse Shefford had ridden, and Lassiter the Indian's roan. Shefford and Nas Ta Bega were to ride the blanketed mustangs, and the sixth and last one bore the pack. Nas Ta Bega set off, leading this horse; the others of the party lined in behind with Shefford at the rear.

Nas Ta Bega led at a brisk trot, and sometimes, on level stretches of ground, at an easy canter; and Shefford had a grim realization of what this flight was going to be for these three fugitives, now so unaccustomed to riding. Jane and Lassiter, however, needed no watching, and showed they had never forgotten how to manage a horse. The Indian back-trailed yesterday's path for an hour, then headed west to the left, and entered a low pass. All parts of this plateau country looked alike, and Shefford was at some pains to tell the difference of this strange ground from that which he had been over. In another hour they got out of the rugged, broken rock to the wind-worn and smooth, shallow cañon Shefford calculated that they were coming to the end of the plateau. The low walls slanted lower; the cañon made a turn; Nas Ta Bega disappeared; and then the others of the party. When Shefford turned the corner of wall he saw a short strip of bare, rocky ground with only sky beyond. The Indian and his followers had halted in a group. Shefford rode to them, halted himself, and in one sweeping glance realized the meaning of their silent gaze. But immediately Nas Ta Bega started down, and the mustangs, without word or touch, followed him. Shefford, however, lingered on the promontory.

His gaze seemed impelled and held by things afar —the great yellow-and-purple corrugated world of distance, now on a level with his eyes. He was drawn by the beauty and the grandeur of that scene and transfixed by the realization that he had dared to venture to find a way through this vast, wild, and unflung fastness. He kept looking afar, sweeping the three-quartered circle of horizon till his judgment of distance was confounded and his sense of proportion dwarfed one moment and magnified the next. Then he withdrew his fascinated gaze to adopt the Indian's method of studying unlimited spaces in the desert—to look with slow, contracted eyes from near to far.

His companions had begun to zigzag down a long slope, bare of rock, with yellow gravel patches showing between the scant strips of green, and here and there a scrub-cedar. Half a mile down, the slope merged into green level. But close, keen gaze made out this level to be a rolling plain, growing darker green, with blue lines of ravines, and thin, undefined spaces that might be mirage. Miles and miles it swept and rolled and heaved to lose its waves in apparent darker level. A round, red rock stood isolated, marking the end of the barren plain, and farther on were other round rocks, all isolated, all of different shape. They resembled huge grazing cattle. But as Shefford gazed, and his sight gained strength from steadily holding it to separate features, these rocks were strangely magnified. They grew and grew into mounds, castles, domes, crags—great, red, wind-carved buttes. One by one they drew his gaze to the wall of upflung rock. He seemed to see a thousand domes of a thousand shapes and colors, and among them a thousand blue clefts, each one a little mark in his sight, yet which he knew was a cañon.

So far he gained some idea of what he saw. But beyond this wide area of curved lines rose another wall, dwarfing the lower, dark red, horizon-long, magnificent in frowning boldness, and because of its limitless deceiving surfaces, breaks, and lines, incomprehensible to the sight of man. Away to the eastward began a winding, ragged, blue line, looping back upon itself, and then winding away again, growing wider and bluer. This line was the San Juan Cañon. Where was Joe Lake at that moment? Had he embarked yet on the river—did that blue line, so faint, so deceiving, hold him and the boat? Almost it was impossible to believe. Shefford followed the blue line all its length, a hundred miles, he fancied, down toward the west where it joined a dark, purple, shadowy cleft. And this was the Grand Cañon of the Colorado. Shefford's eye swept along with that winding mark, farther and farther to the west, round to the left, until the cleft, growing larger and coming closer, losing its deception, was seen to be a wild and winding cañon. Still farther to the left, as he swung in fascinated gaze, it split the wonderful wall—a vast plateau now with great red peaks and yellow mesas. The cañon was full of purple smoke. It turned, it

closed, it gaped, it lost itself and showed again in
that chaos of a million cliffs. And then farther on
it became again a cleft, a purple line, at last to
fail entirely in deceiving distance.

Shefford imagined there was no scene in all the
world to equal that. The tranquility of lesser spaces
was not here manifest. Sound, movement, life,
seemed to have no fitness here. Ruin was there and
desolation and decay. The meaning of the ages
was flung at him, and a man became nothing.
When he had gazed at the San Juan Cañon he had
been appalled at the nature of Joe Lake's Herculean
task. He had lost hope, faith. The thing was not
possible. But when Shefford gazed at that sub-
lime and majestic wilderness, in which the Grand
Cañon was only a dim line, he strangely lost his
terror and something else came to him from across
the shining spaces. If Nas Ta Bega led them
safely down to the river, if Joe Lake met them at
the mouth of Nonnezoshe Boco, if they survived
the rapids of that terrible gorge, then Shefford would
have to face his soul and the meaning of this spirit
that breathed on the wind.

He urged his mustang to the descent of the slope,
and as he went down, slowly drawing nearer to the
other fugitives, his mind alternated between this
strange intimation of faith, this subtle uplift of his
spirit, and the growing gloom and shadow in his
love for Fay Larkin. Not that he loved her less
but more! A possible God hovering near him, like
the Indian's spirit-step on the trail, made his soul
the darker for Fay's crime, and he saw with clearer
sight, with deeper sadness, with sterner truth.

THE TRAIL TO NONNEZOSHE

More than once the Indian turned on his mustang to look up the slope and the light flashed from his dark, somber face. Shefford instinctively looked back himself, and then realized the unconscious motive of the action. Deep within him there had been a premonition of certain pursuit, and the Indian's reiterated backward glance had at length brought the feeling upward. Thereafter, as they descended, Shefford gradually added to his already wrought emotions a mounting anxiety.

No sign of a trail showed where the base of the slope rolled out to meet the green plain. The earth was gravelly, with dark patches of heavy silt, almost like cinders; and round, black rocks, flinty and glassy, cracked away from the hoofs of the mustangs. There was a level bench a mile wide, then a ravine, and then an ascent, and after that, rounded ridge and ravine, one after the other, like huge swells of a monstrous sea. Indian paint-brush vied in its scarlet hue with the deep magenta of cactus. There was no sage. Soapweed and meager grass and a bunch of cactus here and there lent the green to that barren; and it was green only at a distance. Nas Ta Bega kept on a steady, even trot. The sun climbed. The wind rose and whipped dust from under the mustangs.

Shefford looked back often, and the farther out in the plain he reached the higher loomed the plateau they had descended; and as he faced ahead again the lower sank the red-domed and castled horizon to the fore. The ravines became deeper, with dry rock bottoms, and the ridge-tops sharper, with outcroppings of yellow, crumbling ledges.

Once across the central depression of that wide plain a gradual ascent became evident, and the red, round rocks grew clearer in sight, began to rise and shine and grow. And thereafter every slope brought them nearer.

The sun was straight overhead and hot when Nas Ta Bega halted the party under the first lonely scrub-cedar. They all dismounted to stretch their limbs and rest the horses. It was not a talkative group. Lassiter's comments on the never-ending green plain elicited no response. Jane Withersteen looked afar with the past in her eyes. Shefford felt Fay's wistful glance and could not meet it; indeed, he seemed to want to hide something from her. The Indian bent a falcon gaze on the distant slope, and Shefford did not like that intent, searching, steadfast watchfulness. Suddenly Nas Ta Bega stiffened and whipped the halter he held.

"Ugh!" he exclaimed.

All eyes followed the direction of his dark hand. Puffs of dust rose from the base of the long slope they had descended; tiny dark specks moved with the pace of a snail.

"Shadd!" added the Indian.

"I expected it," said Shefford, darkly, as he rose.

"An' who's Shadd?" drawled Lassiter in his cool, slow speech.

Briefly Shefford explained, and then, looking at Nas Ta Bega, he added:

"The hardest-riding outfit in the country! We can't get away from them."

Jane Withersteen was silent, but Fay uttered a low cry. Shefford did not look at either of them.

The Indian began swiftly to tighten the saddle-cinches of his roan, and Shefford did likewise for Nack-yal. Then Shefford drew his rifle out of the saddle-sheath and Joe Lake's big guns from the saddle-bag.

"Here, Lassiter, maybe you haven't forgotten how to use these," he said.

The old gun-man started as if he had seen ghosts. His hands grew clawlike as he reached for the guns. He threw open the cylinders, spilled out the shells, snapped back the cylinders. Then he went through motions too swift for Shefford to follow. But Shefford heard the hammers falling so swiftly they blended their clicks almost in one sound. Lassiter reloaded the guns with a speed comparable with the other actions. A remarkable transformation had come over him. He did not seem the same man. The mild eyes had changed; the long, shadowy, sloping lines were tense cords; and there was a cold, ashy shade on his face.

"Twelve years!" he muttered to himself. "I dropped them old guns back there where I rolled the rock. . . . Twelve years!"

Shefford realized the twelve years were as if they had never been. And he would rather have had this old gun-man with him than a dozen ordinary men.

The Indian spoke rapidly in Navajo, saying that once in the rocks they were safe. Then, after another look at the distant dust-puffs, he wheeled his mustang.

It was doubtful if the party could have kept near him had they been responsible for the gait of their

mounts. The fact was that the way the Indian
called to his mustang or some leadership in the one
he rode drew the others to a like trot or climb or
canter. For a long time Shefford did not turn
round; he knew what to expect. And when he did
turn he was startled at the gain made by the pursuers. But he was encouraged as well by the looming, red, rounded peaks seemingly now so close.
He could see the dark splits between the sloping
curved walls, the piñon patches in the amphitheater under the circled walls. That was a wild
place they were approaching, and, once in there, he
believed pursuit would be useless. However, there
were miles to go still, and those hard-riding devils
behind made alarming decrease in the intervening
distance. Shefford could see the horses plainly now.
How they made the dust fly! He counted up to
six—and then the dust and moving line caused the
others to be indistinguishable.

At last only a long, gently rising slope separated
the fugitives from that labyrinthine network of
wildly carved rock. But it was the clear air that
made the distance seem short. Mile after mile the
mustangs climbed, and when they were perhaps
half-way across that last slope to the rocks the first
horse of the pursuers mounted to the level behind.
In a few moments the whole band was strung out in
sight. Nas Ta Bega kept his mustang at a steady
walk, in spite of the gaining pursuers. There came
a point, however, when the Indian, reaching comparatively level ground, put his mount to a swinging
canter. The other mustangs broke into the same
gait.

It became a race then, with the couple of miles between fugitives and pursuers only imperceptibly lessened. Nas Ta Bega had saved his mustangs and Shadd had ridden his to the limit. Shefford kept looking back, gripping his rifle, hoping it would not come to a fight, yet slowly losing that reluctance.

Sage began to show on the slope, and other kinds of brush and cedars straggled everywhere. The great rocks loomed closer, the red color mixed with yellow, and the slopes lengthening out, not so steep, yet infinitely longer than they had seemed at a distance.

Shefford ceased to feel the dry wind in his face. They were already in the lee of the wall. He could see the rock-squirrels scampering to their holes. The mustangs valiantly held to the gait, and at last the Indian disappeared between two rounded corners of cliff. The others were close behind. Shefford wheeled once more. Shadd and his gang were a mile in the rear, but coming fast, despite winded horses.

Shefford rode around the wall into a widening space thick with cedars. It ended in a bare slope of smooth rock. Here the Indian dismounted. When the others came up with him he told them to lead their horses and follow. Then he began the ascent of the rock.

It was smooth and hard, though not slippery. There was not a crack. Shefford did not see a broken piece of stone. Nas Ta Bega climbed straight up for a while, and then wound around a swell, to turn this way and that, always going up. Shefford began to see similar mounds of rock all

around him, of every shape that could be called a
curve. There were yellow domes far above, and
small red domes far below. Ridges ran from one
hill of rock to another. There were no abrupt
breaks, but holes and pits and caves were everywhere, and occasionally, deep down, an amphitheater green with cedar and piñon. The Indian
appeared to have a clear idea of where he wanted to
go, though there was no vestige of a trail on those
bare slopes. At length Shefford was high enough
to see back upon the plain, but the pursuers were
no longer in sight.

Nas Ta Bega led to the top of that wall, only to
disclose to his followers another and a higher wall
beyond, with a ridged, bare, wild, and scalloped
depression between. Here footing began to be
precarious for both man and beast. When the
ascent of the second wall began it was necessary
to zigzag up, slowly and carefully, taking advantage
of every level bulge or depression. They must have
consumed half an hour mounting this slope to the
summit. Once there, Shefford drew a sharp breath
with both backward and forward glances. Shadd
and his gang, in single file, showed dark upon the
bare stone ridge behind. And to the fore there
twisted and dropped and curved the most dangerous
slopes Shefford had ever seen. The fugitives had
reached the height of stone wall, of the divide, and
many of the drops upon this side were perpendicular
and too steep to see the bottom.

Nas Ta Bega led along the ridge-top and then
started down, following the waves in the rock. He
came out upon a round promontory from which

there could not have been any turning of a horse. The long slant leading down was at an angle Shefford declared impossible for the animals. Yet the Indian started down. His mustang needed urging, but at last edged upon the steep descent. Shefford and the others had to hold back and wait. It was thrilling to see the intelligent mustang. He did not step. He slid his fore hoofs a few inches at a time and kept directly behind the Indian. If he fell he would knock Nas Ta Bega off his feet and they would both roll down together. There was no doubt in Shefford's mind that the mustang knew this as well as the Indian. Foot by foot they worked down to a swelling bulge, and here Nas Ta Bega left his mustang and came back for the pack-horse. It was even more difficult to get this beast down. Then the Indian called for Lassiter and Jane and Fay to come down. Shefford began to keep a sharp lookout behind and above, and did not see how the three fared on the slope, but evidently there was no mishap. Nas Ta Bega mounted the slope again, and at the moment sight of Shadd's dark bays silhouetted against the sky caused Shefford to call out:

"We've got to hurry!"

The Indian led one mustang and called to the others. Shefford stepped close behind. They went down in single file, inch by inch, foot by foot, and safely reached the comparative level below.

"Shadd's gang are riding their horses up and down these walls!" exclaimed Shefford.

"Shore," replied Lassiter.

Both the women were silent.

Nas Ta Bega led the way swiftly to the right. He rounded a huge dome, climbed a low, rolling ridge, descended and ascended, and came out upon the rim of a steep-walled amphitheater. Along the rim was a yard-wide level, with the chasm to the left and steep slope to the right. There was no time to flinch at the danger, when an even greater danger menaced from the rear. Nas Ta Bega led, and his mustang kept at his heels. One misstep would have plunged the animal to his death. But he was sure-footed and his confidence helped the others. At the apex of the curve the only course led away from the rim, and here there was no level. Four of the mustangs slipped and slid down the smooth rock until they stopped in a shallow depression. It cost time to get them out, to straighten pack and saddles. Shefford thought he heard a yell in the rear, but he could not see anything of the gang.

They rounded this precipice only to face a worse one. Shefford's nerve was sorely tried when he saw steep slants everywhere, all apparently leading down into chasms, and no place a man, let alone a horse, could put a foot with safety. Nevertheless the imperturbable Indian never slacked his pace. Always he appeared to find a way, and he never had to turn back. His winding course, however, did not now cover much distance in a straight line, and herein lay the greatest peril. Any moment Shadd and his men might come within range.

Upon a particularly tedious and dangerous side of rocky hill the fugitives lost so much time that Shefford grew exceedingly alarmed. Still, they accomplished it without accident, and their pursuers did not heave in sight. Perhaps they were having trouble in a bad place.

The afternoon was waning. The red sun hung low above the yellow mesa to the left, and there was a perceptible shading of light.

At last Nas Ta Bega came to a place that halted him. It did not look so bad as places they had successfully passed. Yet upon closer study Shefford did not see how they were to get around the neck of the gully at their feet. Presently the Indian put the bridle over the head of his mustang and left him free. He did likewise for two more mustangs, while Lassiter and Shefford rendered a like service to theirs. Then the Indian started down, with his mustang following him. The pack-animal came next, then Fay and Nack-yal, then Lassiter and his mount, with Jane and hers next, and Shefford last. They followed the Indian, picking their steps swiftly, looking nowhere except at the stone under their feet. The right side of the chasm was rimmed, the curve at the head crossed, and then the real peril of this trap had to be faced. It was a narrow slant of ledge, doubling back parallel with the course already traversed.

A sharp warning cry from Nas Ta Bega scarcely prepared Shefford for hoarse yells, and then a rattling rifle-volley from the top of the slope opposite. Bullets thudded on the cliff, whipped up red dust, and spanged and droned away.

Fay Larkin screamed and staggered back against the wall. Nack-yal was hit, and with frightened snort he reared, pawed the air, and came down, pounding the stone. The mustang behind him went to his knees, sank with his head over the rim, and, slipping off, plunged into the depths. In an instant a dull crash came up.

For a moment there was imminent peril for the horses, more in the yawning hole than in the spanging of badly aimed bullets. Lassiter drew Jane up a little slope out of the way of the frightened mustangs, and Shefford, risking his neck, rushed to Fay. She was holding her arm, which was bleeding. Unheeding the rain of bullets, he half carried, half dragged her along the slope of the low bluff, where he hid behind a corner till the Indian drove the mustangs round it. Shefford's swift fingers were wet and red with the blood from Fay's arm when he had bound the wound with his scarf. Lassiter had gotten around with Jane and was calling Shefford to hurry.

It had been Shefford's idea to halt there and fight. But he did not want to send Fay on alone, so he hurried ahead with her. The Indian had the horses going fast on a long level, overhung by bulging wall. Lassiter and Jane were looking back. Shefford, becoming aware of a steep slope to his left, looked down to see a narrow chasm and great crevices in the cliffs, with bunches of cedars here and there.

Presently Nas Ta Bega disappeared with the mustangs. He had evidently turned off to go down behind the split cliffs. Shefford and Fay caught up with Lassiter and Jane, and, panting, hurrying, looking backward and then forward, they kept on, as best they could, in the Indian's course. Shefford made sure they had lost him, when he appeared down to the left. Then they all ran to catch up with him. They went around the chasm, and then through one of the narrow cracks to come out upon the rim, among cedars. Here the Indian waited for them. He pointed down another long swell of naked stone to a narrow green split which was evidently different from all these curved pits and holes and abysses, for this one had straight walls and wound away out of sight. It was the head of a cañon.

"Nonnezoshe Boco!" said the Indian.

" Nas Ta Bega, go on!" replied Shefford. "When Shadd comes out on that slope above he can't see you—where you go down. Hurry on with the horses and women. Lassiter, you go with them. And if Shadd passes me and comes up with you—do your best. . . . I'm going to ambush that Piute and his gang!"

"Shore you've picked out a good place," replied Lassiter.

In another moment Shefford was alone. He heard the light, soft pat and slide of the hoofs of the mustangs as they went down. Presently that sound ceased.

He looked at the red stain on his hands—from the blood of the girl he loved. And he had to stifle a terrible wrath that shook his frame. In regard to Shadd's pursuit, it had not been blood that he had feared, but capture for Fay. He and Nas Ta Bega might have expected a shot if they resisted, but to wound that unfortunate girl—it made a tiger out of him. When he had stilled the emotions that weakened and shook him and reached cold and implacable control of himself, he crawled under the

321

cedars to the rim and, well hidden, he watched and waited.

Shadd appeared to be slow for the first time since he had been sighted. With keen eyes Shefford watched the corner where he and the others had escaped from that murderous volley. But Shadd did not come.

The sun had lost its warmth and was tipping the lofty mesa to his right. Soon twilight would make travel on those walls more perilous and darkness would make it impossible. Shadd must hurry or abandon the pursuit for that day. Shefford found himself grimly hopeful.

Suddenly he heard the click of hoofs. It came, faint yet clear, on the still air. He glued his sight upon that corner where he expected the pursuers to appear. More cracks of hoofs pierced his ear, clearer and sharper this time. Presently he gathered that they could not possibly come from beyond the corner he was watching. So he looked far to the left of that place, seeing no one, then far to the right. Out over a bulge of stone he caught sight of the bobbing head of a horse—then another—and still another.

He was astounded. Shadd had gone below that place where the attack had been made and he had come up this steep slope. More horses appeared— to the number of eight. Shefford easily recognized a low, broad, squat rider to be Shadd. Assuredly the Piute did not know this country. Possibly, however, he had feared an ambush. But Shefford grew convinced that Shadd had not expected an ambush, or at least did not fear it, and had mistaken the Indian's course. Moreover, if he led his gang a few rods farther up that slope he would do worse than make a mistake—he would be facing a double peril.

What fearless horsemen these Indians were! Shadd was mounted, as were three others of his gang. Evidently the white men, the outlaws, were the ones on foot. Shefford thrilled and his veins stung when he saw these pursuers come passing what he considered the danger mark. But manifestly they could not see their danger. Assuredly they were aware of the chasm; however, the level upon which they were advancing narrowed gradually, and they could not tell that very soon they could not go any farther nor could they turn back. The alternative was to climb the slope, and that was a desperate chance.

They came up, now about on a level with Shefford, and perhaps three hundred yards distant. He gripped his rifle with a fatal assurance that he could kill one of them now. Still he waited. Curiosity consumed him because every foot they advanced heightened their peril. Shefford wondered if Shadd would have chosen that course if he had not supposed the Navajo had chosen it first. It was plain that one of the walking Piutes stooped now and then to examine the rock. He was looking for some faint sign of a horse track.

Shadd halted within two hundred yards of where Shefford lay hidden. His keen eye had caught the significance of the narrowing level before he had reached the end. He pointed and spoke. Shefford heard his voice. The others replied. They all looked up at the steep slope, down into the chasm right below them, and across into the cedars. The Piute in the rear succeeded in turning his horse, went back, and began to circle up the slope. The others entered into an argument and they became more closely grouped upon the narrow bench. Their mustangs were lean, wiry, wild, vicious, and Shefford calculated grimly upon what a stampede might mean in that position.

Then Shadd turned his mustang up the slope. Like a goat he climbed. Another Indian in the rear succeeded in pivoting his steed and started back, apparently to circle round and up. The others of the gang appeared uncertain. They yelled hoarsely at Shadd, who halted on the steep slant some twenty paces above them. He spoke and made motions that evidently meant the climb was easy enough. It looked easy for him. His dark face flashed red in the rays of the sun.

At this critical moment Shefford decided to fire. He meant to kill Shadd, hoping if the leader was gone the others would abandon the pursuit. The rifle wavered a little as he aimed, then grew still. He fired. Shadd never flinched. But the fiery mustang, perhaps wounded, certainly terrified, plunged down with piercing, horrid scream. Shadd fell under him. Shrill yells rent the air. Like a thunderbolt the sliding horse was upon men and animals below.

A heavy shock, wild snorts, upflinging heads and hoofs, a terrible tramping, thudding, shrieking mêlée, then a brown, twisting, tangled mass shot down the slant over the rim!

Shefford dazedly thought he saw men running. He did see plunging horses. One slipped, fell, rolled, and went into the chasm.

Then up from the depths came a crash, a long, slipping roar. In another instant there was a lighter crash and a lighter sliding roar.

Two horses, shaking, paralyzed with fear, were left upon the narrow level. Beyond them a couple of men were crawling along the stone. Up on the level stood the two Indians, holding down frightened horses, and staring at the fatal slope.

And Shefford lay there under the cedar, in the ghastly grip of the moment, hardly comprehending that his ill-aimed shot had been a thunderbolt.

He did not think of shooting at the Piutes; they, however, recovering from their shock, evidently feared the ambush, for they swiftly drew up the slope and passed out of sight. The frightened horses below whistled and tramped along the lower level, finally vanishing. There was nothing left on the bare wall to prove to Shefford that it had been the scene of swift and tragic death. He leaned from his covert and peered over the rim. Hundreds of feet below he saw dark growths of piñons. There was no sign of a pile of horses and men, and then he realized that he could not tell the number that had perished. The swift finale had been as stunning to him as if lightning had struck near him.

Suddenly it flashed over him what state of suspense and torture Fay and Jane must be in at that very moment. And, leaping up, he ran out of the cedars to the slope behind and hurried down at risk of limb. The sun had set by this time. He

hoped he could catch up with the party before dark.
He went straight down, and the end of the slope was
a smooth, low wall. The Indian must have descended with the horses at some other point. The
cañon was about fifty yards wide and it headed
under the great slope of Navajo Mountain. These
smooth, rounded walls appeared to end at its low
rim.

Shefford slid down upon a grassy bank, and finding
the tracks of the horses, he followed them. They led
along the wall. As soon as he had assured himself
that Nas Ta Bega had gone down the cañon he
abandoned the tracks and pushed ahead swiftly.
He heard the soft rush of running water. In the
center of the cañon wound heavy lines of bright-
green foliage, bordering a rocky brook. The air
was close, warm, and sweet with perfume of flowers.
The walls were low and shelving, and soon lost that
rounded appearance peculiar to the wind-worn
slopes above. Shefford came to where the horses
had plowed down a gravelly bank into the clear,
swift water of the brook. The little pools of water
were still muddy. Shefford drank, finding the water
cold and sweet, without the bitter bite of alkali.
He crossed and pushed on, running on the grassy
levels. Flowers were everywhere, but he did not
notice them particularly. The cañon made many
leisurely turns, and its size, if it enlarged at all, was
not perceptible to him yet. The rims above him
were perhaps fifty feet high. Cottonwood-trees
began to appear along the brook, and blossoming
buck-brush in the corners of wall.

He had traveled perhaps a mile when Nas Ta Bega.

appearing to come out of the thicket, confronted him.

"Hello!" called Shefford. "Where're Fay—and the others?"

The Indian made a gesture that signified the rest of the party were beyond a little way. Shefford took Nas Ta Bega's arm, and as they walked, and he panted for breath, he told what had happened back on the slopes.

The Indian made one of his singular speaking sweeps of hand, and he scrutinized Shefford's face, but he received the news in silence. They turned a corner of wall, crossed a wide, shallow, boulder-strewn place in the brook, and mounted the bank to a thicket. Beyond this, from a clump of cottonwoods, Lassiter strode out with a gun in each hand. He had been hiding.

"Shore I'm glad to see you," he said, and the eyes that piercingly fixed on Shefford were now as keen as formerly they had been mild.

"Gone! Lassiter—they're gone," broke out Shefford. "Where's Fay—and Jane?"

Lassiter called, and presently the women came out of the thick brake, and Fay bounded forward with her swift stride, while Jane followed with eager step and anxious face. Then they all surrounded Shefford.

"It was Shadd—and his gang," panted Shefford. "Eight in all. Three or four Piutes—the others outlaws. They lost track of us. Went below the place—where they shot at us. And they came up—on a bad slope."

Shefford described the slope and the deep chasm

and how Shadd led up to the point where he saw his mistake and then how the catastrophe fell.

"I shot—and missed," repeated Shefford, with the sweat in beads on his pale face. "I missed Shadd. Maybe I hit the horse. He plunged—reared—fell back—a terrible fall—right upon that bunch of horses and men below. . . . In a horrible, wrestling, screaming tangle they slid over the rim! I don't know how many. I saw some men running along. I saw three other horses plunging. One slipped and went over. . . . I have no idea how many, but Shadd and some of his gang went to destruction."

"Shore thet's fine!" said Lassiter. "But mebbe I won't get to use them guns, after all."

"Hardly on that gang," laughed Shefford. "The two Piutes and what others escaped turned back. Maybe they'll meet a posse of Mormons—for of course the Mormons will track us, too—and come back to where Shadd lost his life. That's an awful place. Even the Piute got lost—couldn't follow Nas Ta Bega. It would take any pursuers some time to find how we got in here. I believe we need not fear further pursuit. Certainly not to-night or to-morrow. Then we'll be far down the cañon."

When Shefford concluded his earnest remarks the faces of Fay and Jane had lost the signs of suppressed dread.

"Nas Ta Bega, make camp here," said Shefford. "Water—wood—grass—why, this 's something like. . . . Fay, how's your arm?"

"It hurts," she replied, simply.

"Come with me down to the brook and let me wash and bind it properly."

They went, and she sat upon a stone while he knelt beside her and untied his scarf from her arm. As the blood had hardened, it was necessary to slit her sleeve to the shoulder. Using his scarf, he washed the blood from the wound, and found it to be merely a cut, a groove, on the surface.

"That's nothing," Shefford said, lightly. "It 'll heal in a day. But there'll always be a scar. And when we—we get back to civilization, and you wear a pretty gown without sleeves, people will wonder what made this mark on your beautiful arm."

Fay looked at him with wonderful eyes. "Do women wear gowns without sleeves?" she asked.

"They do."

"Have I a—beautiful arm?"

She stretched it out, white, blue-veined, the skin fine as satin, the lines graceful and flowing, a round, firm, strong arm.

"The most beautiful I ever saw," he replied.

But the pleasure his compliment gave her was not communicated to him. His last impression of that right arm had been of its strength, and his mind flashed with lightning swiftness to a picture that haunted him—Waggoner lying dead on the porch with that powerfully driven knife in his breast. Shefford shuddered through all his being. Would this phantom come often to him like that? Hurriedly he bound up her arm with the scarf and did not look at her, and was conscious that she felt a subtle change in him.

The short twilight ended with the fugitives comfortable in a camp that for natural features could not have been improved upon. Darkness found Fay

and Jane asleep on a soft mossy bed, a blanket
tucked around them, and their faces still and beautiful in the flickering camp-fire light. Lassiter did
not linger long awake. Nas Ta Bega, seeing Shefford's excessive fatigue, urged him to sleep. Shefford
demurred, insisting that he share the night-watch.
But Nas Ta Bega, by agreeing that Shefford might
have the following night's duty, prevailed upon him.

Shefford seemed to shut his eyes upon darkness
and to open them immediately to the light. The
stream of blue sky above, the gold tints on the
western rim, the rosy, brightening colors down in
the cañon, were proofs of the sunrise. This morning
Nas Ta Bega proceeded leisurely, and his manner
was comforting. When all was in readiness for a
start he gave the mustang he had ridden to Shefford,
and walked, leading the pack-animal.

The mode of travel here was a selection of the best
levels, the best places to cross the brook, the best
banks to climb, and it was a process of continual
repetition. As the Indian picked out the course
and the mustangs followed his lead there was nothing
for Shefford to do but take his choice between reflection that seemed predisposed toward gloom and
an absorption in the beauty, color, wildness, and
changing character of Nonnezoshe Boco.

Assuredly his experience in the desert did not
count in it a trip down into a strange, beautiful, lost
cañon such as this. It did not widen, though the
walls grew higher. They began to lean and bulge,
and the narrow strip of sky above resembled a flowing blue river. Huge caverns had been hollowed
out by some work of nature, what, he could not tell,

though he was sure it could not have been wind. And when the brook ran close under one of these overhanging places the running water made a singular, indescribable sound. A crack from a hoof on a stone rang like a hollow bell and echoed from wall to wall. And the croak of a frog—the only living creature he had so far noted in the cañon—was a weird and melancholy thing.

Fay rode close to him, and his heart seemed to rejoice when she spoke, when she showed how she wanted to be near him, yet, try as he might, he could not respond. His speech to her—what little there was—did not come spontaneously. And he suffered a remorse that he could not be honestly natural to her. Then he would drive away the encroaching gloom, trusting that a little time would dispel it.

"We are deeper down than Surprise Valley," said Fay.

"How do you know?" he asked.

"Here are the pink and yellow sago-lilies. You remember we went once to find the white ones? I have found white lilies in Surprise Valley, but never any pink or yellow."

Shefford had seen flowers all along the green banks, but he had not marked the lilies. Here he dismounted and gathered several. They were larger than the white ones of higher altitudes, of the same exquisite beauty and fragility, of such rare pink and yellow hues as he had never seen. He gave the flowers to Fay.

"They bloom only where it's always summer," she said.

That expressed their nature. They were the orchids of the summer cañons. They stood up everywhere starlike out of the green. It was impossible to prevent the mustangs treading them under hoof. And as the cañon deepened, and many little springs added their tiny volume to the brook, every grassy bench was dotted with lilies, like a green sky star-spangled. And this increasing luxuriance manifested itself in the banks of purple moss and clumps of lavender daisies and great clusters of yellow violets. The brook was lined by blossoming buck-rush; the rocky corners showed the crimson and magenta of cactus; ledges were green with shining moss that sparkled with little white flowers. The hum of bees filled the air.

But by and by this green and colorful and verdant beauty, the almost level floor of the cañon, the banks of soft earth, the thickets and the clumps of cottonwoods, the shelving caverns and the bulging walls—these features gradually were lost, and Nonnezoshe Boco began to deepen in bare red and white stone steps, the walls sheered away from one another, breaking into sections and ledges, and rising higher and higher, and there began to be manifested a dark and solemn concordance with the nature that had created this rent in the earth.

There was a stretch of miles where steep steps in hard red rock alternated with long levels of round boulders. Here one by one the mustangs went lame.. And the fugitives, dismounting to spare the faithful beasts, slipped and stumbled over these loose and treacherous stones. Fay was the only one who did not show distress. She was glad to be on

foot again and the rolling boulders were as stable as
solid rock for her.

The hours passed; the toil increased; the progress
diminished; one of the mustangs failed entirely and
was left; and all the while the dimensions of Nonnezoshe Boco magnified and its character changed.
It became a thousand-foot walled cañon, leaning,
broken, threatening, with great yellow slides blocking passage, with huge sections split off from the
main wall, with immense dark and gloomy caverns.
Strangely, it had no intersecting cañons. It jealously
guarded its secret. Its unusual formations of cavern
and pillar and half-arch led the mind to expect any
monstrous stone-shape left by an avalanche or
cataclysm.

Down and down the fugitives toiled. And now
the stream-bed was bare of boulders, and the banks
of earth. The floods that had rolled down that
cañon had here borne away every loose thing. All
the floor was bare red and white stone, polished,
glistening, slippery, affording treacherous foothold.
And the time came when Nas Ta Bega abandoned
the stream-bed to take to the rock-strewn and cactus-
covered ledges above.

Jane gave out and had to be assisted upon the weary
mustang. Fay was persuaded to mount Nack-yal
again. Lassiter plodded along. The Indian bent tired
steps far in front. And Shefford traveled on after
him, footsore and hot.

The cañon widened ahead into a great, ragged,
iron-hued amphitheater, and from there apparently
turned abruptly at right angles. Sunset rimmed the
walls. Shefford wondered dully when the Indian

would halt to camp. And he dragged himself onward with eyes down on the rough ground.

When he raised them again the Indian stood on a point of slope with folded arms, gazing down where the cañon veered. Something in Nas Ta Bega's pose quickened Shefford's pulse and then his steps. He reached the Indian and the point where he, too, could see beyond that vast jutting wall that had obstructed his view.

A mile beyond all was bright with the colors of sunset, and spanning the cañon in the graceful shape and beautiful hues of a rainbow was a magnificent stone bridge.

"Nonnezoshe!" exclaimed the Navajo, with a deep and sonorous roll in his voice.

XVIII

THE rainbow bridge was the one great natural phenomenon, the one grand spectacle, which Shefford had ever seen that did not at first give vague disappointment, a confounding of reality, a disenchantment of contrast with what the mind had conceived.

But this thing was glorious. It silenced him, yet did not awe or stun. His body and brain, weary and dull from the toil of travel, received a singular and revivifying freshness. He had a strange, mystic perception of this rosy-hued stupendous arch of stone, as if in a former life it had been a goal he could not reach. This wonder of nature, though all-satisfying, all-fulfilling to his artist's soul, could not be a resting-place for him, a destination where something awaited him, a height he must scale to find peace, the end of his strife. But it seemed all these. He could not understand his perception or his emotion. Still, here at last, apparently, was the rainbow of his boyish dreams and of his manhood—a rainbow magnified even beyond those dreams, no longer transparent and ethereal, but solidified, a thing of ages, sweeping up majestically from the red walls, its iris-hued arch against the blue sky.

335

Nas Ta Bega led on down the ledge and Shefford plodded thoughtfully after him. The others
followed. A jutting corner of wall again hid the
cañon. The Indian was working round to circle the
huge amphitheater. It was slow, irritating, strenu-
ous toil, for the way was on a steep slant, rough and
loose and dragging. The rocks were as hard and
jagged as lava. And the cactus further hindered
progress. When at last the long half-circle had
been accomplished the golden and rosy lights had
faded.

Again the cañon opened to view. All the walls
were pale and steely and the stone bridge loomed
dark. Nas Ta Bega said camp would be made at the
bridge, which was now close. Just before they
reached it the Navajo halted with one of his singular
actions. Then he stood motionless. Shefford realized that Nas Ta Bega was saying his prayer to this
great stone god. Presently the Indian motioned for
Shefford to lead the others and the horses on under
the bridge. Shefford did so, and, upon turning, was
amazed to see the Indian climbing the steep and
difficult slope on the other side. All the party
watched him until he disappeared behind the huge
base of cliff that supported the arch. Shefford
selected a level place for camp, some few rods away,
and here, with Lassiter, unsaddled and unpacked the
lame, drooping mustangs. When this was done twilight had fallen. Nas Ta Bega appeared, coming
down the steep slope on this side of the bridge.
Then Shefford divined why the Navajo had made
that arduous climb. He would not go under the
bridge. Nonnezoshe was a Navajo god. And Nas

336

Ta Bega, though educated as a white man, was true to the superstition of his ancestors.

Nas Ta Bega turned the mustangs loose to fare for what scant grass grew on bench and slope. Firewood was even harder to find than grass. When the camp duties had been performed and the simple meal eaten there was gloom gathering in the cañon and the stars had begun to blink in the pale strip of blue above the lofty walls. The place was oppressive and the fugitives mostly silent. Shefford spread a bed of blankets for the women, and Jane at once lay wearily down. Fay stood beside the flickering fire, and Shefford felt her watching him. He was conscious of a desire to get away from her haunting gaze. To the gentle good-night he bade her she made no response.

Shefford moved away into a strange dark shadow cast by the bridge against the pale starlight. It was a weird, black belt, where he imagined he was invisible, but out of which he could see. There was a slab of rock near the foot of the bridge, and here Shefford composed himself to watch, to feel, to think the unknown thing that seemed to be inevitably coming to him.

A slight stiffening of his neck made him aware that he had been continually looking up at the looming arch. And he found that insensibly it had changed and grown. It had never seemed the same any two moments, but that was not what he meant. Near at hand it was too vast a thing for immediate comprehension. He wanted to ponder on what had formed it—to reflect upon its meaning as to age and force of nature, yet all he could do at each

337

moment was to see. White stars hung along the dark curved line. The rim of the arch seemed to shine. The moon must be up there somewhere. The far side of the cañon was now a blank, black wall. Over its towering rim showed a pale glow. It brightened. The shades in the cañon lightened, then a white disk of moon peered over the dark line. The bridge turned to silver, and the gloomy, shadowy belt it had cast blanched and vanished.

Shefford became aware of the presence of Nas Ta Bega. Dark, silent, statuesque, with inscrutable eyes uplifted, with all that was spiritual of the Indian suggested by a somber and tranquil knowledge of his place there, he represented the same to Shefford as a solitary figure of human life brought out the greatness of a great picture. Nonnezoshe Boco needed life, wild life, life of its millions of years—and here stood the dark and silent Indian.

There was a surge in Shefford's heart and in his mind a perception of a moment of incalculable change to his soul. And at that moment Fay Larkin stole like a phantom to his side and stood there with her uncovered head shining and her white face lovely in the moonlight.

"May I stay with you—a little?" she asked, wistfully. "I can't sleep."

"Surely you may," he replied. "Does your arm hurt too badly, or are you too tired to sleep?"

"No—it's this place. I—I—can't tell you how I feel."

But the feeling was there in her eyes for Shefford to read. Had he too great an emotion—did he read too much—did he add from his soul? For him the wild, starry, haunted eyes mirrored all that he had seen and felt under Nonnezoshe. And for herself they shone eloquently of courage and love.

"I need to talk—and I don't know how," she said.

He was silent, but he took her hands and drew her closer.

"Why are you so — so different?" she asked, bravely.

"Different?" he echoed.

"Yes. You are kind—you speak the same to me as you used to. But since we started you've been different, somehow."

"Fay, think how hard and dangerous the trip's been! I've been worried—and sick with dread—with— Oh, you can't imagine the strain I'm under! How could I be my old self?"

"It isn't worry I mean."

He was too miserable to try to find out what she did mean; besides, he believed, if he let himself think about it, he would know what troubled her.

"I—I am almost happy," she said, softly.

"Fay! . . . Aren't you at all afraid?"

"No. You'll take care of me. . . . Do—do you love me—like you did before?"

"Why, child! Of course—I love you," he replied, brokenly, and he drew her closer. He had never embraced her, never kissed her. But there was a whiteness about her then—a wraith—a something from her soul, and he could only gaze at her.

"I love you," she whispered. "I thought I knew it that—that night. But I'm only finding it out now. . . . And somehow I had to tell you here."

"Fay, I haven't said much to you," he said, hurriedly, huskily. "I haven't had a chance. I love you. I—I ask you—will you be my wife?"

"Of course," she said, simply, but the white, moon-blanched face colored with a dark and leaping blush.

"We'll be married as soon as we get out of the desert," he went on. "And we'll forget—all—all that's happened. You're so young. You'll forget."

"I'd forgotten already, till this difference came in you. And pretty soon—when I can say something more to you—I'll forget all except Surprise Valley— and my evenings in the starlight with you."

"Say it then—quick!"

She was leaning against him, holding his hands in her strong clasp, soulful, tender, almost passionate.

"You couldn't help it. . . . I'm to blame. . . . I remember what I said."

"What?" he queried in amaze.

"'*You can kill him!*' . . . I said that. I made you kill him."

"Kill—whom?" cried Shefford.

"Waggoner. I'm to blame. . . . That must be what's made you different. And, oh, I've wanted you to know it's all my fault. . . . But I wouldn't be sorry if you weren't. . . . I'm glad he's dead."

"*You—think—I—*" Shefford's gasping whisper failed in the shock of the revelation that Fay believed he had killed Waggoner. Then with the inference came the staggering truth—her guiltlessness; and a paralyzing joy held him stricken.

A powerful hand fell upon Shefford's shoulder, startling him. Nas Ta Bega stood there, looking down upon him and Fay. Never had the Indian seemed so dark, inscrutable of face. But in his magnificent bearing, in the spirit that Shefford sensed in him, there were nobility and power and a strange pride.

The Indian kept one hand on Shefford's shoulder, and with the other he struck himself on the breast. The action was that of an Indian, impressive and stern, significant of an Indian's prowess.

"My God!" breathed Shefford, very low.

"Oh, what does he mean?" cried Fay.

Shefford held her with shaking hands, trying to speak, to fight a way out of these stultifying emotions.

"Nas Ta Bega—you heard. She thinks—I killed Waggoner!"

All about the Navajo then was dark and solemn disproof of her belief. He did not need to speak. His repetition of that savage, almost boastful blow on his breast added only to the dignity, and not to the denial, of a warrior.

"Fay, he means he killed the Mormon," said Shefford. "He must have, for *I* did not!"

"Ah!" murmured Fay, and she leaned to him with passionate, quivering gladness. It was the woman— the human—the soul born in her that came uppermost then; now, when there was no direct call to the wild and elemental in her nature, she showed a heart above revenge, the instinct of a saving right, of truth as Shefford knew them. He took her into his arms and never had he loved her so well.

"Nas Ta Bega, you killed the Mormon," declared Shefford, with a voice that had gained strength. No silent Indian suggestion of a deed would suffice in that moment. Shefford needed to hear the Navajo

speak—to have Fay hear him speak. "Nas Ta
Bega, I know—I understand. But tell her. Speak
so she will know. Tell it as a white man would!"

"I heard her cry out," replied the Indian, in his
slow English. "I waited. When he came I killed
him."

A poignant why was wrenched from Shefford.
Nas Ta Bega stood silent.

"*Bi Nai!*" And when that sonorous Indian name
rolled in dignity from his lips he silently stalked
away into the gloom. That was his answer to the
white man.

Shefford bent over Fay, and as the strain on him
broke he held her closer and closer and his tears
streamed down and his voice broke in exclamations
of tenderness and thanksgiving. It did not matter
what she had thought, but she must never know
what he had thought. He clasped her as something
precious he had lost and regained. He was shaken
with a passion of remorse. How could he have believed Fay Larkin guilty of murder? Women less
wild and less justified than she had been driven to
such a deed, yet how could he have believed it of
her, when for two days he had been with her, had
seen her face, and deep into her eyes? There was
a mystery in his very blindness. He cast the whole
thought from him for ever. There was no shadow
between Fay and him. He had found her. He
had saved her. She was free. She was innocent.
And suddenly, as he seemed delivered from contending tumults within, he became aware that it
was no unresponsive creature he had folded to his
breast.

He became suddenly alive to the warm, throbbing contact of her bosom, to her strong arms clinging round his neck, to her closed eyes, to the rapt whiteness of her face. And he bent to cold lips that seemed to receive his first kisses as new and strange; but tremulously changed, at last to meet his own, and then to burn with sweet and thrilling fire.

"My darling, my dream's come true," he said. "You are my treasure. I found you here at the foot of the rainbow! . . . What if it is a stone rainbow —if all is not as I had dreamed? I followed a gleam. And it's led me to love and faith!"

Hours afterward Shefford walked alone to and fro under the bridge. His trouble had given place to serenity. But this night of nights he must live out wide-eyed to its end.

The moon had long since crossed the streak of star-fired blue above and the cañon was black in shadow. At times a current of wind, with all the strangeness of that strange country in its hollow moan, rushed through the great stone arch. At other times there was silence such as Shefford imagined dwelt deep under this rocky world. At still other times an owl hooted, and the sound was nameless. But it had a mocking echo that never ended. An echo of night, silence, gloom, melancholy death, age, eternity!

The Indian lay asleep with his dark face upturned, and the other sleepers lay calm and white in the starlight.

Shefford saw in them the meaning of life and the past—the illimitable train of faces that had shone under the stars. There was a spirit in the cañon, and whether or not it was what the Navajo embodied in the great Nonnezoshe, or the life of the present, or the death of the ages, or the nature so magnificently manifested in those silent, dreaming, waiting walls—the truth for Shefford was that this spirit was God.

Life was eternal. Man's immortality lay in himself. Love of a woman was hope—happiness. Brotherhood—that mystic and grand "Bi Nai!" of the Navajo—that was religion.

XIX

THE GRAND CAÑON OF THE COLORADO

THE night passed, the gloom turned gray, the dawn stole cool and pale into the cañon. When Nas Ta Bega drove the mustangs into camp the lofty ramparts of the walls were rimmed with gold and the dark arch of Nonnezoshe began to lose its steely gray.

The women had rested well and were in better condition to travel. Jane was cheerful and Fay radiant one moment and in a dream the next. She was beginning to live in that wonderful future. They talked more than usual at breakfast, and Lassiter made droll remarks. Shefford, with his great and haunting trouble ended for ever, with now only danger to face ahead, was a different man, but thoughtful and quiet.

This morning the Indian leisurely made preparations for the start. For all the concern he showed he might have known every foot of the cañon below Nonnezoshe. But, for Shefford, with the dawn had returned anxiety, a restless feeling of the need of hurry. What obstacles, what impassable gorges, might lie between this bridge and the river! The Indian's inscrutable serenity and Fay's trust, her

345

radiance, the exquisite glow upon her face, sustained Shefford and gave him patience to endure and conceal his dread.

At length the flight was resumed, with Nas Ta Bega leading on foot, and Shefford walking in the rear. A quarter of a mile below camp the Indian led down a declivity into the bottom of the narrow gorge, where the stream ran. He did not gaze backward for a last glance at Nonnezoshe; nor did Jane or Lassiter. Fay, however, checked Nack-yal at the rim of the descent and turned to look behind. Shefford contrasted her tremulous smile, her half-happy good-by to this place, with the white stillness of her face when she had bade farewell to Surprise Valley. Then she rode Nack-yal down into the gorge.

Shefford knew that this would be his last look at the rainbow bridge. As he gazed the tip of the great arch lost its cold, dark stone color and began to shine. The sun had just arisen high enough over some low break in the wall to reach the bridge. Shefford watched. Slowly, in wondrous transformation, the gold and blue and rose and pink and purple blended their hues, softly, mistily, cloudily, until once again the arch was a rainbow.

Ages before life had evolved upon the earth it had spread its grand arch from wall to wall, black and mystic at night, transparent and rosy in the sunrise, at sunset a flaming curve limned against the heavens. When the race of man had passed it would, perhaps, stand there still. It was not for many eyes to see. Only by toil, sweat, endurance, blood, could any man ever look at Nonnezoshe. So it would always be alone, grand, silent, beautiful, unintelligible.

Shefford bade Nonnezoshe a mute, reverent farewell. Then plunging down the weathered slope or
the gorge to the stream below, he hurried forward to
join the others. They had progressed much farther
than he imagined they would have, and this was
owing to the fact that the floor of the gorge afforded
easy travel. It was gravel on rock bottom, tortuous,
but open, with infrequent and shallow downward
steps. The stream did not now rush and boil along
and tumble over rock-encumbered ledges. In corners the water collected in round, green, eddying
pools. There were patches of grass and willows and
mounds of moss. Shefford's surprise equaled his
relief, for he believed that the violent descent of
Nonnezoshe Boco had been passed. Any turn now,
he imagined, might bring the party out upon the
river. When he caught up with them he imparted
this conviction, which was received with cheer. The
hopes of all, except the Indian, seemed mounting;
and if he ever hoped or despaired it was never manifest.

Shefford's anticipation, however, was not soon
realized. The fugitives traveled miles farther down
Nonnezoshe Boco, and the only changes were that the
walls of the lower gorge heightened and merged into
those above and that these upper ones towered ever
loftier. Shefford had to throw his head straight back
to look up at the rims, and the narrow strip of sky
was now indeed a flowing stream of blue.

Difficult steps were met, too, yet nothing compared to those of the upper cañon. Shefford calculated that this day's travel had advanced several
hours; and more than ever now he was anticipating

the mouth of Nonnezoshe Boco. Still another hour went by. And then came striking changes. The cañon narrowed till the walls were scarcely twenty paces apart; the color of stone grew dark red above and black down low; the light of day became shadowed, and the floor was a level, gravelly, winding lane, with the stream meandering slowly and silently.

Suddenly the Indian halted. He turned his ear down the cañon lane. He had heard something. The others grouped round him, but did not hear a sound except the soft flow of water and the heave of the mustangs. Then the Indian went on. Presently he halted again. And again he listened. This time he threw up his head and upon his dark face shone a light which might have been pride.

"Tse ko-n-tsa-igi," he said.

The others could not understand, but they were impressed.

"Shore he means somethin' big," drawled Lassiter.

"Oh, what did he say?" queried Fay in eagerness.

"Nas Ta Bega, tell us," said Shefford. "We are full of hope."

"Grand Cañon," replied the Indian.

"How do you know?" asked Shefford.

"I hear the roar of the river."

But Shefford, listen as he might, could not hear it. They traveled on, winding down the wonderful lane. Every once in a while Shefford lagged behind, let the others pass out of hearing, and then he listened. At last he was rewarded. Low and deep, dull and strange, with some quality to incite dread, came a roar. Thereafter, at intervals, usually at turns in the cañon, and when a faint stir of warm air

348

fanned his cheeks, he heard the sound, growing clearer and louder.

He rounded an abrupt corner to have the roar suddenly fill his ears, to see the lane extend straight to a ragged vent, and beyond that, at some distance, a dark, ragged, bulging wall, like iron. As he hurried forward he was surprised to find that the noise did not increase. Here it kept a strange uniformity of tone and volume. The others of the party passed out of the mouth of Nonnezoshe Boco in advance of Shefford, and when he reached it they were grouped upon a bank of sand. A dark-red cañon yawned before them, and through it slid the strangest river Shefford had ever seen. At first glance he imagined the strangeness consisted of the dark-red color of the water, but at the second he was not so sure. All the others, except Nas Ta Bega, eyed the river blankly, as if they did not know what to think. The roar came from round a huge bulging wall downstream. Up the cañon, half a mile, at another turn, there was a leaping rapid of dirty red-white waves, and the sound of this, probably, was drowned in the unseen but nearer rapid.

"This is the Grand Cañon of the Colorado," said Shefford. "We've come out at the mouth of Nonnezoshe Boco. . . . And now to wait for Joe Lake!"

They made camp on a dry, level sand-bar under a shelving wall. Nas Ta Bega collected a pile of driftwood to be used for fire, and then he took the mustangs back up the side cañon to find grass for them. Lassiter appeared unusually quiet, and soon passed from weary rest on the sand to deep slumber. Fay and Jane succumbed to an exhaustion that mani-

Jested itself the moment relaxation set in, and they, too, fell asleep. Shefford patrolled the long strip of sand under the wall, and watched up the river for Joe Lake. The Indian returned and went along the river, climbed over the jutting, sharp slopes that reached into the water, and passed out of sight upstream toward the rapid.

Shefford had a sense that the river and the cañon were too magnificent to be compared with others. Still, all his emotions and sensations had been so wrought upon, he seemed not to have any left by which he might judge of what constituted the difference. He would wait. He had a grim conviction that before he was safely out of this earth-riven crack he would know. One thing, however, struck him, and it was that up the cañon, high over the lower walls, hazy and blue, stood other walls, and beyond and above them, dim in purple distance, upreared still other walls. The haze and the blue and the purple meant great distance, and, likewise, the height seemed incomparable.

The red river attracted him most. Since this was the medium by which he must escape with his party, it was natural that it absorbed him, to the neglect of the gigantic cliffs. And the more he watched the river, studied it, listened to it, imagined its nature, its power, its relentlessness, the more he dreaded it. As the hours of the afternoon wore away, and he strolled along and rested on the banks, his first impressions, and what he realized might be his truest ones, were gradually lost. He could not bring them back. The river was changing, deceitful. It worked upon his mind. The low, hollow roar filled his ears and seemed to mock him. Then he endeavored to stop thinking about it, to confine his attention to the gap up-stream where sooner or later he prayed that Joe Lake and his boat would appear. But, though he controlled his gaze, he could not his thought, and his stránge, impondering dread of the river augmented.

The afternoon waned. Nas Ta Bega came back to camp and said any likelihood of Joe's arrival was past for that day. Shefford could not get over an impression of strangeness—of the impossibility of the reality presented to his naked eyes. These lonely fugitives in the huge-walled cañon waiting for a boatman to come down that river! Strange and wild—those were the words which, inadequately at best, suited this country and the situations it produced.

After supper he and Fay walked along the bars of smooth, red sand. There were a few moments when the distant peaks and domes and turrets were glorified in changing sunset hues. But the beauty was fleeting. Fay still showed lassitude. She was quiet, yet cheerful, and the sweetness of her smile, her absolute trust in him, stirred and strengthened anew his spirit. Yet he suffered torture when he thought of trusting Fay's life, her soul, and her beauty to this strange red river.

Night brought him relief. He could not see the river; only the low roar made its presence known out there in the shadows. And, there being no need to stay awake, he dropped at once into heavy slumber. He was roused by hands dragging at him. Nas Ta Bega bent over him. It was broad daylight. The yellow wall high above was glistening. A fire was crackling and pleasant odors were wafted to him. Fay and Jane and Lassiter sat around the tarpaulin at breakfast. After the meal suspense and strain were manifested in all the fugitives, even the imperturbable Indian being more than usually watchful. His eyes scarcely ever left the black gap where the river slid round the turn above. Soon, as on the preceding day, he disappeared up the ragged, iron-bound shore. There was scarcely an attempt at conversation. A controlling thought bound that group into silence—if Joe Lake was ever going to come he would come to-day.

Shefford asked himself a hundred times if it were possible, and his answer seemed to be in the low, sullen, muffled roar of the river. And as the morning wore on toward noon his dread deepened until all chance appeared hopeless. Already he had begun to have vague and unformed and disquieting ideas of the only avenue of escape left—to return up Nonnezoshe Boco—and that would be to enter a trap.

Suddenly a piercing cry pealed down the cañon. It was followed by echoes, weird and strange, that clapped from wall to wall in mocking concatenation. Nas Ta Bega appeared high on the ragged slope. The cry had been the Indian's. He swept an arm out, pointing up-stream, and stood like a statue on the iron rocks.

Shefford's keen gaze sighted a moving something in the bend of the river. It was long, low, dark, and flat, with a lighter object upright in the middle. A boat and a man!

"Joe! It's Joe!" yelled Shefford, madly. "There!
. . . Look!"

Jane and Fay were on their knees in the sand,
clasping each other, pale faces toward that bend in
the river.

Shefford ran up the shore toward the Indian. He
climbed the jutting slant of rock. The boat was now
full in the turn—it moved faster—it was nearing the
smooth incline above the rapid. There! it glided
down—heaved darkly up—settled back—and disappeared in the frothy, muddy roughness of water.
Shefford held his breath and watched. A dark,
bobbing object showed, vanished, showed again to
enlarge—to take the shape of a big flatboat—and
then it rode the swift, choppy current out of the
lower end of the rapid.

Nas Ta Bega began to make violent motions, and
Shefford, taking his cue, frantically waved his red
scarf. There was a five-mile-an-hour current right
before them, and Joe must needs see them so that
he might sheer the huge and clumsy craft into the
shore before it drifted too far down.

Presently Joe did see them. He appeared to be
half-naked; he raised aloft both arms, and bellowed
down the cañon. The echoes boomed from wall to
wall, every one stronger with the deep, hoarse
triumph in the Mormon's voice, till they passed on,
growing weaker, to die away in the roar of the river
below. Then Joe bent to a long oar that appeared to
be fastened to the stern of the boat, and the craft
drifted out of the swifter current toward the shore.
It reached a point opposite to where Shefford and
the Indian waited, and, though Joe made prodigious

353

efforts, it slid on. Still, it also drifted shoreward, and half-way down to the mouth of Nonnezoshe Boco Joe threw the end of a rope to the Indian.

"Ho! Ho!" yelled the Mormon, again setting into motion the fiendish echoes. He was naked to the waist; he had lost flesh; he was haggard, worn, dirty, wet. While he pulled on a shirt Nas Ta Bega made the rope fast to a snag of a log of driftwood embedded in the sand, and the boat swung to shore. It was perhaps thirty feet long by half as many wide, crudely built of rough-hewn boards. The steering-gear was a long pole with a plank nailed to the end. The craft was empty save for another pole and plank, Joe's coat, and a broken-handled shovel. There were water and sand on the flooring.

Joe stepped ashore and he was gripped first by Shefford and then by the Indian. He was an unkempt and gaunt giant, yet how steadfast and reliable, how grimly strong to inspire hope!

"Reckon most of me's here," he said in reply to greetings. "I've had water aplenty. My God! I've had *water!*" He rolled out a grim laugh. "But no grub for three days. . . . Forgot to fetch some!"

How practical he was! He told Fay she looked good for sore eyes, but he needed a biscuit most of all. There was just a second of singular hesitation when he faced Lassiter, and then the big, strong hand of the young Mormon went out to meet the old gunman's. While they fed him and he ate like a starved man Shefford told of the flight from the village, the rescuing of Jane and Lassiter from Surprise Valley, the descent from the plateau, the catastrophe to

Shadd's gang—and, concluding, Shefford, without any explanation, told that Nas Ta Bega had killed the Mormon Waggoner.

"Reckon I had that figured," replied Joe. "First off I didn't think so. . . . So Shadd went over the cliff. That's good riddance. It beats me, though. Never knew that Piute's like with a horse. And he had some grand horses in his outfit. Pity about them."

Later when Joe had a moment alone with Shefford he explained that during his ride to Kayenta he had realized Fay's innocence and who had been responsible for the tragedy. He took Withers, the trader, into his confidence, and they planned a story, which Withers was to carry to Stonebridge, that would exculpate Fay and Shefford of anything more serious than flight. If Shefford got Fay safely out of the country at once that would end the matter for all concerned.

"Reckon I'm some ferry-boatman, too—a *fairy* boatman. Haw! Haw!" he added. "And we're going through. . . . Now I want you to help me rig this tarpaulin up over the bow of the boat. If we can fix it up strong it 'll keep the waves from curling over. They filled her four times for me."

They folded the tarpaulin three times, and with stout pieces of split plank and horseshoe nails from Shefford's saddle-bags and pieces of rope they rigged up a screen around bow and front corners.

Nas Ta Bega put the saddles in the boat. The mustangs were far up Nonnezoshe Boco and would work their way back to green and luxuriant cañons. The Indian said they would soon become wild and would never be found. Shefford regretted Nack-yal, but was glad the faithful little mustang would be free in one of those beautiful cañons.

"Reckon we'd better be off," called Joe. "All aboard!" He placed Fay and Jane in a corner of the bow, where they would be spared sight of the rapids. Shefford loosed the rope and sprang aboard. "Pard," said Joe, "it's one hell of a river! And now with the snow melting up in the mountains it's twenty feet above normal and rising fast. But that's well for us. It covers the stones in the rapids. If it hadn't been in flood Joe would be an angel now!"

The boat cleared the sand, lazily wheeled in the eddying water, and suddenly seemed caught by some powerful gliding force. When it swept out beyond the jutting wall Shefford saw a quarter of a mile of sliding water that appeared to end abruptly. Beyond lengthened out the gigantic gap between the black and frowning cliffs.

"Wow!" ejaculated Joe. "Drops out of sight there. But that one ain't much. I can tell by the roar. When you see my hair stand up straight— then watch out! . . . Lassiter, you look after the women. Shefford, you stand ready to bail out with the shovel, for we'll sure ship water. Nas Ta Bega, you help here with the oar."

The roar became a heavy, continuous rumble; the current quickened; little streaks and ridges seemed to race along the boat; strange gurglings rose from under the bow. Shefford stood on tiptoe to see the break in the river below. Swiftly it came into sight—a wonderful, long, smooth, red slant of water, a swelling mound, a huge back-curling wave, another and another, a sea of frothy, uplifting crests, leaping and tumbling and diminishing down to the narrowing apex of the rapid. It was a frightful sight, yet it thrilled Shefford. Joe worked the steering-oar back and forth and headed the boat straight for the middle of the incline. The boat reached the round rim, gracefully dipped with a heavy sop, and went shooting down. The wind blew wet in Shefford's face. He stood erect, thrilling, fascinated, frightened. Then he seemed to feel himself lifted; the curling wave leaped at the boat; there was a shock that laid him flat; and when he rose to his knees all about him was roar and spray and leaping, muddy waves. Shock after shock jarred the boat. Splashes of water stung his face. And then the jar and the motion, the confusion and roar, gradually lessened until presently Shefford rose to see smooth water ahead and the long, trembling rapid behind.

"Get busy, bailer," yelled Joe. "Pretty soon you'll be glad you have to bail—so you *can't* see!"

There were several inches of water in the bottom of the boat and Shefford learned for the first time the expediency of a shovel in the art of bailing.

"That tarpaulin worked powerful good," went on Joe. "And it saves the women. Now if it just don't bust on a big wave! That one back there was little."

When Shefford had scooped out all the water he went forward to see how Fay and Jane and Lassiter had fared. The women were pale, but composed. They had covered their heads.

"But the dreadful roar!" exclaimed Fay.

Lassiter looked shaken for once.

"Shore I'd rather taken a chance meetin' them Mormons on the way out," he said.

Shefford spoke with an encouraging assurance which he did not himself feel. Almost at the moment he marked a silence that had fallen into the cañon; then it broke to a low, dull, strange roar.

"Aha! Hear that?" The Mormon shook his shaggy head. "Reckon we're in Cataract Cañon. We'll be standing on end from now on. Hang on to her, boys!"

Danger of this unusual kind had brought out a peculiar levity in the somber Mormon—a kind of wild, gay excitement. His eyes rolled as he watched the river ahead and he puffed out his cheek with his tongue.

The rugged, overhanging walls of the cañon grew sinister in Shefford's sight. They were jaws. And the river—that made him shudder to look down into it. The little whirling pits were eyes peering into his, and they raced on with the boat, disappeared, and came again, always with the little, hollow gurgles.

The craft drifted swiftly and the roar increased. Another rapid seemed to move up into view. It came at a bend in the cañon. When the breeze struck Shefford's cheeks he did not this time experience exhilaration. The current accelerated its sliding motion and bore the flatboat straight for the middle of the curve. Shefford saw the bend, a long, dark, narrow, gloomy cañon, and a stretch of contending waters, then, crouching low, he waited for the dip, the race, the shock. They came—the last stopping the boat—throwing it aloft—letting it drop—and crests of angry waves curled over the side. Shefford, kneeling, felt the water slap around him, and in his ears was a deafening roar. There were endless moments of strife and hell and flying darkness of spray all about him, and under him the rocking boat. When they lessened—ceased in vio- lence—he stood ankle-deep in water, and then madly he began to bail.

Another roar deadened his ears, but he did not look up from his toil. And when he had to get down to avoid the pitch he closed his eyes. That rapid passed and with more water to bail, he resumed his share in the manning of the crude craft. It was more than a share—a tremendous responsibility to which he bent with all his might. He heard Joe yell—and again—and again. He heard the in- creasing roars one after another till they seemed one continuous bellow. He felt the shock, the pitch, the beating waves, and then the lessening power of sound and current. That set him to his task. Always in these long intervals of toil he seemed to see, without looking up, the growing proportions of the cañon. And the river had become a living, terrible thing. The intervals of his tireless effort when he scooped the water overboard were fleeting, and the rides through rapid after rapid were endless periods of waiting terror. His spirit and his hope were overwhelmed by the rush and roar and fury.

Then, as he worked, there came a change—a rest to deafened ears—a stretch of river that seemed quiet after chaos—and here for the first time he bailed the boat clear of water.

Jane and Fay were huddled in a corner, with the flapping tarpaulin now half fallen over them. They were wet and muddy. Lassiter crouched like a man dazed by a bad dream, and his white hair hung, stained and bedraggled, over his face. The Indian and the Mormon, grim, hard, worn, stood silent at the oar.

The afternoon was far advanced and the sun had already descended below the western ramparts. A cool breeze blew up the cañon, laden with a sound that was the same, yet not the same, as those low, dull roars which Shefford dreaded more and more.

Joe Lake turned his ear to the breeze. A stronger puff brought a heavy, quivering rumble. This time he did not vent his gay and wild defiance to the river. He bent lower—listened. Then as the rumble became a strange, deep, reverberating roll, as if the monstrous river were rolling huge stones down a subterranean cañon, Shefford saw with dilating eyes that the Mormon's hair was rising stiff upon his head.

"Hear that!" said Joe, turning an ashen face to Shefford. "We'll drop off the earth now. Hang on to the girl, so if we go you can go together. . . . And, pard, if you've a God—*pray!*"

Nas Ta Bega faced the bend from whence that rumble came, and he was the same dark, inscrutable, impassive Indian as of old. What was death to him?

Shefford felt the strong, rushing love of life surge in him, and it was not for himself he thought, but for Fay and the happiness she merited. He went to her, patted the covered head, and tried with words choking in his throat to give hope. And he leaned with hands gripping the gunwale, with eyes wide open, ready for the unknown.

360

The river made a quick turn and from round the bend rumbled a terrible uproar. The current racing that way was divided or uncertain. and it gave strange motion to the boat. Joe and Nas Ta Bega shoved desperately upon the oar, all to no purpose. The currents had their will. The bow of the boat took the place of the stern. Then swift at the head of a curved incline it shot beyond the bulging wall.

And Shefford saw an awful place before them. The cañon had narrowed to half its width, and turned almost at right angles. The huge clamor of appalling sound came from under the cliff where the swollen river had to pass and where there was not space. The rapid rushed in gigantic swells right upon the wall, boomed against it, climbed and spread and fell away, to recede and gather new impetus, to leap madly on down the cañon.

Shefford went to his knees, clasped Fay, and Jane, too. But facing this appalling thing he had to look. Courage and despair came to him at the last. This must be the end. With long, buoyant swing the boat sailed down, shot over the first waves, was caught and lifted upon the great swell and impelled straight toward the cliff. Huge whirlpools raced alongside, and from them came a horrible, engulfing roar. Monstrous bulges rose on the other side. All the stupendous power of that mighty river of downward-rushing silt swung the boat aloft, up and up, as the swell climbed the wall. Shefford, with transfixed eyes and harrowed soul, watched the wet black wall. It loomed down upon him. The stern of the boat went high. Then when the crash that meant doom seemed imminent the swell spread and fell back from the wall and the boat never struck at all. By some miraculous chance it had been favored by a strange and momentary receding of the huge spent swell. Then it slid back, was caught and whirled by the current into a red, frothy, up-flung rapids below. Shefford bowed his head over Fay and saw no more, nor felt nor heard. What seemed a long time after that the broken voice of the Mormon recalled him to his labors.

The boat was half full of water. Nas Ta Bega scooped out great sheets of it with his hands. Shefford sprang to aid him, found the shovel, and plunged into the task. Slowly but surely they emptied the boat. And then Shefford saw that twilight had fallen. Joe was working the craft toward a narrow bank of sand, to which, presently, they came, and the Indian sprang out to moor to a rock.

The fugitives went ashore and, weary and silent and drenched, they dropped in the warm sand.

But Shefford could not sleep. The river kept him awake. In the distance it rumbled, low, deep, re-verberating, and near at hand it was a thing of mutable mood. It moaned, whined, mocked, and laughed. It had the soul of a devil. It was a river that had cut its way to the bowels of the earth, and its nature was destructive. It harbored no life. Fighting its way through those dead walls, cutting and tearing and wearing, its heavy burden of silt was death, destruction, and decay. A silent river, a murmuring, strange, fierce, terrible, thundering river of the desert! Even in the dark it seemed to wear the hue of blood.

All night long Shefford heard it, and toward the dark hours before dawn, when a restless, broken sleep came to him, his dreams were dreams of a river of sounds.

All the beautiful sounds he knew and loved he heard—the sigh of the wind in the pines, the mourn of the wolf, the cry of the laughing-gull, the murmur of running brooks, the song of a child, the whisper of a woman. And there were the boom of the surf, the roar of the north wind in the forest, the roll of thunder. And there were the sounds not of earth—a river of the universe rolling the planets, engulfing the stars, pouring the sea of blue into infinite space.

Night with its fitful dreams passed. Dawn lifted the ebony gloom out of the cañon and sunlight far up on the ramparts renewed Shefford's spirit. He rose and awoke the others. Fay's wistful smile still held its faith. They ate of the gritty, water-soaked food. Then they embarked. The current carried them swiftly down and out of hearing of the last rapid. The character of the river and the cañon changed. The current lessened to a slow, smooth, silent, eddying flow. The walls grew straight, sheer, gloomy, and vast. Shefford noted these features, but he was listening so hard for the roar of the next rapid that he scarcely appreciated them. All the fugitives were listening. Every bend in the cañon —and now the turns were numerous—might hold a rapid.. Shefford strained his ears. He imagined the low, dull, strange rumble. He had it in his ears, yet there was the growing sensation of silence.

"Shore this 's a dead place," muttered Lassiter.

363

"She's only slowed up for a bigger plunge," replied Joe. "Listen! Hear that?"

But there was no true sound. Joe only imagined what he expected and hated and dreaded to hear.

Mile after mile they drifted through the silent gloom between those vast and magnificent walls. After the speed, the turmoil, the whirling, shrieking, thundering, the never-ceasing sound and change and motion of the rapids above, this slow, quiet drifting, this utter, absolute silence, these eddying stretches of still water below, worked strangely upon Shefford's mind and he feared he was going mad.

There was no change to the silence, no help for the slow drift, no lessening of the strain. And the hours of the day passed as moments, the sun crossed the blue gap above, the golden lights hung on the upper walls, the gloom returned, and still there was only the dead, vast, insupportable silence.

There came bends where the current quickened, ripples widened, long lanes of little waves roughened the surface, but they made no sound.

And then the fugitives turned through a V-shaped vent in the cañon. The ponderous walls sheered away from the river. There was space and sunshine, and far beyond this league-wide open rose vermilion-colored cliffs. A mile below the river disappeared in a dark, boxlike passage from which came a rumble that made Shefford's flesh creep.

The Mormon flung high his arms and let out the stentorian yell that had rolled down to the fugitives as they waited at the mouth of Nonnezoshe Boco. But now it had a wilder, more exultant note. Strange how he shifted his gaze to Fay Larkin!

GRAND CAÑON OF THE COLORADO

"Girl! Get up and look!" he called. "The Ferry! The Ferry!"

Then he bent his brawny back over the steering-oar, and the clumsy craft slowly turned toward the left-hand shore, where a long, low bank of green willows and cottonwoods gave welcome relief to the eyes. Upon the opposite side of the river Shefford saw a boat, similar to the one he was in, moored to the bank.

"Shore, if I ain't losin' my eyes, I seen an Injun with a red blanket," said Lassiter.

"Yes, Lassiter," cried Shefford. "Look, Fay! Look, Jane! See! Indians—hogans—mustangs— there above the green bank!"

The boat glided slowly shoreward. And the deep, hungry, terrible rumble of the remorseless river became something no more to dread.

XX

WILLOW SPRINGS

TWO days' travel from the river, along the saw-toothed range of Echo Cliffs, stood Presbrey's trading-post, a little red-stone square house in a green and pretty valley called Willow Springs.

It was nearing the time of sunset—that gorgeous hour of color in the Painted Desert—when Shefford and his party rode down upon the post.

The scene lacked the wildness characteristic of Kayenta or Red Lake. There were wagons and teams, white men and Indians, burros, sheep, lambs, mustangs saddled and unsaddled, dogs, and chickens. A young, sweet-faced woman stood in the door of the post and she it was who first sighted the fugitives. Presbrey was weighing bags of wool on a scale, and when she called he lazily turned, as if to wonder at her eagerness.

Then he flung up his head, with its shock of heavy hair, in a start of surprise, and his florid face lost its lazy indolence to become wreathed in a huge smile.

"Haven't seen a white person in six months!" was his extraordinary greeting.

An hour later Shefford, clean-shaven, comfortably

WILLOW SPRINGS

clothed once more, found himself a different man; and when he saw Fay in white again, with a new and indefinable light shining through that old, haunting shadow in her eyes, then the world changed and he embraced perfect happiness.

There was a dinner such as Shefford had not seen for many a day, and such as Fay had never seen, and that brought to Jane Withersteen's eyes the dreamy memory of the bountiful feasts which, long years ago, had been her pride. And there was a story told to the curious trader and his kind wife—a story with its beginning back in those past years, of riders of the purple sage, of Fay Larkin as a child and then as a wild girl in Surprise Valley, of the flight down Nonnezoshe Boco and the cañon, of a great Mormon and a noble Indian.

Presbrey stared with his deep-set eyes and wagged his tousled head and stared again; then with the quick perception of the practical desert man he said:

"I'm sending teamsters in to Flagstaff to-morrow. Wife and I will go along with you. We've light wagons. Three days, maybe—or four—and we'll be there. . . . Shefford, I'm going to see you marry Fay Larkin!"

Fay and Jane and Lassiter showed strangely against this background of approaching civilization. And Shefford realized more than ever the loneliness and isolation and wildness of so many years for them.

When the women had retired Shefford and the men talked awhile. Then Joe Lake rose to stretch his big frame.

"Friends, reckon I'm all in," he said. "Good night." In passing he laid a heavy hand on Shefford's shoulder. "Well, you got out. I've only a queer notion how. But *Some One* besides an Indian and a Mormon guided you out!... Be good to the girl.... Good-by, pard!"

Shefford grasped the big hand and in the emotion of the moment did not catch the significance of Joe's last words.

Later Shefford stepped outside into the starlight for a few moments' quiet walk and thought before he went to bed. It was a white night. The coyotes were yelping. The stars shone steadfast, bright, cold. Nas Ta Bega stalked out of the shadow of the house and joined Shefford. They walked in silence. Shefford's heart was too full for utterance and the Indian seldom spoke at any time. When Shefford was ready to go in Nas Ta Bega extended his hand.

"Good-by—Bi Nai!" he said, strangely, using English and Navajo in what Shefford supposed to be merely good night. The starlight shone full upon the dark, inscrutable face of the Indian. Shefford bade him good night and then watched him stride away in the silver gloom.

But next morning Shefford understood. Nas Ta Bega and Joe Lake were gone. It was a shock to Shefford. Yet what could he have said to either? Joe had shirked saying good-by to him and Fay. And the Indian had gone out of Shefford's life as he had come into it.

What these two men represented in Shefford's uplift was too great for the present to define, but

WILLOW SPRINGS

they and the desert that had developed them had
taught him the meaning of life. He might fail often,
since failure was the lot of his kind, but could he ever
fail again in faith in man or God while he had mind
to remember the Indian and the Mormon?

Still, though he placed them on a noble height and
loved them well, there would always abide with
him a sorrow for the Mormon and a sleepless and
eternal regret for that Indian on his lonely cedar
slope with the spirits of his vanishing race calling
him.

Willow Springs appeared to be a lively place that
morning. Presbrey was gay and his sweet-faced wife
was excited. The teamsters were a jolly, whistling
lot. And the lean mustangs kicked and bit at one another. The trader had brought out two light wagons
for the trip, and, after the manner of desert men,
desired to start at sunrise.

Far across the Painted Desert towered the San
Francisco peaks, black-timbered, blue-cañoned, pur-
ple-hazed, with white snow, like the clouds, around
their summits.

Jane Withersteen looked at the radiant Fay and
lived again in her happiness. And at last excitement had been communicated to the old gun-man.

"Shore we're goin' to live with Fay an' John, an
be near Venters an' Bess, an' see the blacks again,
Jane. . . . An' Venters will tell you, as he did me, how
Wrangle run Black Star off his legs!"

All connected with that early start was sweet, sad,
hopeful.

And so they rode away from Willow Springs

THE RAINBOW TRAIL

through the green fields of alfalfa and cottonwood,
down the valley with its smoking hogans and whistling mustangs and scarlet-blanketed Indians, and
out upon the bare, ridgy, colorful desert toward the
rosy sunrise.

EPILOGUE

ON the outskirts of a little town in Illinois there was a farm of rolling pasture-land. And here a beautiful meadow, green and red in clover, merged upon an orchard in the midst of which a brown-tiled roof showed above the trees.

One afternoon in May a group of people, strangely agitated, walked down a shady lane toward the meadow.

"Wal, Jane, I always knew we'd get a look at them hosses again—I shore knew," Lassiter was saying in the same old, cool, careless drawl. But his clawlike hands shook a little.

"Oh! will they know me?" asked Jane Withersteen, turning to a stalwart man—no other than the dark-faced Venters, her rider of other days.

"Know you? I'll bet they will," replied Venters. "What do you say, Bess?"

The shadow brightened in Bess's somber blue eyes, as if his words had recalled her from a sad and memorable past.

"Black Star will know her, surely," replied Bess. "Sometimes he points his nose toward the west and watches as if he saw the purple slopes and smelt the sage of Utah! He has never forgotten. But Night has grown deaf and partly blind of late. I doubt if he'll remember."

371

Shefford and Fay walked arm in arm in the background.

Out in the meadow two horses were grazing. They were sleek, shiny, long-maned, long-tailed, black as coal, and, though old, still splendid in every line.

"Do you remember them?" whispered Shefford.

"Oh, I only needed to see Black Star," murmured Fay, her voice quivering. "I can remember being lifted on his back. . . . How strange! It seems so long ago. . . . Look! Mother Jane is going out to them."

Jane Withersteen advanced alone through the clover, and it was with unsteady steps. Presently she halted. What glorious and bitter memories were expressed in her strange, poignant call!

Black Star started and swept up his noble head and looked. But Night went on calmly grazing. Then Jane called again—the same strange call, only louder, and this time broken. Black Star raised his head higher and he whistled a piercing blast. He saw Jane; he knew her as he had remembered the call; and he came pounding toward her. She met him, encircled his neck with her arms, and buried her face in his mane.

"Shore I reckon I'd better never say any more about Wrangle runnin' the blacks off their legs thet time," muttered Lassiter, as if to himself.

"Lassiter, you only dreamed that race," replied Venters, with a smile.

"Oh, Bern, isn't it good that Black Star remembered her—that she'll have him—something left of her old home?" asked Bess, wistfully.

EPILOGUE

"Indeed it is good. But, Bess, Jane Withersteen will find a new spirit and new happiness here."

Jane came toward them, leading both horses. "Dear friends, I am happy. To-day I bury all regrets. Of the past I shall remember only—my riders of the purple sage."

Venters smiled his gladness. "And you—Lassiter —what shall you remember?" he queried.

The old gun-man looked at Jane and then at his clawlike hands and then at Fay. His eyes lost their shadow and began to twinkle.

"Wal, I rolled a stone once, but I reckon now thet time Wrangle—"

"Lassiter, I said you dreamed that race. Wrangle never beat the blacks," interrupted Venters. . . . "And you, Fay, what shall you remember?"

"Surprise Valley," replied Fay, dreamily.

"And you—Shefford?"

Shefford shook his head. For him there could never be one memory only. In his heart there would never change or die memories of the wild uplands, of the great towers and walls, of the golden sunsets on the cañon ramparts, of the silent, fragrant valleys where the cedars and the sago-lilies grew, of those starlit nights when his love and faith awoke, of grand and lonely Nonnezoshe, of that red, sullen, thundering, mysterious Colorado River, of a wonderful Indian and a noble Mormon—of all that was embodied for him in the meaning of the rainbow trail.